HER
FERAL
BEASTS

E.P. Bali's
House of Romantasy

Her Feral Beasts is a work of fiction. Names, characters, places, incidents and locations are the product of the author's imagination or are used fictitiously. Any resemblance to actual events, locations or persons, living or dead is entirely coincidental.

This first edition published in 2023 by
Blue Moon Rising Publishing
www.ektaabali.com
ISBN ebook: 978-0-6456909-9-6
Paperback: 978-0-6457846-1-9
Hardback: 978-0-6457846-2-6
Exclusive Edition: 978-0-6457846-8-8

All artwork and words in this book were created by humans:
Cover Design by David Gardias
Case Design by Carly Diep
Chapter Artwork by Wisp Tale
Animus Academy crest by Etheric Designs
Formatting by E.P. Bali

A Note on the Content

I care about the mental health of my readers.
This book contains some themes you might want to know
about before you read.
They are listed at www.ektaabali.com/themes

This one is for those who need a reminder of how powerful they can be.

Her Feral Beasts

L.P. Bali

Prologue

Aurelia

7 years ago

The day my period arrives, I run out of the bathroom screaming for my nanny, Rosalina. It's a scream of joy; shrill, ecstatic, and full of expectation. Because for a female animalia, today is the day my anima will reveal herself to the world.

Rosalina, an elderly python of my court, whoops and opens her arms where she sits in her favourite armchair. I'm thirteen, but I still throw myself into her lap, crying and laughing and babbling about my powers to come.

"A powerful beast lurks under your skin," she whispers, touching my black braid affectionately. "Tonight, we will all be proud to see which powerful serpent form she takes."

When dusk comes and the sky is awash with deepening purple, I giddily trot into the back garden to see a bright half-moon. My father is waiting for me, proud and

1

strong, like he always is: the King of the Serpent Court in a designer suit and shoes that are always shiny. He reaches down and kisses me on both cheeks, his dark eyes glowing with love and I've never felt so cherished in my life.

The dull ache in my lower stomach grows into a roaring fire that explodes outwards with terrible, ancient force.

When my body changes, when my clothes fall to the manicured grass around me, and I've taken on a new body, it isn't any breed of serpent that lies coiled in the grass. The world looks different, but not in the way I expected. Not in the way I was told a serpent could see and sense the minute vibrations of the world. Hollow bones and feathered skin burn like acid and I change again. Bones crunch, ligaments stretch. Then a third time. Then a fourth.

By the time I shift back into my human body, the sharp pains in my bones and an awful, cold shock make tears spill down my face. My father is already storming back into our mansion, tendrils of his dark magic coiling around him, not bothering to control his fury.

Alone and naked, I bolt back inside. Rosalina covers me in a dressing gown, but her head is bowed and she will not meet my eye. Alone, I go to my bathroom, where I look at myself in the mirror, turning my face so I can see my neck—where my new mating mark burns with the light of the stars and the moon. A skull with five beams of light. The sacred connection between me and my mates by destiny.

The sun never really rises again for me.

* * *

The next day, I rise puffy-eyed and look at the simple black dress and ballet flats Rosalina has laid out for me.

"This is my funeral dress," I whisper in a voice like brittle leaves crunching under a boot.

When I look at her in question, she still won't meet my eye. The backs of my own eyes burn again, and silently, I put on my clothes of mourning.

I meet my father in our pristine circular driveway and am surprised to find that he and our driver are already in our black SUV. For the first time in my life, I open my own door and slide onto the cold black leather seat.

As we pull out, a movement at the side of my eye makes me turn. All ten of our house staff, including Rosalina, are standing at the windows of the second floor, staring down at me with grave faces. Rosalina raises her hand to the glass, her face lined with worry.

"Father?" I ask softly, though my heart is racing with trepidation.

The returning cold silence makes all the hairs on my body rise. I know this feeling. I know that the serpents of his court my father isn't happy with sometimes don't return to their families.

I begin to tremble.

According to the most ancient laws of our kind, on the day you become a man or woman, your parents take you to see the oracle. It's supposed to be a day of celebration, a day of revelation, and there was going to be a grand party in my honour. Rosalina and I had been planning it for months.

When we arrive at our city's branch of the Council of Beasts, my father opens his door and strides out, his black trench-coat billowing on a sharp wind.

I scramble to follow before the voice of our driver stops me.

"Miss Aurelia?" His voice is barely a whisper as I turn to look at him.

He touches his hat and says quietly, "Good luck."

It's not his words that chill me to the bone, but the fear in his slitted eyes. Fear for me.

I press my lips together before saying, "Thank you, Mr Chandler."

When I enter the heated formal interior of the council atrium, my father doesn't look at me. He doesn't speak to me directly, and I'm presented to the oracle alone. A ghost of a girl, translucent and silent.

Presenting to the oracle is supposed to be the happiest day of one's life, second only to finding your mates. This oracle is a woman of mystery, from the great and all-seeing House of Phoenix. But at this moment, she's a woman in a burnt orange power suit, sitting behind a grand desk in a corner office with a view of the entire city behind her. Her hair is a bundle of vibrant strawberry blonde curls and her lipstick a perfect shade of fire-engine red. When she smiles kindly upon me, I can't find the heart to return it.

She takes my hand in her red-nailed ones and frowns with delicate brows. "What is your anima, my dear?"

My voice is rough from a night spent smothering my sobs. "I am forbidden to say."

Her eyes flick to the door, behind which my father waits. The phoenix then closes her eyes and everything about her changes.

The halogen lights flicker, a burning wind sweeps through the room and my vision narrows down to this one woman who holds my fate in her red nailed hands.

Her husky voice chants in a whisper, as if it's a psalm for the Wild Mother herself, and I find myself swaying a little, enamoured by its dark cadence:

"Five devils are approaching.

Five black hearts are wanting.

It is five who cry a dark and lonely song, calling for their queen.

Lion, shark, dragon, wolf and...shadow."

My stomach lurches into my throat. "*Five* mates?" I croak. "Are you sure?"

She opens her eyes, and they are aflame with some kind of immortal power unique to her order. Her hand is a vise around mine. "Congratulations Aurelia, you are a regina to five animus' beasts." Her eyes bore into mine and her voice becomes light with wonder. "Dear girl, I wish you luck. Two are already in prison...but somehow that is the least of your worries."

I leave her office feeling like I'm at sea, with my stomach turning, my legs shaking, clutching my stomach as if I can command it not to hurl.

5

"What did she say?" my father asks sharply, and I know I will never get used to this new, cold tone.

"F-five?" What am I even saying? But I know I heard her right because her prophecy is seared into my eardrums. Seared into my soul. "She said I have five black hearts calling for me."

His eyes flash dangerously, and I know the oracle is in trouble now. My father abruptly turns on his heel and storms into her office.

"I want their names!" he roars. "All of them!"

Her reply is calm and cool. "I cannot give them to you, Your Majesty."

My father kicks the office door shut and I can hear no more.

I shiver anxiously, touching the skin of my neck where my mating mark warms my skin in a way that should be comforting and full of golden hope.

Regina to five mates of different orders. Dear Goddess, it will give my new secret away. For the millionth time, I wish my mother was in the world of the living. She would know what to do.

Instead, all I have is my father, who returns fuming; dangerous and unable to speak.

I hope the Lady Phoenix is still whole.

When we return home, the maids take off my diamond earrings and necklace and put them away in a box that isn't mine.

Rosalina whispers to me, her eyes flashing into slits and back to round again with the force of her emotion. "You are no longer princess of the Serpent Court, sweet child. You are no longer a member of the Naga household. You will live the rest of your life as an eagle, like your mother before you."

"But other families keep children of different orders in their houses!" I exclaim. "Why can't—"

"We are *not* other families," she hisses, pointing to the family crest above my fireplace. Two rearing cobras on a field of black, a crown between them, right above a cursive 'N'. I know what she means. My father is a serpent purist; all other beasts are beneath him. And now *I* am beneath him.

Rosalina hands me a dusty black duffle bag. "I am so sorry, sweetheart."

I won't find out that my father executed her until many years later. Both, she and the house staff who were there the day my anima was revealed.

That very same day, my father and his retinue drive me to Aunt Charlotte's house, a smart double story house in a neat serpentine neighbourhood.

But they don't take me *into* her house. Instead, they drive around the side and far back into the compound where, under tall and scraggly trees, a tiny house sits like a weathered toad in the dark.

"This is your home now," Father says.

I gape at the peeling paint, the tin roof, the shattered glass windows. "Father, I don't understand why I have to stay here. None of it is my fault."

"Your *Majesty*," one of his vipers snaps. "You will address him appropriately, *mutt*."

Her words burn like a brand.

I raise my chin, but my father stands over me, once a mountain of protection and safety. But the look in his eyes tells me he is now the opposite.

"There is one thing about life that you must learn, Aurelia *Aquinas*." His voice announcing me by my mother's official surname is a dangerous hiss that makes me go still. "We do not always get what we want."

And in his voice, I hear a deep sorrow, a profound loss. I was his dream, and that dream is now dead. The Serpent Princess is no more.

"You will keep your protections up at all times," he continues. "You will not let *them* find you. If you do, your life will be forfeit. Every power-hungry beast in the country will come for you. Chain you up. Breed you until you are dead. *Do you understand?*"

His words are a cruel blow to the gut, and I bow my head, if only to hide the tears of shame now falling freely. My mates can never be mine.

Nothing will be the same again.

Chapter 1

Aurelia

Present day

There are at least three murderous psychos hunting me and yet all I can think about is food.

I've officially gone loopy. Like proper, doctor-please-admit-me-to-the-grippy-sock-hotel type loopy. I've always known my mental break was coming, and it took being framed for murdering my new husband and being forced to run away in the middle of the night for it to pull the plug on my sanity.

I'm not normal.

None of this is normal.

My current legs are piddly sticks, but they do the job by slowly inching me towards a group of elderly ladies at a fancy breakfast cafe.

They've just been brought their lunches.

It's a tourist town on the coast and the summer holidays are coming to an end, so everyone is out while they can. I know I should be working at this cafe. Living my life free and unbothered. Safe. Happy. Instead, I'm half a foot tall and skulking across the ground like the felon I'm supposed to be.

But I can't care less about that now because I. See. Their. Food.

One has a chicken Caesar salad, the second, a cheese and chive scone, and the third has the most mouth-watering, juicy, succulent chicken burger complete with all the regular trappings.

Ding, ding, ding. The winner is me.

Dear Wild Goddess and all that is holy. That burger is mine.

I know how I sound, but I haven't really eaten in five days. When I left my beloved bungalow in the middle of the night, it was by car, under my special eighth shield of invisibility. I had cash, my phone, and my battered duffle bag carrying my meagre possessions.

But they found me in the first motel I stopped at. Not the three psychos, someone actually worse. And I didn't realise it was possible for someone to be worse.

It was the Deputy Headmaster of Animus Academy, who the authorities no doubt sent to hunt the rabid crim (me) down. They usually send a dedicated retrieval team to hunt rabid or feral beasts to protect the human community, but I guess they thought I was a special case and that they needed to send the best lion in the state. A *specialist,* as it were.

Lyle Pardalia.

The sheer furore on his angelic face when I thwarted him will forever be etched in my mind. Sure, I was grateful he took down my father's scummy retrieval team. I mean, *no one* went against the King Cobra and lived to tell the tale. But when I mentioned it, he scoffed and said he had no issue with it. And a lethal hunter like that? The only way I could get away from him was to shift and fly away, but it meant I had to leave all my stuff behind.

I don't own that much, so the loss of all my savings was a massive blow.

It also means that I have no clothes and no cash. So here I am, in what I hope is an inconspicuous position, eyeing this poor lady's burger.

You don't know real hunger until you've gone this long without a proper meal. My head is fuzzy, like it's filled with cotton wool, and my body feels like it's floating through water, moving in slow motion. Worst of all, I'm *fixating* on this burger like it's a holy relic that'll save me.

Because I will die before I go digging through the rubbish bin. A woman has to have her standards *somewhere*, right?

Dirty pond drinking water I can tolerate here and there.

A dirty burger? Pass. Soft pass, but still.

I hop forwards, keeping low and angling myself so the old ladies don't suspect my intentions.

I'm a predator

I'm an apex predator.

A beast like no other.

If I keep repeating my positive affirmations, I've got

to believe them eventually. That's the way it works. It's science.

It's a beautiful summer's day and there's a cool breeze, so plenty of people are sitting outside this cafe. It's a wealthy area with luxury shops around, so I'm wondering if I can steal someone's wallet while I'm in the area.

I've really descended to a new type of low.

There's a discarded chip on the ground and I purposefully avoid looking at it.

I was a Princess of the Serpent Court at one time. Now, I'm thinking about eating day-old cold chips from the ground. A bubble of mad laughter begins in my chest and I clamp down on it as hard as I can because it'll likely come out as a scary caw.

Hopping right up to the table, I'm about to launch myself into the air when a group of police cars, sirens blaring, race past, followed by a fire brigade.

"Oh dear, I wonder what's happened," one of the ladies croaks, nervously shuffling her orthopaedic shoes under the table.

A young waitress sidles up to the table with a look of 'I've got goss'. "The Opal Feather store just got broken into and set on fire," she says conspiratorially. "I was walking past on my way to work. Glass and flames everywhere. The salesgirl was screaming about beasts barging into her store. A wolf and a dragon, she says."

I freeze.

So does the man sitting alone on the table to my right and the two teenagers to my left.

"Oh, those *creatures* are awful," says Caesar-salad lady. "A danger to us all. I can't believe they let them terrorise us humans the way they do."

"Some of them are so pretty though," says burger-lady, though a little quietly, as if she's ashamed to admit it. "The way the lion men groom themselves? I saw one on the news the other day. Beautiful honey golden hair, and so long!"

"Yes, but they're dangerous, Sybil!" says Caesar Salad. "Criminals and murderers. They can't control their urges, and they act like the animals they are."

The large man sitting on the right hastily gets up to leave. Maybe he's a criminal on the run like me. Fare thee well, comrade. Good luck.

"Well," says the waitress, lowering her voice. "The salesgirl at the Opal Feather said the wolf that came in was gorgeous...right up until they blew up the store and laughed about it!"

Shit. They're here. I need to leave right now.

The ladies titter in fear and judgement as the waitress walks away and I know that it's now or never. I leap up onto the table, black wings flapping, immediately knocking over a pink mocktail and its tiny umbrella.

All three ladies scream.

I launch myself at the chicken burger, grabbing it with my beak and leaping into the air, sweeping my wings to gain some height. But success is a glass bubble that shatters in my beak because the burger is too big for me to clamp around. It slips out and I falter in mid-air, digging my beak in for all its miserable worth. But it does no good.

Caesar-Salad grabs her handbag and swings it double-handed, like a cricket bat, right for my head. I cry out and swerve just in time, catching myself on the recently vacated chair behind her—where a brown paper doggy bag sits full with the man's leftovers.

My beak shoots out, snapping around the paper handles and I launch myself into the air, triumphant, leaving the dramatic shrieking behind me.

I beat my wings as I try to convince myself that I'm going to be alright. That I'm going to get out of this state and the beasts hunting me won't win. That I won't go crazy.

The sun beats down on me and my number one priority is getting the burger I can smell in this bag to safety.

There's a national park nearby, and it has to be the safest place to hide out so I can eat. As an eagle, they'll find it impossible to trace my scent by foot.

The scent I've been trying to hide my entire life.

Ten minutes later, I'm standing at the base of a tall gum tree. After taking a cursory look around and seeing no predators or men in camo gear, I flash into my human form and, butt naked, fall to my knees. Tearing open the bag, I open up the cardboard box and find a mostly uneaten burger ready for me.

I gobble it up like an actual animal, moaning around the still-warm grilled chicken breast as flavour bursts along my tongue. Lettuce, tomato, mayo. I know then for sure there's a Goddess because it tastes like literal heaven to my dry mouth. In moments, a little burst of energy zings through my veins as the calories hit my arteries.

I'm working on tiny amounts of sleep here and there because the thing about being hunted by multiple apex predators is that they're *fast*. And being hot on my tail, I've barely avoided them so far. I can't afford to hole up in a nice cosy place, I *have* to keep moving.

Three of these apex predators had been stuck in a dungeon just over a week ago.

It just so happened that the wealthy eagle who had been keeping them in that dungeon purchased my marriage contract from my father. The place ended up burning down (I suspect my dad for setting that up) and now Charles Halfeather is dead and I'm being blamed for it.

The burger gives me just enough energy to bring back up three of my shields. I usually have seven, when I'm at full power, and if you think that's a bit dramatic, you would be right. But it's been so ingrained in me since the day I turned thirteen—the day my father and I found out how many mates I have.

Yes, there's five of them. And they're all of different orders.

It's a dead giveaway to my secret, so my father instructed me to both hide my mating mark and my scent. That makes for two shields. My third and fourth are psychic shields of different levels, so no one can invade my mind or find me by psychic means. And one of my mates is a shark, so he has the power to do that.

17

The fact that I can make shields like this at all shouldn't be possible, but there you go. I'm a prized sow, and therefore, I *can't* be found. If anyone finds out what I am, I'll be sent to a breeding pen and be forced to make more pups just like me.

It's the reason I've been hiding from my mates my entire life. Usually, your mates are from the same or similar order as you. The fact that I have five of different orders is unheard of.

I shift back into my eagle form and jump up into the tree above me to catch my breath. I'm *exhausted.* Now that my belly is full to the brim, my body is telling me to sleep. Drowsiness haunts my mind and I sway on the spot for some unknown length of time, wondering if I should give up and just nap here in the warm sunlight for a bit.

It seems like a really great idea. If I want to get to the next state, it'll be a long flight for hours. But, if I'm right and the luxury store invasion *was* them, I need to quickly put some distance between us. None of them are able to fly, so I have the advantage here.

Well, Xander is a dragon, but they're only allowed to fly in designated areas. And since they're also on the run, they surely won't risk his big body hurtling through the air.

My eyes droop as I roost on the thick branch of this gum tree. It's deliciously warm, and exhaustion pulls my eyes shut.

I only realise I'm tumbling through the air at the last minute and land on the leaf litter below with a sickening *thump.*

Groaning, I roll my bird body over and lie on my side, feeling a little sorry for myself. But my stomach is full, so no real complaints here.

Eventually, I drag myself to my feet, but it's then that I hear the crunch of heavy boots on the forest floor...and a husky male voice singing what sounds like a children's song.

Chapter 2

Savage

"Hold my chicken."

"Rooster," Xander corrects, accepting the black bird.

I scowl at my pack-brother because he can take his private school education and shove it up his big dragon ass.

"His name is *Eugene*," I snap. Patting said chicken on his red head-frills, I turn back to the trembling cashier of the Opal Feather. The sight of us always makes these humans piss their pants. A dragon, a wolf and a shark walk into a luxury store and, well...they all know what comes next, I suppose.

Or it could be the blood still on my teeth and the bare skin of my torso. On a hunt, I only stop for lunch, you see. Lunch being the two birdie security guards now lying on the shop floor behind me.

"Human woman." I point at the cashier. "Get out. Your boss is in trouble."

As the blonde with the dark fake tan and short, short skirt grabs her phone and scampers out to call to the cops, Xander scoffs again.

"He says that like *he's* not currently human."

Scythe, my brother by blood, says nothing and strides past me to the back of the shop, brushing at the shoulder of his crisp black designer shirt. Scythe has his quirks, and I have mine.

But Xander is wrong. I haven't been 'human' in a very long time.

We both follow Scythe past the dressing rooms and through a curtain in the storage room. There's a narrow staircase leading into a dimly lit basement area.

I grunt at Scythe and he silently holds open the curtain, allowing me to do my thing. Passing him with a smirk, I sing a happy tune, making sure I stomp loudly down the stairs.

"Little birdies, little birdies...the wolf is ready to play."

Chairs scrape in the room below as their occupants jump to their feet. Someone lets out a shout just as I leap over the railing and land in the room with jazz hands.

"Round-a-bout a round table, five birdies, about to pay!"

There are five eagle males in human form, ranging from thirty to fifty, now standing around a table scattered with official-looking documents, wax seals and all.

"Who the fuck do you think you are?" a younger one of them shouts. His hand goes into his pocket, but I'm on him in a flash, leaping across the table right for his throat.

I grab him by his gel-crispy hair and sink my teeth into his throat just enough to draw blood.

He screams.

"Drop the gun, you fool of a bird," Xander drawls as he steps into the basement. Even with my chicken tucked under his arm and the cords of the white headphones hanging from his ears, our glowing-eyed dragon looks scary as fuck.

Eagles are useless in a fight. Their power is healing, so a lot of them carry weapons. This one sets the handgun on the table, whimpering under my teeth. The vibration of it tickles and I suppress a laugh.

Scythe steps out of the shadows of the staircase, and the eagles pin their gazes on him. They take in his silver hair, his sky-blue eyes, and the five lines of ancient marine script on the left side of his neck. The alluring scent of terror fills my nose.

I breathe it in like a sweet perfume and it makes me growl with pleasure.

Even if they don't recognise the signs of his order, they all know who my brother is. Those of us beasts who walk in the dark *all* know who Scythe Kharkorous is and what he does.

Scythe turns to the eagle on my left, a middle-aged guy with a black receding hairline and pale skin that's happily familiar. My brother's voice bears his signature rasp—a predator made into something worse. "Good afternoon, Dirk Halfeather."

"Y-you should be dead," Halfeather stammers.

I chomp down on my prey. Blood bursts in my mouth

as I tear out his throat and throw him to the floor, where he thrashes like a fish. I swallow most of the blood, but the crimson liquid of life spills down my chin to my bare chest, mingling with the dried blood already there.

This is why shirts are useless.

Two of the eagles shout, and one of them reaches for the dying eagle, but I bare my teeth at him and, wide-eyed, he bows his head in submission.

"Good boy," I say, though my wolf-voice is almost too guttural to be clear.

Scythe pulls out a chair and sits down. He leisurely takes out a cigarette from the old-fashioned metal case he keeps in his pocket and lights it with a silver wolf lighter I gave him for Christmas.

He blows out the blue smoke. "No. Not dead. Instead, the two guards at your door, and this eagle, are dead." Dirk Halfeather blanches. "But this is not the price of breaking your agreement with me, Dirk. May I call you that?" We all hear Dirk's audible swallow. "Please," Scythe says mildly, "sit." He indicates to Dirk's chair.

The eagle on the floor finally stops twitching and the four remaining birdies follow the order to take their seats. Xander pulls up another chair and sets Eugene on his lap. I'm too wired after this kill and settle for prowling the underground room to inspect it for anything interesting. There's nothing much in here except that table in the middle and a set of couches deeper in the room. I smell a female eagle and women's perfume—from last night, most likely. There's a glass cupboard of whiskey and other spirits in the corner, along with crystal glasses. A place for business deals and female fun.

Dirk blubbers, "Mr Kharkorous, please, this is all a great mis—"

The temperature of the room suddenly plunges. Ice crystals spread across the walls and I grin as Scythe points his cigarette at Dirk. "*Do not* lie to me, Mr Halfeather. I do not tolerate liars."

Halfeather snaps his mouth shut.

Scythe takes a drag from his cigarette, and the eagles all follow his movements with extreme acuity. He has a voice that violently demands attention, and I even find myself keenly listening in. "I learned the art of business deals from my father. He would have been your age by now, Dirk, but you wouldn't have run in the same circles, of course. One time, he was negotiating the price for a valuable...product. I would have been twelve at the time, but I watched it all quite closely. They couldn't agree on a price. My father wanted a little over a million. They couldn't afford it, but still wanted it. The meeting ended, and that night, those beasts came to *steal* the product. Now, that wouldn't do, and not five minutes later, we had three eagles lying without their wings on our doorstep. My father took their net assets and considered the matter settled."

"'In our world, Scythe, we take what we want and we don't look back', he said to me. Now you," Scythe says, gesturing at Dirk, "are forcing me to look back. And I don't like that. I have no time for that. Halfeather estate is mine."

Dirk spreads shaking hands. "Mr Kharkorous, please, this is my brother's land we are talking about. My *family's* estate."

"Land that was won under the Old Laws forty years ago," Scythe says simply. "Land that is now being relieved from you, under the Old Laws." He pins Dirk with a stare that sets his feathers quaking like the worm-food he is.

"Now, here's what's going to happen." Scythe rasps. "Since you are well aware of the deal I had with your late brother and his subsequent scheming, you will also be aware of what I do to beasts who betray me. Halfeather enterprises and, therefore, this establishment, are now mine."

I'm directly behind Dirk, but I know he's gaping. He glances at the others, though they are wise not to speak. "That was not the deal. You cannot—"

I grab the back of his head and slam it onto the table. The table shakes, his friends flinch, and when Halfeather comes back up, he's gasping. "Please. Oh, Wild Gods, please."

Leaning down, I whisper into his ear. "We know about your little *schemes*, Dirky boy. I'll send your wives pretty black veils to wear at your funeral. You're rex to three sweet tweety birds, aren't you?"

Dirk splutters.

"Thank you, Mr Halfeather." Scythe stands and puts out his cigarette on the table. He beckons to Eugene with two fingers. The bird hastily flaps into air and settles on Scythe's arm.

My brother takes Eugene and stalks back up the stairs. But Xander and I remain in place, looking down at the remaining four eagles at the table. I smirk at my dragon-brother and he smirks back, raising a hand where brilliant red flames aggressively spark to life.

We don't leave until the screaming ends and there are five crispy bodies on the floor.

We head back up the stairs with Xander throwing fireballs behind him, but back inside the shop, he lingers at a rack.

Dragons love sparkly things and I think he's attracted to a shirt with rhinestones on it.

"Let's go," I project into Xander's mind—a quirk of being a wolf.

"Here." He throws me a black T-shirt with a horse on the left side of the chest. "You can't keep walking around half-naked. We have standards, you know."

I roll my eyes because Xander is currently wearing a T-shirt that he's ripped the sleeves off. On the front is a splattered white design of his latest favourite European rock band. But I pull on the shirt anyway because Aurelia is nearby and I want to look nice when we finally reunite.

I hate her, and she's half-mad, but she's my regina, and my animus is howling at me to look my best for her.

Pulling the T-shirt on, I scratch at the rune on my index finger, a little gift from the Serpent King. Blood deals are dangerous, and our kind don't like to mix with them, but *this* particular one we all made an exception for.

Aurelia needs to die. She's a danger to me, my

brothers and everything we've worked for. And if her dad wants to be the one to do it, then by the Old Laws, he has the right to.

We head out and Xander summons a beach ball-sized molten flame between his hands and tosses the entire thing over his shoulder.

Just as I leap out of the store with a *"whoop!"* my eye catches on something and I snatch it up before the entire place explodes in a shower of flames and glass.

We catch up to Scythe, who is casually strolling down the pavement, with Eugene unhappily trailing behind him. Ducking my head down in the way of predators, I sneak up to the chicken and pounce, plucking him right off the pavement. He squawks in terror and pecks at my hand, but I hold him safe against my chest and make gentle clucking sounds. He calms down and Scythe turns to look at me expectantly.

Lifting my nose to the summer air, I stalk forwards, scenting what's on the wind. The breeze is cool, though the air is hot. It smells like roasting eagle, smoke, and food cooking in the cafes across the road.

But something pulls at my blood. Something sweet and ancient calls to me in just the same way as the moon calls to the Earth.

I swear under my breath as me and my cock—*not* Eugene—register our regina's vanilla cake scent.

"This way," I gruff to my brothers. "We're close." A frown pulls at my brows. "And she's weak."

Chapter 3

Aurelia

I n a panic, I flash into my human form, wildly searching my surroundings. I can't see them yet and I scramble to my feet. With my shields being back up, I can't 'sense' them in the way a regular regina would sense the mates of her pack.

"*Lee-uh,*" Savage calls softly.

His voice is like a sweet caress down my naked spine and suddenly I'm as still as a deer, my muscles quivering in anticipation. My anima writhes under my skin, pining for the one who hunts me. The one I've already had inside my body.

My *mate*. Savage is my mate.

Freezing is something prey would do, but I'm too tired to be ashamed. I can't deny that I *want* my mates. That I feel their presence at the corner of all things in my reality. That just the knowledge of them being nearby is sending me mad with the need to run *towards* them.

But I can't. I can't fucking let them have me.

It's my brain that's telling me to run, and right now, I think my brain isn't working properly. I summon the last dregs of strength to fling up my shield of invisibility just as I hear the purposeful crunch of heavy boots.

Freedom from my father and this thing that haunts me is so close I can taste it. I just need a little more time. I'm going to the new blended university. I'm going to live my life away from the clutches of my father and his court and be free of this shit.

A scent like pine and spring wafts towards me and I breathe in a full lungful. The female anima inside of me snaps up its head.

My blood pounds in my ears and every cell in my body stands to attention as I fix my eye on the spaces between the trees.

Shards of sunlight pierce the canopy above, cutting through the air in diagonal slashes, illuminating the space in an otherworldly glow.

They walk into the clearing like three kings of hell.

I suck in a sharp, shocked, *primal* breath.

Because this is the first time I'm seeing all three of them in their solid, physical forms without the bars of a cell between us or in their astral forms, and the sight is a sweet and severe jab to my lower gut.

Savage is in the lead. And as my wolf saunters towards my stricken, invisible body, I can't draw breath at all.

Somewhere in the last week, Savage has had a haircut. A dark curl flops onto his forehead, and he has a fade down both sides. He's also shaved the scruff on his jaw, but even with smooth skin, there is a feral, brutal look to him. Savage is even more devastatingly handsome in the sunlight than he was in the dim dark of Charles Halfeather's dungeon.

Somewhere in the last week, as well, Savage had acquired a small black rooster, which is currently quivering under the crook of the wolf's arm, his red frills vibrating in fear.

I have literally zero time to ponder this new development because Savage's hazel eyes are predatory as they sweep the clearing, his head lowered in the fashion of a beast hunting his prey. He knows I'm close.

They must not be using their shifted forms to hunt me because he's in black jeans and a tight black T-shirt that stretches across his fighter's broad chest. Clothes that hide tattoos and scars from what I've guessed is a lifetime of fighting in illegal underground rings.

Scythe prowls after his brother a little distance away. He's the first shark I've met because none of them like to be land-dwellers, and he has that characteristic out-of-this-world, high cheekboned beauty and the long silver hair of his kind.

But that's where his prettiness ends.

It's his appearance that surprises me the most because he's hunting through the forest in what I'm sure is an expensive black business shirt and slacks. With the tattoos on his neck and black ink across his hands, he looks like some dangerous hitman. Ice-blue eyes search the clearing and a chill consumes me at that purely lethal

E.P. Bali

expression. Unlike the others, he's only ever spoken two sentences to me.

Xander strolls in behind Scythe.

The dragon's got his usual nasty sneer on, but on a face that is sheer fine-boned masculine beauty, he manages to make it look sexy. The last time I saw him, he was strung up, half naked against a dungeon wall, and that is in stark contrast to his chosen appearance now.

His long black hair is currently tied up at the nape of his neck. He's got a black nose ring and a dangling cross on his left ear. In a black tank top and slashed jeans, he's pretty devastating—even without the glowing silver eyes that allow him to see through his physical blindness. He's got one headphone in, but I note that his old music device is gone—swapped for a shiny new black phone stuck into his front jeans pocket.

Put that all together and you have three six-and-a-half foot beasts who would send any normal person running in the other direction.

Instead, my body is trying to lean *towards* them. Stupid, *idiotic*, horny anima.

These are three alpha males and should all be rexes of their own packs. Instead, they're all supposed to be *mine*. I'm supposed to be their regina, the leader and central point of our mating group.

My eyes hone in on the fact that Savage is still wearing my black hair tie—from *one night* of weakness—where he'd slipped it off my hair and onto his own wrist. Oddly, that same hand is also holding a fluro pink handbag. It's tiny, glossy, looks expensive, and is ridiculous hanging off his large, tattooed hand. Completely out of my control, my traitorous anima lets out a silent, sad cry.

All three heads snap towards me.

Dear Wild Mother, I'm so dead.

Xander is little more than a blur and I don't realise that he's circled behind me until I'm tackled to the forest floor. We fall onto the leaf-litter with a crash and my side explodes with pain. My invisibility shield goes down as a pathetic sort of wail leaves my throat.

Some primal part of me relishes the feel of Xander's large, hard body encircling mine, but it's quickly overtaken by a rage borne of the realisation that they've actually caught me despite my best efforts over *five* whole days.

Call me an overachiever, but I thought I could do better.

Xander's arms tighten around my bare stomach as his breath tickles my ear. "You're weak, serpent girl. I could hear your panting from twenty paces away."

I close my eyes with a resigned sigh. Yeah, I *am* pretty weak right now. Is an hour of sleep too much to ask for?

Get yourself together, Aurelia. Think.

Perhaps it's being so close to my mates that gives me a burst of energy, because as Xander roughly hauls me up to standing, my mind is suddenly sharp.

I'm stark naked. Tits out, bits out, buns pressed against some part of Xander I can't afford to think about right now.

My power rises, wild and ready, because this is actually the most embarrassing thing that's ever happened to me. That burger must be kicking in, too.

Xander roughly pulls my arms behind my back, holding both my wrists in just one of his own. And even as I hate him for doing this to me, I can't help but feel how warm his hand is against my cold skin. How his fingers are curling around my wrists. I swallow my desire down and fix a scowl to my face as Savage and Scythe stand like rigid giants before me, glowering with hate.

Oddly, strangely—perhaps disturbingly—neither of the brothers look down past my face.

"Lia," Savage says quietly, and my heart cries at the way he says my name. But he's frowning and fingering the pink handbag.

He comes forwards, bends to place it at my feet, swiftly turns around and stalks off, his shoulders tight like he hates himself for it.

For the second time, I stop breathing.

I know exactly what this is. The male animus inside Savage is forcing him to give me, his regina, a gift. If we were in a normal mating group, this would be the right thing to do. The normal and expected thing. But we *aren't* normal in any way, and I can't give into the powerful urge to reach down and cradle the bag in my arms and kiss it like a baby.

None of them trust me. Or even like me. Savage finds me attractive, I know, and he's been the only one to touch me. He gave me the best orgasm of my life with those strong fingers, and I think that's why his beast feels the urge to gift me things more than the others. Plus, he's a wolf, and they prize family structures more than any other order.

As touched as I am, it's heart-wrenching because I can't accept it.

"You know the price of that bag?" Xander sneers in my ear. "Seven dead eagles, one human with PTSD, and a shop up in flames. Solid two million in damages."

My heart sinks so low into my body that I'm pretty sure it's sitting in my feet.

"And do you know what?" Savage cries, suddenly whirling around to glare at me, his eyes wild and furious. "I'll kill one hundred fucking more beasts to get rid of this fucking rage I feel. I can't believe you tried to kill us, Lia!"

Scythe is silent and pacing behind him as I stare at them in shock. I close my gaping mouth before crying, "I didn't try to kill you! I would never!"

The three of them go stiff and Scythe stops his pacing to stare at me with those icy blue eyes.

Being looked at by Scythe is like having a pair of ice picks spearing into you. Being *stared* at by him? It's like those ice picks are *twisting*. It's cold and calculating, but damn, he looks hot doing it.

To think I'd snuck in track pants to cover his naked ass in that dungeon, when he's used to wearing expensive clothes like this? I'm embarrassed I even tried now.

Xander's grip tightens painfully around my wrists. "Snake's not lying," he snaps. "But you can't deny that you're running away from us. And you lied about not being our regina."

It's a heinous crime to reject your mates. Among our

37

kind, only the truly evil would choose to destroy something so sacred.

I remain silent...until Scythe advances towards me, looking like the devil himself with the darkness that wraps around him. It's then that I see what he has in his hands.

A shining length of obsidian chain.

Terror that's deeply ingrained in my being grips me in its mad fist.

"No!" I scream, bucking like a donkey under Xander's grip. "You can't use that!"

Scythe pauses in his advance, and that's all I need. I slam a shield of power into Xander with every calorie of strength that burger gave me. The dragon stumbles back, releasing me, and I *run*. As I do, I whip three shields over the males behind me, trapping them inside bubbles of my force. They immediately rage against them.

"I'll get you, Lia!" Savage roars from behind me, pounding his fists against my shield. "You're fucking *mine!*"

My heart shatters into pieces at the rage in his voice. That sound is a song no mate should ever hear.

"You can't hide!" Xander shouts, slamming the entire force of a dragon's burning fist into my shield.

I scream, stumbling as pain erupts in my brain and I have no choice but to let the shield holding Xander go.

A shard of fear shoots through my center as Scythe silently rips his jail like it's a piece of paper, instantly freeing himself.

With a primal cry, Savage is out a fraction of a second

later and I have no choice but to take flight. Bursting into eagle form, feathers tear through my skin, a beak bursts through my mouth, and I'm airborne in five jittery strokes. I clear the trees just as the males behind me storm through the forest under me.

Golden success lifts me higher on the wind...until a mighty, guttural roar funnels through the air.

There is only one creature in our world that can produce that terrifying, hair-raising sound.

I feel only dread as I register a wild and ferocious heat chasing me.

In the face of a dragon, I'm nothing but a piddly little pigeon.

Chapter 4

Aurelia

Xander's power hits me like a heatwave from a forest fire; a wall of blazing energy that makes me falter in mid-air.

A huge shadow passes over me like a missile, and panicking, I dive into the trees. I fly at trunk-level through the forest, zipping through the trunks, my mind scrambling to figure how the hell I'm going to escape a real live dragon.

Xander must really be furious if he lost control and shifted. The Council of Beasts places strict rules on when and how dragons fly. Well, either that, or he simply doesn't care about rules.

Something about Xander tells me it's the latter.

My little heart is pounding, my head is throbbing, and I swear some of my feathers are singed. I have no idea where Scythe and Savage are, but they can't be far behind.

As I fly for my life, a roar shakes the very particles of air above me. I don't know what type of restraint Xander has on his magic—or his morals—because he could very well incinerate this forest in one breath. But that would land him in an actual beast prison or he'd become a fugitive they'd have to put down.

Even so, a dragon flying through the air is an issue for the council and he's giving our location away to everyone in the area.

Once they saw the damage at the Opal Feather, someone will have called the animalia police and the state's elite retrieval unit will have been dispatched. My best bet is to head right into town, where my mates will be reluctant to cause a ruckus.

I mourn the loss of that handbag for a single awful second.

Okay, I know they're unhinged, but *seriously*? I need to move faster.

Snapping my beak and swearing bloody murder, I clear the forest and come to the main road that leads up to town. The road becomes a bridge where, underneath, travels a slow-moving river, bordered by tall eucalypts and red bottle brushes.

Hiding is useless because they'll sniff me out right away. But...Savage can't scent me if I'm in water! Thinking fast, I glide towards the bridge where I promptly tuck in my wings and dive headfirst into the river.

The impact hurts when I hit the cold surface and it's

jarring to my already strained nerves. It's murky underneath and eagles were never made for swimming, so I hop out and huddle in the shade of the bridge. A truck zooms past above me and I shiver, trying to catch my breath.

I check in with my power and see that I'm down to my last two shields. I'm severely depleted--the type of depletion that will take me days to recover from. My anima howls miserably.

I know, girl, I tell her. *But we'll figure it out. We have no choice here.*

Huffing through my beak, I try and piece my mind together after seeing my three mates in the flesh. Xander touched me for the first time, and his body is like an imprint on my naked back and his fingers like a brand on my wrists. They were big, firm hands that—

Shit. No, arousal is something I can't have mixing with my scent. Female anima can send sexual signals to their mates without the need for scent at all.

We had a...little incident a week ago when, in a moment of great horny weakness, I accidentally let my guard down and sent out a regina's siren song. That was the thing that revealed who I was. All five of them arrived at my tiny one-bedroom ramshackle bungalow of exile in their astral forms.

Though I hadn't been able to see anyone—except Savage—as shadows, they'd all seen *me* and my mating mark. All five will recognise me on sight now.

A stupid mistake and one I would definitely *not* be repeating.

The memory makes me shiver and I clamp down on my wild anima, who knows that sex with my mates would be excellent fuel for my power.

What to do, what to do. My brain is mush, and the fine bones in my wings burn with strain.

Suddenly, a cold presence at the corner of my thoughts comes slamming into me and I clamp down on a scream.

I would know Scythe's ice and tundra power anywhere. *The water.* He's found me. How could I be so stupid as to sit here, by a body of water, when one of my mates commands that element?

Cursing my horny ass, I make a split decision and leap out from under the bridge. The air is fire in my throat and there's definitely the spicy scent of dragon-made smoke in the air, but I beat my battered wings for all they're worth, shaking the water from them as I do. Neither men nor dragon are anywhere to be seen as I head into open air and away from the forest once again.

There's a group of buildings on my left and I turn around to see a large park full of people...and no less than ten black hunting vans, blue and red sirens flashing.

It's funny because for the past five days, I knew all these beasts were after me, but seeing the vans sprawled out, officers in black tactical gear running around with automatic weapons, blue and red lights flashing? I'm stumped. Actually *stumped* that this is all for me and my mates.

Just as my stomach drops in tortured realisation, a voice like the jagged edge of a knife cuts through the air.

"Don't touch her, she's mine!"

Frantically, I look down to see Lyle Pardalia in a navy three-piece suit standing like the archangel of death at the head of the tactical forces. There's a long black machine on his shoulder that's aimed right at me. His amber eyes flash in lethal calculation.

Seriously? A bazooka...and a suit? What is wrong with this guy?

His tanned jawline could cut skin open, I'm sure, with the signature long blonde hair that lions typically wear, tied off his face. I'm stunned by his figure, by the fact that he looks like he wants to kill little old me.

The lion *really* doesn't like me. I probably hurt his male ego by thwarting him that first time at the motel. He's definitely out for revenge now.

Just as I try to veer backwards, I am held in place by a force so great I think it's going to squeeze me until my intestines burst out of my abdomen. I let out a high-pitched shriek just as Lyle fires his weapon. The ball shooting out of it becomes a black net of tourmaline and obsidian. It swallows me whole, closing around my body and immediately rendering any of my power useless.

The net burns my feathers right through and it's so darned painful as the magic-neutralising properties in it force me to shift back into my naked human body.

It's also embarrassing as all hell due to the audience of well over thirty council hunters, both male and female, staring in disbelief. Lyle levitates me—telekinesis being the feline power—down to land as they all shamelessly stare. But from this high, I can make out a flurry of activity across the clearing. A group of council hunters are surrounding three males.

Savage is putting up, what I'm sure is, a half-hearted fight, thrashing out, kicking and punching as he manically laughs. Abruptly, he shouts, "If anyone hurts my chicken, they're fucking dead! Hear me? Fucking dead!"

Sure enough, the rooster gives a sad, muffled squawk from his own cage, a tiny black hood on his head stopping him from seeing anything.

A very human and naked Xander is laughing as two council hunters are spontaneously set alight, their bodies erupting in violent orange flames. They scream for a single terrifying second before the flames go out and they drop to the grass. I watch the glowing white lights fade from Xander's eyes as obsidian nets are thrown upon him. He merely scoffs at his captors like they're all disappointments.

Scythe is coming willingly, on his feet, already handcuffed in the black shackles, and I'm surprised when I see the hunters keeping a respectful distance from him. The shark's cold eyes are on me, however, as Lyle dumps me unceremoniously onto the grass, my arms bound to my torso, thankfully covering my breasts. But my ass is laid bare to the world in between the thin ropes of the net.

Knowing the deputy headmaster of Animus Academy is in complete control of my body when he comes to look down upon me, amber eyes narrowed, makes me want to punch him in his pretty face. But I can't even snarl at him with my frozen form.

"You made me do this the hard way, Miss Aquinas,"

he says in that flat monotone he seems to enjoy using. I've dubbed it his 'shopping-list voice'. "At Animus Academy, you'll get the help you need. You'll be safe."

A mad laugh is trying to make its way out of my chest, but I'm too tired and it turns into a cough. This beast thinks I'll be *safe* in a prison school? Where the most feral and criminally minded eighteen to twenty-five years olds of our kind try and learn how to be civilised?

Laughs and jokes all around, lion-man.

Mr Deputy Headmaster-slash-jailer grabs a blanket from a council hunter and throws it over me. Even as I grind my teeth together in shame, I'm relieved he at least has the decency to do that.

Because, as he levitates me back up, I can see that now there's a crowd of humans waiting on the other side of a line of police tape, and many of them have their phones out. I die a little on the inside at the humiliation of it all as Lyle levitates me through the open back doors of a waiting military-grade van.

I'm so deeply fucked by this capture I don't even know whether to cry or scream when the doors shut and plunge me into an all-encompassing darkness. As the vehicle rumbles to life and rolls onto the road, my exhaustion comes back in full force. My eyes slide heavily shut and my entire body goes limp, my anima warbling sadly.

A teeny, *tiny* piece of me is relieved that I now get to lie down and rest. That I don't have to run for my life for the next few hours. That was getting really tiring, really fast.

This is just a reprieve for me, right? Only a teensy detour in my well-laid plans.

Except, I know in my heart it's more than that, because Animus Academy is just as much a prison as it is a reform school. And no one in history has ever escaped.

Chapter 5

Savage

I've never been more pissed off in my life.

Aurelia was so close. *So close* I could practically taste her perfect fucking olive skin on my tongue. Taste those rosebud lips and those delicious chocolate nipples. Xander got the first physical touch over me, and as we sit on the floor of the rumbling military truck, I'm ready to pull his brains out of his eye sockets for it.

Snapping out my leg, I strike the ugly dragon where he sits against the wall. "Fuck you, Xander."

Even rendered blind by the magic-suppressing shackles, my dragon brother doesn't take it lying down. He launches himself at me and we break out into a vicious scuffle. Does it matter that we're bound neck to pelvis with tourmaline chains? Not one bit.

As Scythe sits, still and brooding next to me, Xander and I try and break each other into pieces by sheer force of will. He snaps at me with his teeth and I jerk my head

51

to the side before body slamming him against the titanium wall. The entire truck shakes from the force of our aggression.

Just as I'm considering shoving my teeth into his eye holes, there's a shout from the driver's seat. It's only a matter of seconds before they've swerved us off the road and I go tumbling to the other wall. Xander lands on top of me with a grunt.

"Ugly lizard," I snap as he rolls off me.

"Fetid mutt," he spits back.

Once again, Xander proves his entitled upbringing by throwing big words around. What does *fetid* even mean? It sounds like an STD, and the thought sends me growling.

Heavy boots crunch on gravel and the doors are pulled open to reveal a big scary bastard of a wolf and four others flanking him, their automatic rifles pointed at us.

It's Reuben fucking Lunaris. An almost seven foot tall motherfucker with a ruddy beard and even though he must be at least fifty years of age, he's tanked.

"Separate them," Reuben barks like he doesn't know us. "Full gurney restraint." I turn to give Scythe a look to see if he's seen the wolf our father used to call the 'Monster Wrangler', but my half-brother is staring drolly ahead at the wall. He often does that, stares into the distance, thinking dark thoughts. He's probably thinking about how he's going to kill me. Or maybe he's thinking about Aurelia and her long fluttery eyelashes.

Xander and I are dragged out roughly by our scruffs

like we're cubs and dumped on the gravel on the side of the road. Wisely, they leave Scythe where he is.

When I see what they have planned for us, I tilt my head back and give a hacking laugh.

"He's rabid," mutters one of the retrieval mutts.

"Nah," says Reuben, before he shoves a cloth sack with a breathing mesh over my head, "just mad."

I'm still laughing as they begin strapping me, upright, to the wheeled gurney with more heavy metal chains. By the time they're done, Xander and I are covered neck to toe in obsidian with not an inch left to wriggle.

Hannibal Lecter, my personal god, has nothing on us.

As they wheel me to my own vehicle, I squeal a high-pitched, "Weeeee!"

My regina is going the same place as us and that's the *only* reason for my good mood. They've captured her *for* us and I'm thinking of sending someone flowers for it.

The monster wrangler grabs the doors to my new truck and I can just make out a white-toothed grin through the mesh. Before he slams the heavy metal shut, he mutters, "Good to see you alive and kicking, Sav."

Not for long, it won't be.

* * *

Hours later, we arrive at Animus Academy in a style only me and my bond-brothers deserve. At the back of my mind, I wonder what Lyle Pardalia is going to do with us at his cute little school. Xander and I can't be controlled. Scythe has his own agenda and is a menace all on his own. I hardly understand why he agreed to be taken in the first place. I could have done this myself, but my brother always has his own nefarious reasons for doing what he does. The things a shark can see and feel, no one else can.

I begin to smell the ferality of the school forty minutes out. It's a smell that warns civilised beasts to stay away. It's a marker of the type of creatures who are forced to attend the so-called academy.

There's a bump as we pass through the gates and outside, I can hear the ruckus that is enrolment day. There's a general feeling of tension, aggression, and outright violence perfuming the air.

My favourite type of cologne.

After Aurelia's vanilla cake and strawberries scent, of course. A little sweet, a little tart, just like her.

Thinking of her instantly makes me rage, and I feel the chains groan under the strain of suppressing my power. My animus keens for her like a lost puppy and I growl under my breath, telling it to shut up.

The urge to serve her is at war with my hatred. She says she didn't try to kill us, and fine, alright, but she still refuses to acknowledge us as her mates. I can no longer see her mating mark—a skull with five marks on the side of her neck, matching to every member of our mating group—but I'm sure as fuck going to find out why.

No one has the power to mask the celestial mating bond. Literally no one.

All six of us share a unique mating mark imprinted on the sides of our necks by the stars themselves. Only members of your group can see that mark, and beasts spend lifetimes hunting for the other members of their soul-group. Those beasts can then pool their powers. It was our Goddess-given right to be together.

And she didn't want to.

That alone makes her dangerous. A regina has power over her mates, whether we want her to or not, and we can't have someone existing in the world with that much leverage over us.

A roar sounds outside and I know they'll have their hands full with the new intake. This academy is made to rehabilitate feral and rabid adult shifters under the age of twenty-five. They never even bothered sending me an invite, and I was quite offended by that.

But what happens when you put a group of feral beasts-turned-human in one school? Ha! I'm sure Lyle has been fucking around with his success statistics because the entire system is rubbish. I've been to *actual* beast prison and seen first hand the dangerous shifters this school couldn't fix.

A tiny part of me worries about Aurelia being put in here with us. Animus Academy was traditionally made for the male beast spirit we call the animus, as we are more volatile than the female beast spirit we call the anima. When they started taking in animas, they never even bothered to change the name. But importantly, the ratio is something like five males to one female in this place, and she is a beautiful, stunning, physically *perfect* girl.

An *unclaimed* beautiful, perfect girl.

Aurelia reminds me of Princess Jasmine only with blue eyes and a power that makes me feel like lightning around her.

It's a shame we have to kill her.

But she'll get attention from every cock in the place, which is a different problem.

I've worked myself up enough thinking about this so that by the time Reuben slams open the doors again, I'm a growling, snarling mess.

"Quiet, pup," he chuckles. "You'll be allowed out once we get inside."

I haven't been called a pup since I got shoved into my first fighting cage at three years old and it sends me feral.

But the chains work well and I only get a groan out of the metal as they wheel me out. I get a good view of the pretty cast iron and gold gates of the prison-school. Even through my spit hood, I can see the gold glinting in the sun...until I'm wheeled around and get to see the pure carnival of fun that awaits me inside.

The receiving bay at Animus Academy is part zoo, part jailhouse.

When I was little, Scythe told me all about the academy (*threatened* me with it, more like). The main building itself is over a hundred and fifty years old, dating back to the mid-1800s when our kind first arrived in this country during the gold rush. While the core building is an ancient gothic monstrosity that reminds me of a cross between a dragon's lair and a witches' castle, they kept updating the place with the latest technology, extending it one wing at a time until it became a huge complex built to keep the budding crims inside.

There's a line of students going through metal detectors, manned by no less than twelve burly security beasts, most of them with automatic weapons or dart rifles. Two of them are breaking up a fight, but I can't tell what it's about—likely an animus who didn't like another animus' scent. A feeling of nostalgia takes me, because federal prison is similar, except the beasts are older and meaner... and there aren't pretty animas around to *really* fuck us up.

Once the prisoners get through the security check, they go into medical-veterinary where the medics will check them for fleas, scabies, mites and other parasites our kind tend to pick up when we go a little feral.

There are a couple of nervous parents waiting just beyond a steel bar, trying to see if their kids made it through okay. *Their* kids will be the tamer, petty crime sort. They'll complete their three-year program and go back to a loving home to get a regular job, find their mating group and live happily ever after.

The rest of us criminals don't get that. It's lucky I have Scythe, otherwise I'd probably be locked up in the rabid cages like the ones I can see snarling and spitting in the receiving bay.

Six of the thick metal cages on wheels hold shifted beasts. Two scarred tigers, two wolves, a python and a hyena. The tigers have been darted and lie snoring at the bottom of their cages, but the others are staring each other down.

Put us ferals and rabids all together and what do you get? Bedlam.

Suddenly, I can't wait.

The entire bay goes silent as our fleet of guards wheel us into a line beside the sliding glass doors leading to the medical wing. Scythe just walks right through and the two security bears at the doors let him.

Bernie and Ernie work for us and are loyal to all ends. I call them the Forklift Twins because though they're not all that smart, to be on the end of one of their punches is the end of the line for you. I've had Ernie lift the front of a semi once and he didn't even break a sweat as I slid a full-grown lion underneath the tires.

A few metres from me is the queue of beasts in their human forms, around thirty males and five females. They've either been escorted here, or attended as instructed by the council, and are currently eyeing me and my brothers as if we're made of explosives.

They'll soon learn they're not wrong, but I'm not interested in them. I want to know who's already in there and if they can throw a decent nose-shattering punch. My body is coiled tight, just waiting for a chance to vent my rage. I want blood on my hands and this is as good a place as any to get it.

Satisfied this prison-school might not be as bad as I initially thought, I settle back on my gurney, getting comfortable until they release us.

The animalia inside are veterinarians as well as medical doctors, and two academy guards wheel us through within minutes. Mostly because I think we're scaring the parents.

We go past two sets of steel doors which are locked behind us before they take Xander and me into cubicles separated by curtains where there are more armed guards. I know immediately there's no point trying to escape. Scythe can probably get out, but if Aurelia is here, I can't leave until I kidnap her to return her to where she rightfully belongs.

Reuben takes my spit hood off and wheels me against the wall where there are height measurement lines for my celebrity photo. A guard holds a piece of printed paper just under my chin and I think it says my name and inmate ID.

"Say cheese," gruffs Reuben, holding up a large black camera.

"Suck my cock!" I cheer, sticking my tongue out to the side and winking as the flash goes off.

He shakes his head, passes the camera to a guard, and proceeds to unloop my many obsidian chains. It takes a while and five guards have their weapons pointed at me the entire time. They leave me in plain metal handcuffs and footcuffs that bring back all sorts of memories that make me warm and fuzzy.

"Wrangler, I want Eugene back," I say, cracking my neck.

"What is he? Your emotional support rooster?" Reuben is serious as he says it, but his grey eyes are glittering over his full beard as he towers over me and everyone else in the room. It's why they used him to referee my matches when I was a teenager.

"Something like that." I roll my shoulders and try not to laugh at the fully covered guards. They have their faces covered with a black gaiter like they do in real prison. "Kind of like Xander's headphones," I lie. "If I don't have him, I go berserk and start a killing rampage. You know what I mean?"

To my surprise, he nods and I sense him transmitting a mental message to another wolf on his team. Within seconds, I hear a questioning squawk.

"I'm here, Eugene!"

He appears in the arms of a she-wolf with his feathers all ruffled and I snatch him from her.

"You behave for the nice doctor, pup," Reuben warns, "and you can keep your rooster. If not, he goes on a spit for me and my boys."

I'd like to see you fucking try. But I ignore him as the nurse enters, and he steps sideways to guard her.

She's a tiny female with a black bob—an eagle, by her scent—and holds a clipboard that she checks carefully. Since eagles are the order with healing powers, a lot of them become doctors and nurses. I wonder if that's what Aurelia wants, seeing as she is an eagle, too. She's *really* good at healing and it was the entire reason I'd met her. They'd sent her to heal the beast in the cell next to mine when we'd been held captive by Charles Halfeather. At first I wondered why they'd sent this young anima to do a job, but it soon became clear as I stared at her while she worked.

"Is Savage your real first name, Mr Fengari?" the birdie doc asks slowly. I decide she mustn't care much for her life if she works in a place like this.

I glance at Reuben. "Yeah, my parents were assholes."

She nods like she already suspected this and hands me a bright red lanyard with an ID card swinging on it. I take it and examine my picture. Satisfied, I put it around my neck and shake my head because they'd never give us a lanyard in a real prison—they're too good for strangling with.

"What does it say?" I ask, running my finger down the black writing that loops in a repeating pattern all around the lanyard. I can tell it's the same sentence and that it starts with a 'D'.

Birdie is not surprised because illiteracy is common amongst the feral population.

"It says 'Dangerous, do not approach'." Ah, a warning for the other students. Cute. "And I hear you've been to Blackwater Prison."

"They've been talking about me, have they?" I say with a chuckle.

"Your reputation precedes you, yes."

I smile wistfully at the memory as I stroke Eugene. "Yes, nurse, I was sent to Blackwater Penitentiary on my sixteenth birthday."

Her brows shoot up as she stares at me. "They sent you to an adult federal prison at *sixteen*?"

Leaning forwards, I whisper to her as if it's a great

secret. "It was a life sentence. There was nowhere else to put me."

Until Scythe planned his little jailbreak, that is.

I chuckle at the horrified expression she tries to hide and the fact that the guards standing behind her go all tense. Reuben hasn't taken his eyes off me the entire time, but he's always been the clever sort.

"My dad broke me in young," I say by way of explanation.

This place is going to be a piece of cake.

Chapter 6

Aurelia

My hearing returns first and I immediately know that I'm in some sort of hospital, lying on a narrow bed. I groan as I blink my eyes open and realise that I must have passed out in the truck. My throat is sandpaper, every bone in my body aches like it's on fire, and even my eyeballs burn against the harsh white light above me.

I suppose that's what happens when obsidian chains force your bones to shift when they don't want to. It's even worse because I'm so depleted.

Bright halogen lights are above me, the smell of hand sanitiser is in my nose, and there's the constant beep of observation and monitoring machines. I'm in a cubicle sectioned off with blue plastic curtains and there's an IV drip in the back of my hand. I go to sit up and immediately realise both my hands are handcuffed to the bedrails on either side of me.

A quick look outside reveals two armed guards, dressed in all black complete with a helmet, balaclava, and plastic goggles. Honestly, they look more like military than prison guards and I'm sure it's all to scare us.

I can happily say it's bloody-well working.

Grimacing, I put my head back down, and my anima searches the immediate vicinity for my mates. I pull my most important shield up, one grating inch at a time, and tell her to calm the hell down. They'll be here somewhere, I'm sure of it.

There's a patient call bell looped around my right hand, and I squint at the green button before pressing it. Some distance away, a new low beep adds itself to the cacophony of sound.

I wait about five minutes before a tiny lady with brown wisps coming loose from her bun hurries into my cubicle, enthusiastically rubbing her hands with sanitiser.

"Hello Aurelia," she says, flashing me a cheery smile. "I'm Hope, the charge nurse. How are you feeling?"

"Uh, sore, I guess." I do a quick scan of my body and note that nothing is grievously painful to indicate severe injury. It's then that I see they've put a pink cotton hospital gown on me and a plastic ID band with my name. I cringe, wondering how many people saw me naked on the way in here.

"Alright. Well, I'm here to make sure you're in good shape before you start the enrolment process—" There's a commotion a few cubicles down and an alarm goes off just before a loud, angry roar. Heavy-booted feet charge past my cubicle towards it. "Looks like not everyone is happy to be here." Hope waves a hand, chuckling, and I think I like her. "Once this bag of fluid is finished, we can take all this down. It looks like you've not been eating or drinking at all these past few days? You're very dry and your magic is in your boots."

Heat floods my face. I wonder if I should lie, but I haven't had much human-to-human interaction in days and I feel like I might as well tell her the truth. "I-I was running," I admit. "I didn't have time to do much other than...run. Fly I mean."

She makes a disapproving sound as she consults a clipboard. "Do you have a history of doing that?"

Something inside of me is angry at being asked this question. I'm not a felon, nor some feral, rebellious teen. But my voice is soft as I answer. "No. That was the first."

And it won't be the last. As soon as I can get out of here, I will be flying away again. I just need to scope out a way. I can do it. I *know* I can.

She nods. "Any problematic behaviours we need to know about? Your criminal record is clean, but your family doctor's records stop at age thirteen. You just turned twenty, that's seven years of no records."

So she knows whose daughter I am then. Or used to be anyway. "Yeah, I haven't needed to see a doctor these past few years." Because I was exiled from my court and had to deal with healing myself from minor ailments. Being out on my own at thirteen and learning to cook, I got food poisoning a couple of times, and colds, but nothing worse than that.

She asks me more questions about my health, of

which there's nothing much to note other than my periods being painful and irregular and that I am not currently sexually active (to which my anima grunts dramatically). She tells me they took bloods, hair samples and mouth swabs from me while I was out. I feel a little uneasy at that, but apparently people who are charged with major crimes don't get choices. The list of questions is pretty extensive, and it's jarring just to even be speaking openly with another person.

"I noticed you have rather aggressive fang marks on the left side of your neck."

My entire body goes stiff as I realise the cobra bite my dad left on me two weeks ago still hasn't healed—not because I couldn't heal it, but because I'd purposefully let it sit there to remind myself of why I needed to get the hell out of this state. Why I couldn't just give in. My shields have been covering the mark until now so I'm guessing my depleting magic let it slip through.

"It's nothing."

Hope gives me a look. "Were you attacked?"

"No." Yes. Fuck, yes. I was thrown against the wall and everything. All because I told my father that as a legal adult now, I am no longer under his power. He sure rectified *that* misunderstanding.

Hope seems to understand she's not going to get any more from me and tries a different angle. "Do you have a mating group?"

A claiming bite from a mate might have explained it. Alas, no one owns me and they never will.

"No," I lie.

"What did your phoenix prophesy reveal?"

It's usually considered rude to ask, but I suppose in this place, all bets are off. "Um, three other eagles."

She smiles kindly at me, as if I'm a girl with a friendly, sweet mating group of eagles waiting for me in the ether somewhere. "Some anima find their mating groups here, Lia. You could be one of the lucky ones." I give a weak, fake laugh and pretend to look hopeful like a normal girl, who isn't running from her mates, would. "But you aren't sworn in to the Court of Wings, Lia?"

I've avoided this for seven years. Legally, I needed to be sworn into a court. Because I was out as an eagle, just as my mother was listed when she was alive, I should have moved from the Serpent Court to the Court of Wings at puberty. Heat floods my face again and I shake my head. "I... I've been—" I bite my lip. "I'm sorry. I don't know what to say to that."

Fuck, I'm the biggest idiot on the planet. I should have come up with a story for that by now. Something better than, 'oh right, about that. My dad kept me in a ratty bungalow for seven years and forbade me to leave it unless he had secret *jobs* for me to do where I would go invisible to fighting rings and illegal court fights and heal the injured and no one has ever figured out it was me running in and out and not the Serpent King's scary, powerful magic'.

But Hope suspects none of this because she is a kind sort of woman and pats my thigh. "We are a fair court and would be thrilled to have you. Especially given your marks in the healing course you completed last year."

I mumble something, because I *do* like healing. It's my secondary power, which is a rare thing on its own, but it makes a good cover for my actual shielding powers.

Hope finishes her questionnaire and finds me clothes. And when I say clothes, I mean the latest prison fashion straight off the runways of old Blackwater. The orange jumpsuit smells like it's been at the bottom of the box for years. Most of the girls must be smart enough to come with their clothes *on*. The guards have to take off my handcuffs so I can get dressed, but they go back on straight after I pull the curtain back.

The good nurse gives me a zip-lock bag. She puts in it pain killers, a de-wormer, a special shampoo because apparently spending a week in the bush means I might have lice and bird mites now, and a big handful of condoms. When I raise my brows, she nods sombrely. "We give them out for free here."

Our kind are known for our promiscuity, and naturally, with inter-court relations, things have the potential to get figuratively, messy fast. You can only get pregnant by doing the breeding ritual, so that isn't an issue, but that doesn't stop STDs from spreading.

They take a nice mugshot in front of the height lines on the wall outside my cubicle, and within minutes I'm given an ID card that says my name and "Eagle Anima" that's attached to a pink lanyard that says 'Flight Risk' in big black letters.

They have me figured out already.

"Orientation begins tomorrow," Hope says as she leads us out of my cubicle and out into an empty waiting area where another massive guard in head-to-toe black stands with a rifle. "And Aurelia?"

I tightly clutch my zip-lock bag, wary of the sudden change in her tone.

Hope frowns at me. "We increase the security during the first month but...this can be a dangerous place for a young woman, especially a nice one like you. Do not, and I repeat, *do not* ever let your guard down. Stick with the other animas."

Hope leaves me in the waiting room to ruminate on dire thoughts about captivity and bird mites. The prison guard just stands there, his side facing me, dutifully staring at the wall.

Well, shit. Not only did Hope call me a 'nice young woman', she's trying to help me. A feeling of warmth spreads through my chest. Having spent seven years living in exile, it's been so long since an adult has actually tried to help me in an altruistic way. The only other person was my kindly Uncle Ben, who was the one to tell me to run when the Halfeather fire began.

Being visible in this place of so many beasts will be a massive adjustment. My skin erupts with goosebumps and I find myself rubbing my arm with my nose as if it's still a beak I can scratch with.

Cursing myself, I have to admit that I *am* a little feral after all. Spending so much time in shifted form has a jarring effect when you return to your human body and you tend to forget human social rules. Some beasts are so far gone they turn rabid and even forget how to speak completely. Even worse? Some beasts we call 'changed' stay in their beast form full-time. Getting a person back from that state is almost impossible. But this exact thing is what Lyle Pardalia claimed to have done in this very school. They hailed him as some sort of genius saviour.

As for me? I've never had a gram of ferality until now. A real sinking into the gutter moment. A sinking that has led me here, to this prison-school, bursting with the very males I've spent a lot of effort trying to avoid. What if the other two mates I've not yet met are also here? It will be game over. Mating groups are ordained by destiny and it's destiny that brings us together through orchestrated moments of chance.

But I *can* protect myself. I've been doing it for years. The hydration Hope gave me is already helping me recover my power. As I wait, I actually have enough energy now to pull up most of my shields. My magical store is low, at embers level, but I should recover within a few days of eating normally. If I can just wait that long, I'll have the power to use my secret invisibility shield to get the hell out of here.

I flick at my new baggy prison wear. This and my fancy new zip-lock bag are all the possessions I have. Once I'm past the interstate line, I'll somehow need to get a job to start making money. I can't just steal from the innocent.

The day's events catch up to me and I lean my head back against the cold stone wall. Somewhere in here,

Xander, Scythe and Savage are getting processed and being taken to dorm rooms to start the school year.

It's laughable. Those beasts sitting in *class*? Writing essays and learning manners? I imagine Scythe sitting at a tiny desk with a pencil and his tongue between his teeth as he concentrates, copying notes from a blackboard.

Wild Goddess, what am I in for?

Chapter 7

Savage

Birdie doc moves down her long checklist.

"Any health issues or injuries I need to know about?"

Xander's quick as usual when he calls out from the cubicle next to us, "Savage has syphilis! We call him Syphy Savvy."

I snarl over my shoulder, then turn politely to the doctor. "I don't, doc. I check my cock daily, if you know what I mean. And I always use protection."

Used. Past fucking tense.

I look down at my index finger where me and my brothers have a serpent's blood contract marked in black ink. I won't be fucking anyone anymore. Not since Aurelia waltzed into my life that fateful day.

Her father made us swear to bring her back to him so he can execute her for us. We also aren't allowed to mate with her according to this contract. There's just something about an animus that finds it difficult to kill his regina. It's not impossible, it's just tough, and once you fuck your regina...well, your beast might not want to let go at all. Once we deliver Aurelia to him, the contract will be fulfilled, the mark will disappear and we will go back to living our lives as we did before.

We just have to make sure no one finds out about it. Especially our regina.

"Actually," doc says, "you can't always tell just by looking at the penis. May I do a quick body scan?"

"Can't wait."

There's no disease or anything stored in any of my cavities, so I'm not worried. Weapons and drugs are for weaker beasts. All I need are my claws and teeth.

She nods, and her gaze changes, her magic surging towards me in a warm, gentle wave. My animus snarls in annoyance because it now doesn't like any female but my regina touching me with her magic. But I refrain from physically growling because I don't need to kill her. She checks over Eugene for good measure and though his heart beats rapidly under my fingers at the attention, he's a good boy and remains still.

"All done, Mr Fengari and Eugene," doc says. "I hope I don't have to see you here again, but somehow I think I will."

Smart birdie.

After she's done with me, the big wolf takes me to meet Scythe and Xander in a holding bay, bursting with armed guards. Both are handcuffed in plain steel with matching red 'Danger', lanyards around their necks, twins to me. Xander is dressed in an orange jumpsuit to cover his nakedness, though his feet are still bare and he sneers at the guards around us.

The only female in the room, a tall lioness in her late twenties, nods at me.

She gives me the usual once-over before her eyes flick to Eugene under my arm. "The deputy headmaster will see you now." Her shiny red lips curve into a smile before she turns and sashays out of the room. Scythe follows her while Xander and I are ushered through by the guards. She's in a blue business dress which makes me think she's Lyle's receptionist or PA, whatever they're called, and she wears her hair in a long golden ponytail down to her lower back. You can always pick out a lion by their hair; they always pride themselves on the length and colour of it.

I'll give it to Lyle Pardalia, he's smart in sending an anima to get us. The three of us might not be good males, but we don't hurt animas and children if we can help it. None of us take kindly to being ordered around, and it's plain disturbing to see Scythe following anyone's direction. And here we are, at a school that's supposed to *tame* us. It's so funny I snort out loud and Xander gives me his 'what the fuck' look, glowing eyes flashing.

We're taken through a series of corridors to the tune of the lioness' stilettos, the thumping of the guards' steel-toed boots, and Xander's Mongolian throat-singing from his headphones. They didn't even try to take it off him at the park. No doubt it was written on his criminal file with big red ink to leave them in.

Eventually, the floor becomes hardwood and we

come across an elevator that we have to get into. It's a process because they refuse to have us all in there together. The lioness goes in first, then my brothers and I go in one at a time with three guards a piece.

We all gather on the third floor where the senior staff must have their offices because here's a number of important-looking doors and with bronze plaques along both walls. Lyle's office door is the only open one, and when the lion sees us, he gives his assistant a nod and gets up from the redwood desk.

"Mr Pardalia will see them alone," the lioness says loftily. "Guards will wait here."

"Are you sure?" asks one that smells like an Eastern brown snake and I mark his scent.

She flashes him a look that could peel paint and the guard shuts his trap.

The three of us follow her into Lyle's office. There's fancy red carpet and the air-con is set super low, which I appreciate, but I also know it's a known technique to help keep the more violent beasts calm.

The lioness swaggers back out of the office, moving her ass in a way that is meant to draw our attention. While I'm used to blatant female displays, I raise a brow as she passes me because I thought Lyle was supposed to be the stiff collar, rule-following sort who wouldn't tolerate that type of thing. She closes the door behind her and I look at Lyle Pardalia properly for the first time.

I've seen him in his TV interviews before, but the beast is something else in real life. He's a big lion, only a tiny bit taller than me and Scythe, at our six foot six. He wears an expensive navy three-piece suit over a body that's broad and well-muscled enough to tell me he works out daily. His whiskey-coloured eyes are so sharp they don't miss a single thing about the three of us, and I know that he's made an assessment of our ferality in the space of seconds.

That's what Lyle is best known for: rehabilitating rabid—and even changed—beasts. It's brutal and painstaking work, but his success rate is *apparently* super high.

There are three chairs in front of his desk, and the desk itself is super clean and organised. There are only papers, fountain pens...and a small faded blue wooden object that catches my eye. It's in the shape of a person with wings and painted with clumsy hands. I get the urge to break it into pieces.

Lyle wisely doesn't bother to offer the chairs and comes to stand in front of his desk, leaning against it and placing his hands on the edge of the wood in an open position to show us he means no harm.

To my chagrin, he ignores Xander and me and addresses our shark.

"Are we going to have a problem, Scythe?" he asks plainly.

The fuck? He should be asking *me*. I snarl, "I'm going to ruin your life, lion."

"Let the men speak, Savage," he replies smoothly. I know he was waiting for my attitude and there's a dark undertone that I don't like.

"This guy," I say silently to my brothers.

79

Lyle's mouth tightens as if he knows I'm talking telepathically.

I grin because I know exactly why he hates me and it's for a fucking brilliant reason.

Scythe looks out the floor-to-ceiling office windows on our left and stares into the distance for a moment. I have some idea of what he's thinking, but my shark-brother is nothing if not unpredictable.

Eventually, his sapphire eyes flick to Lyle. "There will be issues. I will deal with them. Undisturbed." Scythe's voice is horrifying to people who have never heard it, but they don't call Lyle the Beast Breaker for no reason and he doesn't show any sign of being disturbed by Scythe's damaged rasp.

"I was hoping we could work together," Lyle says.

I scoff, but Scythe says evenly, "Our truce will be dependent on a number of factors."

"Of course." The two beasts stare at each other in assessment. The moment stretches out like a taut band that will snap at any second. Even Eugene feels it and starts vibrating like a phone under my arm. There is so much power in this room that I can feel it burning along my skin like cold fire and it's as exciting as it is annoying. Eventually, Lyle says, "I will ensure your requests are met."

So, he has a brain after all.

Scythe gives a single nod, which is more than the lion deserves.

Lyle turns to Xander. "Will your vision be an issue for you here?"

Xander growls at the insult to his prowess. "As long as I have my magic, I'm the same as any other beast. Even without it, I'll deal."

He's not exaggerating, Xander's hearing is godly. One time, I'd broken a rib and not even known it. That night as we lay in our beds—him with his headphones in—he told me to stop breathing because he could hear the bones of my ribs scraping together.

Then he dodged the lamp I flung at him.

"Alright then," Lyle says quietly, his eyes flicking to the three of us, one at a time. "As long as you follow the school rules the same as everyone else, I don't have a problem with you. And Savage, your emotional support rooster can stay."

"Yeah, yeah," I drone, patting Eugene on the head. "We won't go pissing on the furniture."

Lyle ignores me and hands us each a packet of papers, no doubt a list of the school rules in big letters for those of us who can read. When he tries to hand mine to me, I ignore him and he gives the packet to Scythe instead. I imagine it now, 'No fucking in the corridors. No sniffing the females. No running around naked.'

"We have a judicial system here, Savage," Lyle says pointedly to me. "It's a miracle we were allowed to house you here." By all rights, they should have carted me back to the big boy prison. I can't imagine what strings Lyle's pulled to get me here. "No murder. No maiming. Got it?"

I growl under my breath at his tone of dominance and the only thing that stops me from acting on my impulse to go at his throat is Scythe's returning growl.

Chapter 8

Aurelia

"Got a cigarette?" a bored voice drones. I blink myself out of my reverie and turn to see a girl my age saunter in. The first thing I see are thin gold hoop earrings so large they almost touch her shoulders, a skin tight purple bodycon dress and white sneakers. With one hand on her black rolling suitcase, she pops her hip and wrinkles her nose at me. "Get those prison clothes from a dumpster or something?"

"No, I arrived naked." Although they smell awful, it'll be good to cover the fact that I'm hiding my scent. Animalia can usually scent each other's order and I shouldn't really be able to hide it like I do.

She nods and makes a face that says she's impressed. "Nice. Anyway, ciggie?"

"No, sorry."

She rolls her eyes and sits down on the opposite bench, tapping her acrylic nails against her knee. I stare at the glossy black goodness in envy and avoid looking at my own because I know they're jagged and full of dirt.

But I *do* notice that her pink lanyard has no words written on it. It makes me feel real special to be singled out like this, I'll tell you that much.

Only seconds later, someone comes stomping into the room, but I hear their voice first. "T-Touch me again and I'll b-break your arm, *c-cub*."

"Yeah, yeah, dynamite. Get in there." A male voice, no doubt one of the guards.

The prisoner enters the room growling and sniffing the air—a tall beast with close-cropped brown hair, nose, brow and lip pierced with silver on both sides. Their septum piercing wiggles as they sniff at me. They wear a faded blue denim jacket and matching jeans, leaving no doubt in my mind that they're a wolf. That also explains the stutter. Some wolves can have issues with speech because they use telepathy so much from childhood. Their lanyard is purple and says 'they/them' and their ID is an orange card that states 'Wolf Anim'.

Those beasts that don't differentiate between anima and animus, we call 'Anim'.

"Hey Raquel," cigarette girl says. Raquel's head snaps over to my neighbour and they give the girl a sharp nod, heading straight to sit by her.

Two more girls with 'lioness anima' ID cards enter. One, the blonde and leggy type and the other, an East Asian girl with black to blonde ombre hair. They're excitedly chattering away about some of the males they saw outside.

So they all know people. Great. Am I going to be the only person here who doesn't have friends? It makes my stomach knot to think on it. The walls start to press in on me and I squeeze my eyes shut to try and control the wild thoughts.

I've never felt so alone in a place so full of beasts.

"Are we ready?" comes a bright voice.

My eyes snap open as I flinch, because I can't believe someone has entered the room without me knowing. I'm seriously losing it. I need to calm the hell down.

It's not a threat. It's a short, curvy girl with deep brown skin, long, curly, bubblegum-pink hair and wide, light brown doe-shaped eyes that are staring at me and my handcuffs. Her pupils momentarily shift from round to a long slitted feline version, but it's gone in a flash. Silver bracelets take up most of her forearms and rings take up all of the fingers curled around the handle of her pink plastic suitcase. There's a bright pink folder under her arm that's bursting with plastic sleeves and a rainbow of tabs. Her pink lanyard is plain and her ID card states 'Tigress Anima'.

She's so cute that my protective instincts rise even though I have no doubt that, as a tigress, she can look after herself.

"Hey," I say, smiling at her.

She raises a hand to the side of her mouth and whispers, "Ooh, I recognise you from TV."

My heart stutters. "Sorry?"

She quickly settles herself on the bench beside me, carefully placing the pink binder on her lap. I can now see that it's hand-labelled 'Prison School' in bright turquoise letters that clash violently with the pink background.

"Yeah," she says, eyes wide. "They sent out a fugitive alert. You didn't know, did you?"

I sigh as the other animas pretend not to be listening, but clearly are.

"No, I didn't, but I'm not surprised."

Here I was, calling myself a criminal, when an even better title was waiting for me. *Fugitive.*

"So..." She opens the folder then runs her fingernail down a typed bullet point list. "I read that it's rude to ask inmates about the nature of the crimes that got them in. So I won't ask if you really burned down your husband's house and killed him. But I will ask..." She grins at me with all of her white teeth. "Sagittarius?"

I stare at her for a second. "Actually, yeah. My birthday was three weeks ago. How'd you know?"

She conspiratorially taps the side of her nose with a bright pink nail. "I've got a sense about these things." She holds out her hand. "I'm Minnie. And yes, it's after Minnie bloody Mouse. I was the smallest kitten in the litter and my parents thought it was funny."

Trying not to laugh at that, I shake her hand. "I'm Aurelia—"

"Aquinas. Yeah, I know." She beams at me. "So I made this folder to keep track of everything. You can use it too, if you like. It has the school rules and maps and everything."

I stare at the colour-coded binder as she lovingly runs

her finger down the plastic tabs. "You're my type of girl, Minnie," I say softly. At one time, I'd been that diligent, organised student. It looked like that was all behind me now and my life as a fugitive had begun.

"Then we'll get along nicely!" Minnie kicks her legs as she grins at the girls around us, who all glower back, but it doesn't deter her at all.

I wonder what the hell a girl like Minnie is doing here, but luckily, I've learned that it's rude to ask.

After a few minutes, Hope appears at the door with another woman and two more armed guards. It's pretty unnerving that we can't see anything of their faces except their eyes, but I suppose it's for their own safety. The woman, however, wears a casual t-shirt and shorts. Her blonde hair is buzzed short, she has full sleeves of colourful tattoos on both arms and a silver nose ring.

"Ladies, this is Theresa," Hope says brightly. "She'll be your councillor and guide for the year."

Theresa smiles and nods at us. On her plastic name tag, it has 'she/her', and her name and 'Cassowary Anima'. I instantly know she's a badass because the cassowary, with its lethal kick, is the deadliest bird in the world.

"Looks like we're all here." Her voice is calm and reassuring as she scans us and then the clipboard in her hands. "Alright, we need to have a little chat before we enter the academy." Theresa sits down on a seat by the door.

"Now, Raquel, you've told us that your beast leans a little more toward anima sometimes?"

Raquel shrugs. "Yeah."

"So you don't mind us calling you anima?"

Raquel nods. "D-doesn't matter which one."

"Good to know," Theresa says, looking meaningfully around at us to make sure we got that. "So! As you all may know, Animus Academy was traditionally made for animus students. Now that we've moved on with the times and are accepting all beasts, the school still has some teething issues to sort out." She looks meaningfully around at us. "I want to remind you that although we have many safeguards to look after your welfare, you are unmated young animas in a place with many unmated males, many of whom are more than a little feral. You need to be on your guard. You need to look after each other and watch each other's backs. Go everywhere in pairs, don't go wandering around on your own. Do you understand?"

Minnie nods enthusiastically, elbowing me while the rest of the animas grunt and I sit there in dismay.

Theresa gives us a wary once-over, like she's assessing our ability to look after ourselves. She stops on me, and I see the barest recognition in her eye before she stands up and leads us out another door. One guard follows her. The remaining three wait for us to follow. I think that's overkill, looking around at these animas, but I suppose the fact that they're here means they have 'issues' just as badly as me.

I watch the way in and out of the medical wing with eagle eyes, because if I'm planning a jail-break, I need to know the best way to do it. Unfortunately for me,

Theresa presses her finger to a black pad which, instead of opening the steel door, opens a small panel which reveals a *second* cast iron lock. She opens it with a matching key from her lanyard.

So, Lyle Pardalia takes his security system seriously. Fuck him. I glance at Minnie next to me, who gives me googly eyes as we look at all the security...and then I give a side eye at the pink folder tucked so diligently under her bangled arm. By the way it's bursting with papers, not only does she have maps in that folder, but everything anyone could possibly know about this place. Well, looks like the path to my freedom is pink and sparkly.

Chapter 9

Aurelia

Theresa and the guards lead us through cold corridors lit up with blue-white halogen bulbs. Through my four remaining shields, it smells like fresh paint, disinfectant and anti-flea spray, and I try to listen to Theresa as she talks about the history of the place.

The laminated floors transition into fancy wooden floorboards and the clean drywall turns into high ceilings with ornate carvings on the cornices. I'm reminded a little of the gothic architecture of my father's mansion, and I wonder if they were built around the same time. It should be creepy, but I spent my childhood playing hide and seek in a place like this. I lost my mother in a mansion like this. And I saw my mating mark for the first time in the bathroom of a place like this. Something in me eases, just a little, at the way the air of this place feels against my skin. Like old magic mixed with the buzz of anticipation. It certainly can't be *my* anticipation that I'm feeling, though, but that of the other hundred odd students in this place, waiting to meet us green newbies.

Finally, we walk through a set of glass doors and outside where I get to see the outside of Animus Academy for the first time.

The school is a magnificent gothic monstrosity that was no doubt a part of the old Victorian mansion built by the dragon family that first occupied this land. It's eerily stunning, with a black facade, black iron lattice work all along the eaves, and gold ornate embellishments around each window and doorway. The central building towers above us and it's bordered by wings built along the sides before the more recent parts of the school cages it all inside. They've painted the newer rendered facades black to match the central structure and I can't help but feel amused by the attempt to blend it all in together. It's impressive and intimidating from afar, but not if you look too closely. The Animus Academy crest sits on the highest point of the central mansion: an 'A' is on a shield guarded by a lion and wolf. Bird's wings extend above it like a guardian and a dragon flies beneath it all.

My father's home is much the same, without the new add-ons, and there are carved serpents and the basilisks of myth everywhere. Here, there are no snakes, but the occasional dragon adorns the roofs like gargoyles. And I'm almost sure that if I could see them from here, two dragons would flank the front gate. Classic, and the image of it makes my skin tingle.

Theresa leads us along and points out that the central offices and dining hall are in the old part of the building while newer classrooms are in the outer wings.

The other new addition to this land is the green football field complete with bleachers. On the other side of that, I can see the tall black brick wall that surrounds the entire academy. To my dismay, easy to see by the long rays of the setting sun, there is a blue heat-like shimmer in the sky above the wall.

"What is that?" I mutter to Minnie. "It looks like an electrical field."

"It's old dragon magic," she whispers back. "Security from the dragons who used to own this place. It's to prevent anyone from flying in... or out, I guess now too."

Well, shit. It honestly looks like it would zap anyone to a crisp. I can't just fly out.

Theresa raises her brows at us whispering and I shut up. She gestures to the field. "We host the Hunting Games every Sunday once the transition period is over. If you're interested, you can try out for one of the many teams, but...well, you've seen on TV how rough it can get."

The Hunting Games are a rough, lethal sport us animalia play, and there's even state, national and Olympic teams. Animalia have a healthy prey drive, some orders more than others, and it's one way for us to use our natural instincts healthily without actually killing each other.

We pass the main school and stop by a series of three

warehouses. "You get access to the communal jungle gym when you prove you can handle yourself. The one in the middle is the training gym where we test your prey drive, and the last warehouse is our student-run village. You get access to that a little later also, but it is a privilege, and if you'd like to show your mettle, you can even apply to start a business later in the year."

Minnie elbows me excitedly before a guard behind shouts, "No touching!"

We both jump and turn to glare at him, just as everyone turns to stare at us.

Theresa nods when I raise my brows at her. "We'll go through the full set of rules tomorrow. For now, you need to shower and rest for the night. I've got dinner packs in your rooms so you can eat undisturbed for one night at least."

The way she says that last part has me uneasy once again. I've not eaten with anyone in years, and my diet has consisted of two-minute noodles and an occasional Pop-Tart. My uncle Ben would leave food on my doorstep when no one was watching. My Aunt Charlotte was regina to him and my uncle Ron. Despite the hustle and bustle of their pretty house, they had mostly avoided contact with me except for my shifts at their little grocery shop down the road.

As the sun sets, Theresa walks us back to a five-storey black brick building that's a part of the old structure. The long orange rays light up the windows and gild the scroll-work over each tiny balcony, making it look every part of the wealthy dragon's den.

There's a squat cast iron dragon's head glaring down at us over the double entrance doors and it feels like her eyes are admonishing me for being here. The doors are guarded by two armed guards, one of whom undoes my handcuffs while Theresa shows us how to use our key card to swipe ourselves in. "These are the unmated anima dorms. Mating groups get their own lodgings."

My stomach sinks at the label we've been given and I immediately admonish myself. This is the way it's got to be. I imagine a scenario where I've arrived here, only to be told I have to share a room with those three psychopaths. I'd collapse on the floor right then and there. Share a fucking room? Dear Goddess. No, these girls, at least, don't look like they'll kill me in my sleep.

We are housed on the third level and have to trudge up three long flights of stairs to get there. One bonus of my stay here: my thighs are going to be made of steel by the end of the week.

If I stay that long.

"Room assignments!" Theresa says, pointing at the first wooden door. "Yana and Stacey." The two girls I figure are lionesses get shown how to buzz into their rooms. They wheel their suitcases in and shut the door behind them. Raquel and their friend Sabrina get the room next door, then it's just Minnie and I.

The tigress squeals and throws her arms around my shoulders. "Roomies!" she shrieks before bolting into the room, her suitcase swinging wildly behind her.

Theresa smiles at me. She seems like a kind bird, and I wonder if I can get any information out of her to help me escape. But my gaze is drawn to something behind her.

Our room is at the end of the corridor, and on the wall, hangs a magnificent oil painting in a gilded frame. It's a depiction of a dragon, flying high over craggy mountains. There's a waterfall gushing under him and I just know the view from up there would be spectacular.

"You like that?" Theresa says, pulling me out of my reverie. "It's left over from the old family that used to live here. It's stuck on by some dragonic super-glue, we can't get it down." She huffs at her own joke.

"It's beautiful," I say wistfully.

"We'll chat in the morning, Aurelia. Get some rest for now and then tomorrow morning, head downstairs with the other animas. Alright?"

I say a quiet "thank you" and head into the room after Minnie, who's already thrown herself on the bed on the farthest left. Shutting the door behind me, I turn around to simply...stare.

This will be the first time in seven years I'll be sharing a dwelling with another soul. This room matches the outside of the building. There is white ornate scroll-work not only in the corners of the room, but along the entire ceiling and along the windows. A glance to the right shows me a second bed with a crisp white coverlet and pillowcase. I let out a sigh because sleeping in an actual bed instead of a tree branch sounds like heaven. Past that is a wide wooden door that must lead to our shared bathroom. We each have our own small desk where there sits two paper bags, which I assume holds our dinners. There's a wardrobe and chest of drawers for each of us, and between our two beds is a set of glass doors that leads to a pretty balcony with cast-iron railings. I swallow, clutching the zip-lock bag that holds my medications.

"Did you eat your wormer?" Minnie asks, unzipping her luggage and beginning the process of carefully unfolding her clothes.

Her question is so casual, but it's jarring to be asked about my welfare. In our room. Which we'll be staying in. Together. For the duration of our stay—which is usually three years.

"Not yet," I say hastily, heading over to my bed and opening up the plastic bag to cover up my awkwardness. I laugh and it's a little shrill. "I have to use this stupid lice, flea and scabies shampoo as well."

Minnie opens her wardrobe and stares at the empty space assessingly. "I used LFS a few years ago. It's so gross, but you don't want mites in your feathers, do you?" She sighs and begins laying out a purple cloth on one of the shelves in her wardrobe making it into an altar. "Look, this place is a bit plain, but we can spruce it up a bit with things we can get at the student store—"

But I'm not listening because sitting on the floor next to my bed is a familiar battered black duffle bag.

An involuntary sob rips from my throat as I lunge towards it. Thumping it onto the bed, I roughly unzip it. Inside are all the possessions I packed when I run away. My one pair of jeans, the two dresses I own, four blouses, my underwear and a box of tampons. My little box of jewellery and two of my second-hand romance novels. My cash is nowhere to be seen, but in its black case is the diamond choker Charles Halfeather gave to me to wear on the day I was married to him by force. And to my great and terrible surprise, tucked in the corner is Savage's pink Opal Feather handbag.

The beaten-up duffle is not much, but it's home to me. The expensive handbag is a whole other issue. Both, I never expected to see again.

As I wipe the tears from my eyes, I realise what's different. The bag is neatly packed, my clothes folded in sections—*definitely* not the way I haphazardly threw everything in there. Something cold trickles through my chest.

Someone has organised my things.

I left all of this in my car at the motel when I escaped Lyle Pardalia for the first time, almost a week ago. The thought of *that lion* going through my possessions, my underwear, with his huge paws sends me into a feral, embarrassed fervour. I keel over and press my palms to my eyes, trying to claw out the image of the deputy head-master. Especially the image of him looking unimpressed down at my naked body as I lay in his net on the grass, defeated and pathetic.

The bed depresses next to me and small, gentle arms carefully encircle my shoulders. Bangles chime softly as Minnie presses her warm cheek against my arm.

"It's alright," she says in the softest voice I've ever heard. "We'll be okay, Lia. You'll see."

I sob even more then. Shoulder-shaking, voice-quaking sobbing worthy of a prime-time movie. And it's because I haven't been treated like this since my thirteenth birthday. It breaks something in me a little to think that it took me to come to *this* place, where the worst youth of our kind are sent, for someone to hug me like they mean it.

Chapter 10

Aurelia

Minnie's happy tiger alarm clock goes off at seven in the morning. I rub my bleary eyes open amidst a chorus of "wake up, sleepyhead. You'll miss the bright day!" in an annoyingly cheerful, digital voice.

Minnie is up and bouncing in her rainbow cupcake PJ's, rushing towards the bathroom like she's excited to pee. I take a moment to stare up at the complex scrollwork on the ceiling to steel myself. It looks like whorls of fire encircle the room and I wonder if it's an omen for how our day is going to go. My body doesn't feel like it's been hit by a truck anymore, but I still ache all over and my stomach growls despite the cold chicken sandwich and apple juice I devoured last night.

It had been extremely difficult to go to sleep. In fact, Minnie and I spent the first hour with our noses pressed against our glass balcony doors—which we discovered are locked shut—listening to the noises of the night. I grew up in serpent and lesser order territory, so I was *not* accustomed to hearing night-time roars and the various calls of feline and canine apex predators. Some, Minnie identified as mating calls, and some were howls and snarls of protest by the feral first year animus'. Guards ran around outside all night, and more than once, shots went off, no doubt darting some escaped troublemakers. I have no idea how people were running about in the night, because our room doors were locked at eleven p.m. sharp.

Eventually, all the rebels were subdued and Minnie and I tumbled into bed, where it took me a while to calm my racing heart.

I wondered if any of those wolfish howls were Savage, but I felt like I would *know* his howl if he ever did it. Anxiety clawed through me, thinking about my mates, because I knew that the animus dorms would be down-right rowdy and full of men trying to establish a hierarchy. The medical wing was going to be busy overnight, that was for sure.

Minnie is out within half an hour, showered with a full face of makeup, ready to choose what clothes and jewellery she's going to wear. Dragging myself out of bed, I head to the toilet, where I sit down with my face resting in my palms and try to wake up. Immediately, I notice the giant metal poster screwed into the door. Being so tired yesterday, I was barely able to use that awful LFS all-in-one wash before collapsing into bed.

The metal board has the school rules written in big black letters and I huff a laugh as I read:

. . .

Class A offences-subject to judicial hearing

· Murder

· Torture

· Consuming other students or staff

Class B offences-subject to local punishment

· Permanent maiming or mutilation

Class C offences-subject to remedial classes

· Shifting in non-shifting areas

· Accidental grievous bodily harm

· Marking via urination, furniture or *any* property

· Public nudity (accidental or otherwise)

· Public fornication or acts of indecency

· Disrespectful behaviours towards staff

So, as long as I don't kill, maim, or eat anyone, I'm all good. Sounds like a breeze while I work on my escape plan. I intend to stay as invisible and under the radar as humanly possible, biding my time until I can find a way to get past all the security and leg it out of here to a quiet life of freedom with a fake identity in a blended university. Since the entire place is wing-proofed, my options are limited and I'll need to plan this carefully.

Minnie's positive attitude has spread to me like fleas because suddenly I'm all, 'Where there's a will there's a way', and by the Wild Goddess, I'll find my exit.

When I emerge from our bathroom, trying to

untangle my long mess of black hair, I find Minnie in a black and pink striped dress and shiny black platform shoes, pacing before the altar to the Wild Goddess she carefully set up last night. A stick of incense sends tendrils of smoke over a tiny pink candle and an idol of the Goddess in her human form, sitting on the back of a tiger. Minnie is biting her fingernail, and when she sees me, her face brightens but I scent the sharp tang of her fear.

"Ready?" she asks, bouncing on the balls of her feet, bangles chiming.

I look down at my faded jeans and thin, dark green blouse. I put the red blouse on first and decided against the colour, knowing some feral beasts are attracted to bright and red colours. My hair is super dry and crispy from the LFS, so I try to hide it in a messy bun. For shoes, I only have flip-flops from the donation box in the medical wing. Whatever I look like, it's surely better than the orange prison jumpsuit, right? "Yeah. Let's do this, Min."

She grins nervously, sticking a sparkly pink biro into her dress pocket. I don't even own a pen, so I pretend not to notice that as we put our lanyards on.

"Should I bring my folder?" she asks, hefting up the pink tome.

"Nah, let's leave it for the moment." She looks a little sad at that, so I say, "But I'd really like to look through it page by page tonight, if that's okay."

The tigress brightens immediately, and we wait next to our door for the security locks to open at 8 a.m.

The locks power down with a sad whine and Minnie pounces at the bronze door knob, eagerly yanking it open. "They told us to meet out front, right?" she says as our neighbour's doors open up at the same time.

Raquel and Sabrina walk out. The former in the same double denim outfit with motorcycle gang patches and heavy black boots. Sabrina wears leopard print leggings and a matching crop top, telling us all what order she is. She's chewing gum as she looks us both up and down, delicately sniffing us.

"Morning!" Minnie says enthusiastically.

Raquel grunts and their face bears zero facial expression while Sabrina says a deadpan, "Hi."

"Yeah," I say, trying to sound cooler than I am and coming across much worse. I decide to try my newfound friendship skills and hold up my student card. "I'm Lia, eagle. This is Minnie, tiger."

I'm hoping Minnie being a tiger will hold some sway over the other beasts because as things go, tigers are right up there on the power chain.

Raquel nods in acknowledgement, their piercings shining under the bright hallway lights.

But Sabrina rolls her eyes. She's unimpressed with us and I know that for sure when she turns her back and the two of them walk away down the corridor.

Minnie's mouth drops open and we stare at the obvious display. Abruptly turning your back on any animalia means you think they're too weak to be a threat. It's a great form of disrespect, especially between beasts of the same age who aren't friends.

"Don't worry about it," I mutter, tugging Minnie after them and the two lionesses walking out of the third room. "They don't know us, that's all."

"You're right," Minnie says. "A bit of breakfast and everyone will be much happier."

More animas join us going down the stairs from the levels above and below. There are a few terse mutters exchanged and more than a few glares from the more senior animas. At the end of the day, they want to establish the hierarchy, and Minnie and I are *told*, more than once, that we're at the bottom.

Two lionesses shove us aside as they jog down the stairs and someone yanks on my ponytail. With a yelp, I'm pulled backwards and just manage to stay on my feet. When I turn, black painted lips smirk at me.

Serpent.

Shit. I recognise those slitted pupils from my father's court. This one is called Natalia, and she was a year above me in primary school. She and another serpent girl with heavy black eyeliner glare at us before pushing past and surging ahead to go down the stairs.

Fuck the pecking order, but I *know* this will be nothing compared to the males of the academy. Animas take it seriously enough, but there's usually not the same brutality to it as the animus'.

We manage to find ourselves clustered with our group of first year girls, because Raquel and Sabrina have been pushed back as well, despite their best efforts to remain haughty. There's six of us in total, including the two lionesses, Yana and Stacey, looking off-kilter, eyes darting around. We all might not like each other, but we have no choice but to keep as a group.

And it's a good thing because Theresa and a few other counsellors are waiting for us outside, the older girls already milling around them and eyeing us like we've all got headlice.

"Animas," Theresa says by way of greeting. "If you've all taken a good look at each other for mates, we'll all head over to the field for mating lines."

I choke, but Minnie laughs. "It's where we're shown to the animus' to see if us unmated animas have any mates we've not met before. It's better to do it in a safe environment rather than organically. It could cause chaos."

"Thank you, Minnie," Theresa says, beaming at her. "You're exactly right."

"I read it in the student handbook," my friend pipes proudly.

Sabrina and Yana roll their eyes, but as we make our way to the field, everyone quickly forgets to keep their noses in the air because the males are also streaming from their dorms onto the field not twenty steps from us.

This is actually like my worst nightmare made reality.

It's a precariously controlled chaos of swaggering males, and they only seem to be behaving due to the guns pointed in their faces. Most of them are fully clothed in T-shirts and pants, but many are shirtless, likely showing their order and gang-affiliated tattoos and markings. While they're trying to get a look at us, they're also trying to assert their dominance over each other. Until they've established who fits where in the power chain, there's a danger a fight will break out and us animas can all feel the taut strain of latent power mingling in the air.

There are just as many armed guards today, but even with the six standing by the field, it doesn't stop the overt masculine excitement at the new anima scents in the air and the sight of us.

One of the males walking past says something unintelligible but suggestive, and it's followed by a chorus of deep laughter.

The older girls all seem to be used to it because they just flip their hair and stare them down.

Minnie's smile falters only for a moment before she plasters it back on, but I can't help notice that she discreetly steps closer to my side. Raquel scowls at anyone who looks our way, while Sabrina is thoroughly amused by the attention, flicking her long black ponytail and raising an eyebrow at the wandering eyes.

Me? I don't even know what to do with my face *or* body because I'm trying not to show how freaked out I am. While I'm used to a little male chaos from years of going out on jobs, I'm not used to being *seen* by males. Dodging them while invisible is easy. But being watched? Being assessed? It makes me heat up all over and I'm fumbling to concentrate on maintaining my shields. I've recovered enough to put back up five of my seven shields. No one should be able to scent me, but I'm still sweating under the heat of their attention. My anima is going feral inside my body, trying to see if we can catch a glimpse of our mates, and thumping her down is hard enough on its own.

Theresa herds us animas behind a wall and we wait there, just listening to the buzz of the other students streaming in. After a couple of minutes, I hear the clink of chains and Theresa peeks out.

"The more feral students and first year animus' are coming in," she explains. "They'll be shackled in case they're not sure how to handle themselves around a new mate."

The first-year males are greeted with growls and there is jostling and jeering going on that I try to ignore. Minnie gulps next to me. I take her hand and squeeze it and she looks up at me gratefully.

A male lion appears around the wall, waving in greeting. He's a black-skinned male with a lean build and wears his long black hair in a braid down to his lower back. There are crystal studs in both of his ears, and he grins cheerfully at us.

"This is Connor," Theresa says kindly. "He has an anima but has chosen to stay in the unmated male dorms."

Connor rolls his eyes. "The smell of feral animus really hits you in the face, but I'm having a good time so far."

We laugh and give him a happy welcome. There are plenty of openly LGBTQ members within our kind and having a male with an anima or a female with an animus are less common, but not unheard of. In our world, the spirit of your beast form takes precedence over your outward appearance.

It's why it's so hard for us (me) to fight our anima when it wants something. Like my mates. But she's instinct and spirit only. There's no logic involved. Only *need*. It's not normal to fight your anima, it's just my unique circumstance that makes it imperative that I do.

Moments later, Theresa organises us into a line and leads us out. Luckily, the older girls are put in front of us, which means when we enter the field, I'm given a little buffer for what comes our way.

If you think keeping a bunch of males with horny animuses all together in a place like this for years would drive them feral for unmated animas, you're quite right.

Chapter 11

Aurelia

The Hunting Games field is a tangle of forest in front of us and we're walked out to a long patch of green turf that sits between it and the bleachers. Usually, the medical tents and commentators are set up here, just in front of the metal cages where the hunting teams wait to be released.

No less than one hundred and fifty eyes seated on the bleachers snap towards us with eager expectation. Dozens of wolf whistles and shouts fill the air.

The first-year males are in the bottom row, shackled in black hand and legcuffs. My eyes are drawn to three of the tallest, biggest figures in that row. The three who seem to hold power around them like a wave of dense, latent electricity. Those males forced to be seated next to them are visibly tense.

I do everything in my power to look everywhere but them.

Someone actually barks, "Fresh meat!" and it's

followed by male chortling. The line of guards at the bleachers don't try and stop or dissuade them, making me think that this is *normal* procedure. What the hell, Lyle Pardalia? So much for civilising these beasts.

Theresa instructs us to stand in a line facing them all, jeering at us like we're about to perform some type of show. Is this what strippers feel before they step on stage? I'd always thought about that job in the back of my mind to try and make real money, but never had the guts to actually try it.

But I also can't help but feel like this must be what illegal breeding auctions are like. I've been terrified of them my entire life and as that primal fear grips my chest, I actually feel like my stomach juices are going to erupt like lava from my throat. Against my better judgement, I grab Minnie's hand.

To my utter and profound relief, she doesn't shake me off and grips me tightly back.

I hate that I look weak, but my blood is pounding in my ears and I can't breathe.

I'm a predator. I'm an apex predator, and there is nothing I fear, I chant, over and over again as I stand there trying to keep my face blank.

But I can tell our audience is trying as hard as they can to stare through our clothes to our very souls. A few in the back even get up from their seats to try and get a better look.

They start crying out to us by what we're wearing.

Raquel gets called "Patches."

Sabrina gets shouts of "sexy mama," to which she blows kisses left and right. Go her, seriously.

Minnie gets "Pinky" because of her hair.

And wait for it. I get: "Bun bun bunny!"

"Holy fucking shit," Minnie mutters next to me.

"I knew I shouldn't have worn a bun," I mutter back. But it's all I could manage this morning.

What have I gotten myself into? So much for trying to lie low. Instead, I feel like I've got a crimson target on my chest. Ahead of me, Sabrina preens like a peacock, her hips tilting to show off how great her ass looks in those leggings. A few of the unmated girls from older years boldly stare out at the crowd, but they get called to by their *actual* names.

One of my jobs after my father discarded me was to heal animalia in underground fighting rings. The only thing was, I eighth-shielded myself before I went in, so I was invisible to everyone there. I experienced the most sadistic natures of our culture and got really good at healing bad injuries from a young age, but I did it all without being seen.

This is a whole lot different, and I'd honestly rather burn my eyeballs out than be here with the three males who are hunting me.

"Right!" One of the other teachers, a bald man with a huge, brown huge 'stache is standing before us with a loudspeaker. "Back row, third years, you come down first, pass by, then go straight to the dining hall. If you see a mate, let us know by raising your hand."

I stiffen as the third-year students all but leap down

the steps in a long line. They follow a line of fluoro orange witches' hats to come right at us and walk down the line of animas. There's nothing separating us and them, and they're allowed to get as close as they like.

I'm physically incapable of letting Minnie's hand go and she doesn't seem to mind as the line of males tower over us. Some of them arrive in their packs, looking for another member of their soul-group, and even if they don't see a mating mark on us, it's still intimidating as all hell to be *checked out* up and down by so many animalia.

There's both assessing calculation in their eyes and intense, lusty heat.

"What's your name, pretty girl?" a female lion coos to me, caressing her long red mane with one hand and tugging one of her mates along with another.

I open my mouth, but she's prodded along by the guards and the next one sidles up to lick his lips pointedly at me.

We have no choice but to stand there and wait this *parade* of animuses out as the second row, then third row of students pass us by.

There's no mate-match until the fifth row when a lion animus with long brown hair cuts through the line as if in a trance, making a beeline straight for Yana. The other animus' part to let him through as everyone just stops what they're doing and we all watch, transfixed. The lion extends a large hand out to gently brush the left side of Yana's neck.

Minnie sucks in a shocked breath. I clutch my stomach.

Yana makes a choked, sobbing sound and flings her arms around the male. He rumbles in his chest as he grips her tightly back and then snarls at the males around him in warning.

Other lions whoop behind him and jostle each other but keep a respectful distance. We all stare at the open display and I'll admit I'm a little teary-eyed at the sight.

To find another of your soul group, something ordained by the Wild Goddess and the stars themselves, is perhaps the most beautiful and sacred thing we have in this mad life.

These two beasts, who were effectively strangers just moments ago, have found another fragment of their group. I wonder if Yana is a regina, like me.

I realise I'm furiously squeezing Minnie's hand when I hear her take a shuddering breath next to me. That sound grounds me back in the moment, as everyone else also shakes themselves out of their own reveries.

Breathe, Lia. Just breathe.

I'm just lucky there's a wall of male bodies in front of me, obscuring me from the view of my own mates still waiting on the bleachers. My anima is now violently crying out in my chest and I have no option but to blink rapidly at the verdant grass beneath my flip flops.

Then the line starts moving again as Yana and her mate go hand-in-hand to the dining hall. No doubt they will talk about things that make them who they are. About their lives, their hopes and dreams. They'll get to learn about each other. They will, hopefully, fall in love.

Stacey sighs as she shuffles over to close the gap made

by Yana's absence. They were friends and won't get to bunk together anymore, but she wipes a tear from her eye and smiles at her friend's back as the two mates leave.

There are no more matches until the final row arrives.

Rather suddenly, it feels like fire ants are crawling up my spine.

All I can do is avoid looking at them as steel chains clink and the first years begin to shuffle past us.

A growl suddenly rips through the air and we all turn just in time to see an animus leap for one of the animas in an older year. She yelps as he tackles her to the grass, rapidly moving over her body and sniffing her neck, her breasts, her groin in quick succession.

"Fuck!" she screams. But it's not a cry of fear, it's a breathy sound of pleasure. He pounces back up to her face and their mouths hungrily devour one another in a heated tangle of lips and tongue that has me cocking my head, transfixed. A couple of animas who know her cheer and jump up and down in happiness.

I have to remind myself to close my mouth when Minnie catches my eye with a lop-sided grin. There's hope gleaming in her eyes, as there should be.

The guards let the new mates go at it for five seconds longer before one of the lion-guards telekinetically sweeps them apart. The male roars in protest.

"Alright, you two." Theresa nods at one of the guards. "We'll have a talk about appropriate PDA behaviours later today." And with that, they're quickly taken away by an escort of guards.

I turn back around and find a broad tattooed chest far too close to me. My heart shudders in my chest as I find a wolf tattoo peeking through the open lapels of an orange jumpsuit.

Almost against my will, my head swings up to find Savage's perfectly handsome head, cocked and looking down at me with a very inspired dazzle in his eyes.

My eyes snap into a narrow-eyed look that screams, *'Don't you fucking dare'*.

He promptly ignores it and his eyes flash at the challenge a single second before he leaps for me. I barely have time to let go of Minnie's hand before we crash onto the turf with a thump.

"My regina!" Savage bellows in a tangle of chains and limbs. "This is my regina!"

"No!" I cry as my anima screams with pleasure at Savage's face pressed against my neck. *His skin.* Goddess, his warm skin on mine. His hard body writhes against me. "Stop!" It's sort of weak, but the guards hear it and sweep him off me straight away. Theresa rushes forwards to help me jump to my feet as Savage lets out a reflexive snarl at whoever's got him hanging in mid-air.

"I'm not his mate!" I pant, panicking as my head spins. I desperately grab onto Theresa's shirt. "He's lying!"

Theresa snags my wrists and frowns at me, grey eyes searching. "Are you sure, Lia? Did you get a good look?" She turns me around to face him.

I calm down a fraction at the firmness of her hands

around my wrists and at the fact that I might be able to salvage this. "Yes," I pant. "Yes. He's crazy. He's lying."

Everyone is staring between us in a sort of shock because it's a very unusual thing for our kind to lie about, especially feral beasts, which Savage no doubt is.

Shooting a glance at Scythe and Xander, I find them both stiff-backed and glaring daggers at me. I have to look away, because *fuck*, their anger is a lot this close. Then, to my utter surprise, Xander sighs dramatically, as if this is all stupid and ridiculous. "She's right. He's lying."

Stopping short of gaping at him, I meet Theresa's concerned look. Everyone knows that dragons can tell when someone is telling the truth or not.

"Are you sure?" Theresa asks him suspiciously.

Xander gives a sharp nod and Savage rolls his eyes as he's placed roughly back on the ground. He straightens his shirt with a huff.

A massive wolf security guard, no less than seven feet tall, towers over us all when he snarls, "What are you trying to prove, Savage?"

The wolf just shrugs and turns his back on me.

My racing heart only beats faster.

"One moment, Lia." Theresa gets out a phone and dials someone, walking away so we can't hear her conversation. Her phone case is an anti-hearing one, so us animalia with advanced hearing can't eavesdrop.

She turns around, and after a moment, she nods. She comes back to us. "Alright, let's move on."

Savage and Xander ignore me and move down the line, and before we know it, the animus' are being led away, and the entire ordeal is finally over. I could almost collapse with relief, though I'll admit that it's surprising none of my three tried to force the matter of being my mate. I suppose they want to keep this private, which is fine by me.

Minnie is disappointed she didn't find one of her mates but says darkly, "At least no one pretended to be my mate, I suppose. He's really crazy, that wolf, isn't he?"

Grimacing, I say, "Tell me about it."

As the first-year males are taken away for some type of debriefing, we follow Theresa to the dining hall and an older anima passes us. "Good luck," she says darkly. "Now you're fair game."

Chapter 12

Aurelia

S abrina beams at the anima while Stacey and Minnie smile with a sort of shy hope. I suppose that even without mates, with the number of unmated animus' here, they'll try and claim us on instinct or just for fun. I'll just need to avoid *that* complication at all costs, too.

To my dismay, Theresa waves us through the big sliding glass doors into the dining hall (labelled 'Non-shifting area' in bold red letters) and leaves us there. Alone.

You might have thought the mating lines would have calmed the lot of them down. Instead, in the closed space, the tension just heightens further. Even through my many shields, I can feel the very air buzzing with lust and the will to maintain power.

The dining area is as beautiful and striking as the rest of the academy. It's a large, wood-panelled hall with fancy carvings and cornices. There are small recesses along three walls that hold cast iron dragon gargoyles cemented in place. High above there's even three old chandeliers, though plenty of light comes in through the big stained-glass windows on my right. I'm sure that back in the day, the place was used as a ball-room. But currently the space is filled with dozens of heavy wooden tables with eight wooden chairs around each. A long line of silver bain maries and serving plat-ters are set out at the front for a buffet and there is a second set of doors on the other side, leading to the internal part of the academy. Two exits, that's always good.

But it's full of animus males and one or two females, already seated down and eating, chairs angled so they can see us.

All I can do is avoid eye contact at all costs while we queue for food, because I've had the sudden, heart-sinking realisation that for however long I have to stay here, it's going to be very difficult.

I'm about to cast my eye out to check where my psychopathic mates are—so I can hide behind Raquel's taller frame if need be—I'm not above that—when a waft of buttery fear perfumes the air ahead of me. A soft growl sounds to my left and at the table seated near us are two muscled guys with their gazes fixed on Minnie like she looks particularly tasty.

"Minnie," I say in a low voice. "Clamp down on your nerves. It's activating their prey drive."

She swears under her breath and straightens her spine a little, muttering something about bringing her affirmation cards, while I too try and keep my back tall and my chin raised.

Trying to ignore the keen stares, I distract myself with the buffet breakfast. And by all the Wild Gods, if this is what I get to eat every morning, this place might not be as bad as I thought.

No two-minute noodles and Pop-Tarts here, no siree. Golden toast with knobs of butter on the side, crispy bacon, hash browns and sausages piled so high I can do nothing but stare. And pancakes. *Stacks* of them. Plus, muffins, cereal and waffles further down.

Minnie giggles. "Lia, you act like you've never seen a buffet before."

I close my mouth and don't dare admit that I haven't, not since my twelfth birthday party at my father's mansion. Every girl my age from Serpent Court came to my princess-themed party. I wore an *actual* boa constrictor with pink feathers (one of my uncles, from memory) and the cake was in the shape of two cobras rearing up. They would have been scary if they weren't coloured in pink and gold fondant.

It felt like a completely different lifetime and I'm in no way, shape or form, the same girl of privilege I was then. Now, I'm a discarded scumbag, only considered good for breeding.

My father sees me like that. He married me to Halfeather for money. *Given me* to him like an exotic pigeon for making hatchlings and nothing else. There is no way I would ever let that happen to me again. I will never let myself be a slave. The twin wounds on my neck will remind me of that promise to myself every morning now.

"Whoa, girl. You alright?" a girl behind me asks.

Falling out of my fervour, I'm immediately horrified to see everyone in the immediate vicinity staring at me.

"What?" I ask.

Minnie makes wide eyes at me. "Lia, your power is rolling off you like a heatwave. Calm down before someone takes it the wrong way."

I swear and stop thinking of my past, reeling my power back in and checking my shields. This won't do at all. I'm already slipping up.

"Sorry, Minnie," I mutter. "I'm not used to being around so many animalia."

"Yeah, it's unnerving," she whispers, grabbing a suspiciously flimsy wooden tray from the shrinking stack and piling it high with bacon. A woman after my own heart. "But we're supposed to be here to learn control, right?" she continues, side-eyeing the males taking the opportunity to check her ass out. "This feels like a zoo. I'm pretty sure the guide says we learn good manners in courtship in our first year."

Indeed, it's lucky for the couple of guards standing by the walls. If not for them, I'm sure blood would have been spilled by now.

I take a thin wooden tray for myself and, in a sort of wonder, fill it with a bit of everything. Just when I think I could get used to this buffet, I remember that I still have to escape this place and I groan internally. Just days ago, I was drinking dirty puddle water, and I'll have to go back to that if I don't plan this escape properly.

Us first year animas form a gaggle and find that the only table left is one smack bang in the centre, that seems, to my dismay, to have been purposely left clear for us. The unmated girls from second and third year sit at tables with other animus groups, probably bundling themselves up with their own orders.

We all shovel our food in quietly, but the six of us never look at our food. Our eyes are darting around at the passersby, trying to detect a threat before it catches us off guard. This is the proverbial watering hole, and it feels like more than a few lions and wolves are lurking at the edges, just waiting to pounce.

"Gosh, don't look now, but I think those two are eating each other for breakfast," Minnie says with breathy wonder.

I'm nosy, so I *do* look and see two girls sucking each other's faces. Tongues flash and a guy suddenly joins in, sliding his hand up the leg of one of the girls.

"Obviously mating groups eat together," Stacey, next to me, says. "But the unmated animas also eat with the guys they choose. It's just us losers who need to be careful until we figure out who's who."

"We'll protect each other, though, right?" I say in a friendly voice, looking around and seeing no sign of my three man-shaped problems. "If we watch each other's backs, we stand a chance of getting through our first day unscathed."

"Yeah," she says to me with a smile. "We can do that."

Sabrina, sitting at the end of the table with Raquel, rolls her eyes again, but they still came to sit with us at our table, which means they're more unnerved than they're showing.

Just as I think we've done well at our first breakfast, I understand why our trays are made of the flimsy cardboard. A fight breaks out on the other side of the hall and trays go flying. One huge guy slams his tray down on the head of another and chaos ensues.

Two massive bear shifters appear from the wings and blow a whistle. Everyone around them surges away from the fight. The two beasts are hauled off each other kicking and screaming, and it's not until literal cattle prods are stabbed into both of them that they go limp.

They're slung over the shoulders of the guards and gone within seconds.

I blow out a bated breath. "They don't have cattle prods at the zoo," I mutter darkly to Minnie.

"First year animas!" a guy with a mohawk caws from across the room, his arms spread wide. "Welcome to the fucking jungle!"

Everyone, except our table, laughs.

Chapter 13

Xander

U s first year males are given a solid talking to before we enter the dining hall. The warning is clear: behave or we'll be carted out unconscious.

I can't believe Scythe is forcing me to play school here. We have to sleep in a giant dormitory like a group of pre-pubescent boys at summer camp and Savage and I resort to blows more than once.

This is going to be hell. It's why, as I walk into the dining hall alongside Scythe, smoke streams out of my nose in a black plume.

"Fuck, Xander, have some control," Savage sneers. He's annoyed he has to leave Eugene in a cage in our room and also annoyed that I ruined his fun back on the field.

Scythe gives me a look that could crack stone, and I grimace at him. *"Don't start a fight,"* he drawls into our heads. *"I don't want blood on my hands on the first fucking day."*

"Wait, what was that in the dorm, then?" Savage says, with his hand on his heart, making his eyes wide.

I smirk at the memory of the two lions lying in a bloody mess after two of them shot a shark joke at Scythe. The idiots didn't know who he was and hadn't listened when the others cautioned them.

As a result, they were carted off to the medical wing on gurneys.

The unmated male dorms are a cesspool of pillow-humping illiterates, but we fixed any fight for dominance last night when they put us all in a room with the other animuses and got us to naturally establish pecking order. It was brutal, but time-effective. There'd been no time for much talking though, so we just needed word to spread that we're here now, and in no more than two days, we'll have *everyone* under our thumbs and a couple of beasts six feet under.

I'm highly offended that they have this prison academy in heritage listed, century old architecture made by the Draykaris family. There's the finest walnut panelling on the walls of the central mansion, solid oak flooring—none of that cheap modern pine shit—and I can feel the dragon-magic ingrained in the very crevices of the hallways. It brings back memories I'd prefer not to think about, but there's trick magic here, too, which is interesting, so I'll be inspecting every inch of the place at the first chance I get.

We pass by the security bears hauling out trash as we head into the dining hall. Both nod at us as we pass.

I make straight for the food, leading the way because I'm so hungry I could eat someone. A curvaceous redhead in the queue ahead of me turns to see who's looming behind her. Her eyes widen when she sees my face, and she looks me slowly up and down before promptly sticking her tits out. Some beasts find my white, glowing eyes scary, but plenty of women love it. This one is clearly in the latter camp, so I smirk at her before piling my tray high with as much breakfast as the weak bamboo can take.

No woman is coming between me and my food, no matter what she looks like.

Scythe lets a grumbling Savage queue ahead of him and my wolf-brother fills his tray with rare steak and nothing else. At least Lyle knows how ferals eat and gives us what we want. I'm a little more balanced and take ten fried eggs, twenty pieces of bacon and nine pieces of toast. Scythe looks everything over and chooses not to eat. I immediately see why.

They've not catered to marine beasts because this 'academy' has likely never had one attend. They all get a unique form of psychosis if they're left on land, so most choose to live the ocean life in their shifted forms, often staying that way for the rest of their lives. Scythe, for his part, only eats raw fish and they don't even have a sardine at the buffet at all.

But my shark brother shows no sign of emotion, as usual, and I notice the males in the line behind him take one sniff of him and give a wide berth. Savage smirks when he sees where I'm looking, and when we're ready to leave the buffet, Savage stalks out ahead of me, Scythe behind him as I make a detour to grab an entire urn of black coffee.

The dining hall is buzzing with conversation and shifty, darting eyes. The male beasts are doing everything they can to check out the new females and gather information them so they can capitalise on it later.

Clearly, they're all ignoring the big red poster above the male dorm exit that says, 'Antagonising the animas is a punishable offence.'

I spot the snake girl immediately. She's sitting at a group of clearly unmated females, all looking outright miserable. I refuse to look at her, but she's sitting between two puny girls. One looks like a deer and the other looks like a puppy. Why she's hanging out with animal food is beyond me, because it's a sure way to get caught out in a place like this. But she always *has* come across a little stupid. Maybe she's just insane like her father says.

Savage stalks up to a table right at the back of the hall, ignoring the snake girl as well. He's angry at her for refusing his stolen handbag when he didn't even want to give it to her in the first place. Now my animus? My dragon is horny at the best of times, and he lets out a whine of interest when we pass snake girl, but when I tell him to put his head down, he does. She doesn't fucking want us, and that's a worse insult than spitting in our faces. I won't tolerate it. She'll get what's coming to her soon enough, and once she's dead, I can go back to living my life and forget this thing ever happened.

"*She's—*" I begin, but Scythe cuts me off.

"*I know,*" he says, though his head never moved her way.

We're stared at as we walk through the hall, and I know we're recognised by plenty of students right away. And if they didn't know us before, they know us from the bloodbath that happened last night. Some idiots, however, still bearing the marks from said bloodbath, are growling outright at the memory. They see Savage's arrogant swagger, my creepy-ass eyes, the ice cold shark, and sense something is off about us. They don't like it. Any sane beast would feel uncomfortable at the sheer level of dominance we bring into the room, but they also feel what will happen to them if they don't bare their necks for our approval. I mark out the growling ones for later.

This is going to be amusing.

All the tables at the back are occupied, and Savage heads for a table where a group of the worst monsters are sitting. I don't remember them from last night, but they're hulking, tatted up and scarred; the look of dirty fighters. One is gnawing on a raw bone, another has a long line of stitches on his forehead. Typical. I check the legs of the table for urine marking, but there is none. Surprising.

Savage lets out a growl and commands the mutts, "Off."

Fleeting wide eyed looks tell me that they recognise him--Savage is well known in the wolf community. When he used to participate in underground fights, he was always at the top of the leader boards and no one has won a fight against him since he was a kid. A couple of years ago, we put a stop to him competing because we couldn't find willing opponents.

Three of the six get up, step respectfully away to the side, and wait. The remaining three snarl up at their friends and then at us.

"What the fuck?" the remaining idiot, a lion with scar through his eyebrow, says.

"Just move, Greg." His friend is nobly trying to help him.

"Fuck off. No." Greg proves he has a death wish.

"Do you not know who that is? Fuck man, *move*."

Scythe ignores their disagreement, pulls out a seat and turns it so it's facing the rest of the hall. He sits on it, crossing one leg, the picture of the king of ice at court.

Savage, our king of blood, calmly puts his tray down next to the cretin lion. Before the guy can utter a word, Savage reaches over and violently slams the lion's head down on the table. There's a satisfying crunch as his nose breaks and he slides sideways to the floor, unconscious. Savage's done this so many times over the years that he knows the exact pressures to use to give a concussion, a brain bleed, and a death-blow. In another life, he could've been a surgeon.

Savage puts his tray on top of the blood like it's not even there and sits on the lion's seat, grabbing a steak and tearing into it with his teeth. Chewing, he looks around at the lion's friends and points to the beast on the floor. Two of them immediately run forwards and drag the guy out of there.

Scythe doesn't watch any of it, just quietly observes the hall with his hands clasped in his lap.

I sigh and sit down opposite Savage. Scythe will deal with business while I eat. That's what he does best.

Unlike Savage, I use the ugly bamboo fork and knife, ready to scarf every last crumb on my tray as I sit back and watch the show.

The first to approach is Yeti, a trustworthy Siberian lion we've known for years, an enforcer operating under us and one of the few who we allow to know us on a first name basis. Yeti is a beast who gets a job done, whatever it is. He's a thinker *and* a killer, which is pretty rare as things go. That's why I respect him and his judgement.

"Good to see you, sir," he says respectfully to Scythe, inclining his golden head to us all. "Xander. Savage."

"Yeti, sit with us," Scythe rasps, indicating a chair at the table. "Are you well?"

Those in the vicinity visibly cringe when they hear Scythe's voice, but Yeti breaks out in a smile like he's happy to hear it. "Thank you. I've been well."

Yeti parks himself next to Scythe and promptly gives him the lay of the land, telling us the ins and outs of the academy, and introduces those who approach. For the next half an hour, the young criminals and fighters of the state come to pay their respects.

Those who don't know him personally know him by name and reputation. Within half an hour, we know who is smuggling in contraband and how, who's got drugs, who's blackmailing who, and who's likely to land themselves in Blackwater Penitentiary, as well as any other dirt. We also mark which of the beasts are involved in trafficking and breeding rings in the outside world.

Once business is done and the line dwindles, a few unmated animas saunter forwards and offer themselves. There's not all that many unclaimed women here, but enough to keep the unmated animus' aggressively competing, so it's smart of these ones to come up to us to seek protection.

I'm interested in how Scythe will respond because he's not discussed the snake girl with us, outside of fulfilling our blood pact to deliver her to her father. Even so, she's still technically our regina and the animus in all of us responds to other females differently now. Which is to say, not at all.

My eyes dart over to said snake, and she's watching us with a frown. She notices me looking at her and quickly averts her blue-eyed gaze.

That's a weak snake right there. Prey, more than anything, and it makes my hunting instinct rear its ugly mug.

A pretty brunette in a crimson crop top and matching mini skirt curtseys at Scythe, which is impressive in the black stilettos she's got on. In a sign of submission, she bares her neck by flipping her long hair over her shoulder. I get a whiff of her and there are so many scents there, we all immediately know she's been with half a dozen unmated males this week. Girl's got a healthy appetite.

"Hello, Mr. Kharkorous," she purrs, glossy red lips curving into a seductive smile. "My name is Sarah."

Yeti glances at Scythe. It's well known that our shark doesn't touch women—or men for that matter—but it doesn't stop them from trying. When none of us offer to claim her, Yeti clears his throat. "We see you, Sarah. One of the others will be in touch. Off you go."

Sarah pouts and doesn't move away, glancing first at Scythe then at me. I'm just behind him, and now that I've eaten my food, I'm leaning back in my chair, my legs spread wide and my arms crossed. Her anima must have no sense of self-preservation, because she saunters past Scythe and plonks herself down on my lap.

My animus wants to vomit at the feel of another anima on me.

"You stink of cum," I drawl. "Get off."

It's probably one of the worst things you could say to an anima presenting herself to you, so she recoils while still on me. "Fuck you!"

Smoke billows from my nose and she stares at it.

"If you like your hair on your head, Sarah, go," Yeti warns.

But she doesn't listen and runs her long nails across my chest. "I don't mind a little heat."

I glance at her long hair. It ignites instantly.

Sarah screams at a pitch that might ruin my ears and lurches off me, flapping at the flames and jumping up and down, only making it worse. The acrid smell of burnt hair fills the area, and Savage wrinkles his nose.

Someone throws a jug of apple juice onto her head

and the flames go out with a sizzle and plenty of smoke, leaving her looking like a drowned rat, mascara running down her cheeks.

She shrieks and stomps away, leaving the males around us to chuckle darkly.

But as Lyle Pardalia walks into the dining hall, everyone goes quiet and still. Scythe's voice tickles my brain. *"She's going to try and escape."*

All three of us look at Aurelia Aquinas, who's watching the deputy headmaster like she wants to be sick. *"How do you know?"* I ask.

"Her eyes having been darting around the hall entire time," Scythe says. *"But not at the beasts. At the windows."*

"Well, well," I mutter. *"That won't do at all."*

Chapter 14

Aurelia

Another thing about living isolated and alone for your entire teenage life is that I've never had much access to real non-TV drama. So, sitting at my little table in the dining hall of Animus Academy watching the three beasts who are supposed to be my mates sit like kings while *other* terrifying beasts literally bow to them is pretty bloody high on my 'holy shit' scale. If this is what it's like to be the centre of drama, I don't want it.

Scythe is literally sitting in a chair that he, by his mere cold presence, has transformed into a throne, while men and women shit their pants as they speak to him, baring their necks in submission. Within half an hour, he holds most of the room in his pale, beautiful tattooed hands.

Savage knocked a lion twice the size of him out in one casual blow, then proceeded to shoot daggers my way every three minutes. Xander made all the animas at my table freak out when he walked in with those eerie white glowing eyes. Then, he *lit a girl's hair on fire* without twitching a muscle before or after. She had thrown herself at him, and forced her way into his lap, but still! The poor girl ran out of the hall, shrieking.

I don't know what to do.

Because if they can do *that*, what the hell are they going to do about *me*? Savage has outright told me he'll kill me. Back when I first met them, Xander told me he wished the entire Court of Serpents had all been killed in the '70s purge, and Scythe said he was going to find out all my secrets.

Any plan I could use against them seems infantile. But once again, my loopy trait is kicking in, because the thought of this as a challenge brings out a tiny spark within me. It makes my adrenaline rush through my veins. If I can thwart them, what an achievement that would be for my mental resume.

So I might have a type-A personality. My mum died when I was five, so I can't be sure, but I think I get my mad need to prove myself from my dad or *because* of my dad. Just in my case, it may very well get me killed.

Naturally, all the animas around me notice the new men with their bright red warning lanyards right away.

"Who are they?" Minnie asks in horror.

I think it's best if I pretend not to know them, so I stay silent. Luckily for me, Raquel snorts. "S-stay away, little k-kitten. Bad m-men right there."

Tell me about it.

Minnie gives me wide eyes and I shake my head in dismay, as if to say, 'Gee, I'm sorry for their mates.'

So I still have to run from the psychos, but I need to be smart. Last time, I didn't have a real plan other than to just bolt. This time, I'm going to plan it out cleverly. Phase one is going to be to deny they're my mates completely. They only saw my mating mark in that one moment of weakness and never again. They might just buy the fact that they were wrong. Xander seems to be of the same mind since he basically saved me back in the mating lines with Savage. Phase two is for me to figure out which way my exit lies.

It's not until the deputy headmaster walks in—nay, *prowls*—in like he's on a hunt, that I became stricken and throw all my plans out the window—I wish I could throw *myself* out the window right about now, but they're all locked—because he walks in, staring at *me* like he's ready to tear out my throat. All six-foot-seven of male alpha lion in a perfectly pressed three-piece suit is angled towards my gaping form.

My heart stops. My vision blurs. My throat collapses.

Both times I previously met Lyle Pardalia, he was hunting me. Like the Wild Gods' own personal warrior angel. Wild but refined. Lethal but controlled. He's like a rabid beast with a steel grip on his own tether. It's sexy as all hell and every anima in the room lets out a shudder and swoons. Next to me, Minnie sighs dreamily, and Stacey on my other side squeezes her thighs together. I'm surprised we don't all go into spontaneous heat.

But luckily, everyone has some sense of decency and

there are only a few girly giggles from our table. Lyle's amber eyes thankfully shift off me and sweep around the hall. I almost sag with relief and realise that I shifted my body so I'm in a position to leap out of my seat if need be. I cough awkwardly and concentrate on looking relaxed in my chair.

The worst thing you can do in a room full of male beasts? Unexpectedly run. It sets off their prey drive instinct right away. It's even written on the warning sheet Minnie has in the first page of her binder.

"Is it hot in here, or is he the hottest thing you've ever seen?" Stacey mutters.

The girls murmur in agreement, but I keep my mouth shut because I hate the guy.

I watch Lyle take in the energy of the room, including right up the back where Scythe and the others have set up court. The corner of his mouth twitches almost imperceptibly as he takes them in before he gestures to our table.

"New students, with me. Animas, at the front, if you will." His voice has the deep arrogant drawl of a man who never doubts his authority, and every anima leaps to obey. I'm dubbing it his 'Teacher voice'. I purse my lips and hold back though, because my ego is bigger than my ass and it's currently licking her wounds. This man has seen me naked, taken me against my will, and I'll be damned if I'm obeying him just because he says so.

I mean, I *do* obey, just as slowly as possible. It might sound petty, but in our world, it's a tiny, noticeable message of rebellion. I have to walk past him to get out of the hall, because clearly, he's waiting to gather the animus students, but I just ignore him as I walk past. It means that I catch his scent, and by the Wild Mother, my mouth waters. Under fresh cologne, I smell clean leather and cedar, rich and heady. My anima goes wild like a bitch in heat and I have to clamp down on the need to turn around, press my body against his and sniff at his neck. Instead, I scream at myself not to be needy and all but leap towards the exit, throwing my tray in the bin and hurrying through the doors.

In the hallway, Theresa is waiting for us with a kind smile, and I never thought I'd be happier to see her.

Chairs scrape behind me as the animus students get up to follow us.

"Ladies," Theresa says gently, and I think it's in an effort to calm us down from the aftereffects of Lyle. "I'm taking you to the lecture theatre, and then we'll separate into groups after. Let's get a move on."

Minnie loops her arm through mine like we're in second grade, heading to the bus for an excursion, and for the second time, I wonder how the hell a softie like her ended up here. I'm not judging her though, because the movement calms me after I relax into it.

I know I'm touch-deprived, so I might as well enjoy this while I have it.

We're led to a huge college-style lecture theatre with fifty-odd wooden seats. It looks like a super old parliament room because it was built with the rest of the mansion, with those fancy wood-panelled walls and matching stairs leading up to the thirty-odd rows of seats.

Dragon scrollwork patterns each corner of the room and I can just imagine an entire parliament of dragons, smoke billowing, seated here talking about whatever political issues dragons discuss. Matters of arson? Flight paths? Stock prices? Who knows, but they all come from old money from places like Greece, Italy, and China—where I think Xander gets at least some of his genes from— meaning there's a lot of money to talk about.

Theresa sits us down on the side of the room farthest from the door and right up the back, and I immediately know it's strategic and fall in love with her.

This way, when the males all pile in, glaring or pining up at us, we get a good look at our potential suitors. But they will have to suffer through their backs being turned to us when they sit down.

I make sure all of my seven shields are back up in full force. The morning meal sits happily in my stomach and I feel like I'm ready to be observant and start formulating my plans.

Scythe, Savage and Xander walk in together, all three pairs of eyes finding me as they walk a little way up the stairs. Their faces are blank, though, and they promptly turn around to sit in their chosen seats. I gulp as I stare at their backs.

Savage leans back in his chair, his hands folded on the back of his head, elbows out as if he's here for a summer holiday. Xander's long, silky black hair is neatly tied at his nape and I can't help but wonder what shampoo he uses because it definitely isn't that LFS rubbish. Scythe's silver hair hangs loose and the way his broad shoulders take up his black shirt sends a tiny flutter through my lower belly.

I quickly look away.

The other guys taking their seats have broken off into order groups. There's a large group of wolves; the denim, scruffy, biker types. They're already friendly with one another and talking silently, as is the way of wolves. A group of feline shifters just as big sits as far away from them as possible, their long manes giving them away. A few sit separately, and I know they must be tigers, panthers and lone feline types.

The birds of prey take their seats between the canines and felines, all with short spiky hair and many with shiny piercings.

These separate ways are for us, purely instinctive, and you can see it in the way they all silently just take their places without discussion.

A handsome, familiar face walking in to join the birds has me doing a double take. He's got big biceps that he flexes to get attention and a dark blond spiky hair that, just a few weeks ago, I obsessed over...in Charles Halfeather's mansion.

Beak scans the audience and sees me, the corners of his lips rising into a smile straight away. I raise my hand and he raises his own, before sitting next to a guy with blue and orange stripes in his hair.

Beak was a security guard for Halfeather. He was so kind to me at that cold place and told me he was called to attend Animus Academy. I forgot all about him. But I immediately tense because Savage's head turns to watch

Beak take his seat and the memory of him promising to break the eagle's face sends me into a mad panic.

If it wasn't for Beak, my uncle Ben wouldn't have woken me up in the middle of the night to say the psychopaths were coming for me. I owe this bird, and if he ends up dead, I'll never forgive myself.

Minnie pats my leg as if she thinks I'm nervous about the academy and I smile back at her.

Savage wouldn't just attack Beak in the middle of a crowd, would he?

Would he?

But the wolf stays where he's seated, and I blow out a slow breath.

Scattered in between the larger order groups sit small groups of other orders. I can pick out the serpents immediately because they always dress in a goth style, all black with silver hardware. There are only two of them sitting next to the hyenas, who dress similarly, but have a distinctive curly eyebrow tattoo.

There's a scuffle at the door and someone gives a croaky *bark*. In response to the aggression, three wolves and two birds burst into their beast forms. Our heads whip towards the entrance to the lecture theatre where Lyle stands, roughly pulling two guys apart.

"Feral group," he states calmly, literally taking both growling and snapping guys by the scruffs and hauling them out. He hands them to guards waiting outside before striding back in, not a hair from his long honey-blonde mane out of place.

We all stare in wonder as Lyle assumes his position at

the lectern and, in a booming voice of command that has everyone flinching, says, "Shift back."

A hawk gives a low cry and they all seem to struggle a moment before, one by one, they morph back into their human forms.

Naked male asses appear with the crunch of bones and pops of cartilage. Guards stride around, handing out orange jumpsuits to replace all the torn clothes.

Lyle immediately starts a slide show like this is a normal day at work for him.

Welcome to Animus Academy

Our noble leader talks to us in his deep, grocery list, clipped voice, his eyes seemingly taking in everyone at once. I've never seen a teacher like him, and no one in the audience makes a sound as he speaks. "Welcome. The rabid and most feral students from your year have been taken out for briefing by myself later. Those of you who remain are considered capable of listening to me for the next few minutes.

"The purpose of Animus Academy is to prepare you for a productive and safe life within the wider community, and that includes our non-shifting, human friends. We are a three-year practical program. I do not like to think of this place as a prison, whatever you may have heard. You might be here as ordered by the council, but it can be quite enjoyable if you give it a chance."

More than a few people scoff at that, but quieten

immediately when Lyle levels them with an unimpressed look.

"The rules are plastered everywhere, so you can't miss them, as well as their associated punishments. And I want you to hear me because I have a *zero-tolerance policy* on serious offences. There are no warnings. You will be punished for any harm or damage you cause to a person or object. Class A offences are out of my hands and you'll be taken by the Council of Beasts for a trial. The same laws that apply in the outside world apply here, and if found guilty, you are looking at imprisonment at Blackwater Penitentiary. We are all adults here, and I expect you to start behaving like one.

"Lastly, what you can expect. Your timetable is in the packet of information given to you in your rooms, but you'll be split into smaller groups. There are also some classes where you will be split into anima-animus groups."

I glance at the slide showing our subjects and inwardly cringe as Minnie lets out a giggle as she diligently takes notes with her sparkly pen and a tiny pad. Lyle reads the classes out loud.

Animalia Law 101
Control of Animalia Instincts
Safe Shifting
Safe Use of Powers
How to be Friends with Humans
Practising Safe and Consensual Sex
Safe Courting Behaviours
Self Defence

"I'm so excited by this!" Minnie whispers to me. "It'll be fascinating to see what we learn!"

"Yeah, me too," I say, trying to sound positive...until the silence of the lecture theatre makes us both look with dismay at the lectern—

Where Lyle is staring up at us with a gaze like daggers. My blood runs cold as he snaps, "Do you have something to share, Miss Aquinas, Miss Devi?"

"He knows my name, what the fuck," Minnie mutters.

I shake my head and call, "No, sorry."

He glares at me. Literally tries to kill me with his eyes. "I didn't think so," he deadpans before turning away to point at the screen.

I'm trying not to be dramatic, I really am, but my nerves are literally trying to sew themselves back together as I clench my fists in frustration. There's nothing I'm going to enjoy more than the satisfaction of knowing that when I successfully break free of this place, Lyle Pardalia is going to be left *fuming*.

Chapter 15

Aurelia

Lyle drones on for the next few minutes about the school values, and just when we all start to fidget, he closes off his speech and hands us over to our guides.

Theresa indicates for us to stay with her while the boys trudge after Lyle and the two massive bear shifters to talk about their specific program. It probably includes 'how not to hump the furniture' or 'why you shouldn't chew on carpets' and other important things. Although, I have to admit as I ogle Scythe's broad back swaggering out last, I might very well be needing that lesson soon, too. My anima dismays at the sight of our mates leaving, but Minnie makes for a good distraction while she proudly shows me that she wrote everything down in case either of us forgot.

A red-headed man in a zoo keeper's khaki shorts and button-up shirt enters the theatre carrying a large cage covered with a black cloth.

"Alright animas," Theresa says. "As we discussed yesterday, the unfortunate fact of the matter is that you are only a few anima in the midst of a large number of animus'. A majority of the beasts here are looking for a mate and are highly aggressive in general, at least towards each other. When the academy decided to take on students with animas a few years ago, our noble headmaster found a solution to the concerns of the community. Show 'em, Rick."

The Headmaster, I realise vaguely, has yet to make an appearance. Lyle, being the Deputy appears to be doing all the face-on work.

Sabrina whisper-shouts, "Is she kidding about the 'unfortunate fact'? I'm in heaven over here."

Connor snorts in agreement.

Rick says with great enthusiasm, "G'day, students! I'm the head vet of the changed and rabid beasts of the school. We've sourced these tiny creatures from a small island off the coast of Brazil so that each of you will have a protective companion. Now, nimpins might look small, but they pack a punch when they want to." He slowly removes the cloth to reveal a whole bunch of small, multi-coloured fluff balls, no bigger than the palm of my hand, squeaking, rolling and levitating themselves all around the cage.

We all let out stunned gasps.

"Oh, they're so cute!" Minnie squeals.

"Do they even have legs?" Raquel asks, squinting at them.

"They sure do!" Rick says, opening a door and

pulling one out to show us. The nimpin is no more than a ball of fine downy teal fur, and it blinks up at us with wide, round eyes and a cute little yellow beak that lets out a cute chirp of 'hello'. It has no arms or any upper limbs I can see. Rick turns it around and shows us two yellow oblong-shaped feet, though I can't see any legs. "They also won't trigger your hunting instincts or prey drive, because they let out a pheromone that triggers a maternal or paternal instinct. In the wild, sometimes they're taken in as cubs by other beasts. It's really their only defence mechanism other than their main one, which is to let out a high frequency psychic shriek that will paralyse any person or animal who hears it. It just so happens that I've trained these guys to direct their powers so they can make targeted attacks."

"So..." Minnie pipes, "they'll protect us in case we're cornered?"

Rick nods. "They disable an opponent easily and are trained to act when their owner feels threatened. They're quite empathic, so they double as an assistant animal. They've worked really well for us over the last few years, and your anima will love them."

I exchange a silent, giddy look with Minnie as Rick hands each one of us a nimpin with an information card attached to its foot with a tiny silver chain.

My nimpin is a bright ocean-blue creature that chirps happily when I sit him in my palm. His information card reads:

My name is: Henry

My birthday is: 25th December
My age is: 2 years old
I eat: Insects, spiders, all types of berries and leaves

I instantly decide I'm in love and that I will protect him with my life.

They're supposed to be on loan from the academy, but one look at Henry's sweet round face and large, liquid-black eyes, and I can't care less about that. Looks like I have a nimpin coming with me when I escape. Goddess knows I'll need a little security out there.

Rick gives us each a little baggie which has a tiny litter box they're trained to use and a soft, miniature brush. We are to take them for monthly checks with the veterinary nurses, which would also test our ability to keep our appointments.

Minnie's nimpin is a canary yellow and is called 'Gertrude', though Minnie begins calling her Gertie right away.

The last time I was in a school-like setting was primary school, and it was never as intense as this. It's a novelty to be taught in person instead of online.

There are things they do here that they never did in my old school, though. For one, after Rick leaves, Theresa checks our hygiene to make sure we've showered and taken our de-wormer. It's only Raquel and I who had to use LFS, which is super embarrassing for the both of us. None of us are feral enough that we have actual hygiene problems. In fact, it's mostly the opposite. Everyone, except Raquel and I, dresses to impress, which is a natural thing for both animus and anima to do to try and find their mates.

Minnie is my inspiration through and through, because she carefully curated her spectacular outfit. While Raquel prefers to wear their double denim outfits, I will have to have my three old blouses on rotation. None of Minnie's clothes will fit me, unfortunately, and us new students are not yet allowed in the student village.

It doesn't matter, though; I don't want the attention.

Theresa then begins our first group therapy session where we have to talk about our feelings regarding being here. We all go one at a time and the emotions range from apathy to outright rage.

When it's her turn, Minnie wrings her hands together. "I think I need to be here. I have trouble controlling things sometimes."

"What do you mean by 'things'?" Theresa prompts.

My friend's cheeks turned pink. "When I get upset, I guess." She refuses to say more on the matter and I totally get that. I pat her knee in encouragement and notice her skin glitters with a shimmery powder.

When it's my turn, I barely opened my mouth when Sabrina says, "Did you really murder your husband? I thought you looked familiar, your face was on *Animalia Today*. I thought it was weird they didn't have a picture of you, though. That artist's rendition was rank."

I have to stop from gaping at Sabrina's pretty, perfectly powdered face, because my fifteen seconds of fame have just gone to waste on one useless lie. And of course there were no photos of me, there was no one to take any other than the few selfies I took on my phone then quickly deleted. You couldn't see a mating mark through a photo but I'd been paranoid nonetheless. "I didn't set the fire, but yeah, I got retrieved and I don't really want to be here." I shrug, choosing to go with the authentic rebel route that most of the others seem to be going with. It was the truth, at least.

Theresa nods empathetically and ends our session. We then go through a series of talks by our new 'teachers', including the literal giant bearded wolf called Ruben Lunaris, who will teach us physical defence.

Personally, I can't wait for those classes because I can't fight to save my life in my human form, and I've never had to in beast form. As much as I've watched cage fights over the years, I have no idea how to actually do any of those moves myself.

The rest of the day, us animas and our nimpins take our classes without our animus friends. Little Henry plonks himself right on my shoulder and he is a tiny, softly chirping weight that actually helps to ground me. The three beasts always sit at the corner of my mind, haunting me and my anima. It's like I can feel their eyes watching me wherever I go, even when they're not around. It makes my skin crawl, and then I think about how Savage touched me that *one* time and I get all hot and bothered. Henry vibrates like a phone on my shoulder whenever I get these thoughts. It snaps me right out, making him my new favourite person after Minnie.

· · ·

After a long day of introductory classes, we head to dinner and Connor happily gives us the gossip about the who's who of the unmated male dorms. As we sit down and I scope out the hall, I let out a sigh of relief that my mates are not here. I noticed Scythe didn't eat breakfast, while Xander and Savage most definitely did. Savage once told me that Scythe only eats raw fish and I didn't see any here—but I'm shoving my nose in the wrong place, completely wasting my energy thinking about it.

I'm too busy chastising myself that I don't notice the male with the spiky dark blond hair and tall athletic physique draws up a chair beside me until Beak says, "Hi, Lia."

Violently flinching and then trying to hide it, I cough. "Beak?"

He grins, all handsome, tan, and white teeth. I smile tentatively at him, though I'm not sure how I feel about meeting him here. Before I met the three psychos, I drooled over Beak and he flirted with me. My anima being a lonely and desperate hussy, I responded to him immediately.

He did nothing to help me when I was forced to marry Halfeather. On the other hand, he couldn't do anything to foil the political machinations of powerful beasts, especially when one of them was the Serpent King. I don't see how I can be angry with him.

A few of the beasts from the tables nearby stare at him jealously. Henry hops reassuringly on my shoulder, but it doesn't stop me from tensing up at the thought that Savage and Xander might walk in at any second.

"Are you alright?" he says, searching my face. "I got really worried when—"

"Yeah, I'm okay," I say quickly, eyes darting around. The fewer people who know the details of my escape, the better. "I...ran, but they got me."

He rubs the back of his neck, which flexes his large bicep. I know he does it on purpose to show me his muscles. Peacocking at its finest. He's a good-looking guy, and one time I would have gladly fallen into bed with him. Now I've met my mates, my body doesn't respond the same way to other males.

"Yeah, I heard. It's impossible to get away from the retrieval team." He then lowers his voice, his eyes darting around the hall as if looking for someone. "Have they been giving you trouble? You need to be—"

"Yeah, yeah," I say quickly, wary of the other animas pretending not to listen. "Thanks for checking on me, Beak. Everything's been fine. Just...look after yourself." I make my eyes big to try and indicate the males he should be wary of. I don't understand why they've left him alone. It just seems like a murder waiting to happen.

"Oh, don't worry about me." He actually laughs.

"You're not worried. At all?" I say, exasperated. "I mean, you were one of their jailors."

He shifts in his seat, glancing at the other girls. "Yeah...well, can I talk to you in private?"

"You really need to go, Beak. You could really get into trouble talking to me."

"But—"

"*Go,* seriously." I glance at the door again, but it's empty.

He sighs, running his hand through his hair again. "Alright, well if you...*need* anything, you come right to me okay?"

The suggestion in his voice makes my face heat up. When all I do is blink rapidly at my plate, he does reluctantly leave, and heads back to the table with the other birds of prey. His friends smirk at him while beasts from other orders glare enviously at him.

"Ex-boyfriend?" Sabrina asks a little too casually.

"No. Just someone from a place I never should have been in."

"Girl," Minnie says, shaking her head, "I know exactly what you mean."

It turns out that the animus' have a system surrounding how to approach the animas. Moments after Beak returns to his table, he's confronted by an older hawk and his cronies. The burly males with feathers tatted all down their arms surround Beak and his friends on all sides, bending down to say something clearly threatening.

"He shouldn't have approached," Connor mutters to us. "The most senior students are supposed to approach us first. And then it goes down the hierarchy. Same orders try first and then the other orders get to try. They'll probably tear his feathers out for this."

My heart leaps into my throat as everyone watches the quiet but heated discussion. The guards patrolling the sides of the hall watch the group carefully but don't step in. Then Beak sits back in his chair with his arms resting by his sides and smirks. He says something I can't make out but the older hawk visibly stiffens, his brows twitching up before he gives a sharp nod and...leaves.

"Or not?" Connor frowns.

Beak looks over at our table and winks at us.

"Well shit." Stacey says, impressed. "Looks like birds have a new pecking order."

Chapter 16

Savage

With a cigarette between my teeth, I drag the dead body of the vulture towards the dark of the loading dock at the back of the academy. I wrapped him in an academy branded sheet to save me from cleaning the mess later, but it's soaked through and there's still a trail of blood. Both his arms are out of their sockets and holding on by tendons only—I've never been a neat sort of beast, try as they might to teach us how to be orderly in our class. Sighing dramatically, I dump him at the feet of the two waiting forklift brothers.

"Thank you, sir," says Bertie.

"Bert the bear," I sing around my cigarette, "all dirt and glare." I cock my head, thinking hard. "Or should it be all flirt and glare?"

He grins at me as he hoists the body into his arms like it's no more than a newborn baby. "I like the second one."

"Yeah, me too."

We grin toothily at each other.

I wave them goodbye as they load up their truck, puffing the acrid smoke into my lungs. I find it calming to my overactive mind, even if the nicotine sizzling through my veins does nothing to my wolf body.

After a few seconds, I hum my new tune, shove my hands in my pockets, and head back inside. Xander has fucked up the security cameras in the area, so little Lyle won't have any idea we've even been here.

Scythe's waiting for me when I'm back inside and he's all frowny. "Savage." My brother's voice is disapproving. "What have I told you about leaving blood behind?"

"Sorry," I mutter, exhaling smoke. "I did bring a mop, though." The blood annoys his sensitive shark nose.

Scythe shoots me a dark look before sending Xander a thought-message about bringing the bleach.

With this many beastly noses about, the scent of a vulture's lifesblood is bound to get some attention. There are plenty of enemies for the picking at the academy, but we can't be obvious about our kills. We'd make sure everyone knew about it *outside*, but in here we have to keep it under wraps in case Lyle calls the council executioner on my ass.

Xander turns up with the bleach within minutes, wrinkling his snout—not at its smell, but at the fact he has to clean. Prissy dragon prince.

So I launch myself at him, claws out, with a loud battle cry. "Hee-yah!"

Xander grunts and tries to deflect, but now his arm is just where I want it and I get a swipe at the skin of his wrist. I hit both arteries and they violently spurt open, spraying all over the floor.

"Oopsie!"

"Fuck!" Xander drops the bleach and lunges for me but, flashing my teeth at him, I duck and tackle him to the ground, right onto the long streak of my kill's blood. I slash at his other wrist but miss, and we tussle like animals for a few minutes before heavy feet pound down the corridor. I let Xander get a deep swipe at my chest and blood spills all over him. By the time the guards show up, we're back on our feet, pushing roughly at each other. Scythe is nowhere in sight and neither is the bottle of bleach.

The floor is a mess of blood. Vulture mixed with dragon and wolf. Xander should be thanking me. He doesn't have to clean this now. Some bugger on detention will have to do it.

I'm helpful like that.

"Cut it out!" one of the guards shouts, a small wolf I could eat for breakfast. But behind him strolls Ruben.

"What's going on now, Savage?" he says casually, eyes darting around to assess the scene of the crime. Grampa wolf doesn't even carry a weapon, he's enough on his own.

"He looked at me funny," I whine, pointing to Xander, who's angrily staunching the blood still spurting from his wrist. Reuben thinks he has me cornered now because they've got me in *remedial* classes, don't they? I want to be in Aurelia's class, but apparently she's not feral and doesn't need the extra security or help of Class

B. They're forcing me to learn to write properly, which Scythe is happy about but I'm not. The only bonus is that we get extra fighting classes to burn off our energy. That's where I appreciate Ruben, because he's the only one who will spar with me now. The rest of them are too weak.

Ruben rolls his eyes at me, which sends me growling. "Sure he did, bud. Come on, let's go to medical, then."

He treats it like such a great task while Xander's fiery glare promises murder. When no one's looking, he shoots a burning flame towards my ass. It hits me and burns like a motherfucker, though I don't make a sound just to piss him off. Dragonfire hurts in a whole new way that regular fire doesn't, and if it hits you bad enough, it can melt your bones.

I think Xander goes to the hospital for something to do because his dragon magic will heal his wounds in minutes. Neither of us mention it, but I want to see the medical wing again too, so I happily go along with it.

Afterwards, with useless wound dressings on, because the healers don't waste their power on simple injuries, Scythe reappears and he and Xander leave for the dining hall. For dinner, everyone is piling into the cafeteria because they have cheesecake for dessert. Someone got Scythe the sashimi he likes, so he's keen to make a beeline right for it. I'm not hungry and settle for irritably prowling back to our dorm.

I know I hate Aurelia, but the beast inside me has my brain in a chokehold. It wants to dominate her, to make her submit and claim her as my regina.

Sometimes the wolf inside me wins, and I have to tap out. This is one of those times.

I find myself drifting towards her room, yet again. We identified where she's staying straight away, and maybe that's a bad thing because now my wolf is able to go there every day.

During lunch break, we sniffed around the room to see what was in it, purely for security reasons. We went through her things and were confused by her lack of possessions. Why didn't her family bring her clothes? It made my wolf whine in protest. From our investigating, we know that her mother died years ago, but she must have *some* relatives helping her. Her family is super wealthy, and why she lived in that tiny hut at the back of her aunt's property, even as an eagle, doesn't make sense. Why didn't she go to live with the eagles in her family?

Now, I can't contain my need to be in her space. If I can't physically be with her, this is the next best thing because her scent is all over her stuff.

The two guards outside the unmated female dormitory are a nuisance, and one of them is the Eastern Brown I had my eye on from yesterday. It takes me fifteen precious minutes to deal with them both.

Once I'm done, I use the security pass Scythe arranged, and I excitedly bound up the stairs and into her room with a mad grin.

"Lee-uh," I sing into the empty space, triumphant. I take a sniff of the room. The bed on the left is the tiger cub's bed, and the one on the right is Aurelia's. I head for

171

it without a single thought, kicking off my boots, pulling the covers back and climbing inside the cool sheets.

I'm a bit annoyed they aren't still warm with her heat, but as I become enveloped in her delicious vanilla cake scent, I let out a mournful whine. Pulling the blankets around me, I lie on my side and snuggle in, burying my nose in her pillow.

Sleeping has never really been my thing since I was a kid, and here in this place, I didn't sleep a wink last night, my wolf sensing that somewhere nearby our regina slept in a cold bed, alone. I allow my eyes to droop as I get drunk on her and the memory of her heaving, sweaty skin and soft, needy moans in my ear.

It's not until I'm getting hard that I sigh and climb back out, looking around. I want her to know I've been here, in her private space, touching everything because it's now mine too. She needs to know.

She needs to *fucking know* that I own her.

I growl to myself as I look at the set of drawers assigned to her. I pull open each one and rummage around for good measure. Only the top two drawers are being used, the rest are empty. What she does have is mostly neat to start with, but by the time I've held everything to my nose, it's all a happy mess.

Then I find her underwear drawer.

Excitedly, I check each and every single piece, and I'm growling with rage well before the end. She has seven pairs of underwear, mostly threadbare, faded and some even with holes. It's really strange for the once princess of the Serpent Court. Even if her anima was an eagle, her father should be providing for her, with all the money he has.

One pair is yellow with the face of a familiar character and I immediately pocket it because she'll have no man's face on her underwear, even if it's a cartoon sea sponge. Fuck him. Fuck her for making me lose control. Everything here is mine as well and I will take all of it if it means she understands me.

Next time, I'm going to take *all* of her underwear. She can go without for all I care. All the better for us to scent her as she walks around. I'd have to leave her one pair because what if she has her period and uses pads? I'm not rabid. I know about women's needs. *My regina's* needs. Scythe keeps me educated on everything. When we were kids, he told me all about periods when he first learned about them. Because of his nose, he took an interest in anything to do with blood.

My wolf keens again because if she gets her period, then she'll need us and we can't be here to rub her stomach.

Fuck this shit.

I slam down the present I brought for her on to the dresser and then angrily go through her trash to check for anything suspicious. I quickly check the tiger cub's side to find any clues as to who she is and mess up her drawers while I'm at it.

Then I leave, slamming the door shut behind me.

I miss her scent as I walk down the corridor and shake myself to get rid of the idiotic thoughts.

We have group therapy tomorrow and I smirk

because it's hilarious to see Scythe refuse to participate in the lessons. I'm just waiting for some type of punishment to be dealt, because then I'll get to have some real fun. On the way back to my dorm, I see a big sheet stuck to the wall with the state symbol for the Hunting Games, some writing, and lots of empty space underneath. I take the pen attached to a chain next to it and carefully write my name down in my big messy scrawl. It takes me a few minutes to sound out the letters, but this is important. Being able to hunt each other in a tournament definitely sounds like something I want to do, especially since we're allowed to maim each other in the arena. It has to be a priority for me.

They do stuff like this to help us temper our instincts. We can't get rid of them, so they found an outlet. The Council of Beasts invented the Hunting Games as a way to let us legally do that. Since my need to hunt is endless, despite my constant bloody fights, I need as much of an outlet as I can get.

Otherwise, the wolf in me is likely to continue to hunt and stalk Aurelia until it gets what he wants.

Which is to be buried balls deep inside my regina while she screams my name.

Chapter 17

Aurelia

We're leaving after dinner when Theresa stops us at the door, a grim look on her face. "Sorry, girls. No bed for you two just yet. You've landed yourselves detention."

"What?" Minnie gapes because Theresa is pointing to *both* of us.

"Why?" I say in protest. I've never had detention in my life, never so much as had my name written on the whiteboard, and I'm not about to start now.

Theresa hands me a very official-looking notice on *red* paper and everyone crowds around me to read it, including the beasts trying to get out of the hall.

A male behind me lets out a rude snorting sound.

Notice of Detention for joint crime
Name (1): Aurelia Aquinas
Name (2): Minnie Devi
Crime: Disrespecting a member of staff

177

Punishment: Cleaning duty, left wing. Central building.

Lyle's signature is beneath it in a professional cursive that looks like calligraphy done in a fountain pen.

A bastard through and through.

"When were we rude to a member of staff?" Minnie shrieks as if this is the worst thing to ever happen to her.

Sabrina starts laughing. "In the lecture hall when you two were whispering!"

I groan. "You've *got* to be kidding."

"We take this seriously," says Theresa sternly. "Now, follow me."

Minnie and I grimace at each other as Sabrina and Stacey cackle on their way out. Connor and Raquel are more sombre about it but can't help smiling anyway.

Theresa collects two mops and buckets on our way to the left wing while I stew on the idea that Lyle Pardalia is taking his revenge on me. This is beyond unfair, and I've just dragged my brand-new friend into it as well.

"Look," says Minnie, waving her mop around like a flag. "We've done the wrong thing, now we make up for it and let's never—"

We both abruptly halt because Theresa has led us to the scene of our detention.

There's blood splattered *everywhere* along the corridor as if someone has actually been butchered right here. There's a small clotted pool in the middle, with streak marks leading out in every direction as if there was a scuffle. And there's also splatters all along both walls.

"Who died?" Minnie asks softly.

"No one," Theresa says. "It was just a fight. Now get to work and I'll be checking on you in half an hour."

And then she just leaves us there.

I gulp at the blood and gently set my bucket down. Henry clucks softly in my ear, as if he knows this is a distressing situation. Gertie, sitting on Minnie's shoulder, does the same.

And then, before our very eyes, some areas of blood on the floorboards start to *dissolve*. No, not dissolve but—

"Is the wood *absorbing* the blood?" Minnie breathes.

I swear. "I think so, Min."

After a minute of staring, the process seemed to stop, the rest of the crimson pool just sat there, congealed.

After exchanging a dark look, Minnie and I set to work mopping up the mess as best we can, wringing it out in the bucket and refilling it with clean, soapy water from the bathroom nearby. The two nimpins zoom around us, chirping in encouragement.

"Lia," Minnie says slowly, turning off the sink tap. "It smells like *dragon*."

My heart drops in my chest.

If one of my mates is dead, I would know, I'm sure. I slowly turn towards her. "Are you sure?"

She frowns at me. "Can't you smell it?"

With my seven shields back up, I actually can't smell all that much. "Uh, I guess it's a mess. I sort of blocked it out."

She nods as we head back out. "Yeah, it *is* a mess. But there's more than one scent. Wolf, too."

My heart gives an uneven thump as I eye the blood

smeared on the walls. What the hell were *they* doing here? I know Theresa said no one died, but she had no reason to tell us the truth, either.

Theresa returns just as we've scrubbed away the last of the spots on the wood panelling. She approves our work and walks us back to our dorm building.

But when we get there, we find at least four animas milling around the outside, looking uneasy. One of them has shifted into her wolf form and is sniffing the ground outside the front door.

"What happened?" Minnie asks.

"Nothing you need to worry about," Theresa says far too quickly, in my opinion. "Head on inside and I'll see you tomorrow." She turns to the wolf. "Layla, shift back, *now*."

The girl does and crouches on the ground, naked.

"Smell anything?" a vulture asks.

Layla frowns and vigorously shakes her head. I pause on the doorstep because I get the distinct impression that Layla looks frightened...and I'm suddenly sure she's lying.

Frowning at each other, Minnie and I go inside and climb the narrow stairs to the third floor. Sabrina and Raquel are talking to Stacey. All three of them look a little pale, if I'm honest, and the nimpins on their shoulders are agitated, looking this way and that with their big liquid black eyes.

"What happened?" Minnie asks.

"You two smell bad," Stacey complains.

"Someone killed the two guards at our door," Sabrina says softly.

Henry and Gertie give little squeaks of indignation.

"No way," I say, my stomach doing a dive into my pelvis. A dark feeling winds its way around my insides, and I want to be sick for a second time tonight.

"Who do they think did it?" Minnie asks quietly.

"W-We all need to go back into our r-rooms and c-close the doors," Raquel says, jabbing their finger around the circle of us girls. They take a deep breath. "I-If you know what's g-good for you, d-don't open the door for anyone e-except s-staff." With that, Raquel angrily stomps into their room and holds the door open, glaring at Sabrina.

"Alright, alright!" the leopard says, holding her hands up and striding in. Raquel slams the door shut so hard the frame rattles. Charlotte gives us a wide-eyed look and goes into her room, too.

But when Minnie and I get back to our room, Minnie let out a loud gasp. When I see what's happened, my entire body freezes.

A tornado has hit our room. Only in certain places.

Both Minnie's and my drawers have been opened, the contents all spilling out in a complete mess. The lid to our trash cans have been taken off and thrown to the floor.

Though Minnie's bed has been untouched, the sheets of my bed have been tossed around and every single one of my drawers is open.

Henry and Gertie leave our shoulders and zoom

around the room, trying to see everything at once.

"Someone's been through our things," I say in stricken disbelief.

Minnie chokes as she looks at her side, then mine. She points to my bed. "Do you know anyone here?" she asks. "Because I...don't."

"Um, not really." I feel bad for lying, but I don't really *know* know the three psychopaths, do I?

"How about that eagle-ex of yours? Beak?"

"Not an ex. We never did anything," I say quickly. Why is my blood roaring in my head?

"Hmmm, because usually if an animus is stalking you, they've thought about it beforehand."

If an animus is stalking you.

My heart falls into my nether regions. I clutch at my stomach.

Shit. Fuck.

Raquel's suspicious behaviour. The wolf shaking her head outside. Wolves always stick together. They don't spill each other's secrets.

Minnie sniffs at her things while I'm still staring at the room. She then hurries to my side and sniffs my bed, her little button nose twitching. After a moment's hesitation, I do the same.

I freeze when I catch it.

Ancient cold forests, pine, and deep, rich earth. A feeling of dread winds itself around my lower stomach. Savage *has* been here. The bastard has actually been in my room. Was he trying to scare me?

"Do you recognise the scent?" she asks, sniffing again

with interest. Gertie and Henry levitate in circles around my pillow.

I busy myself with hastily shooing them away and straightening my bed again. Without a word, Minnie helps me, tucking in the sheets on the side I can't reach. My movements are jerky as I try to control my panic. Savage has been by my bed before, when I was at home, that one night I let out my siren call. The flash of memory makes me heat up and sends my head spinning.

"It's alright, Lia," Minnie says in a too-calm voice. "We'll just report it to Theresa and she'll sort it right out. Says so on page two-forty-seven of the handbook. Stalking is not permitted without prior consent."

"No!" I say quickly. My friend looks at me with her brows raised.

I clear my throat. "I just mean that I don't want the staff involved in...my love life?"

Minnie nods slowly. "Okay. I understand."

"You do?"

She shrugs. "Yeah, I had a similar thing with an ex. But—" She flaps her hand at me as if it was nothing. "He was trouble, so I left him. Anyway, we're not in danger from *this* animus, are we?"

Her question catches me off guard because suddenly I realise how this looks. I'm immediately ashamed of myself. To have her stuff messed up, maybe things stolen too? I go from scared to furious within seconds.

"I'm going to kill him," I say, angrily, rummaging through my drawers to check if anything's missing. "Don't worry, Minnie. I'll take care of this. I'll—"

I stop dead when I see the tiny fluffy bear on top of the dresser. It's definitely not mine; I don't own any bears. It's blue and white with a rainbow on its belly.

"That wasn't there before," Minnie says softly. "Lia, someone is courting you."

This is Savage's second gift.

My stomach plummets and I whirl around to look at her. But she shrugs. "I dunno, it's kind of cute."

Both nimpins levitate themselves towards the small teddy bear. They sniff at it and make low cooing sounds.

"They like it too." Minnie lets out a disbelieving laugh. "What the hell, Lia? This guy is unhinged. Who is it?"

"Is it bad if I can't say?" I ask tentatively.

Minnie bites her lip. "Did he give you that pink Opal Feather handbag too? It's pretty." I stare at her and she waves her hands in the air, exasperated. "I know you don't have that much money, Lia! They're thousands of dollars."

Squeezing my eyes shut, I rub my temples. In the history of people trying to hide things, I am, perhaps, the worst at it.

"Shit. Yeah, I know it looks bad, doesn't it?"

Minnie giggles. "If he's giving you presents, he's courting you. You need to set boundaries, Lia. This animus needs to know— Wait a minute!" She points at me. "The only person unhinged enough to do this is the wolf who jumped you this morning!"

I stiffen because my safety literally depends on me keeping my mates a secret.

The fact that they are all from different orders is the issue. Nearly all mating groups are from creatures who are in the same order. On the rare occasion, like with Scythe's and Savage's parents, the mating group might have one beast from a different order. So the fact that I'm a regina of a mating group with all different orders? That's a dead giveaway that something is suspicious about me.

If it gets found out, I'm literally done for. I'll be hunted down and kept as property. My worst nightmare.

All I want is a life of freedom to live as I please. Is that too much to ask for? The thing is, no one from the council or from the underworld beast groups would care.

Minnie is now sniffing my sheets and nodding like she's recognising his scent. "Yeah, it's definitely him. And..." She looks at me meaningfully. "It was his scent I smelled in detention."

Shit. I plonk down on my bed and groan into my hands. "Minnie, you're a regular Sherlock Holmes!"

Minnie throws herself on top of me, sending us both crashing to the bed. "Oh my God, I'm so excited, Lia. We need to make a plan! He probably went through my stuff to see if I was a threat to him or something! It's so cute!"

She's a complete mess and I'm a complete mess because my anima *is* actually excited by this, and soon enough, we're laughing and breathless like teenage girls.

"Fuck, Minnie. No, it's not like that. I can't even tell you the trouble I'm in."

She sits up off my bed and pushes a pink curl off her face. "Is it about that old eagle you married? Does it have something to do with that?" Then she gasps and points outside our window. "Did *he* kill Halfeather? He killed the guards as well, I think. Wowsers, Lia! He's going to land himself in real prison if he's not careful."

My stomach churns as I realise that Savage must have killed the guards outside to get in here. Because of me.

I'm also a little alarmed by how little Minnie's bothered by the murdering and stalking as she merely straightens her side of the room, giving me a commentary as she does it. Her altar is untouched, with not a wrinkle in the purple material or any shift in the bronze Wild Goddess statue. I say nothing during her Sherlock Holmes-ing, but she seems content that she's right and takes my silence as confirmation.

This is what happens when you bunk with a nerd. If the positions were reversed, I might have put just as many things together.

I don't have the headspace to come up with an opposing argument, so I just sit on my bed and watch her.

Minnie gives a satisfied nod to her drawers before she and Gertie head to the bathroom for a shower.

Henry and I are left to stare at the teddy bear. I can't help but bring it up to my nose and inhale. It's fresh yet alluring, and as much as I know that it signals danger, my anima keens, low and satisfied. Henry chitters in amusement, immediately rubbing himself on it and leaning against it as if allocating himself as protector of the thing.

Minnie and I get ready for bed in a sort of post-shock silence. That night, I sleep surrounded by Savage's scent and it's the best sleep I've had in over a week.

Chapter 18

Aurelia

We wake up to *four* guards at our dorm entrance but no one makes a comment about it, with us first-year girls just sticking a little closer together than the day before. Even Sabrina doesn't have anything sassy to say.

But me? As we go down to breakfast, I'm *seething*.

Not only did he mess up Minnie's things, but Savage killed two people to get into my room. Needlessly. For no good reason other than to mess up my room and leave me a teddy bear. Two innocent people with families—mothers, brothers, just doing their job—are now dead.

That thoughtless waste of life, that sheer disregard for the innocent, makes my blood simmer. I didn't *hate* him before, but I sure do now.

Everyone is a little jittery because of the murders, and I get the feeling the staff and other guards are trying to downplay the entire thing because there are fewer guards around than before. Minnie says that our first day has more guards around in case of teething and posturing issues, but subsequently, we won't have as many around to make it as much like a normal environment as possible. Looks like Lyle doesn't think the murders should change anything.

Of course, when the three of them finally arrive, they enter the dining room like they own the place. Today, they get to wear normal clothes. Savage wears a black T-shirt and track pants, Scythe seems to enjoy his business shirt and slacks, and Xander is wearing a red and black band T-shirt with black shorts. I suppose he runs hot.

I determinedly cut and shovel my bacon and waffles while Minnie makes eyes at me. "What are we gonna do?"

The fact that she's using *we* makes me fall in love with Minnie even more. But I don't want her caught up in this. These males are far too dangerous, and the game my anima wants to play is going to be dangerous in the worst way.

I desperately want to get out of here, and in the back of my mind, I'm cataloguing what I need to do to run. If my mates are stuck here, I won't have to worry about them in the outside world and will have a clear path to leave the state. So maybe Lyle came in useful after all.

As the three of them sit down with their meals (Scythe *does* have a meal today) I want to let him know I'm not intimidated. Like he knows that I'm staring at him, Savage looks up from his slice of rare steak. My eyes are narrowed as they meet his hazel ones. The bastard quirks a brow and maybe it's the regina in me, but it makes my blood boil. He thinks he can just go through my things and I'll *let* him? He thinks I'll let him touch *Minnie's* things? No one has that right over us.

And then, like a volleyball shot through the air, a thought lands into my head in the sound of Savage's arrogant growl.

"Did you like my present, princess?"

His nickname for me strikes me speechless as I hear it like a soft caress to the inside of my head.

I shove down the urge to lean into it and send him a reply. *"I hated it. It's the ugliest thing I've ever seen."*

Savage's dark brows rise and I know immediately that the other two sense something is up by the way Scythe puts down his chopsticks and sits back in his chair. Xander continues eating, but his head is slightly cocked.

Savage's face morphs into something resembling fury. I've rejected his gift, and it's struck a chord with the wolf animus in him.

I snarl, *"Stay out of my room, wolf."*

"Are you going to stop me, princess?" Even telepathically, he's biting his words out.

"Maybe I will."

He presses his lips together just before he tears into his steak without taking his eyes off me.

The girls start to leave the table to head to our first class, and without another look at Savage, I follow.

* * *

191

Our 'Interacting with Humans' class is a hoot because two senior eagles are giving a presentation as part of their own studies. My mates sit at a table far away from me, thank the Goddess.

"Now, what are some things you shouldn't do?" the eagle with a bubblegum-pink bob says. "Yes?"

Minnie has enthusiastically raised her hand and says, "Um...smack them on the ass?"

More than a few people laugh, and I cast her an appreciative glance. A jaguar animus did that very thing to her this morning at the buffet, making Minnie scream at the top of her lungs. The entire dining hall had turned to stare, and quickly, that guy was presented with a detention slip. But I like that she can make humour out of that sort of thing.

"Sometimes that's okay if you know the person," Pink Bob says.

Theresa lets out a small cough and the eagle roughly corrects, "If you have consent beforehand, of course. But you'll learn about appropriate methods of courting later in the year. What else?"

Raquel raises their hand and says in her deep alto, "Y-You c-can't sniff them."

The second eagle, a male with a black mohawk nods. "Yeah, they get offended if you're obvious about it. Humans can't smell half as well as we do, and besides, their scent isn't always so nice."

"Nothing smells as good as one of your mates though," a scruffy wolf with an untamed beard says loudly. "My rex smells like peppermint."

I glance at Xander, who sits closest to me. He's leaning back in his seat, his long legs stretched out and his arms crossed like he's unimpressed with the world, which I've realised is his default look. I can't help but wonder what I smell like and if it affects my mates. To me, Xander smells like warm glowing embers, molten spices, and something like a vast cavern deep in the earth. It's hard to explain, but there is so much dimension to what I smell it's like seeing a whole new part of the world. A new part of *him*...as loath as I am to admit it. But I have to remind myself that it's only natural and nothing to be ashamed of.

Once I get out of here, I won't have to deal with it.

The day I realised the three psychos were my mates, it was by accident. As unprepared as I was, stepping out of their dungeon into the light of day was an assault to my senses. Everything looked different. The way I physically saw the world completely changed.

It was like going from standard definition to 4K.

I wonder if it was the same for Xander.

As if he knows I'm watching him, the dragon swivels his head towards me and I find myself unable to look away from his glowing white eyes. There is a moment of stillness between us and I just stare into the white abyss of light. How the hell does he make them do that? Is it his power shining through his eye sockets, or what? The more I stare at them, the more beautiful it gets and I begin to see other colours in there as well. Flashes of blues, purples, greens, and even a colour I can't quite name...

But then Xander sneers in disgust and snaps away as if he's smelled something off. With my heart pounding in shame, I tear my gaze off him and sink deep into my seat. I think I'm going to pretend that didn't just happen. Henry nuzzles my neck from where he sits on my shoulder as if he knows I'm a complete idiot and is trying to make it better.

"What else?" the presenter with the blue mohawk asks us.

Maybe I can forget, but my anima sure can't. Quite suddenly, I'm furious at Xander's dismissal of me and I throw my hand up in the air. "You shouldn't set them on fire."

Raquel, Sabrina, and a bunch of other people turn around and gape at me and my audacity. Minnie grabs my arm as if she's trying to rein in my apparent death wish.

Blue Mohawk and Pink Bob exchange a look before the latter clears her throat and, pointedly refusing to look at Xander, says, "Yeah, you shouldn't use your powers on humans either. Telepathy or telekinesis is the worst. It freaks them out and makes them scared of us. Er...let's move on, shall we?"

At dinner time, I loiter behind to make sure the three males head to the dining hall ahead of me. They're always eating a lot, so I know they won't miss this meal.

"I just need to get a tampon," I say to the girls.

I wink at Minnie as I leave and dart into the nearest toilet. My plan for retaliation is a good one, I think, but I'm still nervous as all hell.

The bathrooms are the one place guaranteed to have no security cameras, so I eighth shield myself inside a stall. Once I'm completely enveloped in invisibility, I speed-walk out. With a quick check to make sure the men are seated at their usual table in the dining hall, I follow a random unmated lion out of the hall.

Connor speaks at length about the chaotic, unmated animus dorms during our meals, so I think I know what I'm in for when I get there. With the majority of students in the dining hall, there are a couple of guys who have eaten quickly and are taking animas back to their dorm—to fuck, I'm assuming—because by the way they're all groping each other, they're definitely not going there to play cards. I follow them all into their dorm, slipping in when the door is opened. Up three flights of stairs, I assume that, like us, they've put the newest guys on the upper floors. It smells like male, deodorant and what I think is perfume. Sure enough I pass an A2 black and yellow poster that outlines the hygiene regulations. ('Shower twice a day, use soap and deodorant is your friend!'). It's there that I sneakily un-shield myself in an alcove and snag a hyena, skulking down to the communal bathroom they have to use.

Hyenas are matriarchal so I try and put on a dominant voice to appeal to his instinct. "Hey you, where's Savage's room?"

He frowns at me, his curling family tattoo stretching

E.P. Bali

along his brow. "Why do you wanna go in there? Are you nuts?"

"I'm going to surprise him. I want to fuck."

His face brightens. "Will you fuck me?"

"No."

He sighs dramatically and points to the end of the corridor, right at a painting of a dragon that someone has stuck a blue paper party hat on. "There are trick stairs there. When you pass through, you'll see it."

"Trick stairs?"

"Old dragon magic," he explains. "To hide secret rooms. They're using it to hide from the guards now."

Oh, those sneaky bastards. Of course Xander noticed dragon tricks right away. What other trickery is there in the old parts of this place?

I nod and cautiously make my way there, though my heart pounds as I do. Sure enough, the end of the hall looks like a solid wall, and so does the painting, but as I press my hands against the canvas, it gives way like jelly and I press myself right through it. I end up at the bottom of a completely new staircase that curves left.

Awed, I eighth shield myself again and climb up the stairs carefully in case one of them creaks. At the top, is a whole other level that you can't even see from the outside, complete with a dining table, comfy chairs, and many adjoining rooms. Muttering darkly about dragons, I decide I'll check the rooms sequentially.

A soft whimper stops me in my tracks.

Slowly, I turn to see that in the far corner, behind the dining table and almost hidden from view, sits a male student with long shaggy hair. His tongue slips out to taste the air, so he's a snake, but that's not the most alarming thing.

He's tightly bound to the chair with magic dampening obsidian chains, and his face and bare torso are a bloody mess, lacerations and grazes marring his pale skin. Both his eyes are black and I think some of his teeth are missing by the way his mouth is swollen. My power lurches, wanting to heal his terrible wounds.

My breath seizes in my throat. I make a split-second decision. Crouching down behind the dining table so he can't see me, I unveil myself, then rush over to him.

He's gagged, so when he sees me, he makes a muffled, desperate scream.

There's a black padlock locking the chains in place by his belt. "Where's the key?" I ask quickly.

I place my fingers around the gag and carefully pull it down. He chokes on a breath and I know his jaw is broken when he cries a muffled, "Get me the fuck outta here!"

"Have you seen the key to this thing? I need the key!" I panic, wildly looking around for some sign of a way to get him out.

"I don't know! I don't know! Get me out!" He thrashes around in his chair, clearly losing it, and fair enough, because I would totally be doing the same.

"Alright, wait." I have no choice but to do a search. It's just as well I came up here because I can't imagine what they're doing with a snake hostage and what they would have done if I hadn't found him.

Bolting to the first door on my right, I find a bathroom. I shut that door and open the next. This room is huge and opulent. Three single four poster beds with red velvet curtains form a line. Bingo.

It's not uncommon for members of the same pack to prefer to sleep together in the same bed or same room. Even anima or animus who are heterosexual. In fact, to see these three monsters share a room makes the anima in me *whine*. There should be two more beds in here and a regina would share her time between each—

The sudden yearning for my pack to be whole and complete hits me like a train at full speed. I keel over and clutch my stomach as a very real physical sensation *burns* my insides. Henry coos with worry, rubbing himself against my neck.

I need to get the fuck out of this room.

But as I turn to leave, something unusual catches my eye. There's a cage on one of the carved ornate bedside tables and Savage's black rooster from the national park is sitting inside it on shredded newspaper. He's staring at me as if I'm a ghost, his beak a little open in shock.

Henry makes a surprised noise and immediately zooms over to look at him.

Two prisoners will be released today if I have something to say about it.

I rush over to them both and unlatch the cage. "Get out, chicky!" I hiss. "And don't attack me while you're at it!"

The bed it sits next to has to be Savage's, so I yank off the fancy red velvet coverlet and black sheets and strew them about messily. The rooster hops out of his cage, looking between me and Henry but not leaving. There's a strange light in his beady black eyes, but I don't have time to ponder it. "If you've seen a key for that serpent out there, I'd be super grateful," I say, yanking open each drawer under his cage. Bronze glints in the bottom of the last one and I grab at it, holding it up. It's key alright, long and slender, a match to the lock. Brilliant! Spinning around, I hurtle towards the door.

The rooster caws sharply, but I ignore him and run out of the room—

Only for Henry and I to be thrown back by a blast of ferocious red magic. A scream tears from my throat and I land on my ass on the wooden floorboards. Henry falls with a thud onto the floorboards. Thankfully, he bounces right back up, shaking himself and hurtling back towards me, where I catch him to my chest with relief.

We both gape up at the curtain of red glittering magic that now covers the doorway.

A dragon lock. I've never actually seen one in real life.

The rooster gives a mournful caw, and it sounds like a balloon deflating.

"Well, well, well." Xander's drawl is cold fire down my spine. "Look what the cat dragged in."

Chapter 19

Aurelia

A cold-faced Scythe steps through the dragon lock first and now stands barely a foot from me, flanked by Savage and Xander. Their energy crackles and snaps around them like a living flame that takes up the entire damned room.

I gulp.

How the fuck I didn't think they'd have their stuff protected is beyond me. I'm a complete fool, and in the wake of utter embarrassment, my face gets hotter by the second.

I clench my teeth to staunch my rising panic as I scramble to my feet and glare at them like *they're* the ones in the wrong. Were they always this intimidating up close? Did they always take up this much space? Shit, that day in the forest seems like a lifetime ago.

Scythe's cold blue eyes fix me to the spot. This is the closest I've stood to him without the bars of a cell between us, and his presence is sending me tumbling like

I'm in an ocean rip. Savage is the only one wearing his red 'Dangerous: do not approach' lanyard, and he wears it like a trophy.

Xander is leaning against the doorframe with his hands in his pockets like he's bored by this whole thing, staring into space as he listens to whatever music he's playing. His black and red T-shirt reveals his swirling dragon tribal tattoo down his impressively muscular left arm.

Henry bops in greeting on my shoulder but doesn't do his psychic squeaking thing yet. Clearly he hit his head on that fall.

"What are you doing?" I snap angrily to try and dispel some of the adrenaline coursing through me. It annoys me that I have to look so far *up* at them.

Savage raises a dark eyebrow at the mess of his bed, but Scythe's stare turns vicious. The apparent king of sharks takes a single, meaningful step forwards, and I have *no* choice but to take a step back if I don't want to be chest to chest with him.

It irks me to no end that I have to do that. That movement alone is me waving a giant red flag that says 'submissive'. Worse? The corner of Savage's mouth twitches the second I do it.

Instinctively, I double my scent shield because I'm frazzled and in bloody danger. Scythe looks furious as he notes the messed-up bed, but says nothing, prompting me to lose my mind in the silence.

"Who is that you have chained up?" I snap. "Angry you couldn't catch me? So you went for someone else?"

"You know," Savage says, casually. His eyes are not trained on me, but Henry, sitting on my shoulder. The pure predatory wolf I see in his eyes makes me grab my little nimpin straight away. "He looks tasty."

"Don't you dare!" I say, cradling Henry to my chest as if I can protect him with my tits. Savage clearly has no paternal instinct for Henry's pheromones to work on.

"I'm sure his bones are nice and crunchy." Xander cocks his head as if he's actually imagining Henry's bones in his mouth, and I swear those white eyes glow with interest.

I gape at them and take another step back. But then they all take a step forwards and I know I'm in deep shit.

"You look different when you're not behind bars," I say slowly, trying something to delay whatever it is that's coming—anything to catch them off guard and give me some leg to stand on.

None of them respond, but Savage suddenly looks furious. He's *still* wearing my hair tie, and when he sees my eyes flick down to his wrist, he clenches his jaw.

"What are you doing in here, snake?" Xander spits at me. "Trying to steal something?"

"Trying to save your many prisoners, apparently!" I exclaim around Scythe.

"He a relative of yours?" Xander says, jerking his chin toward the living room with disgust. "A cousin?"

Suddenly I'm fucking annoyed.

"What do you want with me?" I say angrily, as if I didn't just storm in here on my own. "Whatever you're looking for, I can't give it to you."

Scythe's icicle eyes flick down to Henry and I turn away from him defensively, bringing Henry up to my neck.

The creature wriggles out of my grip and I'm forced to open my hands and watch him levitate up, but the moment Henry opens his little beak, Scythe lashes out quicker than a viper and snatches him out of the air with his tattooed hands

Henry makes an offended sound as Scythe brings the nimpin up to his own perfectly cruel face, but all he does is stare down at Henry.

To my utter surprise and dismay, Henry bops up and down on Scythe's palm as if they're having a silent, cheery conversation. Everything gets worse when Scythe puts Henry on his own shoulder and my nimpin sits there, blinking all innocently at me.

"Traitor!" I gasp, glaring at my blue fluff ball. "You're supposed to protect me!" But Henry just blinks serenely, as if there's nothing at all wrong. Horrified, I take another step backwards, but my ass bumps into the rooster's cage. I'm going to be having words with that zookeeper, Rick, because Henry is clearly faulty.

And then Scythe speaks, and it turns my body into a statue of horror and fear.

"Aurelia." I forgot that haunting, dark rasp. A sound that should belong to some monster lurking in a cemetery. "I am going to give you one chance, just one, to explain why you are lying about not being our regina."

My stomach turns to a jelly that is now trying to escape up my throat. The implication in his voice. The threat of it. The way it caresses my skin like fingers is extremely terrifying and arousing at the same time.

Am I scared? Heck yes. Am I more fearful of what awaits me if I tell them my secret? Also, heck yes. I have no choice but to lie. These guys already hate me. Even if these maniacs are safe for me, if I agree to be their regina, I'll be in danger of every beast here knowing what I am.

Then I'll have a mark on my head. A big red neon sign that says, 'breeder' and 'money' and 'catch immediately and sell'.

But it's still hard, because in the cage of stubbornness I've placed her in, my anima is keening, whining, *wailing* that these are my mates. That this is the pack I belong to and there are only three lonely beds in this room.

But it gets much worse than that because Henry is not the only traitor. My body is responding to the closeness. My *pussy* is throbbing and I can't help but clench those muscles in frustration.

Shit.

Their very presence strikes my body like a flood of warm honeyed heat and there suddenly surfaces a deep desire for Scythe to hold me, to caress me, to fuck me silly.

But the repercussions of that are a level of danger I just can't tolerate.

So I say through gritted teeth and flap my hand at my neck where I know they can't see our mating mark. "I'm not your regina. It doesn't make sense."

The temperature of the room plummets below zero. Xander sort of moves his head in an arc that tells me he's rolling his eyes, and he scoffs like he expected my response. Savage literally bristles with rage and Scythe has gone so still that I don't even think he's breathing.

My instincts are screaming at me to run. My anima is screaming at me to jump into Scythe's arms. In short, I'm a confused puddle on the floor.

"Aurelia." Scythe's rasping voice makes my skin flush and crawl at the same time. "I will not be disrespected by you. I do not tolerate liars. And there is nothing I won't do to destroy those who wrong me."

I'm literally going to vomit and I only just stop myself.

Danger and lethal promise lace his words, and I know this is a beast who is never disobeyed. But his words take me aback because this is about survival.

"It's not about respect," I blurt like a fool. "It's just that you have it wrong."

"I think they call this gaslighting," Xander drawls. "That's what they told us in therapy. Are you gaslighting us, snake girl? Because we fucking saw your mark when you spread your pretty legs for Savage. Or do you not remember when you *pined* for us on a siren call in the middle of the night and all five of us rocked up to your disgusting hovel in astral form?"

I don't know if I'm more taken aback by the fact he called my legs pretty or that he called my cute bungalow a disgusting hovel. It kind of was, but still, he had *no* right. Also, how can I explain the siren call if I'm not their regina? He has me in verbal and literal corner.

Naturally, my only move is to deflect. "Are you going to let me out or not?"

"I think." Savage's nostrils are flaring, and I can even see the thick veins in his neck. "We're going to keep you chained up here as a pet."

I cross my arms. "You wouldn't d—"

I'm abruptly cut off by Scythe grabbing me by the throat and shoving me backwards. My back slams against the cage and I wheeze in shock.

Scythe's huge, cool palm presses against my windpipe, and his fingers squeeze my carotid arteries. My own hands fly up to claw around his.

I *know* this is a threat, but the regina in me can't help but love the fact that he's actually touching me. His *skin* is on mine. Skin-to-skin, and by Wild Goddess, he is so strong—

My anima cries out to him and the force of stifling it makes my eyes water. I can't help but remember this beast had the entire academy dining hall at his mercy within minutes. That beasts were bowing to him. That when I met him down in Halfeather's dungeon, he killed a hyena for perving on me *and* that was before he knew I was his regina. The space between my legs throbs with each rapid heartbeat and I close my eyes for a second.

I'm caught up in a hundred emotions and perhaps that and the threat of going to prison for a crime I didn't commit has made me unhinged because I do something risky.

Something insane.

I open my eyes and let my scent shield down. Rapidly.

Scythe is hit by the full force of my regina scent and arousal. He visibly flinches.

A part of me can't believe I'm so needy that a threatening touch is a touch nonetheless and is turning me on. Is that pathetic? I think it is. But the primal beast in me yips in approval.

Savage begins growling, deep and low in his chest, and it only serves to make me wetter. Xander scoffs in disgust and turns his nose away.

My eyes flit back to Scythe. The powerful shark is staring at me, his pupils blown out, encasing his sky blues almost completely. His beauty is so mesmerising in that out-of-this-world way. And then his scent hits me like a monsoon.

He doesn't wear cologne. With frost and salt, his scent is *vast*. As if the entire Pacific Ocean is at his calling. It fills me up like an ocean tide that then rushes out back to sea and drags me along with it.

And I *want* to be dragged if it means being closer to him. My right thumb moves, caressing the skin on the back of the hand he has around my throat.

He stiffens.

Then slowly, so slowly it's painful, Scythe leans forwards and his body heat sends my anima nuts. Just when I think I'll feel his nose against the skin of my neck, he pauses just short and *inhales*.

The torturous moment extends into eternity and, just

for a moment, I'm swooning and revelling in the hold of this powerful beast.

Quite abruptly, he lets me go and steps back.

I just manage to keep my legs strong under me so I don't slide onto the floor like a worm. I'm left reeling and dizzy, but have enough wits to gather my senses together and slam my scent shield back up.

All three men visibly shake themselves.

But I'm kicking and cussing myself out because I've just screwed up. Big time.

I've just confirmed two things for them. Even if they can't see my mating mark, that level of arousal is not possible outside of a mating group. I've also confirmed that I can control my scent. I'm a blistering idiot and am royally ruining everything.

Scythe turns his head just slightly to Henry on his shoulder, and silently, the little creature levitates himself happily back to me.

Then I remember.

Marine beasts have psychic abilities, and Henry is a psychic creature by nature. Therefore, Scythe is the only beast in this place who can control the nimpins.

Exactly what I need. Let's just add this to my basket of woe.

I almost groan in dismay as Henry's tiny weight settles back on my shoulder, his little feet wiggling happily.

Scythe gives me a look that can only be described as a lethal warning.

Naturally, I ignore it.

"Are you going to let me go?" I ask defiantly. I'm literally poking the shark. After this, I'm going to ask Theresa for extra therapy.

Will there be an 'after this'?

"Go, Aurelia." Scythe turns his back to me.

Savage growls. "I don't want to let her go."

My anima cries out at his words. But I know he doesn't mean it in a nice way.

"I think we should give her a parting gift," Xander says. "Come here, snake girl." He turns around and leads the others into the sitting room. I have no choice but to follow, glaring at the rooster, now standing as far as possible from me on the far bed.

There are some beasts walking in from the other side of the room, making me think that there's a way for them to get into this room from the *outside*.

Trying to hide my surprise at this revelation, I stalk into the room with my head held high. There's the feline they call Yeti, some wolves and to my great surprise there's Beak, who's giving me a deep frown like he disproves.

It hits me then, the way he's sauntering in here like he's used to it. Beak is *with* them. He's a part of their group.

But I don't have time to confront him about this because Xander is dragging the chained serpent by his chair into the centre of the room. The gag is back on and he screams around it, his dark eyes wide with terror.

Savage aggressively paces back and forth before us, like he's a hairsbreadth away from killing someone.

"Put him out of his misery, Sav," Xander says. "We're done with him anyway, right, Scythe?"

My blood turns cold.

Everyone, including the serpent, looks to Scythe.

He gives a single nod.

From inside the bedroom, the rooster lets out a sound akin to a blood-curdling shriek just as Savage explodes into his wolf form. I only have time to register the midnight monstrosity that is Savage's wolf before he leaps for the serpent, his jaws wide open, showing massive white canines. The chair crashes to the ground.

"No!" I scream. My hands fly for Henry to cover his eyes.

The man makes wet, choking sounds, but they're replaced by the sound of Savage's growling and gnashing as he devours the man's throat.

Beak strides over to me and prods me towards the entrance. Scythe gives a low warning growl and Beak immediately stops touching me, jerking his head towards the stairs.

"This is what they are, Lia," Beak hisses. "This is who you're dealing with. Leave. Now. And don't ever come back here unless you want to die."

I withhold a sob as I look back at the two men and the wolf who is raging so bad I don't even want to look at what he's made of the man. The other two tall, muscular frames dismiss me as if I'm nothing. My anima cries out a lonely, mournful hymn.

All I can do is run.

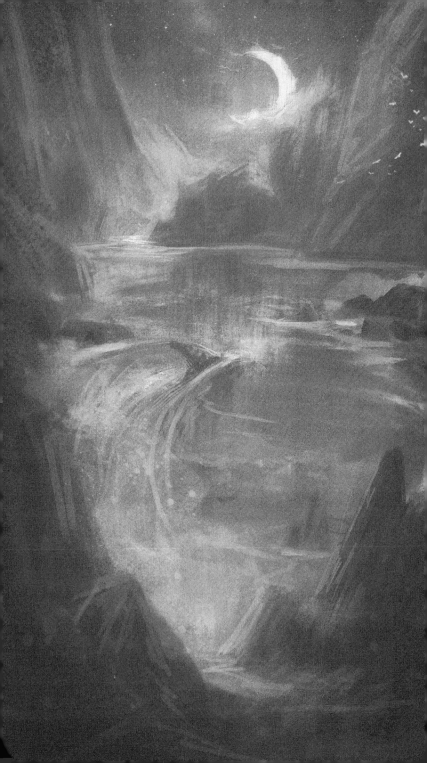

Chapter 20

Scythe

As our regina flees from us, the great white shark inside of me thrashes around like a rabid creature. In the joy of watching my brother kill, but also, in violent protest.

My regina is running away from me and my birth-given, *star-given*, right.

And I cannot follow her.

I still can't believe that I actually touched her bare skin with my own. The velvet soft warmth of it will be etched into my palm for the rest of my Goddess-damned life.

Swallowing that bitter feeling down, I take a seat on the couch as Savage finally stops mauling the serpent's face and shifts back into his human form. Naked and covered nose to chest in the snake's blood, he stalks over to the alcohol cabinet where Xander is pouring whiskey.

My brothers are so different from one another and

yet the same in many ways. They carry violence around their shoulders, and to my shark eyes, I see it as colours of crimson and blood red, roiling over their muscular frames. Right now, both of them also carry swathes of dark colours. Our regina is responsible for *that* darkness.

While Beak and Yeti prepare to get rid of the serpent's body, Xander hands Savage one crystal glass and brings me a second, drinking his own, his face drawn.

I knock it back in one go. Blood and whiskey, our favourite combination.

The apparition that has been following me around for the past eleven years appears by my side.

I ignore it.

Back in Lamington National Park, I scented Aurelia for the first time, and her presence hit me then, right in a deep-seated part of me. It was like nothing I've ever experienced before. Ambrosial, heady, as earthen as deep parts of the sea and as light as dawn. But her desire just now had been something unfathomable. Unquantifiable.

Some people think that the mating bonds we share with other animalia were created in the stars at the dawn of creation. That our souls have followed each other in groups since then, pining until we meet up each lifetime.

Fish exist in schools, whales and dolphins in pods, but sharks generally like to live their long lives alone.

But that option was stolen away from me a long time ago, by a father who held greed and violence as his gods.

The ocean still calls to my blood and bones in the same way it always has, but there are things on land that pull me just as strongly.

And I saw one of those things with my own eyes today. Or smelled it, when I scented her neck so intimately.

My regina desired me with the full force of her entire being. I could see it, scent it, taste her primal desire in the very particles of the air. The soul-crushing need to consume her, to spread her legs and feast from her centre might have destroyed me if I wasn't the man I am.

And yet, she did not want us. Lied to us. To me. She looked me dead in the eye and tried to manipulate me. I'm still vibrating with rage and desire, my cock uncomfortably hard and straining against the seam of my slacks.

The apparition prances past me, his long, silvery hair swinging, his eyes dark and sunken, face gaunt. He hums a familiar song under his breath. A funeral chant.

"Leave," I mentally command.

There are spirits and ghosts haunting or watching over this land, and most of them fled when I came along this week. But this one is no spirit. Is no ghost of the dead. I could say that he is a shadow of the darkness and madness that haunts the edges of me and creatures like me who walk this plane. Sometimes Xander calls me an alien, and at those times, it doesn't feel like he's wrong.

So, as usual, the apparition doesn't obey me and continues to skip around the room.

"Kill her," he mutters. *"Destroy her. Liar. Widow. Dangerous."*

I sigh and block out its noise and face the same way I've been doing for eleven years.

But today it's right.

Aurelia is a bad regina, and that *is* dangerous to our mating group. It defied everything I thought I knew. No beast has denied me in a long time and now my own regina? It's so vastly wrong it makes me itch from the inside out.

I know madness when I see it, and yet Aurelia isn't mad. A little unhinged, but there is no psychosis behind that face of celestial beauty. So then why lie? Anyone who lies to me is strongly punished for it. That's the way I've run my business from the beginning.

As my regina, I own her like I own my own body and soul. And if she needs to be removed, it's my responsibility to do it. Perhaps we can try again in the next life, when she isn't this way. And when *I'm* not the way I am either.

Savage is still oozing anger from his pores while Xander pours him another glass and I can taste it in the air. He's normally as wild as the Wolf Father himself, but now that we've met Aurelia, his world has suddenly changed. He's struggling with his desire for her, and his wolf is not helping. Affection is a wolf thing, but also, it's a Savage thing. He's already tasted her, and his obsession is making our task here difficult.

Yeti, Beak and the wolves leave out the dragon door down the corridor. It's dark now, and Ernie and Bernie are always patrolling our back door in case we need them.

"We need to close this." Savage holds his index finger up where the King Cobra's blood covenant is etched. "Things are getting out of hand."

That's as close as Savage will come to admitting *he's* getting out of hand.

"I agree," Xander says. "She's had her one chance, and that was more than generous. Let's get this done, Sy."

I grunt in agreement.

The Serpent King wants his daughter back for a within-court execution. I condone execution for uncontrollable beasts. It's the best way to keep the wider community safe. Serpents use venom to punish their court, and it will be a slow, painful death for Aurelia. Savage doesn't know that, and I'm not going to tell him. Xander definitely knows, because though he would never admit it, snakes and dragons are eerily similar.

The primal part of me wants to steal my regina away and keep her safe from death. But the logical part of me says that this is needed. That her power over us is a special kind of danger.

I want to kill someone. Break something. Throttle Mace Naga until he's lifeless in my hands. But I have his magic in me now and the deal is fixed. There's no going back from the moment she rejected us.

There's only one thing standing in our way and that is the fact that this institution is near impossible to breach. The lion who runs the academy will never allow her—or any of the students, for that matter—to be taken out of the school. This is supposed to be a safe house where all the orders have a truce. He took great pains to make it that way. It's his life's work. I respect that in a beast, but this time it goes against my own agenda.

Every previous attempt to steal someone out of Animus Academy has failed. But now I'm here.

"I'll need seventy-two hours and it'll be done."

Savage stiffens, but nods in acceptance. "Friday then."

Chapter 21

Aurelia

When I arrive back at our dorm, Minnie is outside, shrieking at the guards, her pink hair wild as she tears at it.

"I'm telling you! She's been—"

One of the guards point at me and Minnie whirls around, her face crumpled in distress. She sees me and her dark brows fly up into her hairline. "Lia?" She rushes up to me, but I shake my head at her in warning. She must see something on my face because she silently follows me as I swipe my card and jog up the stairs.

My body is shaking, vibrating as I fall apart at the seams. I storm back into our dorm, stand back to let Minnie in, then slam the door shut.

"Fuck!" I scream to the walls. "Fuck, fuck, fuck!" Sitting down on my bed, I bury my face in my hands, my tears falling hard and fast. Henry quivers, flush against my neck and I feel Gertie landing next to him, cooing softly like she's trying to help.

221

A man was killed before my very eyes, mauled to death by Savage, who was nothing more than a violent, vicious creature who seemed to kill and *enjoy* it.

I knew they weren't good men, but seeing Savage like that? Seeing what they are capable of? Beak's parting words haunt my mind.

This is what they are. This is what you're dealing with.

"Lia." Minnie's voice is a whisper as she comes to sit next to me. "We were sitting at dinner when the three crazies just got up and stormed out. Something clearly alerted them and you weren't back and I just knew it was you! Please don't tell me you did something insane!"

"I *did* do something." My voice is muffled as I try to suffocate my words like it'll quash the memory of me thinking I could just walk into their dorm and get away with it. "And I fucking didn't achieve anything." One man is dead, and for all I know, that rooster is up next.

Minnie groans. "Lia! I thought you were a goner. You can't fuck around with people this dangerous."

Finally, I raise my head and look at her. I must really look awful because her face softens, and she reaches for my hand. "Lia," she says seriously. "You don't really know who these people are, do you?"

"What do you mean?"

She smacks herself on the head. "Wait a second." She leaves the dorm, and I hear her banging on Raquel and Sabrina's door. Within seconds, Minnie returns, dragging Raquel in by their hand. "Tell her!" Minnie says to

Raquel. "Tell her what we've heard about the Slaughter Brothers!"

"W-What did you do, p-pup?" Raquel asks, brown eyes wide. I shake my head and the wolf says, "Stupid h-hatchling. Scythe K-Kharkourous is a m-mob boss. His wolf b-brother is an enforcer. A h-hitman. They b-black-mail, extort, k-kill people in the u-underworld."

"What?" I ask, horrified. But suddenly this isn't a surprise.

Raquel and Minnie roll their eyes at me as if I'm a naïve idiot. "I *know* what goes on in the underground fighting rings," I cry. "I've heard people making deals. Hell, my father is one of these people! I knew all of this, but it's just... I'm at a loss for words because..."

Because I'd just dreamed this entire time that my mates were alright people.

"Because what?" Minnie asks.

I gulp because I can't say anything. But perhaps I can tell them something that will make them understand why I have to leave. So I say, "They're after me."

Raquel's eyes almost bug out of their head. "Is t-that why S-Savage j-jumped you?"

"He's come in here to muck with our stuff too," Minnie breathes.

"A w-warning," Raquel gruffs.

We all stare at each other in a sort of mutual horror, and I jump to my feet. "They're going to kill me. Or capture me. Or something! I have no idea what exactly, but it'll be bad."

Raquel is looking at me like I've grown a third tit. "Why?"

I sigh. "I suppose they don't take rejection well."

"Shit!" Minnie says, jumping up and down. "Shit!"

"The only thing I can do is..." I glance out the glass doors. "Get the fuck out of here."

"You're not going to run away?" Minnie's voice is a shocked gasp.

"I have to, Min." A shiver wracks my body. "They threatened to chain me up."

Raquel swears loudly.

"You see? I have no choice."

Raquel heads over to the glass doors that lead out to the balcony. "H-How are you g-gonna d-do it? This p-place is F-Fort Knox."

It's a relief Raquel isn't trying to persuade me not to. It probably helps that they're a delinquent, just like me. On the other hand, the fact they're not arguing with me tells me just how dire the situation is.

"There has to be a way, right?" I say desperately. I have the invisibility up my sleeve and my scent shields. No one has a better chance than me.

Then I think on what I've just seen.

"So..." I say slowly. "We know they're killing people here, right? There was our two guards, and now this serpent I just saw. How are they getting rid of the bodies? They must have some method of getting the bodies out?"

Both Raquel and Minnie exchange a look. Raquel runs a hand through their hair. Minnie says, "It'll be sus if we ask around. But Sabrina has just started seeing a lion in the unmated dorms. Maybe she can find out something."

Involving another person in this is risky. The more people who know, the more people to blab.

I can't help but think maybe I need to do more snooping. The thought of going back in there, though...

My sigh is long and dramatic because I'm really not in the right state of mind if I think I can get away with this.

"Sorry to tell you this, Lia," Minnie says nervously. "But you literally come with a flight risk warning label. They'll be watching you."

I tug mournfully upon my lanyard. But now I'm smelling a challenge, and the fact that Minnie thinks I can't do this is only egging me on. My fists clench of their own accord. "Well, fuck them and fuck Lyle Pardalia. I'm leaving this week and I'm *going* to find a way."

* * *

In the two days that follow, I formulate my plans to escape. Savage, Scythe and Xander do all they can do ignore me and it makes my skin crawl every time I look at them. Savage cannot help but send me dark looks now and again and I can't help but feel that their lack of overt action means that they've got something up their sleeves for me.

In the dining hall, our table is approached at least

once per meal where the animus' of the school try their luck in approaching us. Raquel flat out growls at any wolf that comes their way except for a female animus with long black hair down to her waist and a lacey black corset. Raquel nods while they have a silent conversation and the rest of us hide our grins as they appear to make plans for later that day. Sabrina and Stacey are quickly taken up by a group of lions, who shoot little notes folded up into paper cranes to our table. It's a new, impressive version of sexting that amuses us to no end. Minnie, to my surprise, brushes off all advances with a shy smile and instead has her eye on one of the senior animas from our dorm.

For my part. I'm *focused* like an eagle should be, and my prey are those black and gold gates that lead out of the academy.

I need supplies so I don't fall into food desperation again like I did the first time. We don't have access to the student-run village just yet, so I make do with thieving.

I hate them for turning me into this. A thief. A person who has to steal to get by. A person who has to sneak around just to survive. But my goal is absolute and I've been given no other option.

During Hygiene class, where we learn about showering and washing our bits properly, I take extra samples of deodorant and soap.

During dining etiquette class, I ask Theresa about how food gets delivered to the school. She's not even suspicious of me because Minnie makes a good show about being excited to learn how to make tuna bake.

There are deliveries made every Friday night and I can barely contain my excitement because I think I just found my getaway vehicle. This way, I can still be invisible in my human form and carry a couple of bags with me.

It's simple, it's brilliant, and I can take food and water aplenty. My only problem then becomes money.

I have none and I'm not willing to ask anyone for any because my pride is the size of Greenland. I have the diamond choker Halfeather gave me on my wedding day, but I'll need to find a way to pawn it. A simple pawnbroker isn't going to have that type of money in their shop, so I'll be without cash for a little while.

That's fine, I'm used to sacrificing. I can handle this.

So I just wait it out, but at some point on Thursday, being around my mates becomes unbearable.

In elocution class, some of the students have to be taken to extra special classes because the more feral you get, the less a beast likes to talk. Some of them can't enunciate words properly, or forgot how, so they need a speech therapist to re-learn how to do that. Raquel has a small speech impediment with their stutter and so gets time with the speech therapist along with the others.

Xander has been so quiet for all our classes that his supervisor, a threatening-looking wolf, gestures for him to follow the feral students. Xander snarls and grabs *Animal Farm* out of his hand and reads from it in a smooth, formal tone that is so beautiful I can't help but stare at him, my stomach flopping on itself at his deep cadence.

I wonder yet again how a dragon ended up with the

Slaughter Brothers. They are wealthy and snobbish folk who get private school education, and yet Xander landed himself in Halfeather's dungeon with no one to bail him out. I thought it odd at the time, but now that he's *here* it's even more suspicious.

I get the feeling it has something to do with what happened to his eyes.

Minnie and I are the last to leave class because I need to loiter behind to swipe more perfume samples left over from the class before. I've been using it to hide the fact that my scent shield is up at full force and leaving me with no scent at all.

I exit the room ahead of Minnie when the sight of *him* wipes the triumphant smile clean off my face. My three plastic sample tubes go clattering to the wooden floor.

Scythe is leaning against the wall opposite me, his powerful arms crossed over his wide chest. Terror laced with deep yearning strikes me in my sternum as his ice-blue eyes bore into mine like a sign of my doom.

With his gaze alone, he holds me prisoner.

It's like in a horror movie where the main character is walking through the haunted house and you just know the demon is going to jump out and get them, but you hold your breath and don't look away, enamoured by the fear, the tension.

A sheet of power as cold as ice spreads between us, its fissures spider-webbing out long and wide. I know then that Scythe has a power like I've never known. That he has the ability to do torrential and profound damage to whatever lies in his path.

Just like he told me back in their room.

I can't breathe. I can't blink.

And yet I know in the deepest part of me that I want him.

I'm sure I'm going to shatter into pieces when he suddenly kicks off the wall and prowls down the now-empty corridor. All I can do is watch that body; that slow, languid walk of pure power as lazy as an afternoon tide.

When he turns the corner, the spell is broken, leaving me in a puddle of my drowned wits. Henry vibrates on my shoulder as Minnie pats my back to ask me to move. I step to the side and sag against the door frame, clutching my churning stomach. Henry makes a small sound on my shoulder and Gertie replies to him like they're having a conversation. I don't have time to ponder it as Minnie stares at me with concern.

I can't help the irrevocable feeling that I've been given a warning.

If all sharks are like this, they could take over the world. Except none of them want to, preferring to stay in their watery-blue realm beneath all things. Or perhaps above them.

And yet, here Scythe is. Watching *me*. Threatening me and my underwear, which is currently on fire because my anima wants him so badly she's weeping hot tears from between my legs.

I don't know how I'm going to survive this. What just passed between us is something I can't even explain.

"Are you alright, Lia?" Minnie asks, picking up my fallen samples.

Henry clicks his beak in emphasis.

"One day," I murmur faintly. "One day, I'll be alright."

Chapter 22

Aurelia

Friday arrives and I just have to get through this day until 2 p.m. when the delivery trucks arrive. I'm excited and tense and Minnie notices right away.

"Lia?" she asks as we get ready for breakfast.

I'm checking my duffle bag, which is currently crammed full of stolen items. Aurelia, the thief. My father would be so ashamed. My mother too, I'm sure, although I like to think she'd be proud of me for surviving this.

"Yes, Minnie?" I say softly, tucking my duffle back under my bed.

"You really think this is your only option?"

I don't even need to clarify what she's talking about, because I've thought about nothing else since I made my decision. And honestly, Minnie has been the sole person who's gotten me through the last few days. She's hilarious, and the inner nerd in me is amused to no end to see

233

the extensive, organised, colour-coded notes she has in her pink folder, which goes everywhere with us. She's so proud of it that even when Sabrina and Stacey tease her about it, she doesn't even care.

"I really think so," I say honestly. "I've just been trying to get through each day until..."

"You leave," she finishes for me in a whisper, as if the room is wired. I seriously hope it's not, and I look around the room with new interest. Though Lyle doesn't seem like the wiring type.

"I respect that you don't want to tell me your plans, Lia," she says softly, tucking a pink curl behind her ear as she applies her blush. "But I just want you to know that I've appreciated your being friends with me this past week. Wherever you end up going, maybe I can visit you after I get out of here."

Minnie has never spoken about why she's in here to start with, and our respect for privacy has gone both ways.

But her sentiment makes me well up because, fuck, this is scary and she's been my only real friend in, well, ever. I tell her so and her face crumples.

I rush over to her and hug her tightly. She makes a squeaking sound and so does Gertie on her shoulder. Henry returns a sad croon.

"Oh, I'm sorry," I say, pulling back. "Theresa said we have to ask consent before we hug each other."

"You have my fucking consent," she sobs, pulling me back towards her. I laugh and kiss her on her pink head. "Will you take Henry with you?"

"I've stolen everything else, so I might as well steal him, too." I take the nimpin from my shoulder and look into his liquid-black eyes. He bops up and down on his tiny feet, clearly having no idea what I'm talking about. I've made sure I've packed his food and grooming brush so I know I'll be able to look after him. I won't be able to live with myself if Henry has to eat rubbish out of a bin.

There's a knock at our door and all of us violently flinch. Neither me nor Minnie moves to answer the door. We just stare at each other, wide-eyed, as if a predator is on the other side. But whoever it is slides a piece of paper under the door and our spell of terror is broken. Minnie leaps to grab it.

She reads it and her brows shoot up. "It's for you."

Gingerly, I take the thing, noticing that it's on a fancy piece of thick card, like our previous detention notice.

But this is no detention notice. It's something much worse:

Reform Therapy for Aurelia Aquinas
Session: Saturday 9 a.m.
Therapist: Lyle Pardalia, Deputy Headmaster
Location: Senior offices, top floor, central building (use elevator)

"Why do I have to see *him* for personal therapy?" I ask, horrified.

The date is listed for tomorrow, and Lyle's elaborate signature is below it in his trusty fountain pen. I run my fingers over the bold, black script and shudder.

Minnie chokes. "Lia, I don't think you realise the gravity of your situation... other than the three monsters. According to the handbook, the deputy headmaster sees the worst students, and you're literally wanted for murder."

All I can do is stare at her because she's right. But the thought of sitting down with *that* lion and talking about my thoughts and feelings? Unthinkable. Laughable.

It's just as well, then, that I won't be here for it. I almost wish I could see the look on that angelic face when he realises I've stood him up and thwarted him all in one swoop.

We attend our hygiene and human interaction classes as normal and I'm a little bummed because Theresa tells us we get to see the student village on Wednesday and I was excited to see the little town made by decades of academy students. We also would have started 'Healthy Dating' classes in a few weeks, and I know I'm missing out on a good time.

But my freedom is far too important. Minnie, Raquel, and I have been watching the three monsters closely for anything weird. Savage is still determined to ignore me, and Scythe and Xander have just been apathetic today. I don't have time to ponder it though, because far too soon, it's time for lunch and I know the delivery truck will be arriving.

We walk out of hygiene and I say to Minnie, "I just need to get a tampon."

Minnie immediately realises I've used a code phrase. "Oh."

The thought saddens me a little because we've developed a secret language like best friends would, codewords and shifty eyes included. I put a hand on her shoulder and grip it, trying to convey my emotion through touch alone. "It's alright." I don't know if I'm telling her or telling myself because my heart is pounding like one of Xander's rock songs.

She presses her glossy mauve lips together and her eyes go all shiny to match. All she does is nod, and I make my exit before I start crying.

Going to the dorms is easy, the four guards are still stationed there and when I tell them I need sanitary products, they stand aside.

Henry and I go up into our room. I carefully take off my student lanyard, wind it around itself and put it on my dresser. I grab my bag, then eighth shield both nimpin and myself. The cool calm of my invisibility shield cloaking my entire body feels like slipping into an old favourite pair of pyjamas. I'm more at home and used to this state than in any other state and it makes my heart rate slow down. I've done little missions like this before, I can do this.

Blowing an *almost* relieved breath, I say, "Henry, if you so much as make a squeak, or chirp, I'll let Savage eat you like he asked. Got it?"

Henry makes a small, frightened sound, and for the

first time, I wonder if I've made a mistake in bringing him along. But it's too late to change my plans now.

Henry and I leave our dorm and I cast one last glance around in farewell. The dragon oil painting at the end of the hall catches my eye like it always does. And just for a moment, I wonder...

But I have no time to ponder dragon house-magic because I need to leave right now if this is going to work. Turning around, I rush down the corridor and down the three sets of stairs.

I have to wait a little while for one of the guards to enter the building on their hourly patrol, but when they do, I sneak out after them on quiet feet.

The loading dock is behind the school, past the kitchen, and I've never actually been this way before, because it's off-limits. Heading down the eastern side of the school at a swift walk, I dodge a number of patrolling guards, walking on the grass when I can to muffle my steps. I have fifteen minutes to get to the dock and that should be plenty of time.

But I'm doing this. I'm actually escaping. They'll call me the escaped queen and Minnie will start a movement at the academy in my honour.

You want a fugitive? I'll give you a fugitive, Lyle Pardalia, you bastard. Fuck your school. Fuck your therapy. I have my assistance animal, I don't need anything more. I don't need *anyone*, either.

I make it through the side gate that leads to the arrival area for new students, according to the map. The driveway goes down to my right, which is the main entry/exit. The huge gold and black cast iron gates are currently closed and manned by four armed guards. It's super pretty how the gold parts of it glint in the afternoon sun, and it almost overpowers the sinister feeling of the dark, curling parts. Old trees stand like a guard of honour leading up to it and their leaves rustle and dance in the warm end of summer breeze.

I cross the driveway and head past the medical wing around to the back. The road leads to the place that should be the loading docks, according to Minnie's maps.

Our student map doesn't have this part the school on it because students shouldn't have access. However, Minnie's pink folder came to the rescue with a map from online she'd printed 'to prepare' for the Academy.

Am I going to send her a box of roses with my first pay in a real job? Hell yes.

Henry shifts uncomfortably on my shoulder, as if he knows we shouldn't be here. But it's all going to plan so far and he's been obedient in making no noise. Excitedly, I dart across the grass, following the building around to the back of the academy...and promptly stop dead.

The first thing I see is a big chain grocery truck already in the loading dock. The second thing is a tall, muscular back with loose silver hair brushing the collar of an expensive black business shirt.

Immediately, I walk backwards and press myself against the side wall so hard I might crush my kidneys.

What the hell is Scythe doing standing there? And I think, perhaps *he's* thought the same thing as me and is going to escape. Two peas in a pod, us two.

Except...he's standing out in the open like he's supervising.

My scent shield is strong and I've literally never been caught in all my time being around particularly good feral noses. How hard would it be just to sneak around the other side and slip through the open doors at the back of the truck?

I literally won't have another chance, because someone will have already found it strange that I've been gone this long. The guards will soon go into my room to see why I've not come out yet. The animas around here are closely supervised by guards and students alike, and in the dining hall the eagle animuses will notice I'm not there.

I'm a predator. An apex predator. A beast like no other.

I can do this.

Sucking in a measured breath, I ease myself off the wall and, clutching my duffle bag to my chest, peek around the corner. The shark isn't there anymore, only the two big bear shifter guards, helping to move boxes out of the truck.

And then a voice like cold, suffocating death says, "I can hear your heart beating, Aurelia."

I freeze before slowly looking upwards. Scythe is sitting on the lip of the roof, his legs hanging off the side as he casually smokes a cigarette.

Henry bops up and down excitedly because he's clearly not right in the head.

Slowly, I back away from the building. My legs are

quaking, but I command them to *move*. Scythe's eyes, a lighter blue than the sky, track me with hair raising, lethal focus.

"How do you hide yourself?" he asks, quietly, his eyes fixed on my chest, my *irregularly beating heart*, as he blows out blue smoke. He shakes his head as if he can't quite believe it. "It's a real shame you have to die, Regina." He pushes himself off the roof.

All I can do is run.

Invisible, I fucking bolt for my life, darting right for the loading dock so I can get into the school fast.

I don't hear Scythe's feet land or dare look behind me as I kick off my flip-flops and pass the truck, bolt past the two confused bears, up the ramp and through the open roller-doors. There are boxes and guards crammed in here and I bump into one, who lets out a shout of alarm.

But they have no idea what's happened and the other guards just stare at him like he's nuts. Does Scythe know these guards? How is he just walking around here?

I'm running so fast that Henry is forced to dig his tiny claws into my shoulder, but he manages to stay with me as I swerve into a narrow entrance that leads into the school proper. I pass the kitchens, bolting down the long corridor as fast as I can. My bare feet pound against the floorboards and I have no idea if anyone is pursuing me or not. Everyone's at lunch, so I luckily don't bump into any more people. This is the exact wing where Minnie and I mopped all that blood on Monday night, so I know the way to the outside.

I take a left, then a right, then another left and shove a door open.

Sunlight bursts upon my face as I make it outside and continue running across the pavement. I've come out with the unmated female dorm right in front of me, where the same four guards stand as they always do.

It's then that Henry loses his grip and tumbles off my shoulder. Frantically, I skid to a halt, the hot concrete painfully scraping my bare feet. I hiss as Henry recovers, catches himself before he hits the ground, and levitates back up to me, his shiny black eyes wide with fear.

Then, faster than I think is possible, an impossibly strong hand slaps over my mouth. Another snakes around my waist and *yanks*.

Chapter 23

Aurelia

I 'm pulled into the shadows between the tall buildings. My back is crushed against a tall, hard body.

"Your breathing," Savage breath tickles my ear. "Your breathing gives you away."

He whirls me around by the waist, his large palm still covering my mouth, and pulls me into his body. I'm so shocked that he's caught me unawares that I'm wheezing as I try to drag in air.

Savage's hazel eyes are blazing as they search the air in front of him to try and see me. He lets out a slow exhale, his lips parted.

His eyes flick out past the mouth of the alleyway. "Those guards are not ours, regina. We have to be quiet."

It's the first time he's called me *regina*, and it shakes me to my core. My blood pounds in my head as I pant through my nose.

"Can't smell you," he says, hazel eyes trying to focus

on my invisible face. "Can't see you, but I know it's you." His hand slides down the curve of my back, and down lower to grip the full round of my ass. "Yep." As if this confirms it.

A pulse of desire tears through me, and I let out a squeak of indignation. I buck, trying to break out of his grip, but his hold on me is like steel.

The hand covering my mouth moves to cup my cheek and his thumb gently sweeps across my lips. He brings his face so close to mine as if he's fixated on the feel of it. "Yep," he whispers.

I buck again but he just crushes me harder against him. I feel every inch of his fighter's frame and something languid and smooth inside of me responds to it in the worst, traitorous way.

The lids over his hazel eyes stutter as if he's fighting something inside of himself, too.

"Just once," he says, as if to himself. "I need to do it once."

My anima grips me in place as he leans forward and brushes his lips against mine. I stiffen. Heat flares through my body. His lips. By the Wild Goddess, his lips are soft and warm on mine. Even through my shields, his masculine, fresh pine scent drifts into my nose and hits me right between the legs.

My anima keens. This wolf is mine. Has been mine for weeks.

The primal sound that escapes up my throat is *thoroughly* unbidden. But it's a sound of pure need.

And my mate responds.

A rumbling growl vibrates through his chest to mine.

I part my lips.

He pounces. Hoisting me up, I wrap my legs around his waist on instinct and he slams me against the brick wall. He invades my mouth with his own warm, wet, masculine one. My chest expands in a tornado of desire so powerful that I lose sense of everything that isn't Savage. My nose fills with his scent, my head fills with the feel of him, and I *crave* for him to be inside me. My own hands are demanding on his body, tearing at his shirt, his skin, like a desperate woman.

It drives Savage off the rails.

Growling like he's given in completely to his wolf, Savage kisses me down my face, his tongue hot against my neck.

My anima tells me that this is right. That is what it should feel like for a regina to kiss her mate properly for the first time.

I moan, and he opens his mouth, his teeth scraping my neck. Not very gently, he bites.

It's the faint pain that makes me realise what the fuck I'm actually doing. Shoving at his chest, I push him away. Savage rears back, his face taut with conflict as he allows me to set my feet back on the floor.

I'm gasping, and Savage's breath is ragged as I glare at him.

"Fuck," he says gruffly. He covers his eyes with one hand as if he's trying to control his wolf. Or perhaps it's in shame because he can't bear what he's just done.

I'm so annoyed with myself, and I'm about to tell him to go fuck himself, but I stop dead.

Because what I see on the index finger of his hand turns every particle in my being still. My eighth shield falls and I don't even care.

There are very few in this country who can write in the text of the old Naga.

And I recognise my father's script immediately. The black, sinister, curling tattoo trips my mind into a storm of terror. My hand snaps out like a viper. I grab his finger and, with laser sharp focus, interpret the lines and whorls.

A blood covenant. It wasn't there when I first met Savage in Halfeather's dungeon, which means it was made between their escape and them finding me in the national park.

This marking is tied to three others, including my father.

They made a binding contract with my father.

For the first time in months, I use my serpentine power and send it into the marking, searching through the ink to read the nature of the contract.

Blood magic was taught to me from infancy. I know it like I know the English language, and it takes me seconds to read it.

They have to retrieve me and return me to my father. They also vowed not to mate with me; it's written here as plain as day.

I drop Savage's hand and step away from him in

horror. His eyes focus with sudden awareness and he straightens, extending *that hand* out towards me.

"Lia."

My voice is a hoarse whisper. "Don't you fucking *dare* speak to me."

Henry is suddenly levitating next to me, making sounds of alarm, but all I can hear is the roaring in my ears, the sickening terror of the betrayal of a whole new kind. My father has commissioned my mates to hunt me. To bring me back to him. To never mate with me.

It's a violation the likes of which I never thought I'd live to experience.

It also means my father knows these three beasts are my mates.

He. *Knows.*

All I can do is grab my dropped duffle bag, lurch out of the alley, slap my eighth shield back up, and run. For some reason, Savage lets me.

The wind is on my face and the pounding of my heart resounds in my head like a death gong. I rapidly pass the four guards standing sentinel by the anima dorm, and I don't even realise that Henry is not on my shoulder until I'm passing the central academy building.

But then Scythe is stepping out of the dining hall, followed by Xander, both their faces transformed into something frightening.

I screech to a halt, leaving two feet between us, my chest heaving as I look between them, wiping the tears from my cheeks.

These are the lengths my father will go to. He turned my own mates against me.

And my mates agreed.

My anima cries out in fear, desperation and confusion, but all it takes is Xander striding towards me with a malicious, very dragon-like fixation in his eyes that I come to my senses.

Some instinct speaks to me, and before I know it, I'm holding my breath and heading through the glass doors of the dining hall, clutching my duffle to my chest like a shield. My heart pangs a little, but I think it's a good thing that Henry had the sense to abandon me. He'll be much safer without me.

Everyone is in the dining hall for lunch, so there are many witnesses, meaning they can't do a thing. Staying invisible, I jog inside, where the buzz of voices and laughter settles my terror a little.

I glance behind me to find Scythe and Xander entering the hall, closely followed by a stony-faced Savage. I rush over to my regular table where Minnie is picking at a barbeque chicken and pasta salad with Raquel, Sabrina, Connor and Stacey. Coming up next to her, I mutter a quiet "Minnie, it's Lia."

Minnie drops her bamboo knife. Gertie squeaks from her shoulder. I swear internally and look up to see all three men have their eyes on my Minnie.

"Minnie. Emergency," I mutter. "I don't know what to do. Don't talk now. Hide your mouth with your hand before you speak."

Bless my little pink-haired Sherlock Holmes because

Minnie rests her elbow on the table, resting her chin on her hand and whispers, "Lia?"

Raquel looks up and frowns at her and I know I need to get Minnie out of here, but I also don't want to get her hurt.

But Savage is pushing the other two aside and is now in the lead, prowling over to the table, his eyes fixed on my best friend.

"Shit," I whisper. "They're trying to abduct me. They've made a contract with my dad. I don't know what to do."

Minnie looks up with alarm when she sees the three beasts making a beeline for her. But I can't wait any longer. I dart between tables, making a sharp left and heading back outside, hating myself for getting her involved. But they don't need her, they'll track me right out here, if Savage is right about my breathing being so loud.

Fresh, warm air hits me and I look up at the cloudless sky and know at once what I'll do. I need to fly, maybe get up onto the roof of the school where they can't track me, but that would leave my duffle for them to find and they'll know my plan at once. I break into a full sprint, heading as far away as I can towards the warehouses where I can dump my bag.

"Lia." Savage's voice cuts through the air like a brutal knife and I hear a small squeak of protest. "I have your little Minnie Mouse."

I skid to a halt on the grass, whirling around to see the three monsters with Savage gripping a frightened Minnie by her bicep. A snarl tears from my throat and I know they have me.

"Don't you dare!" I cry. Both Gertie and Henry are in Scythe's hands and he drops the blue and yellow fluff-balls to the grass where they stay, eyes closed. Fury rips through my being. I sprint towards them.

"Run, Lia!" Minnie cries, her eyes searching the area. "Don't worry about me! Go! Run!"

We're far enough away from the dining hall that no one hears us and I curse myself for this trap. There are no guards in sight.

"Tigger tiger talks big talk." Savage shakes Minnie a little. "She wants to play with the big boys."

"No!" I cry.

They search the area for my voice, but I keep moving so they don't know exactly where I am.

"Reveal yourself, Lia," Savage growls, no sign of the hungry mate from before. "However you're fucking doing it."

I swear and make a wide berth so I'm behind them. But as I do, Scythe and Xander turn around, following my sound.

"How is she doing that?" Xander mutters.

Minnie looks up at him with alarm.

"Let Minnie go," I call. "And I'll come with you."

"No negotiating," Scythe rasps. "You'll reveal yourself *now*."

That voice of command almost has me, but Minnie cries out and suddenly Savage leaps away from her.

Bones pop and Minnie shifts. Her clothes fall to the

ground in shreds as orange and black striped fur bursts into existence.

A snarling tiger stands between us now, her canines white and bared. She snaps at Savage, her eyes furious. In response, Savage explodes into his big black wolf form, baring his own huge teeth and viciously growls at her to submit. Minnie hisses, refusing to back down, and Xander laughs as Savage throws his bigger body at Minnie, leaping onto her and shoving her onto her back, his jaws aimed at her throat.

I scream Minnie's name, and a primal force tears my very body open. My blood rushes like electricity through my veins and I explode. There is no thought in my mind, no semblance of logic or rationality.

My body changes and I am nothing but fur and teeth and claw and violence as I charge at Savage with the full force of my rage behind me.

Chapter 24

Xander

Scythe swears as he sees what we're all seeing. Aurelia is a black wolf, her blue eyes dilated and almost rabid with uncontrolled rage as she launches herself at Savage. I'm thoroughly confused as I see my supposed regina tackle Savage off Minnie and take him to the ground, allowing the tigress to jump up and follow. Minnie leaps onto Savage's back, digging her claws in.

The three of them begin tussling.

Scythe and I let it play out, knowing Savage will win this fight. But if we don't stop them, we'll be looking at two seriously injured girls within minutes. The bears are waiting with the truck and I'm getting impatient as my Hungarian rock music blares in my ears. Anyone could come out at any second and try to stop us.

My shark brother takes a causal step forward and Minnie seizes, falling to the ground, her paws sticking up

255

in the air like a fainting goat as Scythe grips her mind in his mental fist.

Lia falters as she's caught by surprise. Savage takes advantage and leaps onto her, and with his bigger size, pins her down onto the grass.

She growls and snaps, her dark fur glistening under the sun, her eyes as vibrant as the sea on a summer's day. But what the actual fuck? She's a wolf, too?

Scythe steps forward and Lia goes limp, shifting back to her human form, her naked olive skin bare to us all. Savage sits on top of her, resting his big furry head on her naked chest as if he's claiming a possession. His tail wags. Even though he knows she's going to go away now, his beast enjoys being close to his regina.

It's sad for him, but that's life.

Lia's eyes are screwed shut, glistening tears streaming down her face.

"When the fuck did we start abducting women?" I mutter under my breath, because even my skin prickles as we execute this plan and Scythe crouches down next to her.

Oh, I know when. When our own regina rejected, betrayed and lied to us. That's when. When our regina turned out to be the daughter of a snake and became a threat to us all. *That's fucking when.*

Scythe exhales through his nose. The shark in him doesn't like this either, but it has to be done. The threat needs to be eliminated.

"*At any cost, Xan,*" he growls, crouching down to stare at Lia. "*We do this because it's what we need to do.*"

Lia's lips are pursed shut as if it hurts her to have Scythe inspect her psychic defences.

"I've never seen this before," Scythe projects to us. *"She has seven fucking layers of protection."* Then he does something that surprises me. He reaches out a hand and strokes Lia's tear-streaked cheek with a finger. But it's not in an endearing way, it's more in a fascinated, inspection sort of way. But Savage takes this as permission to lick her chin with his big wolf's tongue.

Scythe says to the snake girl, "I'm going to tear down your shields one at a time, Aurelia. I need to see what you've been hiding from us before you go back to your father."

Lia's face screws up and I sigh, turning away from her face to look at Minnie, who is in a hilarious position with her paws frozen straight out. I get my phone out and snap a picture. Maybe use it as leverage later on, I don't know. Things like this are always useful.

Scythe's power thrums through the air, brushing my skin, and I know it's doing a lot more than brushing the snake girl. Lia whimpers as she feels its effect and Savage whines, but I know Scythe won't stop until he gets to the bottom of this: our regina and her strange powers.

I always assumed our regina would be a mythical creature like me, because who else would be powerful enough to be regina for the likes of us? But now I don't know what to think.

Scythe makes a noise of approval as he mentally tears into her and I register her regina scent immediately. Like flowers and sunlight mixed with something heavy like thunderclouds. Her fear also perfumes the air, making me flinch with disgust. I can't stand that smell, let alone on *her*. My animus huffs in annoyance. I turn my music up louder as I turn to look at what has Scythe excited, when he's never excited over anything.

He turns Lia's head to the side with a thumb and now visible on her neck for us all to see is our mating group mark. A skull with five streams of light erupting out of it. Silver and bright.

A massive, powerful body roars to life inside of me, followed by a feeling of satisfaction and heat. So much heat that it makes me clench my fists in anger. It's the fourth time in my life I'm seeing my sign on the neck of another and it should drive me to my knees. But it doesn't. I refuse to let it.

Lia the Liar. It fits like a glove.

Chapter 25

Aurelia

Scythe's voice is like the Grim Reaper's above me. "I'm going to tear down your shields one at a time, Aurelia. I need to see what you've been hiding from us before you go back to your father."

Cold terror wracks through my insides, even as Savage's huge wolf heats my naked skin with his own, his tongue swiping eagerly at my chin.

There is violence around me and possessiveness over me, and it's as alluring as it is terrifying. Scythe has a power that I've never experienced before and I can't believe it excites me like it does. It's like the sharpest tip of a blade, precisely, *cleanly* slicing through each of my shields one at a time.

I want to scream, but my voice is stuck in my throat, choked up with terror and confusion. They've forced me to submit to them, literally and psychically, and as Scythe slices my shields, my vulnerability escalates one layer at a

My physical protective shield goes.

My scent shield is torn apart.

My blood shield crumples.

My mental shield dissolves.

My two psychic shields fall away.

Finally, my last defence against a world that will destroy me, my mating mark shield, disappears with a puff like it wasn't even there.

The full force of our mating bond hits us all in a visible wave of sheer celestial power. Something that existed before we were born and will exist long after. Something bigger than us. Something mightier than us.

I struggle to breathe through the desire, the pure need to bond with each of them, to join anima and animuses and be whole once again.

But my brain is scrambling. It's truly a terrifying thing to be under Scythe's control. As he looms over me, his mating mark now visible to my eyes on his neck. It takes my breath away; that golden skull gleaming with celestial light. Its sight is vicious and demanding; a sheer order to claim my mates. To love them and let them have me in all ways.

But they attacked me.

Hunted me like prey and pinned me to the ground like meat.

They made a contract with my father and nothing can forgive that.

But just as Scythe opens his mouth to speak, he and Savage are torn away from me as if by a giant's hand.

I gasp as Savage's heavy weight is abruptly removed

and I can breathe again. Coughing, I fling back up every single one of my shields. Minnie makes a sad sound nearby as she's unfrozen and we both roll over to see what the hell is happening.

Students are streaming outside behind an animalistic Lyle who has both his palms facing the men who hang limply in the air, and a face full of rage. Behind him, Theresa and the other staff rush towards us, including feline guards who hold their palms up to help to restrain a violently protesting wolf-Savage with telekinesis. Xander and Scythe remain still and tense in the air.

Minnie lopes over to me, shielding my naked body with her tiger's body.

"I trusted you, Scythe," Lyle roars. "You didn't honour your agreement. You took advantage. You're all in fucking lockdown."

Reuben, our head fighting instructor, jogs out with his team behind him. He bursts into a vicious white wolf and his team follow suit. They form a pack that rushes under Savage's body, forming a snarling, snapping circle to receive him. Lyle lowers Savage and the five other wolves growl and bare their teeth, ready to make him submit.

Savage growls right back, but he's surrounded by too many grown snapping mouths and has no choice but to be escorted out. He snarls the entire time and looks back to give me a pining glance, but I just scowl at him over Minnie's back.

Xander is lowered to the ground next and received by a group of so many guards I can't even count them. They throw obsidian shackles on his ankles and wrists straight away. Neither he nor Scythe put up a fight as the shark is also taken away in shackles. Xander does not look at me as he leaves, but Scythe's eyes find me and those blue ice chips are unreadable.

The buzz of students' voices rises in the air as, no doubt, rumours spread right before me. Theresa crouches next to Minnie and I, orange jumpsuits in her hands. She snatches up my old duffle bag, still lying on the grass from before I shifted and hands it to me.

She gives me a look that says something like, '*Really* Aurelia? Running away?' but spares me anything verbal just yet.

Wild Mother bless her, honestly, because I don't think I could take a telling off right now.

Not when escape had been *so* close.

Not when I've had my plans foiled. Thwarted once a-fucking-gain.

Not when I've been betrayed by the very men fate had destined to love and protect me.

This is a wound that has cut so deep, I can't even see where it ends. That primal thing inside of me breaks a little.

I quickly unzip my bag and realise I have no pants left because I tore through my only pair of jeans when I shifted to save Minnie. Sighing, I grab the musty orange jumpsuit and yank it on while Minnie shifts back into human form and does the same.

The students are all sent back to the dining hall with curious, backwards glances at us and it's only then that I see Lyle is standing there, glaring at Minnie and I. Well, he reserves the glaring part just for me.

"*You*," he hisses, his amber eyes blown out into their lion form. I'm taken aback by his anger, by the rare loss of control of his animus.

But I'm also wired and still trembling with adrenaline, my own growls echoing in my head. So I snap back a feral, "*You!*" I hate this man so much.

He blinks. In shock, I think, because I have some audacity right now.

Between one blink and the next, his eyes return to human and he glances at Theresa. "I want bars on her door and their guard doubled."

Lyle bends down, scoops up the unconscious nimpins, turns on his heel and storms after the guards. Shit, I hope Henry and Gertie are okay.

Minnie casts me a disturbed look. "What's going on, Lia?" she asks. "None of this is normal. I heard everything they said. Why can you turn into a—"

I clap a hand over her mouth. "Later."

Theresa silently leads us away and Minnie frowns but remains silent.

"They tried to kidnap me, Min," I mutter, shaking my head, rage bubbling at the memory of my father's mark on Savage's finger. "They were going to fucking take me back to my father!"

Her eyes widen, but she doesn't look at me. My anger and anxiety are a horde of angry bees in my chest. I don't want to lose the first friend I've made. But I've put her in danger. Perhaps it's best if she doesn't want to be friendly with me anymore.

"I understand," I say darkly, "if you don't want anything to do with me after this." Minnie folds her arms around her body like she's hugging herself for comfort, and proceeds to chew on her lip. Fuck. I've really done it. Because of me, she's traumatised. "*And* I'm going to murder those bastards for it," I mutter.

"I'm going to pretend," Theresa says loudly in front of us. "That I didn't hear you say that, Lia. Especially considering your situation."

Oh right, because I'm already accused of murder. Threatening others isn't a great look.

By the time we reach our dorm room, I'm a tangled raging mess of heat and electric energy. I angrily pace the room, my fists clenched, fury roaring in my ears. I need to do something. I need to hurt them for what they did. For thinking they could hunt me down, chase me, throw themselves on me, and tear my shields apart like they were nothing. I want to tear apart my father for thinking he has a right to do *any* of this.

And to think he knew! *Knew* these three were my mates. He probably blackmailed that lady phoenix back when I was thirteen and then lied to me about it. I just can't believe he would send me to Halfeather's mansion, knowing they were in that dungeon. What is he playing at?

"Aurelia." Theresa's voice seems far away as I pace the length of our dorm room.

"She's losing it." Minnie's voice sounds muffled as the

vision of Scythe and Savage bearing over me flicks through my mind like an aggressive slideshow.

"I'm not losing it," I snarl, not caring that my voice is all gravelly. "I'm fucking *angry!*" I clench my fists so hard, sharp pain bursts across my knuckles, but I relish it. "I want to fucking tear their heads off for what they tried to do."

Theresa moves behind me and I'm so wired that I whirl around, ready for it. But she's not trying to attack me. She's holding one of Minnie's massive European pillows.

Chapter 26

Aurelia

"Punch it," Theresa commands.

I frown at her serious face. "What?"

"You want to hit someone, Lia? You want to hurt them for what they did? Well, you need to learn healthy outlets for your anger. Take it out on this."

I stare at her for a moment longer until Minnie groans, "Do it, Lia."

There's so much energy vibrating through me that I don't question it further. I launch myself at the unicorn printed pillow, pummelling it with my fists in rapid succession. But I've never been the most physical person, so I'm red, sweaty and gasping for air within seconds. "Fuck!" I bellow, blowing a strand of hair off my face. My knuckles and biceps burn and I press the heels of my hands into my eyes. "Fuck!" I cry again.

"Let it out, Lia," Theresa says, calmly. "You're doing good."

"Please don't tell the deputy headmaster," I groan. "He's going to think I'm feral."

"That's a little of what it is," Theresa admits. "You haven't appeared all that feral before, but I have reason to believe that you've just been keeping it tucked away. Do you need to go again?"

My muscles suddenly feel loose and now a weariness makes my bones heavy. My anima cries out in sadness because, yes, I've been keeping that part of me locked away. "No," I say weakly. "I'm done."

Theresa throws Minnie the pillow and sits down on Minnie's bed, clearly knowing I need space. "I can't see any physical damage on you two, but there was a fight, by the look of it. Do you need to see the healer?"

I shake my head. In between my own sweat, all I can smell is Savage on my skin; ancient forest and pine, a heavy masculine scent. I shiver in memory of his hungry mouth devouring mine.

But *I* was also starving for him. And I hate myself for it.

"Are you going to tell me what happened?" Theresa looks at me. So does Minnie, from her bed, still chewing on her now swollen lip. "Why you tried to run away? You're an intelligent girl, Lia. I admit, I didn't quite expect you to be the one trying to run." She glances at my neck where my stupid 'Flight Risk' lanyard should be. It's still on my bed side table as a sort of 'fuck you' to Lyle. Instead, it's now a 'fuck me'.

I shake my head because I'm not intelligent at all because that escape attempt was a shambles. I screwed it up massively, though it might have worked if it weren't for the Slaughter Brothers.

"I just feel stupid," I admit.

Weariness clings to my bones. Likely from having Scythe tear my shields apart and also the guilt of seeing Minnie, Henry and Gertie get hurt.

Theresa makes a thinking sound. "Lia, your feelings are justified. I think you have every right to be angry."

I stare at her blankly because this is the first time someone has validated my feelings. "You do?"

She nods. "Yes. You don't want to be here, right? Your choice was taken away from you. You're an adult, and it's a hard thing to come to terms with. Then...*that* happened. Whatever that was."

My skin suddenly feels itchy, like I need to scratch it off and get out of myself. "I... I think I'm in shock," I say slowly. "I just need a moment, Theresa."

Theresa accepts this and gets up. "I'm going to return tonight, and we'll need a statement from the both of you. Write them down before the details get hazy, alright? Savage is a convicted felon, Lia. The authorities will want the full story. And... if you need to rage again, use the pillow."

All I can do is nod as Theresa leaves. The moment she closes—and locks—the door behind her, I drop onto my bed and bury my face in my hands. The tears come hot and fast.

"I'm so sorry, Min!" I choke. "If you never want to see me again, if you want me to move out, I will— Actually." I get up from my bed, rubbing at my eyes. "I'm going to pack my stuff now and tell Theresa it's safer for us to—"

"Lia!" Minnie shouts, throwing her hands up in the air. I stare at her. Her face is pink when she says, "Honestly, Lia? That was the most exciting thing that's happened to me in a while. Being friends with you is... something."

I stare at her in disbelief.

"Sorry, that came out wrong." She blushes, rubbing a tear away, and for the first time, her wrists don't chime with all the bangles. They were torn off her arms when she shifted. Now I feel worse. But she continues, "I know they hurt you. I'm sorry. I just meant that I... sort of felt alive, you know?"

My mouth drops open because Minnie is the last person I expected to be an adrenaline junkie. "What the hell, Min! I thought I was nuts, but you're nuts too!"

Minnie levels me with a look. "Here's the thing, Lia. I heard what they said. I also saw Scythe turning your head to look at your neck."

My heart stops in my chest as she takes a deep breath, like she's hammering the final nail on my coffin.

"And they were all staring at you..." She takes a deep breath. "Like you were their mate."

Her words ring with surety, and her eyes are steady on me.

I look at her, my face no doubt a mess, and immediately hide my face again in my hands. "No one was supposed to know."

"Oh, Lia." Minnie's voice is thick with her own

emotion as the bed depresses next to me and she leans her body against mine. "Holy shit. I don't blame you. This is... This is..."

She doesn't even know what to say. Hell, even I don't know what to say.

"No one was supposed to know," I repeat, because my brain is a scrambling mess. She's seen too much. Knows too much.

"It's hard to hide something like that in a place like this," she says softly, like she's trying to calm a startled animal. "I started to suspect when I kept smelling Savage around you and the room. His scent is strong. They all have a strong scent, because they're so powerful, I guess. But what the hell happened? I was honestly trying to come to terms with the fact that you were leaving... and now *they* tried to attack you? They're your mates. What the hell!"

"Please stop saying it out loud," I whisper, sagging into her and finally looking her in the face. "You can't tell anyone, Min. Like, I mean, *no one.*"

Her eyes are wide as she takes me in, like she's looking at me for the first time. I feel thirteen years old again when my nanny, Rosalina realised what I am. How I have to be kept separate. And secret.

"*Please*, Min," I whisper. "Please don't tell anyone."

The look on her face is serious, I realise. She understands the implications of what she saw and how it makes me *different*. Something calms in me a little. My terror abates as Minnie nods slowly like she's considering this carefully.

"Shit, Lia," she whispers. "I totally get why you needed to run this whole time."

"I'm sorry for getting you involved, Min. I really am."

But she shakes her head. "Honestly, I think I'm the best person for this job."

I stare at her in disbelief, but she's nodding like she's convinced. "You are going to tell me everything. That is the price of my forgiveness. I want to go into our friendship fully prepared." She slices her palm through the air. "You have a big fucking secret, and I want to know all about it. I think I have the right now, don't you? You wouldn't let me help before and it's gotten us nowhere."

I replayed the events in my head, thinking her words over and the implications of telling Minnie *everything*. But above it all, the vision of my friend bursting into her tiger form and charging at Savage, a wolf with more fighting experience and ruthlessness than anyone at this academy... "Min," I say slowly. "You literally shifted and attacked Savage to defend me. Why would you do that?"

"I like you, Lia." She shrugs. "And it was a dangerous situation. I think you're a woman who's had a difficult lot in life, and from what you've told me so far, I want to help."

Tears spill all over again as Minnie yanks me back down onto my bed. "I'm getting that bag of caramel popcorn my aunt sent me, and you're going to start from the beginning."

It's the sternest voice the tigress has ever used with me, and as I stare up at my friend, I realise I've been yearning to tell *someone* the truth for years now. I owe her. This girl took on Savage for me and I realise now that I would have done the same for her in a heartbeat.

"You could have run from them back there," I say quietly. "A lot of beasts would have just left me to fight for myself. Hell, Raquel and Sabrina would have left me. I know it. But you didn't."

"You stood up to those monsters, Lia. And the fact that your mates are those beasts? Ovaries like that? Girl, we're sticking together."

I let out a choked, slightly hysterical giggle because I thought I'd take this secret to my grave. Instead, I fling myself on Minnie's bed and start talking.

I tell her about the day my anima was revealed and how I went into exile. How my father sent me on secret healing jobs over the years, and how he sent me to Halfeather's mansion to heal a beast behind a steel door, and in that dungeon is where I met three of my mates. How I was really only there because Halfeather was looking me over to purchase me as a bride. Then I tell her about the wedding and the fire and how my uncle told me to run in the middle of the night.

By the time I'm finished, Minnie's mouth is open, her caramel popcorn forgotten. "I've never heard of someone actually activating a siren song!" Her voice is a breathy whisper. "I thought it was a myth! So you never actually—"

"I haven't really touched any of them, no." Until today, when Savage's lips were all over me. I shiver at the memory, but don't want to admit to that just yet.

She puts the bag down and begins pacing between our beds. "This is complicated. Very complicated."

No kidding.

I can see the gears turning in her mind. The shifting was a big muck up on my part, but I know it was just a response to Savage being on me that my anima must've just... bugged out and responded.

"We'll get through this, Lia," Minnie says. "I'll help you in whatever way I can."

I pinch the end of my nose. "Thank you. My problem now is that there's no work around for the blood covenant my dad has on them. They have to seal the deal."

Minnie swears. "Okay, look. It's getting on in time. We need to come up with a statement for Theresa. And I'm sure Mr Pardalia will want to speak with you. He looked *angry*."

We pull out exercise books and come up with a story we both agree on. Minnie ties her pink hair in a ponytail and puts her pen between her teeth. "Just two nerds out to take over the world, Lia," she says.

I nod glumly. Minnie lights a candle and incense and her altar of the Goddess. Then we write down our stories, which is really just the same thing, leaving out the blood contract and the fact that I turned into a wolf. We just said I turned into my eagle form instead.

Theresa comes back, and when she does, there are four new guards with her. Men this time, big ones with tools and a new door.

While Theresa reads our papers, Minnie and I look on with dismay as our wooden door is taken down and replaced with bars like a real, actual prison cell. They then put bars on the balcony doors, too.

Theresa nods in satisfaction after they're done.

"You're safe, Lia," she assures me. "The nimpins are getting checked at the clinic and will stay there, but they look fine. Those three beasts are caged now and the deputy headmaster is dealing with them."

Minnie exchanges a look with me. She says, "But they'll come out eventually, right?"

Theresa makes a non-committal gesture that tells us to worry about ourselves for the moment. But Minnie and I know that this is only the beginning.

Chapter 27

Savage

When I wake up, I feel like shit and I know I've been darted. When I saw where they were taking me, I tried to take out the guard-wolves, but within seconds came three sharp pricks in my hind leg, followed by three more in my side.

There are black shackles on my wrists and my body feels like it's been thrashed around. There's a lump on my head the size of Australia and there is only one wolf in this place who could've managed to knock me out. I smell sea salt and blood and earth in the air, and as I pull myself up, I see that I'm in a cage, set against the wall of a vast cavern. The air is musty, but an industrial fan whirrs nearby, sending cool air through the humid dark.

Thick steel bars encase me on all five sides, and on my left, there are two more identical cages where Xander and Scythe sit silently on plastic chairs. The air is electrified and I know from the low hum that our bars have electrical currents running through them.

"What the fuck!" I say loudly from the stone floor.

"You've finally decided to join us," calls a baritone I know only too well.

I groan to my feet to see the massive lion sitting on a steel chair in front of our cages. Behind him is a deep pool of water, which explains the briny smell.

"Where is Lia? What is this place?" I say, plonking myself into my own plastic chair. There are track pants folded at the corner of the cage, but I ignore them. Shit is about to go down, and I'd prefer to face it in my naked skin. I need to get the fuck out of here and see Aurelia.

"This is one of the underground caverns where I train the rabid beasts," Lyle explains evenly. But he's cracking his knuckles and staring at me like he's ready for murder. Maybe we'll finally get to see this man become the Beast Breaker.

"Do you know what you did, Savage?" His voice is dangerously quiet. "What you and your brothers did?"

I look down at my hands. I can still smell Lia's perfect vanilla cake scent on my skin. Still feel her naked, writhing body beneath mine. I even got to taste her soft lips in the alleyway. All my dreams came true in that moment. The heavens opened, and I felt... holy shit. Well, I felt like I had come home. Like every bad thing that has happened in my life faded away just by being close to her. My regina. My animus gives a pining whine.

"Don't answer him," Xander calls to me, aggressively clanking his black chains. I look over at my dragon, but his eyes are closed over his empty sockets. When they take his magic away, they take his magical sight away too.

"You'll be quiet, Xander," Lyle says. "I turned away when students started to go missing. I let it go when my video feeds started turning up blank. But I will not tolerate you kidnapping animas."

"Animas?" I snarl. "*Animas?*"

"Let it go, brother," Scythe rasps.

"Where were you taking her?" Lyle rests a leg on his knee as if he's settling in for a long interrogation. "Some type of revenge for what happened at Halfeather's?"

The three of us stay silent. Because yeah, while it wasn't revenge, we needed Aurelia gone. But also, she just turned into a fucking wolf, and for me, that changed... some things. I glance at Xander again, but he's just sitting in his chair, stony.

Lyle sighs. "We can do this the easy way or the hard way."

Is he kidding? That's usually my line.

"I want to see Lia," I growl, knowing it's a stupid thing to ask for, but my animus is making me pine for her. "I want to see if she is okay."

"You care about her?" Lyle uncrosses his legs and sits forward with interest. "Or is it just you being possessive?"

Yes. No. Fuck. My animus wants her. By all the stars in the universe, my animus fucking wants her, but the man in me can't let it happen.

"How many times has she rejected you now, Savage?" Lyle says mildly, but it's a sharp knife at my throat. "Say it out loud."

My animus takes over and lunges at the steel bars with a feral growl. Pain explodes as the electricity sparks and throws me backwards onto the concrete. The smell of burnt skin and blood fills the air, acrid and sharp. I know it's my own damage, but I savour the pain like a three-course meal.

"Come on, Savage." Lyle's voice is closer, like he's standing by my cage, and deathly urgent. "Let the man take over. *Think*. Don't let your animus control your cock."

But all I can see is Aurelia as a wolf. Dark and beautiful, with a pelt like the night sky. She *glittered*. My animus replies, deep and guttural, "I fucking need her."

"All wolves know this, Savage," Lyle sighs. "If your alpha says no, it means no."

I know what he's saying. I get it, I really do, but I can't *let* it be true. "She's been accepting my gifts and keeping them," I rasp. "She's not been throwing them away."

Xander sighs dramatically because he gets the need I have to provide for her. Dragons hoard their wealth after all, and the gifts he'd give her would be gold and jewels, but he has too tight a claw on his dragon to do that.

"Don't you feel bad?" Lyle asks quietly as I lie on the floor, letting my skin fire up. I deserve this punishment. "For hurting her? For pinning her down naked and forcing her to submit to you? She was crying, for God's sake, Savage. You made her cry."

My animus whines out loud and I know it's true. *We made Aurelia cry.*

"We'll see her cry more before this is done," Xander says quietly.

Scythe doesn't say anything because he probably agrees.

"This could send you back to Blackwater, Savage," Lyle says to me. "I could have you put down with just a few words to the council."

"I'd get out," I shoot back, finally sitting up. "We know plenty of beasts in Blackwater."

But Lyle gives me a wry smile. "So do I, Savage. So do I." He brushes off a piece of lint from his suit and I can't imagine how the hell he'd look in prison. He left Blackwater before I got there, so I never saw him. But he continues, "I could also make it so that Aurelia ends up in Blackwater, too."

This motherfucker.

My eyes flick back up to his and we both know that he's got me there. I wasn't expecting Lyle to be as ruthless as us.

They'd ruin Aurelia in the federal penitentiary. As growly as she is, she's soft and sweet as chocolate pudding on the inside. She'd be out of my grasp and I'd never be able to fulfil Mace Naga's stupid blood covenant.

I'm surprised when Scythe interjects. "Her father won't let that happen."

"Ah, the Serpent King," Lyle says, turning to look at Scythe. "He's an interesting beast. Did you know he spent every day of the last week sending me subtle threats?" He rubs his jaw like he's imagining the letters he's received. "He's kept her separate from him for half of her life and now he desperately wants her back? Why could that be?"

I know why. Aurelia has two forms. It's unheard of. Impossible. Such a thing is a myth these days, but if anyone would know why, it's Scythe. I glance at my blood-brother, but he's looking straight ahead.

Any father in their right mind wouldn't want her out of his sight. The thought of Mace Naga getting her back sends me spiralling with thoughts and images I can't control. I charge at the electrified bars again.

I hit it like a battering ram and it throws me back ten times as hard. Xander swears under his breath.

"*Stop*," Scythe commands.

I groan and flop onto my back, my skin on fire, my heart trying to tear out of my ribcage. "I'm going to kill you," I say to Lyle.

He sighs. "Let me help you, Savage."

"I don't want your fucking help."

"Here's what's going to happen," Lyle says to the three of us. "I'm not going to go to the authorities about this. I'm not going to send you back to jail, Savage. But what we *are* going to do is be honest with one another." He turns. "Scythe."

Lyle strides towards my brother's cage, the big keys at his belt jangling. "I was under the impression we had an understanding."

"This could get a lot worse for you, Lyle," Scythe rasps.

To my surprise, Lyle sighs and says, "I know. That's why we're going to come to another agreement. In exchange for not reporting on you and having council executioners in here, you're going to tell me why you all have made a blood covenant with the Serpent King. Don't try and deny it because I've seen the serpent magic on your fingers and the markings are exactly the same. I've seen this type of magic in Blackwater."

As I look at Lyle, I realise this bastard *will* actually call for our execution. I can see that rabid beast lurking behind his eyes, calling for blood. He enjoys violence just as much as I do.

As I stare at the lion in realisation, my blood thrums with a single word, and I can only just hear Scythe's low rasp as he talks.

Afterwards, Lyle exhales deeply. "You needn't have bothered with the abduction," he says. "If Lia loses the tribunal, her father will demand she be dealt with according to the Old Laws and that means she will go back to him anyway."

My animus roars in my ears and I have no choice but to ride it out.

Chapter 28

Savage

Eighteen years ago

"**C**ome on, pup. Put your hands up," my dad growls at me from outside the octagon.

I quickly put my tiny fists back up, determined not to get hit again as the tiger cub opposite me snarls through a broken lip. He also has the beginnings of a black eye, but I'm not much better.

We move around the ring, our eyes fixed on each other like eagles. It smells like ciggie smoke and weed in here, as well as the blood of the cubs who fought before us. They wiped the plastic mats of the ring, but I can still smell the iron of it.

The cub rushes at me, and I duck and swing out with my wolf claws out. I get him on the belly and he cries out, lunging back at me. I'm too clumsy and he swipes at my side. Fire burns through my skin and I realise that he's got me.

"Fuck!" I cry.

The men and women outside the ring laugh because they like it when the pups swear. My dad gives a low warning growl.

I know what that means for me. That growl.

I attack the other cub with everything I've got, landing punches at his head, his neck, his chest. My knuckles split open, but I keep going, smearing blood all over him. The cub's face becomes covered in his own blood, shiny as new paint, and I hear crunching, but I keep going because all I can hear is my father's growl in my head.

"Enough, pup," comes a low rumble by my ear. I'm lifted off him, right into the air as grown-ups jump into the ring to check on the tiger cub, now lying all floppy.

"Let me go!" I scream to the wolf who has me by my scruff.

"Calm down, pup. Fight's over. You won."

Relief is a warm shower over my head, and I stop flailing. "Really?"

He sets me down and I look up at him through my swollen eyes. Reuben is super massive, bigger than my dad even, and he doesn't hit the pups like the other grown-ups do, so we all like him.

"*Savage,*" my dad growls, and I hobble back to him as he gives me daggers from the side of the ring.

"He fought well, Fengari," Rueben says, following me. "Managed to get his claws out. But he needs to learn restraint. Control."

Pups usually can't pull out parts of their beast form

until puberty. You gotta beat 'em until it comes out, and it hurts every time because my skin is soft. But dad got them out of me quick smart. I puff out my chest because Reuben's words sound good.

My father grunts in reply as I hop off the platform and onto the ground. "Let's go, Scythe." He flicks his fingers at my brother, where he sits next to a nice serpent lady. My brother is so pretty, and even at my age of five, I can see how the grown-ups think he's pretty, too. He's not allowed to cut his long silver hair, and it's down to his elbows now, though you would never think he was a girl. Eyes as blue as the morning sky check my injuries and he reaches for me.

Scythe takes my bloody hand as we leave the warehouse, and I think he does it so I don't lick my knuckles. It's not until we get home and my dad pulls me into the garage that I get into trouble.

My mother huffs as my dad punches me in ribs. "Don't cry, Savage," she calls out in a voice like a tin can. "It'll only be worse if you do." She sits on an old milk crate with Scythe on her lap, and she brushes his hair with her best brush. She used to be pretty my mum, but now her eyes are all sunken in and her teeth are all yellow with the white powders she takes.

I try not to, I really do, but I can't stop it when the tears fall. My tummy is already bleeding, and when I fall backwards, I skid along the cold concrete of the garage floor. Scythe cries out and tries to leap off my mum, but she grabs him around the neck and sits him back down.

Scythe makes a choked sound, and from her special corner, Scythe's mum wails.

"Don't do that," my mum coos to Scythe. Then she throws an empty beer can at Lily. It bounces off her cage and I flinch at the sound.

"This is what Savage gets when he doesn't fight properly," my dad says angrily. He's a beastly rex, my dad, with dark hair and eyes like me. He's got big muscles covered with tattoos that he uses to hurt people. No one likes to speak out against him because they'll end up six feet under.

I lie still on the floor, bleeding, as my dad prowls out of the garage and back into the house where he throws himself on the couch and turns on the TV. I lick at the blood on my knees, but Scythe tuts and says, "I'll get the antiseptic."

"No, you won't," my mum says crossly. She glances at me. "Get the tape, cub. The dirt is good for you, and so is the pain. It'll make your wolf come out better."

Silently, I obey, heading over to the table where Dad keeps the medical tape and the tools he uses on me.

Through the bars of her cage, Scythe's mum looks up at me with those big blue eyes, the exact same as Scythe's.

"Please," she whispers to me. And then I realise that she's not talking to me, but to someone I can't see behind me. Dad says that she's 'as mad as a hatter, just better looking.'

Scythe thinks she's beautiful and I think she looks like a mermaid, only one who's always crying. She reaches up with a long-fingered pale hand and touches the lock to her cage, then touches her heart. Her weepy eyes stare at mine and she smiles, but it's sad.

Lily hardly ever talks because she is mostly rabid, but for some reason, she says a full sentence to me now. Maybe she's been listening to the TV, or maybe it's just the voices in her head.

"One day..." Her voice sounds like she's swallowed sandpaper and rubbed it against her throat. It makes my skin go all bumpy. "One day, your regina will make you weep, little wolf."

Chapter 29

Aurelia

The next morning, Minnie and I are let out of our jail cell. Neither of us slept very well, and I had a strange dream about Savage and Scythe. The wolf was fighting in a ring and both of them looked young enough to be children. It was so vivid and the fact that I remember every detail shakes me more than I like to admit.

Worse, I didn't even have Henry to cuddle to my cheek when I woke up covered in sweat with my heart pounding. My little nimpin had really helped me this past week, and I didn't quite realise how much. He was an assistance animal in the whole meaning of the phrase.

As soon as our cell door disarms, Minnie and I immediately go to the veterinary clinic to pick him and Gertie up.

The poor nimpins squeak and throw themselves at us when we reunite, their huge black eyes telling us they were super worried, and I feel awful. The nurse reports that they were hysterical when they woke up, but calmed right down once the situation was explained. They've been given a bath and berries to eat, but were otherwise occupied with watching the goldfish in the tank set into the clinic wall.

With them cuddled to our chests, we head to the dining hall to join Raquel, Sabrina, Connor and Stacey. The entire hall goes quiet for a moment as we enter, before the noise kicks right back up again. Henry vibrates against me in reassurance, and I kiss him on his clean, fluffy head. I glance at the end of the hall and find *that* back table has been left empty.

It's really strange not to see any of the three monsters holding court and knowing they're not going to be sitting there.

But my anima gives a woeful cry that sets me trembling.

Stop that. They tried to kidnap me, dammit!

I don't even know what I *would* do if I saw them again. I'm still angry. I'm still hurt and betrayed. Just pretending they don't exist seems safest and is now going to be my signature mental gymnastic move.

The animas of our little group try not to ask us too many questions, though I know they're bursting with them. The entire academy knows that the three psychos tried to kidnap me and that Lyle Pardalia saved Minnie and me. Once again, he is the hero of the school and I'm the butt of the joke. This academy is not short on drama, but a kidnap attempt is still out of the ordinary. I avoid their questions with the grumpy, don't-start-with-me look that's now on my face at all times.

Resting bitch face?

Try resting don't-fuck-with-me-or-I'll-gouge-your-eyeballs-out face.

Besides, I'm nervous for my 'therapy session' with the boss lion of this fine institution and it's occupying my mind for the moment. I never thought I'd actually have to go to it, and it seems especially cruel of the universe to have the session on the very next day of my escape attempt. I'm not even sure how much he knows about exactly what happened, but he's going to rub it in, I'm sure of *that*. And not rubbing in a good way, either.

And the look on his face yesterday told me everything I needed to know about how the appointment is going to go.

What does he expect me to say? "Oh, so sorry I ran, sir. Won't happen again." Are we going to talk about my deep, dark fears about being chained up? My twisted relationship with my dad? I would rather stick my drumsticks in hot oil.

I drag out breakfast as much as I can, but Minnie gives me a wide-eyed look as she points to the clock hanging above the buffet. "Wish I could be a fly on the wall for this therapy session," she sighs. "It's even hotter that he's a psychologist. Swoon!"

The rest of the animurs, including Connor, who catches up with us for breakfasts, giggle in agreement. Raquel even gives me a smirk.

I'm disgusted by their adulation of him and let my

face tell them I'm very disappointed. "Yeah, well, you'll get your chance, Min."

This morning, Minnie got her notice for a session with Lyle for after lunch, and we guessed it was to debrief for her own part in her, as she's dubbed it, 'hostage situation'. "It's going to be awful," I mutter as I heave myself to my feet. "I'm telling you, I'm going to come out even more mentally unstable than I already am."

Minnie chuckles as if that's a cute joke, and I leave the six of them and their nimpins to their leisurely breakfast. After a longing look back at them, I walk up to one of the guards by the door and show him my appointment note.

He nods and two of them escort me deep into the central building where all the offices are supposed to be. Without Minnie or one of the girls by my side, I suddenly feel very alone.

My skin prickles as a few passing males look me up and down as they pass in the opposite direction. It's not uncommon to see beasts being escorted around the school by two or more guards, but I'm one of the few with the warning sign on my lanyard, and the males get curious about it.

The fact that I come with this literal warning label around my neck is another sort of humiliation. The other beasts take it as a point of pride if they have one, but for me, it becomes a running joke.

"Hey *Flight Risk*," jeers a passing lion.

"More like flight... *failure!*" says his friend. They both

chortle at their great joke and I know at once that I'll never live this down. Gods, I preferred 'bun bun bunny'.

The guards say nothing to admonish them. Great lot of bastards, the lot of them. And don't think I've forgotten about the fact that Savage outright told me that some of the guards are on their payroll. Like some mafia shit.

If it *is* mafia shit, that makes Scythe a mafia *don*.

The thought makes me shudder, right down to my bones, because it makes so much sense for that shark to be in a position like that. I'd known from the moment I saw them all in Halfeather's dungeon that they were into illegal business.

We make it to the deputy headmaster's office after the guards loiter to talk to another set of guards about who's on break next, so I'm pissed off *and* late. But as the elevator opens to the top floor, revealing a plush, carpeted seating area worthy of the Prime Minister's offices, I'm chewing my lip with anxiety. I'm still frazzled from yesterday. Couple that with the lack of sleep and I'm practically jittery. Henry vibrates on my shoulder to try and settle me down.

The guards take up positions by the elevator and my panic ramps up a notch. Am I going to be in a room alone with the guy? He has a vendetta against me because I escaped him that one time, and that detention he gave us was out of spite. But surely the guards will be with me for the meeting?

A sophisticated lioness with a long mane of golden hair and a sexy pink business dress that hugs her curves gets up from a receptionist's desk. I suddenly feel very drab in my faded old shift dress. She's smiling when the elevator opens, but when she sees it's me, her smile drops immediately. For some reason, that irritates me, and I pointedly look around for Lyle's office door. But there are only closed doors in the lush burgundy ambience. Potted ferns are strategically placed around the room, bringing a little nature into the corporate space.

"Hi, I'm here for—"

"You're late," she snaps.

I'm about to say I'm sorry when she turns on her black red-bottomed stilettos and strides to an ornate door on the far wall. She knocks briskly, then opens it without waiting for a response. I think that's a little rude, but what do I know? I'm just a felon.

"She's here," the receptionist announces. I don't like the way she says 'she's' like I'm a dirty tissue.

The deep male voice from within says, "Thank you, Georgia."

Georgia, whose dress clings to her body in all the right ways, narrows her eyes at me and jerks her head towards the room.

She's trying to show her dominance, and for some reason, maybe instinct, it sets my anima off. My spine straightens, my chin comes up, and my walk becomes more of a stride. Henry lets out a warm, reassuring warble on my shoulder as I don't break eye contact with 'Georgia', and walk right up to the door with bristling purpose. My new flip flops slapping against my heels ruin the effect but still.

Sweeping past her dismissively, I enter the room—

And promptly trip on the edge of a thick carpet. I let out a little squeak before I catch myself and straighten. Henry leaves my shoulder for a moment, but lands right back down with a low, annoyed cluck.

Behind me, fucking Georgia snorts before closing the door. My anima and I decide we hate her and both of her supermodel legs.

So it's with great attitude that I lock eyes with the massive suited beast sitting behind the redwood desk. His long honey blond hair is neatly tied back, and his grey three-piece is so perfect I feel sick. It's like I've walked into purgatory only to be met by an archangel who's about to interrogate me in front of a set of golden scales. Will I be allowed into heaven, or will he judge me as only worthy of hell? It's easy to forget that he's twenty-seven, if rumours are to be believed.

"Don't be late again, Miss Aquinas," he says tersely.

His deep voice moves across my skin like heavy silk. I'm so annoyed by this and the receptionist that I just stand there and seethe. Lyle's perfectly clean-shaven jaw clenches and my heart becomes a racehorse when he says in a cold clip, "It's customary to apologise when you are late to an appointment. I expect better of you."

What a prick. But I do remember that this guy is the archangel of feral and rabid beasts because he's supposed to teach us how to operate in society and not just be animals. But I'm also still annoyed he brought me here against my will. And... he 'expects *better*' of me?

I cock my head at that statement. "Do you?"

His face is so cold that I feel a chill down my spine

and the anima in me begs to submit to his sheer alpha dominance. But he literally foiled all my well-laid plans. Enemy number one, whether my anima likes it or not.

He says nothing and I realise he's not going to proceed until I apologise. I sigh so deeply it moves my shoulders.

But I'll be damned if I'm *submissive* as I say it.

So I keep my chin up. "I'm so sorry for being late, Mister Deputy Headmaster." Was that a mocking bite to my voice? Shit, there definitely was. Why am I literally poking the lion with a stick? A smarter woman would bare her neck, then stab him in the back afterwards. But I just can't stomach that, because right now, defiance is all I have left.

"Sit," he orders, pointing to one of the two chairs sitting opposite one another by a set of fancy bay windows.

My anima shoves me forward as soon as the pure command hits my ears. I hate my beast so much, but I can't resist without tripping over again, so I just shuffle over, then plonk down in the hard seat. I take Henry in my palms and pet his fluffy goodness to distract myself. He's so cute; he just blinks up at me and bobs up and down on those silly feet. I keep my eyes on his liquid black ones as Lyle gets up and strides over to sit opposite me.

But oh-fucking-no. Because now, he's too close.

Even through my seven shields, I scent him immediately. On the surface, he smells like cologne and freshly pressed books. But underneath that is a feeling of sheer power that has me quivering in my old dress. Why do we have to sit like this? I don't look up at him and just continue to pet Henry's soft blue fur with two fingers. His hair will grow long, and eventually I'll be able to braid it. Connor already has tiny diamante clips in his nimpin's hair, and I want to treat Henry just as well.

I can see Lyle's legs from this angle. He's resting one shiny business shoe over one knee and I can't help but notice how the grey slacks strain against the muscle of his thigh.

My anima keens and I slap that bitch down. Henry blinks as he senses my discomfort and leans into my fingers to try and comfort me. As soon as we get back to the dining hall, he's getting the juiciest blueberry I can find.

Everything in this office is perfectly straight and organised. There's not a speck of dust, nor anything that doesn't serve a purpose. It's giving elephant-sized control freak energy.

Lions are known for their aesthetics, but Lyle has taken things to a whole new level.

He's silent for so long that I glance up at him. His amber eyes are staring at me so intensely that I'm struck into a stupor for a long moment. But I recover and break from his gaze, shifting in my seat to mask my discomfort.

He's got me intimidated, and I'm sure he's doing it on purpose. Bastard.

"What are we supposed to be doing?" I ask.

He's not happy with what I'm saying yet again, and

just replies, "Why did you try to escape yesterday, Miss Aquinas? Do you have no common sense?"

The nerve of this man. "Common sense is exactly what had me trying to leave."

I really shouldn't have said that because that piques his interest and he says, "What do you mean by that?"

I exhale heavily out my nose because I have no idea what to tell him. Men like this, men in positions of power, are rarely the empathetic, forgiving sort. Just like my father. You have to be ruthless to get into power like that. He might have no idea who *I* am, but I know his type sure enough. I also know that avoiding the question will piss him off.

So I say nothing and stare fixedly through the bay windows that overlook the front of the school. The Hunting Games field stands there, lush and untamed. A place a person could get lost in. A place like that, up in the sub-tropical north, means freedom for me.

"You shouldn't have bothered," he goes on in a low voice. "There is nowhere on this wild earth you could hide from me."

Chapter 30

Aurelia

My eyes snap back to his at the open, bloody threat, and I'm like a live wire under his predatory gaze. It's clear, I *had* wounded his pride. I slipped from his fingers once and he would never let it happen again.

But I can't accept that I *have* to stay here.

And then Lyle Pardalia proceeds to further ruin my life. "The reason I called you here today was to discuss your crime."

"Which one?" I ask absently.

He gives me an unimpressed look. "The one where you set your husband's mansion on fire. The one where a very rich and influential eagle is dead because of you."

My insides turn cold. Tundra cold. Antarctic cold. "But I didn't do it." Even as I say that, I know it sounds pathetic.

"The Council of Beasts has sent us notice of a trial."

My mouth drops open and I clutch Henry to my

chest, suddenly panicking. "Wait, what? I thought *this* was my punishment?" I gesture around his office to indicate the academy.

He looks at me as if I'm stupid, and honestly, I believe him. "Attending Animus Academy does not acquit one of murder. The law still exists. You'll be tried, and either found guilty or innocent."

Do they want to send me to *federal prison* for Halfeather's death? My head is shaking back and forth as if my very muscles can't believe it, either. "My father set me up. I can't believe this. I can't fucking—"

"Language, Miss Aquinas," he snaps at me.

My voice emerges shrill and out of control. "I'm screwed, and you're worried about my language!"

"Control yourself," he commands in that heavy tone.

Get. Fucked. But my stupid anima wants to obey.

My eyes are burning and I know I'm going to cry, but I can't let him see me like this. He's my enemy, like the rest of them. I clutch Henry to my chest like a shield. If the council wants a trial, I can't run. If I'm wanted for *murder,* I'll have the best teams in the country tracking me down and skewering me dead. They'll dart me and have me put down. That's what they do to rabid murderers. They're not considered safe for society. My plans fall to tatters on the plush carpet of Lyle's office.

I have to stay here.

I can't just run. Everything I've dreamed of is actually dead at my feet.

Looking back at him, I find his amber eyes are

assessing me, tense and intent, as if he thinks I'm going to bolt at any second. In truth, I want to.

Suddenly, I realise how alone I am.

But this guy is supposed to help feral beasts, right? He boasts about his high success rate on the national news. This place is supposed to rehabilitate people like me. As I stare at him with this realisation, his face softens just a fraction. It's so small that I think I imagine it, but I suddenly know it's really there, and a strange feeling settles at the base of me.

It pains me to ask for help, because when has anyone except Minnie ever offered it to me? But I steel my pride and ask in a resigned voice, "What do I do?"

I'm in such a hyper-alert state that I'm attuned to his every micro-expression. The corners of his lips twitch as if he's pleased that I've asked him.

"Your situation depends on your behaviour, Miss Aquinas. The council will hold their trial, but since the school is a safe-house, they cannot touch you for your first month. The trial is set four weeks from now."

The rope around my lungs that is my panic loosens just a little.

"In that time, you will have to show your character. You will have to show improvement. I am the one who will assess that, and I have to say that we're off to a bad start."

Just when I thought he was going to help me, it turns out he's to be my judge and jury. I clench my teeth in annoyance. So I have to impress *him* now? It sounds like a set-up. Some dark joke played on me by the Wild Mother.

But he's not laughing. In fact, his face is suddenly so impassive as he observes me that I don't think he even cares about this much at all. I'm just another bothersome student he has to deal with. This is his job.

"Okay," I say begrudgingly. Henry makes a choking sound, and I realise I'm clutching onto him like my life depends on it. I ease up my grip, placing him back in my lap. He shakes out his fur and looks up at me accusingly.

"Your student history will help in your trial. You've proven yourself to be a satisfactory healer, and your grades are good."

Satisfactory? Oh no he didn't! "I'm the best healer of my age in this city," I bite out. "I assure you."

He quirks a brow. "Arrogance does not a good healer make, Miss Aquinas."

I refrain from rolling my eyes, but honestly, he's right.

Holding up one large hand, a piece of paper from his desk shoots so fast towards us that I flinch. I'm sure he's showing off, but he's staring down at the paper like he does this all the time and says in his shopping-list drone, "You will assist in the healing and medical clinic on Friday and Saturday nights. Those are our busiest shifts."

And thus depriving me of any recreation time. I suppose felons don't get that luxury. He hands me the paper with instructions for the medical wing.

"Usually, we wait until second year to assign you a job, but in this case, I will take pity on you and we can fast track it."

I barely contain my anger at his jab. *Pity on you.* I hate myself when I say, "That's very kind."

"And you will attend weekly sessions with me to discuss your issues until the trial."

My frown is back because I don't have any *issues.* Any that I want to talk about with him, anyway. "I beg your pardon?"

He actually smiles at me and my heart does a little jump. "I'm pleased to see you have some manners."

I take a jab back. "I was once a princess of the Serpent Court, Mr Pardalia. You would do well to remember that."

His smile drops quickly. "But no longer." He pauses as I rage internally. "Your father has been very vocal about your guilt."

Fear is an obsidian hewn sword in my chest. "What?"

"Indeed." I can tell he finds this interesting. "He was the one who presented the evidence of your alleged crime to the council. He was sure you were trying to kill him, too."

I close my eyes and pinch the bridge of my nose. Henry starts vibrating again.

"We need to work on your temper," Lyle says.

Remaining in that position, I say darkly, "It's a new development."

He huffs through his nose and I drop my hand to stare at him. He asks, "*Do* you want your father dead, Miss Aquinas?"

The question is a loaded gun that could go off in my face. Do I want him dead? I don't even know. Half my problems would go away if he died. But do I want his death? I sigh because this is all too much. "No. And if you're going to ask me if I'm going to kill anyone or have any plans to maim, destroy, murder, manslaughter, or burn anyone's house, the answer is also no. Even being forced to marry Halfeather, I would not have tried to kill anyone. I was just going to run."

It feels good to admit it, but when I look back up at Lyle, he's gone rigid in his seat. But his voice returns to shopping-list flat. "Your father told me you were a liar."

"And you believe him?"

"He is a respected member of the council. And Halfeather was an unmated eagle with substantial wealth. He had a long line of animas wanting to wed him."

"You're implying that I tried to marry him for his money?" I say in disbelief. Beasts often marry if they don't find their mates, often for protection or if they're getting older and want children.

He shrugs. "It's a claim that makes sense. They will use this at the trial."

I want to vomit and sucker punch him at the same time. In all my time living in my bungalow, I never tried to steal or obtain more money other than by working. Until I was literally starving and forced to steal, that is. Now they're going to use this against me in court.

My voice is deadly quiet when I say, "My father sold me, Mr Pardalia."

But he's sitting there shaking his head as if I'm full of it. "Your father actively speaks out against bridal and breeding contracts. He's been trying to improve the image of serpents in society, which is a noble thing for him to do. To do what you are saying would make him a—

"A Liar," I hiss. "A hypocrite. A manipulator."

And that is why he's so good at what he does.

"Funny," Lyle deadpans. He looks me straight in the eyes. "He said the same thing of you."

I want to scream. The rage that pours from me at this injustice is a tempest that wracks my very bones. As if he knows, Henry scrambles out of my grip and begins pecking me on the cheek, but it does not stop my shaking.

"Well," I bite out through clenched teeth. "Looks like you have it all figured out then, don't you? If you're so friendly with my father, why do you need to speak to me at all?"

"I am trying to help you, Miss Aquinas." His eyes flash. "Like I *helped* you when those beasts tried to kidnap you."

"Thank you for doing your job, Mr Pardalia," I reply smoothly. And a beam of wicked inspiration springs through me, wild as an autumn wind. "As grateful as I am, you hardly have a handle at your school. Did you know, for example, *those beasts* have their own dragon trick floor in the unmated dorms?" When he stares at me, I know that he didn't know and I run with it. "That's right. And did you know they killed a serpent up there? Right in front of me, to prove a point."

His entire demeanour changes.

Lyle seems to darken at the edges, and though he remains perfectly still, his stillness changes from that of a contemplative repose to coiled, lethal predator preparing to strike. I can *feel* the contained violence rolling off him like summer heat.

My hackles rise in warning as alarm bells ring loud and clear in my head. Henry puffs up on my shoulder, as if he's ready to finally do something.

His voice is nothing more than deathly quiet when he says, "What were you doing up there, Aurelia?"

I'm so taken aback by the sudden change that I open and close my mouth like a blowfish. My voice is stuck in the depths of me as my anima cries out in warning.

"Get out," he says in a voice of pure command. "This session is done."

I stare at him, because he did *not* just dismiss me like—

"*Get. Out.*" His voice holds a lethal punch of command and my anima has me lurching out of my seat and stumbling towards the door like our life depends on it. Yanking it open, I rush past Georgia and the guards and stab the button for the elevator. Thankfully, it opens with a soft whoosh and I stumble in. It's not until the guards file in and the door closes that I clutch onto Henry and gasp a full breath.

One of the guards chuckles at the sight of me and says with a grin at his comrade, "They don't call him the Beast Breaker for no reason."

What the hell just happened?

Chapter 31

Aurelia

My guards take me straight back to my dorm. Henry and I tremble the whole way. Maybe this is normal. Maybe this is who the deputy headmaster of this school is. Violence kept hidden behind an Italian three-piece suit.

It's both shocking and completely makes sense. A weak beast couldn't run this school. And a beast who walks around with that much power and arrogance is going to show it sometimes.

When I get back to my dorm, I'm surprised to find Theresa and Minnie are waiting for me, chatting away about something I'm not listening to.

Minnie pats me on the arm before the guards take her for her own meeting with Lyle and I don't get to warn her to be careful.

Somehow, I don't think he'll speak to Minnie the same way he just spoke to me. She won't give him attitude. She won't taunt him.

"Are you alright, Lia?"

I shake myself because I realise this is the second time Theresa has just asked that question.

"Sorry, Theresa. Yes, I'll be fine."

Henry is still puffed up on my chest, his cheeks rounded like he wants to bellow.

"It's alright, Henry," I murmur, holding him up to my cheek. "The threat is gone. We are fine. We are well. We'll be okay."

I hardly believe it, but you can't tell small creatures the truth like that.

"So, I'll need you to sit down." Theresa points to my bed and speaks softly.

Immediately, I'm worried. Once I'm seated, Theresa sits on Minnie's bed so we are opposite each other like in a meeting. "Savage, Scythe and Xander will be locked up for seven days and they will be released the following Monday." I suck in a breath. Will they have a trial like me? "And then they will be released back into gen pop."

My stomach hollows out.

"That's not possible," I whisper. Under my skin, my anima hoots with joy because we'll get our mates back. But what the hell? "Theresa, they literally tried to kidnap me."

"Mr Pardalia has sorted it out, and it seems it was a bit of a misunderstanding."

I gape at her because what I saw in that blood covenant was *no* misunderstanding. But Theresa frowns. "Did you not discuss this with him?"

No, I was alpha-ordered out of his office before he could. "Shit." I clutch at my stomach because my insides want to escape up my throat and are doing a very good job of trying.

"Seven days is a long time, Lia," Theresa reassures me. "They'll have obsidian shackles on. They won't be able to use their powers and will be guarded more heavily."

Ha! Guarded by their own employees!

"This place is a joke. This system is rigged."

Theresa grimaces. "Lia, in four weeks, you have your trial, correct? I think you need to put all your efforts into that. This is serious. A murder trial is a big thing."

Like I don't know that. "I don't have a lawyer."

"You'll be assigned one. And I suggest you go to the library and have a look at what to expect. We have quite a few legal resources for you to use."

"And I have Minnie. She's a good researcher."

"And you have Minnie," Theresa confirms with a smile. "And Henry."

My good little nimpin chirps in agreement.

She asks me if I have everything I need because from tonight, the monthly lockdown begins. I read about this in Minnie's folder.

Once every month, mated females ovulate and go into heat. Being in close proximity 24/7, most of the females in the academy have their menstrual cycles synced. For mating groups it's fine, they dorm together anyway and get to fuck each other silly until it's over. But the pheromones make the rest of us—especially the animuses—rowdy, and things can get out of hand between the unmated beasts. On the night of the heat and the days before and after, the school goes into lockdown for three days. If we have classes in the mornings, we take them online and stay in our rooms. The dorms literally lock down with steel doors that nothing can get through and we have microwave meals for those nights.

After Theresa leaves, Minnie returns a little while later with a big grin. "He was so lovely, Lia. I have no idea why you don't like him. I was all quivery, but he pretended not to notice. Such a gentleman!"

I snort in response, suddenly feeling exhausted. I decide I'll take a nap to start off the lockdown and change into the old purple T-shirt and flowery shorts that have been serving as my pyjamas for the past three years.

Minnie claps as if this is a good idea and gets into her own rainbow coloured unicorn PJ's, suddenly shooting me a wry smile. "You're not going to try and put your hands down my pants because you're not with your mates?"

I throw a pillow at her and she hoots with laughter as she catches it.

"No!" I groan. "I'm still not a *mated* female, am I? Not fucked any of them yet."

"Don't know how you've avoided it so far," Minnie says. "They're pretty sexy, even if they are evil."

I blush profusely because she's right on both accounts, and the alleyway moment Savage and I shared still makes me all hot and bothered. But I don't get to reply when there's a banging on the bars that have been left unlocked for the three days.

"Let us in!" It's Sabrina, dramatically clinging to the bars as if she's in jail herself.

Minnie rolls her eyes. "They've come for gossip."

I sigh, but it's not just Sabrina who's standing there with our group of first-year animas. It's an entire gaggle of girls from second year as well, in their pyjamas, with packets of cookies, chips and lollies clutched to their chests. Their nimpins are excitedly bobbing up and down on their shoulders and chirping. Someone has a hair curler and another a film projector. Connor is here as well, because apparently it might be a little dangerous for him in the animus dorm.

"It's singles' night!" Sabrina shouts, wiggling her hips and waving the two bottles of gin in the air as she kicks the cell door open. "It's time to party. Woohoo!"

"A-Also," gruffs Raquel, "W-w-we want to know w-what h-happened yesterday."

They all squint at me as they file in, sitting themselves on every surface in the room. Red plastic cups are tossed to each person, and Connor passes a smuggled joint around.

I take an offered cup as Minnie brings out multiple bags of chips from her wardrobe.

"So, why does the mob boss want to kidnap you?" Stacey asks point blank.

Lying back on my pillow, Sabrina holds out an eye mask and I stay still while she puts them under my eyes. Minnie exchanges an amused look with me because apparently, all it takes is a kidnap attempt to make a person popular.

I tell them the adjusted story, embellishing the part when Minnie faced off with Savage, making it more of an actual fight.

"We start proper fighting classes soon," Sabrina sighs. "You need to learn to use those eagle claws, Lia. It's all you've got going for you."

Grimacing at the underhanded gibe, I nod.

"So you have no idea why they want you?" one of the two second-year lionesses in the corner asks. They're curling each other's long honey-coloured manes.

"They made some deal with my father," I say, thinking it's no harm if I tell them that part. "And he's...dangerous."

"Shit," Sabrina says. "Sounds like my dad, dude." She holds up her hand in a high-five and I smack her hand with a dark laugh. "When I was in primary school, my dad used to lock me in the cupboard for hours. Used to piss my pants and everything. That's how I learned to pick locks with a bobby pin. I'd go out to wee and lock myself back in for when he got home after work. Came in handy when I started to steal other things."

We all gasp in dismay, but the thing is, you put a whole bunch of feral delinquents together in a room and stories like that are commonplace. Feral children often come from feral homes. Not all of us, like Minnie, but some. Sabrina passes around her neon pink vibrator like the 'speaking ball' we use in group therapy and everyone gets their chance to tell their fucked-up story.

"My m-mum used to f-feed me these weird b-biscuits made of dog f-food and grass mashed up and f-fried," Raquel admits. "She p-put salt in them s-so it t-tasted alright. Then we f-finally f-found a commune and we g-got to eat meat. M-most of the time it was raw." They shrug like they don't mind it, and then turn to Minnie. "We l-literally k-know nothing a-about you, M-mouse."

Minnie sighs and accepts the vibrator, tapping it against her chin as she thinks. "Well, I finally got asked out by that girl in third year."

"What!" I say, getting up on my knees and pointing at her. "This is the first I'm hearing of it!"

"In the p-past!" Raquel shouts. "That l-lion is h-hot, though."

"They're having an orgy downstairs," Sabrina says wistfully. "I wanted to go, but I wanted to hear your goss more."

I make a face because an orgy sounded like a great distraction right now... if only I was actually able to find someone else enticing other than the three monsters.

Minnie nods. "I'm totally going down there tomorrow. But yeah, well, I got mixed up in a bad crowd as a teenager. My parents weren't really social and..." She rolls her eyes as if she's embarrassed by herself. "When this *really* sexy tiger gave me some attention, I fell for him."

"He was a bad boy, wasn't he?" Stacey says as she sets up the speakers for the movie.

Minnie nods. "The baddest bad. Maybe even worse than the Slaughter Brothers Pty Ltd. When you got on his bad side, he had an attitude worse than Xander Drakos."

"Ugh!" one of the lions from second year shouts. "That asshole *dragon* is so fucking hot with those glowing eyes. But he knows it! He refuses to fuck *any one* of us, and we've all tried! Katrina offered herself to him in a stunning lace playsuit and he *ignored* her. Imagine!"

There's a collective groan as my anima makes a very disgruntled sound. Minnie shoots me a look and I try not to show my discomfort.

"Well," Minnie continues, "he's been taken away for his crimes, so I'm safe now."

Raquel and Connor swear in solidarity and I suddenly realise why Minnie might have empathised with me about my situation.

I say, "That sucks, Min. I'm sorry I didn't know."

Minnie smiles gratefully at me. "It's okay. I don't like to think about it too much."

We all shut our mouths after that because we're allowed to have our privacy, aren't we? And Goddess, I understand playing the 'ignore it and it'll go away' game all too well.

By nightfall, we're tipsy and giggling, bobbing our heads to new RnB music on the phone and speakers Stacey smuggled in.

Connor brings out a little tub and we give the nimpins the full day spa experience, washing them with strawberry scented bubble bath and painting their tiny nails.

As I watch Connor blow dry a line of five nimpins,

including Henry, I sit there in a tipsy wonder. Finally, at the ripe old age of twenty, I get to experience a slumber party, and just for a moment, I allow myself to feel like I belong. I suppose that just sometimes, good things *can* come out of a kidnapping attempt.

Chapter 32

Aurelia

We watch rom-coms and K-dramas late into the night, and eventually, we all fall asleep in precarious positions around the room

By morning, everyone leaves our dorm to head to the bathroom, get more food or get themselves off, I'm guessing, by the way Sabrina lovingly picked up her vibrator and took it to her room.

Minnie prances off with some caramel flavoured lube to find the aforementioned orgy and she's gone for hours.

I'm not aroused all that much, so I'm left to mope and try and mentally recover from everything that happened in the last two days.

I know that my father is trying everything he can, including framing me for murder, to get me back into his clutches. He has a plan for me, and if his previous plans are any indication, he's likely going to sell me yet again. Perhaps to someone worse than Halfeather. To males like them, I'm a useful tool that shouldn't be allowed to go to waste.

And my mating group is the key to everyone knowing just what a *tool* I am. Being open about my mates will lead to my demise. I will never be safe.

That evening, Raquel, Sabrina, Stacey and Connor return to set up for another night in our dorm.

"They're going to be out in one week," I say after a drink of something Stacey calls a 'rabid lioness martini'. It's got a gummy bear on a toothpick across the top instead of an olive. "I can't believe they get *one week* of jail time for what they did to me." But none of the animas look surprised and Connor shakes his head in dismay.

"I fucking want revenge," I mutter. "But I wouldn't even know where to start."

"Piss in his underwear drawer?" Raquel fiddles with their lip piercing, thinking deeply.

"That's a class-C offence," Minnie says sagely. "No urinating anywhere except the toilet, unless you want remedial classes."

"Throw all their clothes out?" Sabrina says around a mouth full of chocolate. "Ooh, I know, steal the dragon's headphones."

Before I can say that would be disastrous, Minnie sits up abruptly. "Do you know what?"

"What?" we all say at once.

"Lia, I think you need to begin your villain slut era. Now's the time."

We all stare at Minnie with a mixture of shock and awe.

"H-How's that g-going to h-help?" Raquel asks, but I'm already nodding, a massive shit-eating grin on my face because I know where this is going.

"They want you, right?" Minnie says, giving me a significant look. "Let them, especially Savage, know that he *can't* have you, in the best possible way. Rub it in his dirty old face."

Connor snaps his fingers. "Minnie, you're a genius! I mean, you have a stunning body underneath those old T-shirts, Lia. We need to get it out! Let them know who the fuck they're dealing with. Animuses like that need a smack to face type of lesson. They need a shock."

"Yeah," Sabrina says excitedly. "Who needs subtlety?"

This entire time I've been hiding. Trying to keep low and out of sight, but look where that's gotten me? Nowhere.

And the other animas might not know that it's going to be worse than they think because a regina flaunting their body to other beasts is the worst type of jab to the heart of a mate. They might hate me even more, but. Oh. Fucking. Well. Revenge is called for. Revenge will be had. They made a covenant not to mate with me? Well, I'm going to make them regret that choice.

"We get to go to the village this week," says Sabrina excitedly. "I've been nagging Theresa about it this entire time. There'll be clothes there, even handmade. We have a whole week to prep for this, Lia. *Finally*, I won't be embarrassed to be seen with you."

I roll my eyes at Sabrina as Minnie's eyes light up. "Oh yes, baby. We're going to wipe the floor with them."

It's a really great plan, but there's one major thing in the way. "I can't buy anything," I groan. "I lost all my money when I flew away. I'm sure Lyle took my stash of money when he caught me the first time because it's not in my duffle."

"What?" Minnie frowns at me. "No, if you didn't come in with an account, you get a stipend from the council. Here, use the academy tablet."

We jump onto the academy network on the tablet Theresa gave us. We're not allowed access to the internet or smartphones while we're here, so the school has its own dedicated network we can access from the new tablets. Older students get to use special phones they can message each other on, but us newbies don't.

I log in using the credentials I was given in my information packet, and when I click on the dollar sign icon, my mouth drops open. Listed there is a figure I've never seen in my bank account.

"That's the stipend?" I gesture wildly at the tablet.

Connor and Sabrina choke on their drinks when they look over my shoulder.

Minnie frowns, then picks up her pink folder, opening it up to a green tab. "No, the council allowance for financial assistance is... one tenth of that."

"Wild Goddess," I whisper. "They've made a mistake."

"Check with admin," Stacey says. "They helped me when I forgot to bring my Valium."

I end up shooting admin an email and a reply comes back from Georgia, no less, within minutes, saying it wasn't a mistake.

Scratching the back of my neck, I glance at my meagre possessions. They only take up two drawers of the dresser I've been given.

"Lia," Sabrina says slowly. "Your father is the Serpent King, isn't he?"

"I know what you're thinking, and it's impossible. He never gave me money. I had to earn it at my aunt's grocery store. I've been saving coins for ages."

"Okay." Connor claps his hands. "Let's thank the Wild Goddess for your good luck and not question it!"

I frown at the figure again, and he shakes my shoulders. "Come on, Lia! You have money to spend now!"

"And if you feel bad about having so much money," Sabrina says pointedly. "You can always buy us something too!"

Stacey and Connor cheers with their cups.

For the first time in a long time, I'm excited.

The rest of the lockdown is spent in a sort of tipsy daze as we plan my revenge. Sabrina teaches us how to pick locks using bobby pins and a set of purple fluffy handcuffs from Raquel's stash of sex toys. Sabrina can even get herself out of them using her telekinesis and after hours of practice, so can Minnie.

Lockdown finishes and the following week of classes are *so* much easier now that I know I don't have to keep looking over my shoulder. It's almost a breeze, and I don't even notice the other males ogling me as we go from class to class. Their jabs of 'Hey, Flight Risk,' don't even hurt so much now that I have something to look forward to.

My comeback.

The most exciting thing by far is our new access to the village on Wednesday night. The last time I was *this* excited was the night before my twelfth birthday, because my father always ran big parties for me, pink jumping castle and all. And the thing is, memories of my life back then are good. My uncles were scary men to others, but to me, they wore pink feather boas and let us play with them in their serpent forms. After my mum died, Aunt Charlotte fed me, brought me pretty dresses and danced with me and my friends.

Oh, how things changed.

I might not have had close friends back then, but at least I had people excited to be there with me.

But now, I finally have *real* friends to share excitement with.

The village is the student-run retail precinct in warehouse three, and we need fingerprint ID that'll allow us first-year animas access only on Wednesdays. There's a metal archway manned by four security wolves who pat us down when we exit. Through it, I'm surprised to see a white cobblestoned street lined with colourfully painted two-storey buildings. Theresa explains that the entire thing was made by hand, mostly by those on detention in the seventies when the school was first established.

While the Village was constructed decades ago, one of the tasks students have is maintaining and cleaning it. It's supposed to replicate the outside world, and teach us how to behave properly in a simulated environment. There's grocery stores, clothing boutiques, a cinema, cafes, and even a couple of nightclubs that serve alcohol on certain nights to really test the final-year students.

The entire simulated city is run by the students after classes until the bedtime bell, and they even make fake money called animus credits as they work.

It's a theme park for the likes of me.

There are security beasts and cameras everywhere though, so it just misses the mark for reality, but I don't mind at all because once Theresa finishes her tour, Minnie, Connor and Sabrina drag me to one of the more feminine clothing stores immediately.

"Slutty," Sabrina announces to the jaguar owning a pretty black and pink boutique. There's a crystal chandelier, a pink velvet loveseat and everything. "Lia needs skanky, attention-seeking outfits that scream, 'fuck me'. *Many* of them."

The jaguar arches an eyebrow at me as I blush. "I'm making someone jealous."

"Jealous?" Sabrina repeated, outraged.

"More like rock hard and sweating!" Connor cries.

"We want them to regret the day they were born!" Minnie concludes, waving imaginary pompoms.

The jaguar nods in solidarity. "Well, we have plenty of what you need here, girlfriend. Now blue has to be your colour, right?"

I try on multiple outfits with the animas sitting on a little sofa as I shyly walk out. They adjust me, pulling material here, demanding for more skin there, and before

I know it, they have me in a new push-up bra and lace thong, drunk on their own laughter.

Thank the Goddess for my crazy stipend.

By the time we leave the village at nine p.m., I'm thoroughly exhausted and carrying so many paper bags that it's a struggle to get back to our dorm.

"This is going to be amazing," Minnie giggles. "I can't wait to see the looks on their faces!"

Stacey giggles back, holding up her own purchases. "Oh, please wear that one that shows your side boob. It's so sexy. I promise you, by the end of day one, you'll have a beast hanging off your arm."

"All of our arms!" Sabrina cheers.

Raquel is the only one who's squinting at us like we're mad. "Y-You w-*want* this attention, Lia?" our wolf asks in their serious voice. In the dark, all I can see is Raquel's extensive facial jewellery glittering, and I find it beautifully mesmerising in my giddy state.

"Uh-huh. I really do," I say, looping my arm in theirs. "I want revenge and I want it bad. I want to cause *pain*, Raquel. I want to *hurt* them."

Our five nimpins chirp sadly as if they know this will bode trouble for them.

"They'll be adjusting their erections all day!" Connor squeals. "Imagine the mixed classes all week!"

The guards by our dorm door shush us and, I'm sure, roll their eyes as Sabrina and Stacey shimmy their way through the door.

It turns out that a wardrobe update can do wonders for one's mentality.

Chapter 33

Aurelia

The next few days pass with a sort of routine. It's almost scary just how easy it is without those three beasts in my vicinity. No heart palpitations for me anymore. No freezing or shivering or neck prickling. No wet panties either.

Even the other males don't bother me with their longing stares and suggestive questions. There are fewer guards around due to it being the second week, but even that doesn't bother me. Heck, everything else is *child's play* in the absence of my monsters.

Minnie and I, being nerds and proud of it, go to the library every night after dinner to try and find something to help for my trial. We are accompanied by Stacey, because Raquel, Sabrina and Connor go off with their sneaky links most nights before eleven, when we have to be locked inside our dorms for the night.

In the library, we look up previous cases like mine, where a young woman has been sold for a bride contrac to someone from her order. We also look up murder cases.

To my dismay, we find hardly any of the former and a lot of the latter. It seems people like my father are good at avoiding court, likely by paying beasts off or blackmailing them. The murder cases are always interesting, and we spend most of the night gasping over scandalous court testimonies.

Does any of it help me? Do I find comradery with the women involved? Not really. I've not actually murdered anyone. I can't find anything remotely similar to my situation and plan on telling Lyle as such.

Friday night means I have my first shift at the medical wing. I bid the girls and Henry goodbye at dinner and have the guards escort me to my shift. Because of the potentially volatile beasts who come into emergency environments like the medical wing, nimpins aren't allowed. Henry, on Minnie's shoulder, gives me a sorrowful look as I leave. If he had lips, I'm sure he'd be pouting.

The plus side is that the lovely charge nurse Hope has volunteered to be my buddy nurse and show me around.

She makes extra sure to tell me that the glass sliding doors we came through on enrolment day are barred and locked shut with fingerprint ID. I nod sombrely, like I've never thought about escaping that way, but more than once I catch myself looking longingly out into the carport through the bars.

It's all going well as I restock the bandage cupboard

until a commotion through the academy side-receiving bay makes me snap my head around.

A voice is mentally projecting through the entire room and I lurch towards it on pure reflex.

"Lia!" Savage shouts into every head in the vicinity. *"Where is Lia?"*

Four bloody lions are hauled through the door, all unconscious, followed by another massive beast I recognise instantly. All I can see of Savage is black fur made darker than ink, because it's wet and splattered with blood.

Cold fear shoots right into my throat as Hope and several other nurses turn to give me raised brows. I force myself to shrug casually and shake my head, trying to make it look like he's crazy and I have no idea why he's calling for me. The fact that Savage can blast his voice into the entire room without any trouble is alarming.

Hope is astute, giving me a side eye, and I know she's wondering what relationship we have. The idiot is giving us away and I *don't* appreciate that. Though it kills me to see his blood spilled and my anima roars with outrage, I take every last reserve of discipline and turn my back on him, busying myself with tidying up a messy bundle of wound dressings. The two security bears haul his wolf body onto one of the wide veterinary tables while his victims are taken to the other side of the wing, far away from him, as is protocol.

"Calm down, Mr Fengari," says one of the veterinarians as Savage thrashes on the table.

"Don't fucking touch me!" Savage projects again. *"I want Lia!"*

I'm blasting expletives in my own brain when I see them getting a dart gun ready. Hope jerks her head at me to get over there.

I stride over to Savage, lying on his side, whining low in his chest as everyone except the two bears give him a wide berth. These bears are under their employment, from memory, because they've been all around the school and were at the loading dock that day of my escape attempt.

"I'm here, Savage," I sigh. He goes still and turns his big wolf head to look at me. "Where is it hurting? There's a lot of blood."

"You should see the other guy." His voice is an annoyed grumble and he licks his chops.

I want to say that he deserves to be injured because of what he did to that snake in their dorm, the guards outside the anima dorm, and likely countless other beasts, but my need to heal him is overriding everything. After steeling myself, I say begrudgingly, "Honestly it'll be easier if you turn into your human form. But it'll—" With a groan he changes, his joints audibly popping. "Hurt."

Before me is a naked Savage, who promptly flops onto his back, giving us all an uninhibited eyeful of the entire length of his spectacular, tattooed naked body. Completely out of my control, my gaze flicks down to his cock before hastily shooting back up to his eyes. He's looking at me half-lidded, covered in sweat and blood, but there's a lazy smirk on his lips as if he knows how massive his manhood is.

Someone clears their throat behind me before a blanket is thrown over him. It's only when the dart gun is put away that I take a breath and take a look at his arm, which looks like someone has tried to take a bite out of his bicep.

He points to his arm as if I can't already see that's his only injury and I roll my eyes as Hope wheels over a dressing table with equipment on it.

But then he says, "Bray-*kee*-al artery."

I realise that he's saying brachial artery. How the hell does he know that?

"Are you alright to do this?" Hope says, watching me carefully. "I can take over—"

"No one will take over," Savage growls. The violence in his voice has me glaring at him.

"Behave yourself, Savage," I snarl. "Don't you *dare* think I've forgotten what you did." I look at Hope. "I'll do it. I'll just pretend he's someone else."

She gives me a smile. "Very professional, Lia." She gives Savage a look of warning before locking the wheels on the dressing table. "Looks like we're putting you to healing sooner than I thought."

I give her a small smile, slipping on the sterile gloves and seeing what equipment she's given me.

There's definitely a nicked brachial artery, so I don't waste time. Slapping on a wad of gauze to the wound, I press down to staunch the flow and close my eyes to start the healing.

I can feel Savage's eyes on me as I work. I can feel him breathing, the movement of his muscled chest, the way the wolf inked there is hot and shiny with his exertion. My body is so attuned to his that the rest of the room fades away as I stand there, enraptured by his heavy presence. Does he feel me in that same way? Is he wondering about what he saw last week? Is he thinking about how our bodies were roughly pressed together when our lips met?

As I knit the fibres of his muscle back together, my anima flutters in contentment, fluffing its feathers and preening itself, extremely happy at being watched by our mate and even more happy that we're healing him.

At the most fundamental level, I know that denying my mates is a primordial level of wrong. The only person who'd faced this problem was my mother before me, and she's no longer alive to give me advice.

It doesn't change the fact they tried to kidnap me.

As soon as I've knitted his dermis together, I open my eyes and find Savage's eyes are fixed on me with a scary sort of focus. His hazel irises glimmer with something I can't interpret. What the hell is he thinking right now?

"Are you hurt anywhere else, Mr Fengari?" I ask in a clipped, professional voice, lifting up his arm to wipe the blood off it with a wet swab.

He watches me but doesn't reply. I raise my brows.

"No. I only let him get me there."

I frown down at him and see at once there is something unhinged about the smile gracing his pink lips.

"You did this on purpose," I say, horrified, dropping

his arm.

He smiles at me, raising his hand as if he wants to touch my face, and then dropping it when I glare daggers at him. "Lia." He grins absently.

"He's delirious," Hope says from where she's observing by the wall.

"No, just crazy," I reassure her. "I'll do a scan to make sure he's not lying."

"Great work, Lia. Don't close the curtains. I'm just next door." She bustles away to the patient in the cubicle next to us.

The two security bears have disappeared and I'm suddenly alone with Savage.

"I thought you weren't supposed to get out until Monday."

Savage puts his hands behind his head like he's leisurely sunbathing by a pool. The blanket slides down, exposing more tanned skin of his lower stomach. He's surprisingly well groomed for a wolf, with a neat scattering of hair trailing down beneath the blanket. Heat suffuses my body.

"Lyle said if we promised not to get into trouble, he'd let us out tonight."

And Lyle thought they'd keep their promise? Idiotic lion.

"Right," I deadpan. "And who did you coax into a fight?"

"*Coax.*" He says the word slowly, like he's testing it out for the first time. "I took Xander's headphones. The lions and a few others just got caught up in it." A grin

341

spreads across his face and I have to look away, busying myself by cleaning up the bloody gauze.

"And Xander did that to you?"

"He can do a lot worse, believe me. I gave the headphones back in the nick of time."

My anima does not like my animuses fighting with each other. But with males like these, it's probably a daily thing.

I narrow my eyes. "Do you not care about the others who got hurt?"

"No. It's their fault if they get in my way."

I sigh. "Why are you here? What do you want?"

He tuts at me like *I'm* the child. "Ask me nicely, and maybe I'll answer."

"Then we're done here." I make to turn away.

"No we're not." With a speed that's downright scary, he sits up and swings his legs around to sit at the edge of the table. "They always give me a sandwich. It's protocol. And I have to sign the release form."

Always? He's literally been here two weeks.

I take a step forward, bristling at his sheer audacity to be this light-hearted when he's done what he did to me.

My voice is a low hiss. "I should cut that off your finger." I point to the blood covenant tattoo. "You let my father mark you? You swore not to—" I can't even say it out loud.

"Fuck you," he finishes in a low voice. "I swore not to fuck you, Lia." He looks at the mark and my anima writhes with sorrow.

I can't even speak.

"We killed a lot of beasts on our way to you, Lia," he says, all too casually. "And I would kill many more."

I stare at him in disbelief as he hops off the table and, naked, saunters over to the mini fridge in the corner where we keep our snacks for the patients. There are many things that can help a beast recover, other than outright healing them. Sex is one, food is another. Savage's cock swings with each step and when he turns, I get a view of a perfectly taut ass. Gulping, I look away.

He takes a wrapped sandwich and brings it back to the table, casually draping the blanket back across his lap.

"Why are you so violent?" I say, shaking my head as he takes a massive bite. "How do you kill and hurt people so easily and not care?" I really expect him to scoff or ignore that completely, so I'm surprised when he answers seriously.

"I was made to be like I am. Cut and hammered, Scythe says. And our dad was the carpenter."

"Was your dad like…"

"Me?" His jaw clenches and he looks away. "In the ways of being a wolf, yes."

"How do you mean?"

"You have to be worse than them, to be better than them."

"That makes no sense."

He considers me with those piercing hazel eyes, and goosebumps erupt all over my body. I wish I could control the way he makes me feel when he looks at me. I desperately do.

As he muscles his way into my head, he shoves the

rest of the sandwich into his mouth and swallows it down.

"*I saw your anima, regina. And she was beautiful. I want to see what you look like when you let your tether go. Fully. Wild and free. And vicious. Wouldn't it be nice to be free? To feel that power in the tips of your claws? At the feathery ends of your wings?*"

I suck in a shocked breath. I can't. I would never...

"*I want to see it again.*" His voice is whisper soft. Reverent, almost. "*Let. It. Go.*"

"Savage—"

His mouth drops to my lips, and he lashes out so fast that I'm completely unprepared. He yanks me between his spread legs, crushing his mouth against mine. I squeal in protest as he captures my lower lip in between his own and sucks hard.

My body heats up even as I try to shove him away. My entire body tingles in delicious awareness even as I punch him in the chest. His powerful scent is in my nose, but we can't... I can't—

Guards rush in with Hope and Savage finally releases my lip, pushing me away from him. I stumble backward as Savage is tasered. He doesn't make a sound as he grimaces and crumples sideways onto the table.

I watch the scene in disbelief as Hope helps steady me. I gently press my fingers to my swollen lip, trying to push away the feeling of delicious dissatisfaction. I didn't want more. I didn't, damn it!

But Savage's eyes never leave mine. As his face is roughly pressed into the steel table, he laughs. "Worth it."

Chapter 34

Savage

Twelve years ago

Mum and Dad are screaming at each other again. It's loud and nasty, as always, but this time, Scythe doesn't roll his eyes at me. At thirteen, he's already broadening at the shoulder and developing muscle. My father only lets my mother trim his hair, and so it hangs in a long curtain of liquid silver to his lower back. He is already five foot ten, his jaw squaring off and his hands large and veined. When he comes with me to fights, female beasts shout things to him, and more often than not, male beasts too. He hates it, but Dad makes him come, parading him around like a prize bull.

"It's called marketing," Dad always says. "We need to show them the goods, Sky."

My brother keeps telling Dad that the c in Scythe

silent but Dad just keeps telling him he doesn't give a flying fuck.

As big as Scythe is, Dad is bigger, and I get the feeling he might *always* be. I train with Dad twice a day and he is really the devil in the ring. "I'm making a monster out of you, pup," he says, smashing my jaw with a hammer until my wolf fangs come out. "No beast except me will ever be able to beat you." We'll spar for a bit and then he'll proceed to beat the shit out of me. I heal fast, and we'll do it all over again in a few days.

I'm proud to say that it's working. Even though I'm only eleven, they have to put me with the teenage fighters because the other pups can't keep up with me and my sharp claws and teeth. Because it's not only Scythe who's tall now.

I make them into meat if Reuben doesn't pull me out of the ring. My dad laughs when that happens and pats me on the head. It's the only time he smiles at me and makes me feel warm inside my heart.

Scythe and Dad disappear for longer periods of time between my fights now. My mum pouts at them when they leave, but dad ignores her. I think maybe Scythe is fighting people too. He has pretty good reflexes because sharks have natural brutal instincts, but he never returns with bruises and broken bones like I always do.

But if it isn't fighting, what else is it? Scythe won't tell me, but he *does* share his secret money. He stashes the green notes away under the floorboards of his bedroom and uses it to buy his mum special creams for her dry skin and the food she likes, but we have to hide that from the other two parents.

Tonight's parent-fight is about something to do with Scythe because he sits on the couch pretending to watch *Home and Away,* but his shoulders are all tense and his hands are in fists, thick blue veins popping up all over his forearms.

"He's ours!" my mum screams. "I won't share—"

Dad backhands mum so hard she crashes to the floor with a yelp. I try to go to her, but Scythe clamps a hand on mine so tightly that I grumble under my breath and settle back on the couch. Mum is also a fighter, so she shakes herself and climbs to her feet. Her cheek is bright red, but she holds her ground and I'm proud of her.

"He's taking the client, and that's that," Dad snarls. "Let's go, you two."

It's a Saturday, so I have a fight today. I pick up my backpack and see that, weirdly, Scythe also pulls his school bag over his shoulder, but it has no books in it. He's allowed to go to school for now, but Dad says it will be his last year because 'he might get ideas'.

But when we get to the ring, in an abandoned ware-house on the outskirts of the city, Dad sits me down by the ring and goes off with Scythe. As I smear globs of Vaseline on my cheeks for the fight, I curiously watch them walk over to an anima/animus couple in the corner. The anima runs her hand down Scythe's arm and then touches the strands of his silver hair, smiling at him. She and Scythe are the same height, and I think the smile on her face is sort of ugly. The man is looking at Scythe like he's prey, and I don't like that at all. Before I know it, Scythe is walking off with them, his hand white around the strap of his backpack. I'm about to get up and see where they're going—I'm angry now and I don't even know why—but Dad returns and what he says to me makes me forget what I saw. "Listen, pup. You're going to rip out his throat tonight."

"W-What?" I stammer.

He gives me a look of feral warning that promises pain if I question him again. "Remember how I taught you about the arteries in the body?"

I list them off on my fingers. "Carotid, jugular—"

"Yeah, yeah. Those ones. You're going to rip out the ones in the neck. Quickly and properly, but only in the third round. You understand me?"

I look over at the fifteen-year-old boy I'm supposed to fight today. He's a python shifter (only the non-venomous snakes are allowed to fight), big and brawny, with meaty fists. It might even be a tough fight.

"That'll kill him, Dad."

"Yeah, it will, but it'll get us a lot of money." He catches someone's eye in the crowd and gives them a nod. I look over and see a tall man dressed in all black. He makes my skin go bumpy and I know him right away—the King of the Serpent Court.

Dad grips my shoulder painfully. "Do you understand me, pup? Toy with him for the first two rounds, then bring out your fangs like we practised, and tear out his neck."

I run my tongue over my teeth. One of them is loose

because my baby teeth are still coming out. I'm collecting them for the tooth fairy, even though I know it's Scythe who puts the coins under my pillow. He told me his mum knows the tooth fairy from under the sea, and I think Lily knows lots of weird and pretty people just like her, so he's probably telling the truth.

"Okay, Dad," I say.

When I do as I'm told, it's messy and tastes yuck. Someone screams, but it's not me. All I do is stare at the python and the colour spreading across the floor. My red crayons are not as bright as this. Red traffic lights are not as bright as this either. Then my dad is steering me away, and it's the first time in my memory that he hugs me.

Chapter 35

Aurelia

Tonight, I dream of Savage again, and what I see chills me to the bone. It's disturbing, to say the least, and I'm still processing what this means: that I'm seeing Savage's memories.

The worst of our kind make money fighting their pups in cage matches. I've seen teenagers fight, but never a child. I know beasts fight to the death, too, but making pups and cubs do that?

Savage killed and maimed people and just continues to live his life. I'm not sure what happened to his parents, but I have a feeling I won't like the answer.

The next morning is Saturday, and that means I have to see the bastard lion again.

After our previous altercation, my skin is positively itching at the thought of going back in there for another one-on-one session.

But as I come out of the shower to grab my clothes, I open my underwear drawer and stare.

It's empty.

All my underwear is missing. Like, gone. Including my pretty new thong. The drawer is empty except for my tampons and a plastic packet that I lift out.

"He didn't!" I screech like a cockatoo.

Minnie rushes over from where she was lighting incense at her altar and gapes at my drawer too.

"Do you think it was Savage who took your under-wear, or Scythe?" she asks, clearly trying not to laugh. "Honestly, it seems like something Savage would do. That and the chocolate give it away."

Holding up the bag of Freddo Frogs, I touch my still swollen lip, because of *course* he would. I groan, "Somehow, Xander and Scythe don't seem like the panty-stealing type."

"Anyway," Minnie continues. "Just buy more." To be honest, it's kind of disturbing that we're just used to Savage coming in here now. Just another day at Animus Academy. Murder, theft and chocolate.

But the one thing I'm thinking of that dominates my mind is: I simply can't go commando to a meeting with Lyle.

"We can't go to the village until Wednesday!" I groan.

Minnie makes a face. "Oh, shoot. You're right. So you're going to go a whole five days sans knickers?"

"My period's due at some stage," I groan. And I don't say that my pussy has been weeping every time I think about the psychopaths and that they're due to return to classes on Monday. While I can clamp down on my scent, the weeping pussy, I cannot. I need underwear like Minnie needs her pink folder.

"Message Theresa and tell her we have an emergency."

I do just that on our tablet, but the reply comes back with the fact that she knows I have a meeting with Lyle now and that I need to get permission from him.

"I think I'm actually going to cry." I throw myself on my bed. "How will I explain it to him?"

Minnie giggles. "Make something up! You have to go now, anyway. If you're late a second time, he might spank you."

Casting her a dirty look, I storm out of the room, her chortles following me.

I stomp down to the guards at the dorm entrance and two of them take me to Lyle's top floor office. But the trip there is excruciating because all I can think about is my pussy lips flying free in the wind and the fact that I sprinted out of his office that last time like a fool. The fact that he *ordered* me out like an insubordinate.

My clothes need to be washed—which we have assigned days to do them on—so all I have left is one of my *appropriate* dresses, if I don't want to wear the sexy ones I have planned for classes. It's deep blue to match my eyes, but far too nice for the likes of this school. I decide it will be the dress I'll wear to the trial. No harm in looking nice, right?

But the dress is more than *nice*, it shows a little cleavage, and I'm very happy with my decision when the elevator doors open and Georgia catches sight of me and *seethes*.

Yeah, lion-girl, I can dress with style too.

We now have a thing, Georgia and I. We've decided to hate each other. Her eyes drag up and down my body, but she makes no move to get up from her desk. So I leave my guards to wait, stalk past her with my nose in the air and knock on Lyle's door.

"Come in." His deep voice hits me right in the ovaries and I wonder how it would sound right up against my ear.

Shit. Focus.

I steel myself and open the door. Luckily, Lyle is busy with something on his desk, so I get a chance to collect myself in his striking presence. He's in a blue shirt and slacks today, as if on the weekend he lets himself off with the three-piece, though he looks no less impressive and sexy as all hell. I suddenly realise that we're almost matching. My dress is practically the same colour as his shirt.

My entire body heats up like I'm standing in an oven. The space between my legs throbs and I command my vagina to control herself.

I look away from him to his desk, where there is not a speck of dust nor pen out of place. The one thing that is a little odd however, is a small wooden, winged doll propped up against his pen cup. It's roughly carved, as if hewn by clumsy hands and the blue paint on it is faded and chipped as if small hands have held it for years. I wonder if it was a gift from a niece or nephew.

Lyle doesn't even look up at me when he says, "I'm glad to see you can read the time, Miss Aquinas."

After two weeks, I'm getting used to bantering with people now, and Minnie is an excellent verbal sparring partner. But I still can't look at him to give him lip, so I glance outside his window as I say, "Oh yes, Mr Pardalia. I can read numbers and everything."

From the side of my eye, I see him look up at me in mild surprise. His pen pauses above the piece of paper he's writing on and he stares at me for so long that I turn to look at him, brows raised. His features harden as he looks down to continue writing.

"We're going for a walk today," he says mildly. "I don't think you like sitting down."

I stiffen because how the fuck does he know that I don't want to sit so close to him? What do I even say to that?

"I sit down all the time."

He chooses to ignore that stupid, idiotic comment and gets to his feet. "Let's go." Grabbing a big black phone from his desk, he pockets it and nods to the door behind me. I turn and go right back out, heading towards the elevator, Henry making soothing sounds in my ear.

I *feel* him behind me. Like the midday sun, his heat warms my back, his fresh paper and male musk scent wafting around me. I want to wrap myself in it like I'm a letter inside an envelope and if Lyle could lick me shut, I'd be the happiest woman on earth. My anima slinks around my body, extremely happy we're going somewhere with this lion.

I realise I can't even blame Georgia for having the hots for him.

We get into the elevator without the guards and I suddenly realise how huge this man is. He takes up the whole space and I press myself up against the steel side wall to avoid touching him and grab Henry from my shoulder just for something to do. The space between my legs throbs mournfully.

Shit. Shit. Shit.

It's a chant, a prayer to the Wild Goddess for my sanity.

My anima is so desperate for my mates' touch that it's going off with a hair trigger at any man! Combine that with no underwear, and my labia are suddenly gliding along as I hurry out of the elevator.

I'm swearing so much internally that I don't realise he's asked me a question.

"Pardon?"

From his considerable height, he looks down at me in disapproval as he leads me outside. He opens the glass door with a flick of his telekinetic fingers, and holds it open for me as if the whole thing is dull.

He only pretends to be a gentleman. He's a real barbarian underneath.

"How was your week?" he asks.

"Great. Lots of fun." It's not a lie because Minnie and my new friends are a hoot and successfully distract me from my awful plight. Lyle makes a sound of disapproval.

Is he ever happy? Will his face split in two if he smiles? Hell, I'd probably split in two if he— I'm losing it, so I talk business. "I'd like to talk about what to expect at the trial."

"We have time for that later," he says dismissively. "I need to see the type of person you are. You need to prove yourself to me."

These statements suddenly feel extremely intimate. Prove myself? I've spent the last seven years trying to prove to myself and my father that I didn't deserve to be cast out. Bastard. I change the subject.

"I need access to the Village for emergency reasons."

"And what is the nature of this *emergency*?" I can actually hear the air quotes in his voice. His arrogance knows no bounds.

"Women's issues." That usually gets men to stop asking questions in movies. But apparently, Lyle is not a regular man—he has even *more* audacity.

"You can get sanitary products for free from the medical wing."

"Ah, yes. I know. Great idea. Innovative."

"So then, what is it?"

"I, um..."

He stops abruptly and turns to look at me. I actually pull to a stop and cross my arms. In the beast world, for a beast to do that is an antagonistic stance, indicating they are threatened, and remembering this, I uncross my arms, huffing at my misfortune. *Wild Mother, help me.*

"I need clothes."

He pointedly looks at my dress.

E.P. Bali

I bite the bullet. "I need underwear. Mine are gone."

Lyle stops breathing. I know, because a moment before, his shoulders moved dramatically up and down. After a second, his amber eyes seem to glow as he says, "What do you mean, *gone*?"

I shrug, avoiding his gaze, having no intention of telling him about my thief. "I seem to have lost them."

He remains silent until it's so uncomfortable that I'm forced to look at him. His face is marble. Tanned, beautiful, scary marble, and it makes my core quiver.

"Miss Aquinas," he warns.

I know I'm going to get a telling off by his 'deputy headmaster' tone.

"Yes?" I say innocently.

"A part of being a productive adult is communicating properly. Use your words. Explain to me."

"Don't talk down to me," I snap. "They're gone. I need more. That's all you need to know."

The space between us heats up and I know he's furious. I'm *sure* he's furious when he steps forward, towering over me. Is he even taller than Scythe or is it just his bad attitude?

"Miss Aquinas, if you take that tone with me again, you won't like what happens."

Minnie was right. I think he is going to spank me after all. I look up at him with my mouth open and I'm incredulous as I say, "What will happen?"

"Punishment."

As if that's a complete sentence! But he continues. "I don't tolerate disrespect."

360

I sigh at his chest. "You sound just like Scythe," I mutter and then freeze when I realise what I've just said.

Lyle stiffens. Slowly, I look up at him and try to deflect. "Can I get my panties or do you expect me to walk around without them for the rest of my sorry life?"

He just stares at me, those pretty eyes seeing right through me. Through my dress, through my organs, and right into my very being. Before I know it, my eyes are wandering over his face and I can't breathe at the intense masculine beauty. Those perfect angles of his nose and cheekbones...

Then I shake myself, because fuck, women must fawn over him all the time and I don't want to be a simpering idiot. I drop my gaze and stare at my cuticles as if I'm unbothered by him and his proximity.

"Is he talking to you?" his voice is whisper soft, but it's furious.

Instinctively, I take a step away, and Henry titters on my shoulder as if he knows there's an angry, powerful beast standing right in front of us. "Uh. No. Not really."

"This is the second time you've lied to me, Aurelia. You'll be punished for that."

I look up at him, exasperated, because I don't want to clean up anymore blood. "I'm here to talk about how to get out of this mess my father put me in. None of this is productive."

He rubs a thumb along his jaw, his shoulders visibly settling. He should get a nimpin too. I'm sure it would help him. But he says, "You're right."

Excuse me? I need to stop myself from gaping so

much because I'm going to get TMJ. But he continues the conversation like he wasn't just lethally angry.

"What do you want to get out of Animus Academy, Miss Aquinas?"

"I don't really know. I don't think I need to be here."

He makes a dismissive sound. "Where were you running to when I was hunting you? Did you have a plan or were you just seeing where the wind took you?"

So it's communication he wants? Well, communication is what he'll get. "I take that in high offence, Mr Pardalia. I've been planning my escape for years. I thought I'd be a healer and live a quiet life."

"Is that right?" The bastard sounds amused. "Why do you say 'escape?'"

Oops, why is he so sharp? Coming here, I didn't intend to share so much of a personal nature. Minnie knowing everything is bad enough, although I'm glad I told her. I stay silent, trying to figure out what to say. But he's relentless. "During the hunt for you, I took a visit to where you lived. Your Aunt Charlotte lied to me."

I freeze mid-step and he pauses to look back at me, intently watching me as if my face and body will give clues to what he wants to know. It's lucky that there are only guards around on their patrol, and there aren't any students to snigger at me.

"What did she say?" I ask slowly, proceeding to walk alongside him again.

"She said that you lived with her in the house. But I saw the... property at the back and got curious. She didn't stop me when I went to look at it."

Embarrassment crawls up my spine like acid. The vision of Lyle seeing where I lived—in my *hovel*, as Xander calls it—is truly awful. I didn't mind so much when the others saw it. But this refined beast who dresses like a European model and is responsible for this school? Mother, take me dead. I can't look him in the eye.

"Now, if I ask myself why a father would put his daughter in a place like that, I can only come up with one answer."

I swallow the lump in my throat. "And what's that?"

"You did something. It was punishment for something *you* did."

The backs of my eyes burn because I'm triggered. Massively.

Serpents are the most hated court of animalia kind. So hated that there was an effort to kill them all off in the '70s. They called it The Serpent Purge. A group of other orders got together and tried to eradicate them. It all happened because the king at the time was heavily using blood magic and poison, like he was addicted to it.

Because of this, my father has spent his whole life doing everything he can to turn that around. He's carefully constructed himself a reputation of being a kind and generous man. He goes to council meetings, buddies up with rich, influential people. Does illegal favours for them, often using me. If anyone suspects he's a power hungry, devious, conniving, sinister man, they ignore their instincts. In fact, Xander is the only one who openly expressed hate for him.

All I did to deserve my exile was genetically take after my mother.

So when Lyle Pardalia accuses *me* of being in the wrong, I want to cry. Instead, what do I do? I abruptly turn around and storm away.

As if it somehow confirms my guilt, he lets me.

Chapter 36

Savage

I'm soaping myself with my new Aurelia-scented liquid body wash, because obviously I had to get the same one as she just starting using, when a black energy hurtles down the corridor on the floor below. Fear spikes within the wolves of the building and I jump out of the shower, not bothering to put clothes on, suds still sliding down my abs when I step into the bedroom I share with my brothers. On the level below, every door of the dorm corridor slams shut, leaving it deserted. The beasts here have the good sense to flee. A fight between powerful beasts can get nuclear-level nasty.

The door crashes open—no, it *flies* into the room completely torn from its hinge—and standing there with a look of pure murder in his whiskey-coloured eyes is Lyle Pardalia.

Scythe and Xander are already on their feet. Eugene gives a scared squawk from where he's perched on my headboard.

"What's wrong, Lyle?" Scythe says in that heavy, calm rasp of his.

Lyle can't even speak he's so angry, and it makes my hackles rise, a growl beginning in the depths of my chest. He's looking at me like he wants to fight, his fists clenched, his eyes on fire.

I like that look. It means I'll get to taste blood.

"What did he do now?" Xander puts out his joint, ready to defend me in his own way.

But Lyle only has eyes for me, and the challenge in them sets me off. I'm never matched in a fight, but I think rabid Lyle might just be a beast who actually stands a chance. I shift on instinct. My joints pop, my bones change shape, fur bursts from my skin, and I relish that sweet burn because I was born to be a wolf, and no one does it better than me.

Landing on my four massive paws, I snap at Lyle, my long, loud growl filling the room.

But our deputy headmaster doesn't move an inch, and his fear doesn't perfume the air for my pleasure like it should.

"Change back, wolf," he snarls. "Or I will string up your carcass from the ceiling."

Well, now I'm so fucking excited I could get hard. But my brother goes and ruins it.

"You won't." Scythe takes a step forward and tries to poke my brain with his psychic power, but I don't let him. I'm too angry. This lion has been seeing *my* Aurelia in private sessions, so I'm ready to mutilate him. But my brother is a ruthless bastard and knows me too well because he slams into my brain and commands, *"Control, brother."*

Growling, I shift back, remaining in a low crouch on the floor, my eyes on Lyle's perfect face, imagining his face would be even prettier with glistening red slashes.

"You've been stealing her underwear," Lyle states down at me.

I go still and so do Scythe and Xander. They both turn to look at me at the same time and I sigh, standing up.

"Oh, is that all?" I drawl, leaning on my dresser where I've hidden my loot in a scent-proof box because they're *mine*.

"What the fuck, Sav?" Xander scoffs like the child of nepotism he is.

"Don't tell me you've never done it." I wave my hand dismissively.

"It stops now, Savage," Lyle orders. "Get them out. I'll return them to her."

My voice is my low octave alpha growl. *"Like fuck you will."*

"I've never seen him like this," Xander says, shaking his head in disappointment. "You've been sniffing her underwear every night, haven't you? Feral fucker."

"If you take them away from me, I'm going to tear your school apart," I say quietly, meaning every word because I only got them last night. And I wasn't going to sniff them *all* the time, just hold them to my chest *some*times.

"Savage, I will put you in a cage."

369

"No one's going in a cage right now." Scythe's voice is sharp as he strides towards me, getting in my face. "Give them back, brother. They belong to her. You can't have her. She doesn't want you. You're clinging on to a ghost."

He slices my chest open with his words and my head hangs in defeat. He's right. He's fucking right and I've been rabid about her this whole time. She's going back to her father and I'm just *clinging on to a fucking ghost.*

"Can I keep one?" I ask.

Scythe turns to stare down Lyle, and gives me a firm "yes."

I sigh and turn around to pull out the drawer, reverently taking out the black scent-safe box. Shielding it with my body, I open it to take out one pair, quickly shoving the pink material back into the drawer before tossing the box over my shoulder.

Lyle catches it easily with one paw. "Well done, Savage. We'll talk about your behaviour tomorrow. And you'll be in black shackles from Monday."

Hil-fucking-arious.

Rolling my eyes, I exchange a glance with Xander because if Scythe has never been able to tame me, how is this guy going to?

Before he leaves, Lyle tosses a live grenade over his shoulder. "She came to me today without any underwear on and I could smell her the entire time."

Roaring, I launch myself at him, but my brothers tackle me to the floor. They have to pin me down with the combined weight of their heavy bodies and all I can do is watch the lion's shiny black shoes stride out. For the next hour, I rage while Scythe strokes my hair, trying to get me to calm down like he used to when we were kids. Xander is quiet and occasionally pats me on the back in between his quips. Even Eugene comes to peck at my head.

Eventually, my thundering brain calms down, though my heart still aches like it's been branded.

It *has* been branded in the shape of my regina's name.

"Sav," Scythe says gently in my ear. "You know we have to give her back, don't you?"

My animus whines, *"mine"*, but the blood vow on my finger throbs as if it's reminding me that I'll literally die if we don't fulfil the vow.

"I hate her," I bite out.

Xander sits on my back and takes a long draw of his joint. He blows out the smoke. "Don't we all."

Chapter 37

Aurelia

The next morning, in a show of solidarity, Sabrina and Stacey come to get dressed in our room. Connor promises to meet us for breakfast, and Raquel point blank refuses to join my new venture. But even that can't stop me from feeling excited.

Years ago, I bought a lingerie set for myself off a super cheap website, but that was as far as it went as I never had money to burn. Whoever is in charge of my new stipend is surely going to be grateful that I'm using it well.

Minnie and I already chose what we were going to wear last night, with Sabrina's approval. Our leopard friend wears her new bodycon dress in her favourite leopard print and matches it with shiny black stilettos. I don't know how she's going to walk around campus all day with those on, but she's confident in them, and paired with red lipstick, looks like a fifties pin-up model.

Charlotte wants to be lolita-type cute, so she wears a

ruffled lemon-yellow playsuit she altered herself with knee-length white socks with lace ruffles. She even adds a white bow to her high ponytail for a bit of show.

Minnie, on the other hand, wears a deep pink skin-tight dress paired with gold hoops and gladiator-style lace-up sandals. We help her curl her hair so she can wear it in a long ponytail, and by the end, she looks like a little dessert. There's that lioness in third year she wants to impress, and I know she'll be head over heels.

Raquel doesn't want the attention, but in solidarity, wears sexy fishnets and black denim cut-offs that show off their spectacular legs.

And me?

Fire engine red, skin-tight matching set—check.

Push-up bra—check.

Super short hem that shows my legs—check.

Skimpy crop top—check.

Commando—against my will, but check, and at least I'll have no panty lines (I'm all about positivity these days).

Make-up on point—check.

Lastly, I dress it down with brand new white sneakers and straighten my hair so I can wear it sleek and loose down my back.

Do I want some attention? Not so much, but I want to prove a point even more. I want to show them that we aren't frazzled by what they did. In short, it's a big ol' *fuck you*.

No matter how hard they try, they *aren't* going to get me. They don't have their powers and Theresa told me that they've put the guard numbers back up. *And* I'm not about to go to prison without having my fun first.

As we exit our dorm, we get a couple of raised eyebrows from the other girls, but plenty of the animas dress up here anyway. It's in our nature to show off in front of the animuses to try and lure in our mates. I just haven't done it so blatantly yet.

The dining hall is another matter though, and even as we walk up to the outside doors, the guards standing either side exchange a dark look and adjust their guns.

A butterfly in my stomach moment, for sure.

Sabrina tosses her head, and the five of us enter the dining hall with swaggers and smirks.

The buzz of the busy hall fades into silence.

I know at once that I'm not prepared. These boys are thirsty on a bad day, and Minnie and I are not used to the level of attention we get.

We get catcalled straight away, and one of the wolves even howl.

"Shiiiittt, ladies!" someone calls.

"Come sit with us, Flight Risk!" another shouts.

"Mouse, bring those muffins here!"

There is more than one feral bark and growl as we walk up to the buffet, trying to ignore eye contact.

But the thing about the buffet line is that we now have our asses to the hall.

Sabrina and Stacey are preening and definitely in their element.

Connor comes waltzing up to us in a tight red dress shirt, his long black hair straightened and loose, and a massive grin on his face. His canary yellow nimpin is chattering, but not excitedly. Our nimpins respond with squeaks as if they're complaining about our lack of self-preservation.

"Get used to it, animas," Connor sniggers, slapping Sabrina's ass when she happily sticks it out for him. "You've just put a signal on your back and every beast is going to come calling. Small pool and all." He grins at someone approaching from behind me, and I scent a lion animus.

"Hello, ladies," comes a deep, seductive voice. I turn to find a stunning broad-chested male standing there with pretty green eyes gleaming with interest as he hones in on Minnie. "What's your name?" He holds out his large hand.

Minnie shyly gives him her hand, and he leans down to kiss it. "Minnie," she says softly.

He smiles, though his eyes are predatory on her cleavage. "I'm Ashton. Please make my week and sit with me."

Oh, he's smooth—so smooth that if I didn't see him punch another lion so hard he had to be taken to the hospital, just for stealing his fork, I'd have encouraged my best friend to go with him.

"Oh, I..." Minnie glances at me, then Connor.

Connor catches on immediately and pulls Minnie away. "We eat together," he says hastily. "Another time, Ashy."

Ashton frowns but says nothing more, stalking off back to his table where he's met with stifled laughter.

"I like your hair," comes another deep voice. This

time, we turn to find three wolves eyeing us from their front-row table. They are all over six feet with five o'clock shadows in the way this pack likes to present themselves. The one who spoke has a nose ring and says, "Wait... Aurelia, right?"

I force a smile. "That's me."

They're silent for a moment and I realise they're having a telepathic conversation with each other. Then, abruptly, they turn back in their seats away from me. "Sorry, uh... nevermind."

Sabrina makes a disgusted sound. "Pussies."

The males freeze and my stomach drops in my gut as I fight the urge to smack the leopard. All three males immediately turn back around. "What did you just say?" The leader's voice is low and dangerous.

"Ignore her," Minnie says quickly. "She was talking to me."

"No she fucking wasn't." His nostrils flare and he points a dirt-ridden finger at me. "Savage claimed you already. We're not going anywhere near you."

My mouth drops open as they get up and move away from us. "Wait, what?"

Minnie says. "No they didn't!"

The wolves don't say anything as they leave, heading to the far side of the dining hall.

Raquel, standing behind me, clears their throat. "Uh, you d-don't remember w-when you were on the g-grass, naked, and Savage l-lay on top of you? In wolf-language, that's a c-claiming. As far as all t-the wolves in this place are c-concerned, you're the k-king wolf's p-property." They shrug. "We have a t-telepathic notice b-board."

I stared at her for a moment as the memory of Savage's giant, terrifying black wolf's face hung over me, his powerful body warm on top of mine, his scent heady and intoxicating. Within the context of being kidnapped, I thought he was just detaining me. Apparently, I was wrong. Wolves are the most social order, and their unwritten social rules are followed by the book. Savage, being considered the strongest wolf here, means that no wolf is going to challenge his claim.

"Shit, I'll have to up my game," I mutter. So attention from the wolves is out, but screw them, there are plenty of other beasts here.

Raquel gives me an incredulous look, but I'm determined as all hell.

We get our breakfasts—bacon and eggs for me, Minnie gets an acai bowl—and we head to our table where Raquel sits down with their massive stack of pancakes.

"H-How are we going t-to get anything done with a-all this?" Raquel waves their fork to indicate the staring males on every side.

Minnie scopes out the hall. *"They're* not here yet."

"I-I'm sure we'll know w-when they get h-here," Raquel says darkly.

Sure enough, halfway through my scrambled eggs, I feel them. The proximity of my mates advances like a blazing fire sweeping through dry brush. It's at once terrifying and alluring. And just like a bushfire, its smoke makes my breath seize in my throat.

My entire body shivers and I rub at my bare thighs. Minnie, sitting opposite me, notices right away and she nods at the entrance to the hall. Raquel, Minnie and Connor on the side of the table that can see the entrance, all stiffen.

"Don't turn around," Connor advises firmly. "Stay strong, Lia. They can't hurt you."

I nod gratefully at him, apparently the only one with any sense in our group because Sabrina and Stacey turn around to look.

The lioness swears and I breathe deeply to contain the butterflies flapping up a hurricane in my abdomen. I *love* my outfit and they're not going to ruin my day. In fact, their reactions will *make* my day. That's one point for me and no points for them. I'm the top dog on this leaderboard.

Breathe. Just fucking breathe, Aurelia.

The dining hall falls quiet in the wake of their entrance. As if someone is turning down the volume knob and turning up the tension one. The room was positively rowdy just moments before, but now it's reduced to a tense muttering as the male beasts avoid eye contact to be respectful.

Within moments, they come into my view.

They walk down the centre aisle with a cloud of darkness shrouding them. I swear no one in the hall breathes or blinks as they make their way to their usual table with

Scythe in the lead, prowling with his plate of raw fish. None of them so much as look my way, and I don't look up from my food until they are well past our table.

But my anima, now a force greater than me, shoves my head up to look upon them: three of the other parts of my being.

They look impeccable as always, and not as if they've spent an entire week in a cage. Freshly shaved, recent haircuts, and not a wrinkle in their usual dark clothing. The only new addition is that Scythe and Xander have thick black metal around each wrist. Magic dampening shackles.

This means that Xander gets the most side-eyes stares because what we see—or don't see—is terrifying. Xander is not just blind. He has *no* eyeballs at all in his sockets, with red scars around them as if they've literally been cut out.

My anima screams at the realisation.

Xander's shoulders tense the barest fraction as if he hears it. He's back to normal within seconds, but I'm so caught up in trying not to cry and scream and leap out from my chair at the fact that—

Someone has brutalised my mate.

"Lia!" Minnie hisses. She leans over the table to grab my hand because she's the only one who realises what's happened. "Lia, stop," she growls with a little push of her power behind her voice, and it snaps me out of my rage and shock. I realise that Henry has been violently pecking at my earlobe.

"Breathe, Lia." Stacey grabs my other hand and squeezes. "Come on, you can do it. You're safe with us."

I blow out a steady breath as Stacey squeezes my left hand, Minnie digs her nails into my right and Henry pinches my ear with his beak. The pain grounds me and I nod at them in thanks.

Henry squeaks softly, his reminder for how I should pace my breathing.

The healer in me wonders how something like Xander's injury could be fixed, if at all, and I know the answer. Unless you're a mythical starfish shifter, you can't grow back entire organs or body parts.

Despite not having any magic to see with now, Xander still manages to take his seat with his back toward me with no trouble. He seems not to need eyes at all.

Savage and Scythe sit at the table and are soon joined by their entourage of scary beasts, including the Siberian tiger Yeti and the huge, bearded wolves.

Slowly, the dining hall seems to relax now that we know no one is going to be maimed, and the talking resumes again at a low murmur. Our anima table is so silent that I can hear Minnie's erratic breathing as we finish breakfast and Gertie's chattering in her ear. We're all getting up in an unspoken, unanimous agreement to leg it out of the hall when a brazen hyena decides to shoot his shot.

"Going so soon, ladies?" he says, rubbing his hands like a villain from a black and white movie. I want to point and tell him that if he wants to learn how to be really evil, he should go to the mafia table, but he just starts blabbing about some party on Friday night.

Someone drops a plastic cup at the other end of the dining hall and then everything moves slowly.

Like a revolving clown at a fair, my head swivels of its own accord towards said mafia table. Minnie and the animas follow the sound, too.

We watch as all the blood drains from Savage's handsome face and he goes *white* as plasterboard. His pupils blow out, engulfing his hazel irises completely, taking me in from head to thigh. His empty hand is poised in midair as if he was taking a sip from his cup and dropped it on the way there.

It's then that Scythe, his silver hair catching the morning light like pure starlight, turns in his chair to look at me. When he does, his ice-blue eyes, too, become consumed by his pupils.

Minnie giggles nervously under her breath, but I can't stop looking at my mates. The entire room, including the babbling hyena, disappears until it's just the four of us.

Xander turns to look at me, his nostrils flaring, his head cocked as if he's listening to something. I'm not sure how much he can 'see', but he knows something is up.

A logical part of me remembers I came here with something to prove. These bastards tried to abduct me, and Savage threatened Minnie.

I make the executive decision to turn my head in dismissal of them and then proceed to turn my body towards the hyena. The spell is broken, and I feel like I've surfaced from a deep dive.

"Did you say party?" I ask in a sassy voice, popping my hip. My Aunt Charlotte would be so proud.

The hyena runs a hand through his oily black hair as his eyes stop at my cleavage and he nods. "Yeah, I was saying—"

But I don't get to hear him because a spear of telepathy is thrown right at me and Savage's voice is an assault to my brain.

"Get rid of him, regina, or I promise you, his intestines will be in my teeth in five fucking seconds."

My heart thunders under my ribs as I slowly turn to glare at Savage. His teeth are clenched so hard I'm surprised he's not crushing them to powder. Scythe's eyes are pure predator on me and he's not even blinking. I swear I can see the shark in him *moving* in there.

"Five. Four." Savage's counting is a low, menacing drone.

Wait, is he serious?

"Three."

Oh shit, he *is* serious.

As much as I hate this, I can't let this guy die because of me. That'll be the second hyena in just as many months and I can't have that blood on my hands.

"Bye!" I say to the still-chatting hyena, physically grabbing his shoulders, turning him around and shoving him away. His friends hoot with laughter as he returns to his table, head hanging in dismay.

"Good girl," Savage says. *"But you've touched him. Now Xander is going to have to cauterise his skin for us."*

"No," I breathe out loud.

The girls standing around me are looking between my mates and me, bewildered. Minnie's hand flies to her mouth.

But Savage nods slowly, once, then picks up his steak and continues to eat. Scythe, however, remains staring at me.

"Fuck, that's scary," Sabrina mutters.

Connor prods at her shoulder, "Let's get the fuck outta here, animas."

"Say no more." Raquel grabs Minnie's and Stacey's arms and hauls our friends out along with the others. I hurry after them, feeling eyes on us as we leave. There are a few snide mutters made in our wake, but I can't even hear them because Savage's dark voice is still ringing in my brain.

Chapter 38

Savage

What the fuck. What the fuck. No. Yes. I mean, no? My regina is a goddess and I want to cover her body and shove my cock so deep into her that she screams my name. I want to pull her into my lap and bite on her neck hard enough to leave a permanent mark so everyone in this fucking school knows she's mine.

"*Calm down,*" Xander says irritably through our bond. "*Someone tell me what the fuck happened.*"

I don't—*can't* say anything because I'm too busy obsessing over Aurelia's ass as she flees the hall.

Shoving down my instinct to chase, I flash Xander a mental image of our regina's outfit. His fork pauses on the way to his mouth and he makes a surprised noise.

"*She looks amazing,*" I say.

"*Lyle really should have shackled you.*" Xander says, ignoring me. "*And Scythe is in shark mode, He hasn't taken a breath for two minutes now.*"

Wolves and birds usually get free passes with magic dampeners because we can't attack with our gifts. Xander resumes shovelling his bacon into his mouth in the most gentlemanly way possible as I turn my attention to my brother. Scythe is staring at the dining hall door even though there's no one there. And, fuck, he's still not breathing.

"Brother. The blue fairy has left the chat."

But Scythe says nothing. He's preternaturally smooth as he gets to his feet and I know his prey drive is activated.

"Oh, fuck," I mutter out loud, getting up to follow him.

Scythe's prey drive is worse than mine. Worse than anyone I've ever met, actually, *including* in Blackwater.

"What is it?" Yeti says, alert for anything. The wolves shift uncomfortably.

I nod to indicate Scythe, who's walking, his head lowered, shoulders a little hunched, *stalking* after Lia. Tracking her. Yeti's face pales.

The males in the tables around us all freeze as they recognise what this is.

"We'll handle it," Xander sighs, following me. *"It's because of the giant red flag she's wearing."*

Scythe is already out the door, so we jog to catch up. "Ah, fuck it *is* the red," I smirk at him. I'm ready for a fight and missed out just moments ago when Lia saved that hyena's life, so I'm pumped and ready to handle Scythe.

The girls are nowhere to be seen in the corridor, but

we know we're due for a nine a.m. class on, well, wouldn't you know, interacting with marine beasts. Though her scent is not in the air, as usual, Scythe is following Lia's blood itself and I signal to the Forklift Brothers to follow, just in case. Hell, we might actually need the help this time.

"Ready?" Xander asks, his voice an octave lower as, even with the shackles on, his dragon comes out a little.

"Not yet," I say. "I want Lia to have a look."

He chuckles evilly. *"You just want to see her do the thing again."*

"I mean, yeah," I say, scratching my jaw. *"I still think I imagined it."*

"Wishful thinking, more likely."

I'm not convinced of anything at this stage. But I have to admit: add everything about Aurelia together and it's suspicious.

We enter the lecture hall and my eyes find our regina instantly because her group is the first here. Her breasts are nothing but the sweetest, softest, mouth-watering mounds over the red crop top and I salivate instantly. Pavlov's dog, eat your heart out. I'm so aroused that I almost miss Scythe heading up the wooden stairs towards her.

Xander chuckles because Raquel sees Scythe's glazed eyes and shouts, leaping off their seat.

We take our cue and I take a running jump right onto Scythe's back. He roars and I bellow dramatically back, punching him right in the head.

But my brother's head is made of titanium because he

doesn't blink and proceeds to fall backwards to body slam me to the floor. His mating mark is blazing and I get to say a little, "oh fuck" as I realise that this is not an ordinary prey drive, but a shark's *mate* drive, which is supposed to be a thousand times worse according to Scythe himself.

"Xander?" I choke out. He's actually managed to wind me. "Now might be a good time to get in here!" Scythe turns around and throws a fist at my jaw. I see stars as it lands.

"You look like you're handling it, Sav," Xander says casually.

"Fuck you!" I shout, and then say,"*Look at his mating mark.*"

"*I can't see it, you fuckwit,*" Oh, good point. "*But he smells different.*"

Xander falls heavily on top of Scythe, body slamming the both of us, and I'm wheezing instantly. There's only one solution to this problem and we both know it.

With his magic out of action, it's just pure blood and violence as Xander punches Scythe on the head from the back and I go at him from the front. We then grapple to get into a better position so Xander can get behind him to choke him out.

"We have an audience," Xander mutters as he rolls Scythe on top of himself and elbow chokes him from behind, while I hold his arms down. There's a purely rabid struggle for minutes on end because Scythe can go ages without oxygen, but without his magic, thankfully, he eventually goes limp and I get to jump up.

I look around the room and see the animas all on their feet, staring down at us from their wooden lecture seats with horrified faces. Minnie has a pink water bottle beside her. "Minnie mouse, sweetie-pie," I coo. "If you toss me that water bottle, I'll forgive you for attacking me."

The tiger cub gapes at me in the cutest kitty cat way, and Aurelia crosses her arms. "Fuck you, Savage. I'm still waiting for *my* apology."

"Mother Wolf, you're gorgeous when you're angry." And I do mean it because her cheeks are flushed, her skin is glowing, and I get to see all of that delicious thigh that's begging for my tongue to lick it up and up and up... Then I remember that everyone else can see her thighs and I turn around angrily at the crowd waiting to enter the lecture hall behind the Forklift Brothers.

"Water!" I snap.

Someone tosses me a plastic water bottle and I snatch it out of the air and open it. I dump it all over Scythe's face and he wakes up with a gasp.

"Shit," he splutters. "Did I—"

"*Yeah, brother,*" I say as Xander saunters up the stairs to choose our seats. "*Full on mate drive.*"

"*Why didn't you get me earlier?*" he says irritably, getting to his feet. The water makes his silver hair glow even more under the downlights. He fits right into this medieval-looking hall.

I glance at Aurelia and he knows right away why. "*Asshole,*" he mutters. "*But good job.*"

That's my brother, always giving credit where credit

is due. I take a valiant bow in front of the audience and the wolves obediently clap for their king.

We take our seats up high, where we get a good view of Aurelia and the Forklift Brothers allow everyone else to file in. Lyle Pardalia brings up the rear. I watch as his nostrils flare. His eyes immediately flick down to where Scythe's blood spots the carpet. The corner of his mouth presses in annoyance before flicking to Aurelia and then right to Scythe, whose black eye is starting to form. It'll be gone in a day, but it's still evidence of the altercation.

It's going to look real pretty in about thirty seconds.

"Welcome to today's session," Lyle booms from the lectern. "Living with marine beasts is a new course we're able to start this year, courtesy of one of our students, Scythe Kharkorous."

Everyone shifts in their seats with interest, and lo-and-behold, the only person with balls big enough to actually look at Scythe is our regina.

I decide I like playing with her now that I know I can get into her mind. *I know your secret,* I whisper to her, sounding creepy as fuck.

Xander hears the telepathic waves in the air and sighs, knowing it's me. But my regina says nothing. *"Also, it's rude to stare."* She turns away, pink-cheeked, and I instantly miss her.

Lyle finishes his speech about how grateful he is about Scythe, completely pretending that he didn't just have us locked in a cage for several days. My brother exhales through his nose and stalks back down the stairs to the lectern.

As one of things we have to do to make up for trying to kidnap Lia, Scythe agreed to give his talks to the different year levels of the school. Who would have thought that our boss lion would use *education* as a bargaining chip? Weird beast. I still don't like him.

Scythe clears his throat, as he has everyone riveted just by breathing. My brother is a stunning creature with his silver hair, porcelain skin, sharp cheekbones and alien beauty. It's not often land beasts get to see his kind, let alone permission to look at him for a good fifteen minutes. Scythe used to *hate* getting stared at and his looks had once been the absolute bane of his existence, but once we were free of our parents, he made sure that the only way anyone ever looked at him again was with fear, not desire. As a child, I felt lucky to have him as my brother and that feeling hasn't changed.

His rasp is mesmerising as he speaks. A slideshow with ocean pictures runs of its own accord as he talks about land-sickness, what it's like to swim in the deep parts of the ocean and breathe underwater, what he eats, and how his teeth randomly fall out only to be replaced by another within days. He also talks about land psychosis and how it's really scary for marine beasts to have it, like your worst nightmares have become real and that we need better ways of keeping those beasts safe.

If we hear about a marine beast on land, Scythe tends to have them monitored in case they need to be saved. In which case, we scoop them up into a portable tank we had specially made years ago. It's pretty rare, but when it happens, those beasts need help quickly.

At the end, Lyle has people ask questions, though everybody is too scared to ask him anything. To my surprise, Minnie Mouse raises her tiny hand. Scythe's lip quirks in amusement as he nods to her.

She clears her throat. "How, uh... How come you're not crazy?"

I'm surprised by her guts, but am more interested to see how Scythe will answer this one.

"Some would say I *am* mad." The room is quiet, but he cracks an uncharacteristic smile and everyone gives tiny chuckles of relief. He runs a hand over his silver hair and a couple of the girls sigh as it catches the halogens in the room, sparkling like liquid light. "Honestly, I don't know why I haven't had the land psychosis. I think having a wolf for a father might have helped stabilise my genes. That pairing is unusual, so I think my dad might have just been dominant enough to override it. I guess we'll never know."

His eyes flick to me as he says this. I know the reason why Scythe stayed sane and it has more to do with our father than anyone will ever know.

The first question clearly gives the crowd courage because a she-wolf at the front of the room asks, "Is it true you can see spirits and ghosts? Could you see my mum if she was around?"

Scythe takes this question seriously because sprits don't like fucking around with him. "I can. But if they're the troublesome sort, they... leave when I come along." Run, he means. Or float, whatever ghosts do. "If they are looking to send a message, they usually don't choose me to do it, or I send them away. I don't like them hanging around."

Everyone goes quiet at this until a male taipan I've had my eye on has the nerve to ask, "Is it true that sharks always feel the ocean, wherever they are?"

Scythe nods. "Yes, we feel water wherever we go. I know exactly where and how far away the ocean is from wherever I am. Even in this room, I can feel the water in your bottles... even the blood inside your bodies. I can feel it and track it. Manipulate it if I wanted to."

Xander and I smirk as the entire room goes still at this dark revelation and Xander laughs darkly under his breath.

Lyle strides forward and quickly says, "Everyone thank Scythe for his time today."

Everyone rushes to clap.

Chapter 39

Xander

We head to our next class, which is cooking skills in the student kitchen. Lining up at our steel benches, we watch the red-haired tiger chef show us how to make a Pad Thai.

Savage gives me a detailed description of what the snake girl is wearing and what she's doing through our mating bond. I might not be able to see her outfit with my own eyes, but I can hear the movement of new material across her bare skin easily enough. That soft scrape also tells me that she's wearing no underwear. But I don't tell Savage because he's driving me insane as it is. Having her submitting under him that day we tried to kidnap her has really driven him off the rails.

"It hugs her ass like a dream and that push-up bra is giving me a second life, I swear. I would kill a man just to pull that skirt down and be ears deep in that sweet pussy. I need to taste her properly, you know? It was great in astral form, but in real life it'll be something else."

Unfortunately for me, I have to turn my Tibetan throat singing down for now. When I'm without my magical sight and physically blind, it's necessary because the sound waves bouncing off the objects in the room give me an echolocation sort of 'sight'.

I'm definitely not attracted to the snake girl, even in her new outfit, but with the mental images Savage keeps sending me, I have to admit the other males don't know what to do with themselves around her and the other animas.

Disgusted with this revelation, I write down the recipe of the dish we're supposed to be making because Savage will have no idea with how little attention he's been paying.

The chef starts barking orders and the Forklift Brothers have to separate two lions fencing with meat cleavers when I nudge aside Savage to get the wok out. They've put the rest of the ferals with the main group and there are, let's just say, teething issues.

Savage discreetly adjusts himself as I set the wok on the stove. His eyes haven't left the snake girl's body or face the entire time, and it's starting to piss me off.

Scythe shifts in warning as if he thinks our brother wolf is going to hump the snake girl at the first opportunity, as if he didn't almost try to eat her himself not long ago.

When I first learned that we didn't have to kidnap her, I had a moment of relief. Somehow, sitting here and watching her, I still feel uneasy. Like the lava burning under my skin wants to burst out of me. It's annoying as all hell.

"Look at her handle that knife. She's so pretty," Savage sighs at the snake girl, who's currently giggling over something stupid with her little tigress friend.

"If you don't shut the fuck up, I'm cutting your dick off," I snarl. "I'm trying to make Pad Thai."

And then all at once, everything turns to into bedlam.

I hear the snake girl bend over to take something out of the cupboard below the counter. At the same time, a serpent, a taipan, jabs his friend and whispers, "Take a look at that," pointing at the snake girl's ass. By the sound of it, her lower ass cheeks are bare for all to see.

Naturally, every animus in the room almost breaks their necks to look.

Savage lets out a sound of animalistic fury I've never heard come from him before. Snake girl snaps straight, but before anyone can do anything, Savage is brandishing a carving knife and leaping over the counter toward the taipan. The snake runs for it and because the room is full of long kitchen benches, Savage has to chase him, weaving all around the kitchen. The taipan shifts into his snake form. Chaos breaks out as everyone rushes for the door and the chef screams at Savage to stop.

But my wolf brother is out of his mind with rage as he chases the snake around the maze of the kitchen. Scythe and I watch on and I chuckle a little, because for me, there's nothing better than watching a snake get murdered. Just when I was having an off day, too.

The Wild Gods are gracious, sometimes.

All at once, the snake gets it in his head that he's going to use a human shield and slithers straight for our regina, standing stricken like a doe by her bench. The serpent lunges behind her, just as Savage screeches to a halt.

Lia raises a small paring knife just before he can lunge around her and says a stern and low. "*No.*"

Savage freezes on the spot and, to my utter bewilderment, drops his knife. It clatters to the floor and Lia and Savage just stare at each other like time is frozen for them. I don't hear any movement except the slither of the taipan as he escapes the kitchen. Next to me, Scythe stops breathing again.

"I can't believe how violent you are, Savage," Lia says in a low, calm voice. "You need to stop it."

Savage lets out a slow, measured exhale that tells me he's coming to his senses. "Give me a kiss and I will."

I could knock him out right now.

"No!" snake girl says incredulously. "Now, turn around and go back to your bench before someone gets hurt, *yet again.*"

To my radical surprise, Savage does as she asks, and he comes stomping back up to me. The nimpin on Aurelia's shoulder gives her a tiny reassuring chirp, and she pets him back. Her movements are so quiet and I realise for the first time that Aurelia isn't wearing any jewellery. Now that I think about it, I've never seen her in anything except a simple pair of cheap crystal studs. It's pathetic, honestly. I have so much gold and silver I should really let her have some.

I shake that thought immediately out of my mind because what the hell? Savage is quiet as he comes up next to me, but the chef is fuming so badly I'm surprised there's no smoke coming from his ears.

"You!" he cries. "To the deputy—"

"It was just a bit of fun," Scythe rasps in a voice that won't be argued with. "Leave it, Hector."

Scythe is acquainted with all the staff here, so the tiger immediately drops his case and leaves the kitchen to bring the other students back to where I can hear them all cowering in the room next door. Lia turns her back to us, her breathing a little shallow, as if she's coming to terms with what she's just done.

Savage is frowning in disbelief. *"Did she just regina-order me?"*

I snarl, *"Yes, and your little bitch-ass complied."*

Chapter 40

Aurelia

"This day keeps getting crazier and crazier," Minnie says, smothering a yawn as we sit down for lunch.

"I t-told you guys," Raquel says. "You shouldn't b-be t-taunting them like this, Lia. A shark's p-prey drive is no j-joke, and it was the s-scariest thing I've ever s-seen."

"Amen," mutter Stacey and Sabrina.

"No m-more red," Raquel warns.

"What would he have done if he'd gotten to Lia?" asks Minnie.

"Let's hope we never find out," I mutter darkly. Because hell, what does an animus want with their regina? I cast an eye over to a table full of lions where Yana, our fellow first year anima, is sitting on the lap of her rex, while she feeds him potato chips. His hand is on her thigh, stroking slowly up and down. The other animuses give them jealous looks now and again.

The sudden image of Scythe pulling my skirt up and

feasting on my pussy takes me by surprise and I almost fall off my chair.

"And what the fuck happened in Home Economics?" Sabrina hisses. "One second Savage was about to murder Cheston, and then the next second, he's standing with his tail between his legs at his bench?"

"I don't even know!" I try to parse what I did. "Cheston ran right towards me and I recognised him from my father's court. We played together as kids. He was nice to me. I... remembered that and just raised my knife and said *stop*."

"And he just did it?" Minnie levitates a cupcake from the stand at the buffet and it shoots it to our table, where she catches it in one hand. What a useful skill. "Dear Goddess, he obeyed you." She gives me a significant look because we both know I *regina commanded* him. There was a sort of power to my voice, and it was a completely foreign feeling.

Sabrina swears as she considers this. Any intelligent beast would put two and two together and I can't help but think Savage's overt possessiveness over me is starting to look suspicious. I need to have a word with Savage... without actually having a word with him.

We have lunch in relative peace, because my psychos are not in the hall. It's a heavy weight off my shoulders given everything that's happened today.

For some reason, Beak decides to approach us from his table of eagles. He's handsome in a black polo shirt and his hair is in the signature spiky style. Beak's always been a guy who likes to be well groomed. It's definitely an eagle thing, but underneath that, he has a devilish sort of charm that turns the anima's heads. He slides into the empty seat next to me.

"How are you, Aurelia?" Beaks brown eyes are concerned as they take me in, and his arm brushes mine. I scan the hall again, just to reassure myself my mates are not present. As if I'd ever forget what he said to me the day Savage mauled that snake right in front of me.

"They're not here," he says quickly.

"You've got big balls coming over here, eagle," Sabrina warns. "The alpha wolf has his eye fixed on her."

"So does the shark," Minnie adds. "You need to be careful."

"It's alright, I know them." Beak waves dismissive a hand. "Don't worry about me. I want to know if you're okay after everything that happened."

I stare at him incredulously because what the hell? The sheer audacity that he has to be working for Scythe and now coming up to me? I can't help but feel a *little* betrayed.

So my voice is a little harsh as I say, "I'm fine. Alive and kicking, obviously. Did you help plan my kidnapping, by the way?" Did he help them with their other murderous exploits?

He grimaces. "No. For the record, I didn't know about what they had planned."

I glare at him. "And you've been working for *him* since..."

"Yeah." He says quickly, completely oblivious to my death stare. "But we don't talk about that. I knew you were a tough one, but you also need to be more careful, Aurelia." His eyes flick down to my clothes. "But... if you need anything, you only have to ask me, alright?" I raise my brows at him, because why would I need anything from him? "You know," he says in a low voice.

Minnie is making eyes at her macaroni and cheese while the other girls are avoiding looking at us. Raquel is gaping at him.

There was a time where I would have happily taken him up on his offer, but now? I'd be signing his death warrant. And... well, he's not really doing it for me since I've met my mates. That's what happens when you scent the other parts of your soul group. No one else quite looks as good ever again.

"Thanks, Beak," I say stiffly. "I'll keep that in mind. My uncle told me that you gave him the heads up that day of the fire. It was because of you and him that I got to run. So thanks for that, I suppose."

Abruptly, his energy changes, and he shoots off his seat. "Anytime, Lia." He's back at his table so fast that I don't even register what's happened.

"Incoming," Minnie warns.

I look up to see Savage at the door, joining the buffet lunch by himself, though he hasn't shown any sign of noticing me. A sudden flash of the vision I had on Friday night beams through me and I almost choke on my pasta salad. The sheer violence in it makes me cold to the core. But there is also a cruelty in it borne of something *not* Savage. I know the cruelty of parents. Of a father. How it can ruin you and turn you into something you had no intention of being.

* * *

At group therapy, Theresa and Rylan, a cheetah with a lazy smile, make us arrange our plastic chairs into a big circle so we can see each other all at once.

Everyone immediately hates this position because there's no hiding, and it's the first time we've had therapy with the male beasts. I make sure my legs are squeezed shut against the many eyes scraping down my bare legs and arms and realise that Scythe and Xander are pointedly looking everywhere but me. I shiver in the air-conditioned room and rub my arms.

"Do you want my shirt, Lia?" a hawk whose name I don't know, says eagerly. Beak gives him a look but the hawk ignores it.

Every animus stares at him. The way they're all hyper-alert to us animas is really unnerving.

"Uh, that's nice of you, but no thanks." I'm trying to be nice, but it's hard when I'm pretty sure Xander is paying close attention to every minute sound in the room. That's my current theory anyway.

"I'll take it, Gregory," Sabrina purrs, holding out her hand. Gregory grins at her and goes to take off his shirt before Rylan makes a choked sound.

"Greg, you need to keep your clothes on," the cheetah says patiently. "Remember we spoke about this yesterday? It's not polite to sit shirtless in human society, unless you're at a pool or beach or in the privacy of your own home."

"Oh, right," Gregory says slowly, shoving his shirt back down. "Forgot, sorry."

Theresa nods. "Well done, Gregory. You forgot and took direction from a friendly person. Remember, it's our job to help our friends make better choices if we can." She walks towards him with a sticker sheet in her hand and peels off a gold foil star. Gregory puffs his chest out and Theresa slaps it on him good-naturedly. He proudly pecks at it with his nose.

I stare at the hawk for a moment, looking as happy as any kindergartener when Theresa explains, "In Class B, we give out stars to show we appreciate effort. Sometimes the little things count, you know?"

Most of Class B merged with us, but Savage, as demonstrated by the knife episode, must not be quite so ready. I wonder where he is.

"She's right," Minnie whispers to me. "Now I want a star too."

I grin at her because it's sweet, but also, the guys don't seem to mind it because they see it as a competition.

"Alright everyone, how are things at the moment?" Everyone mumbles half-hearted positive things. "What's everyone's favourite things about the academy?"

Sabrina's hand shoots up in the air and Theresa throws her a blue sparkly ball marked, '$peak3r'.

"I like the village. It has a great selection of clothes."

The girls all nod in agreement.

"You look lovely," Theresa says, "but I'm not sure how practical the six-inch heels are."

Sabrina grins and kicks her heels off to show us. Sure enough, she has two blisters forming at the sides of both feet. "Yeah, it'll be kitten heels tomorrow."

"Don't lick them," advises a wolf with a bandage on his forehead. "Is not hygienic."

Rylan nods in approval and gives him a gold star.

A lion raises his hand and Sabrina throws him the ball. "I like that the Hunting Games will start soon. It's cool we're allowed to be aggressive."

"Excellent point," Rylan says. "What are some other ways we can take out beastly aggression?"

The ball gets chucked around. "The fighting mats!"

"Very important," Rylan explains. "Once you've proven control, you'll get to practise fighting in your beast forms."

"Lia," Theresa calls out to me and I freeze. "What did we do for your anger a little while ago?"

The ball gets thrown into my lap and my face grows hot as Scythe's eyes land on me. I say begrudgingly, "I punched a pillow like a boxing bag."

A few of the birds snigger and Minnie and Raquel glare at them.

"It works really well, if you're in a pinch," Theresa says. "Now, today we get to talk about appropriate courting among animalia because we're seeing some inappropriate behaviours."

I pass a glare in Scythe's direction because surely the

409

height of *inappropriate* is kidnapping. But he's not looking at me and Xander has his usual sneer on.

"What kinds of things have we been seeing around the academy?" Rylan prompts.

"How about girls wearing skirts so short you can see their ass when they bend over?" Xander says snidely.

I immediately heat up.

Theresa makes a sound of disapproval. "The anima likes to preen, that's normal. They dress up in fancy clothes, often showing skin to present themselves to their mates. But you're right, Xander, we do need to be careful about appropriate clothing in public. Showing your buttocks in non-swimming places is definitely indecent. We shouldn't be nude in public where humans find it offensive."

I try not to look embarrassed and then decide to take an offensive approach. I raise my hand and Theresa passes the ball back to me. "How about kidnapping and abduction? Those are *inappropriate* courting behaviours, aren't they?"

Sabrina chokes mid-sip on her water bottle and Minnie nods in solidarity. She gestures for the ball and I pass it over. "Holding animas hostage is also rude."

"Yes, and yes," Rylan says enthusiastically. "In the Old Times, kidnapping was commonplace and accepted courting behaviour. But today, we know better. Both anima and animus must choose their partners willingly, it's only fair."

"I've got a question," Xander sneers.

"Then raise your hand," Theresa says.

Xander does so and Minnie stands up and throws him the ball as hard as she can. Xander catches it with a grunt.

"That wasn't nice, Minnie," Rylan says. "You need to apologise to Xander."

"He still hasn't apologised to *me* for my newly developed PTSD," Minnie shoots back. "That's really not fair, Rylan."

Rylan taps his chin. "Has he not? Well then, I think you two will need to write a formal apology to Lia and Minnie for your abduction attempt. I'll let Savage know too."

Airing out our dirty laundry in public is a surprisingly cathartic experience, and I'm very pleased to see Xander's fingers angrily digging into the ball.

"Fine," he says stiffly. "So my question is: is it wrong for a rex or regina to reject their pack?"

More than one person gasps and the male beasts shift uncomfortably. My stomach churns and I can't help but hug myself.

"It's pretty uncommon," Theresa admits. "How do we feel about something like this?"

"It feels gross," Connor says. "Like, the *entire* pack? You'd have to be pretty screwed in the head to do that."

My insides feel like they're going to erupt.

"What if there's a good reason?" Minnie pipes.

Everyone stares at her. A lion with purple hair asks, "What's a good reason?"

"Well, what if the pack committed a really bad

crime?" Minnie says in a soft voice. "What if they're really *evil* beasts?"

I feel like I'm being watched and I look from Minnie to find Scythe's cold gaze on mine. I meet him stare for stare in a challenge. We've rejected each other now, the men and I. I refused them, and they in turn tried to force me back to my dad 'to be dealt with'. It feels to me like their betrayal was worse though, because I never tried to hurt them, only run away from them.

The room is silent as we all digest Minnie's words.

"If we consider that," Theresa says, "then a rejection is fair. It is perhaps the only acceptable reason."

Chapter 41

Aurelia

After dinner, Minnie and I bid our friends farewell and I scan my card to open our cell door. We don't have so many guards out the front of the anima dorm anymore, but they won't give us back our normal room door until further notice.

But as I yank the cell open, I stifle a cry.

Savage is reclining on my bed, boots and all. He's throwing my teddy bear up in the air and catching it. When he sees me, he leaps to his feet, throwing the teddy behind him, his face a mask of animal rage.

"Minnie. Leave," I order.

"What—"

"*Please* go."

She legs it and heads back down the corridor. Quickly, I step into the room to confront him.

I want to run. I really do, but the constant glares Savage has been sending me has given me some type of adrenaline that lasted all day. Coupled with the fact that

I regina-ordered him back in the kitchens, I think I stand a chance against him.

"My *regina*," Savage snarls, his voice an octave lower than usual. My body responds as only a regina would, and I'm throbbing between my legs immediately, desire skittering over my skin like electricity. I can't fucking breathe, but I force air down in a steady, slow wave. I try to use my calm, collected voice, channelling the energy I used to regina-command him. "Savage, get out of my room."

His expression darkens. "No. I don't know what that was in the kitchen, but you don't get to do that."

I should be frightened at the pure rage in his voice. But no, my regina wants to *play*, and it's completely out of my conscious control when I cross my arms to push my tits up and purr, "But you were such a good boy."

His response is immediate. His head cocks to the side as he drags his narrowed hazel eyes up and down my body. "What do you think you're doing dressing like this? Are you *trying* to rub it in my face that I can't fucking have you? Or are you trying to get my attention?"

"Absolutely not!" I snap a leash around my aroused anima and Henry clucks in agreement. "Why would I want *your* attention? I hate you! You tried to turn me back to my father!"

His jaw clenches but his voice is even when he says, "Mine is the only attention you *should* want, Lia." He steps closer to me and I'm aware of his. Every. Minute. Movement as he does. The way his skin is flushed, the heaviness to his breaths, the ravenous look in his eyes.

The way his scent is caressing my nose like a delicious spring wind.

The room seems to darken around him as we stare at each other, but I stand my ground, even as my anima is screeching at me to get on my back and spread my legs for him. To let him fuck me, to come inside me as my mate. I *want* him to bite me, mark me as his. As *theirs*.

In short, I'm losing it. Henry pecks at my cheek to calm me, so I take a breath, but am embarrassed to find it shaky.

The wolf's voice is deathly quiet as he says, "Just what the fuck do you think you're doing talking to Beak?"

I cross my arms to hide the fact that I'm trembling at his nearness. "I talk to who I want. What's it to you?"

Savage's long strides eat up the space between us and then he's towering over me like a ferocious, angry giant. "What's it to *me*?" he growls.

There is electricity between us and I think it's going to ruin me.

I clench my teeth to steel myself. "He's a nice guy, Savage. Unlike you lot, he's always been kind to me."

Savage roars and shoves me backwards into the bars of the door. Slamming his hands on either side of me, he leans down to snarl in my ear. "I own you, Lia. You are my regina, you are *my* possession. Do you understand me?"

I'm trembling where I stand. He could easily overpower me, do as he pleases, how he pleases, and I wouldn't be able to do a thing. It's only then that I realise he's got his fist around Henry, covering his little beak entirely. The nimpin gives a muffled sound of protest but can't do anything more. Scythe's definitely conned him somehow because he definitely isn't doing his job.

"I will *never* be property," I whisper, but my voice cracks as I say it.

Savage goes still, and he sighs, resting his forehead on my shoulder. I'm so shocked that I just stand there, blinking rapidly. My anima screams at me to let us scent him. To let down my scent shield and bury my nose in his neck because it would be *so* easy to do that.

But I can't. I just can't let myself do that. I've had his fingers in me before, and he made me come so hard and so easily. I've been craving that again ever since. The way he kissed—the way *we* kissed each other with our entire mouths and bodies—was something out of this world entirely and I can't handle any more.

"Lia," Savage whispers to the floor. "What are you doing to me?"

The vulnerability in his voice gives me whiplash, and the broken thing inside of me whines. The safest thing for me is to stay silent. So I do just that.

He takes a deep breath, still refusing to look at me. "You're my regina. And don't you dare tell me you're not because I saw our mark on you." He rubs at his jaw with one hand then looks at me. His face is so close to mine that we could kiss. His breath tickles my face, his eyes penetrating my skin, and I just know if I let my shields down, I'd let him take me against this door and it would be fucking amazing.

"I've been inside you Lia, and there's nothing in this universe that's going to replace that."

The backs of my eyes burn like they've been struck. My anima screams for him so loudly that I can't hear anything else. She's roaring in my ears and my vision goes blurry. Savage lifts his hand to my face and gently strokes my lip with his thumb, as if remembering the feel of it.

I turn into stone because I want to kiss him so badly that I think I'm literally going to shatter into a million pieces if I don't.

And then, his face turns completely feral, his voice dropping a further octave, as if his wolf has taken over. What he says cleaves me in two, ripping my control away. "I own you. You are my possession. I will do as I please with you. When I say *jump*, you say *how high?* Do you understand me?"

My anima is completely in control now and forces me to nod.

Savage bristles. "This wolf likes your pretty voice. He remembers how you moaned for us. I need to hear you say it. *Do you understand?*"

"I understand," I whisper. Oh Wild Goddess, it feels good to say it. It feels *right* to accept my mate's wishes.

He growls and I would have jumped into his arms if I wasn't in complete submission to his dominance. He says, "Use my name when you address me, princess."

His old pet name for me suddenly brings me to my senses, as I remember when he first used it in Halfeather's dungeon. I'm able to slam a cage onto my anima. Triumphant, I say, "You're an asshole."

The corner of his mouth lifts. His hazel eyes glitter. "This asshole has a name." He strokes my cheek with his knuckles, his lips parting slightly as if he's mesmerised. But my skin screams where he touches it, and I can't tell if it's a noise of pain or pleasure.

I stare at him, refusing to say it and his eyes focus again. He places the same hand around my throat. "If you think your life is bad now, Lia, it's nothing compared to what I could do to you." I know he's telling the truth.

Fate is demanding that all my choices be taken away from me and I wonder how I've angered the gods to end up in this miserable position. Between clenched teeth, I bite out, "I *hate* you."

"This could have gone another way, but *you* chose this." He presses his lips together as if he hates to admit it. "I could have given you the world."

My stomach hollows out the same as my heart.

It's not my choice at all.

Now again, I have no choice but to submit. So, I project as much hate into my eyes as possible and say, "I understand, Savage."

He closes his eyes for a moment. As if he's savouring the sound of his name in my voice. Abruptly, he removes his hand and pats me on the cheek like a dog.

"Good girl." Turning away, he looks at my wardrobe. "Now, what are we going to wear tomorrow?" I can't help but watch his ass in those black sweatpants as he yanks open my wardrobe. "Hmm." Leafing through the hangers, he grumbles under his breath because everything I've purchased at the village is short, tight or bright. "I know, you'll wear this." He pulls out an old T-shirt and the holey leggings I usually wear when I have my period. I make a face and he lays it out on my bed.

"Wear this tomorrow, regina, or we're going to have a problem."

I stare at the clothes, and he cocks a brow at me. "What do you say to me, princess?"

Grinding my teeth, I bite out, "I understand, Savage."

He smirks, shoves his hands in his pockets and saunters towards the door, whistling. I move aside for him to leave, and he does so without looking back.

Sagging against the wall, and glaring at a confused-looking Henry, I wait a minute for the evil wolf to leave our dorm building.

I count to one hundred, then hurry next door to where, no doubt, Minnie is hiding with Raquel and Sabrina. All three whip open the door right away, wide eyed.

"What did he want?" Minnie asks, her arms crossed angrily.

"I don't care what he wants," I grumble. "But I need you guys to help me with the best outfit possible."

"Oh, you're g-gonna get in t-trouble," Raquel groans as we all return to mine and Minnie's room. The other nimpins are irritated and they don't seem to be under the same spell as Henry because they zoom about the room, sniffing the air.

But I'm determined not to be scared of *that wolf* or comply like a submissive pup. Minnie gets that, as a devious smile spreads over her lips. Sabrina seems to understand as well as a mischievous look catches in her eye.

"You know," our leopard says, pulling out a top that's no more than a bra. "I had no idea you guys would be this much fun. I thought you were nerds."

"I can still be a nerd and wear sexy clothes," I say smugly.

"Oh, babe." Sabrina's eyes practically shine as she pulls out a coat hanger, holding up the outfit like a trophy. "You're not wearing a *conservative* old crop top tomorrow."

Chapter 42

Aurelia

I make sure we show up to breakfast late so I know Savage will be there, waiting to see me obey his so-called order.

Today, I'm the predator, *bitch*.

Savage thinks he can tell me what to wear? He thinks he can try and kidnap me and I'll just forget that? Well, I'm going to make them regret the fuck out of everything they've done and assumed about me.

My dress is black, the original colour of rebellion, and much to the taste of my mood. While it's midi length, down to my shins, the side panels are cut out *all* the way down from the armpit to the hem and joined together with criss-crossing black strings. It shows side boob, and the sides of my hips so that everybody can clearly see that I'm wearing neither underwear nor bra. I thought Lyle would have tried to investigate my stolen underwear, but turns out he didn't care about it as much as I thought, so I still have to wait until tomorrow night to buy some more.

In solidarity, Sabrina wears a strappy body con dress and Minnie a teensy yellow skirt and crop top combo with her hair in a high pony. Stacey chooses super tight jeans and a red top that's more bra than blouse. Raquel blushes when they see us but shakes their head in dismay because we all know shit is going to go down. They put on heavy black combat boots, as if kicking someone is going to be our way out of this. And it might be, I don't know.

I saunter into the dining hall with my nose in the air, in the lead because I want to make sure I'm seen. I'm not catcalled anymore and beasts only make comments to my four friends. *Everyone* seems to know that Savage is out for me and are too scared to take him on. Savage seems to have a soft spot for Minnie, and it might have something to do with the fact that she was bold enough to tackle him, when none of the other animuses in this place would dare.

But I point blank *refuse* to see my plans foiled yet again.

My war is with the king wolf and no one else. I sidle up to the buffet, fully aware of the three monsters already seated at their usual table.

"He's s-seen you," Raquel mutters. "The look on his f-face is actually s-scary."

My heart leaps in my chest. "It's alright," I say mostly to myself, focusing on ladeling maple syrup onto my pancakes.

I don't even get to the end of the buffet line when someone clears his throat behind me. I turn around to see a pimply-faced wolf no older than eighteen. He's in double denim with an eyebrow ring and nervously looks at his own feet.

"Um, Miss Aquinas?" he says to the floor. "Mr Fengari says you have to come sit by him now."

My eyes flick up to Savage.

He's brutally handsome with his fresh fade, the almost-black curls at the top of his head arranged perfectly. He's wearing a black singlet, which shows off all his tattoos and muscles, completed with a heavy gold chain. He's never looked more like a cage fighter, so it looks like he came in ready for battle. The scariest thing is on his face, though: a wolfish grin that shows all his teeth and tells me he's *that* furious.

"Well, you can tell *Mr Fengari* that I cordially decline." I turn away from the boy and proceed to saunter to my table with the animas close behind me.

Raquel mutters expletives while Minnie gives a small, "You tell him, Lia!"

Connor joins us with a nervous laugh, and he's wearing shiny red heels and black hot pants, making his long legs look amazing.

I feel Savage in my head before he speaks, and it's like a mean black cloud of shadow looming over me. *"Oh, my regina."* His laugh is cruel. *"I'm going to make your life hell."*

The challenge makes something definitely not human in me claw at my insides. Maybe it's the fact that I have a tribunal in less than two weeks that's sending me batshit crazy, or the collective, feral smell of arousal in the air, but I decide that I've had enough. He thinks *he* has power?

I'll show him fucking power.

I slam down my scent shield with a *bang*.

The girls sense the change first and glance at me warily, but it's only Minnie who asks, "Lia, what just happened?"

Okay, so I might have forgotten that my friends can smell me now too. Oh well, mess is made.

"It's all right, Min." I'm trying to sound confident so they don't question me as we sit down.

It takes a minute for my scent to get all the way to the other side of the hall, but I know when it hits them. Scythe turns around to stare at me first, his gaze narrowed. Xander's dark brows furrow over his closed eyes, then his face morphs into something that resembles pain.

But it's Savage who shoots to his feet, eyes trained viciously on me. I stiffen and realise that maybe I've made a mistake in playing this game. The beasts around him visibly flinch away and I'm surprised when I hear his dark voice in my head.

"Come here, regina." There's power behind that command and it makes me gulp.

I also can't believe he's calling me that name now, so I just ignore him and focus on my pancakes with the determination of a soldier in the trenches.

"Um, Lia?" Minnie says quickly, clearly panicking.
"Yeah?"

"They're coming over. Like, all of them."

My head whips up. Sure enough, their *entire* group is stalking over to us, the three monsters, plus their team of wolves and felines. My heart turns to ice, and that's when the real panic sets in. I look around and suddenly realise the only two guards here are the two bears. Their employees.

The nimpins start clucking with worry.

"We need to go!" Raquel hisses.

"Let them come," Sabrina says breezily. "I like the look of one of the wolves."

I nod stiffly.

"You guys are crazy," Connor whispers. "I fucking love it."

Minnie and Raquel groan in unison.

The smell of feral males surrounds us like a multilayered blanket. It's the scent of sunlight mixed with untamed forests, cold earthen caves and the icy depths of the ocean.

My body erupts with goosebumps.

"You wanted my attention, Lia?" Savage's voice is a wolfish growl. He roughly pulls up a chair next to me, sets his tray down, patting Henry roughly on the head before draping an arm over my shoulder. "Well, you have it. Animas, I'm sure you don't mind company."

Though I stiffen, his scent is around me, warm, delicious and inviting. But I get my shit together because everyone in the dining hall is watching.

"Such lovely manners," I say darkly. "Is that what they teach you in the ferals class?"

Savage, damn him, leans down and puts his nose

flush against my neck. I stiffen as his touch sends feathers of arousal fluttering through my entire body. I'm wet within seconds and struggling to breathe. I need to buy underwear asap.

"Fuck, regina, you smell amazing. Climb into my lap right now and I'll fuck you in front of everyone."

I know he's just saying that to rile me up, but wouldn't it be funny if I actually did that, with that treacherous mark on his finger? The image sliding through my brain is telling me there'd be nothing *funny* about it.

The wolves and felines are all drawing up seats and crowding around us, huge and intimidating. Sabrina and Stacey are batting their eyelashes and smiling flirtatiously while Minnie shrinks when Yeti takes a piece of bacon from her tray. Scythe sits at the end of the table with his sushi, his eyes cold on me, still a king at court.

Three kings at court who are out to make my life hell.

I'm so suffocated by the smell of male and my own mates that I'm rapidly dizzy and lightheaded. But I asked for this, it's true. I need to show strength right now. For Minnie, whose face looks as if she's eaten a firebomb chilli, I need to be strong, and for Gertie, who's looking worriedly at each animus.

Raquel suddenly growls and snaps their teeth at the wolf trying to put his arm around them.

"Leave Raquel alone," Savage orders, pointing a finger at the male.

The wolf promptly raises his hands and quickly says, "Yes, boss."

"Apologise," Savage says, picking up his toast.

"I'm sorry, Raquel."

Raquel grunts as if to say 'apology accepted'.

Dear Wild Mother. His absolute command over them is unsettling.

Savage devours his toast with this right hand, licking his fingers one by one when he's done. I can't help but watch and it's all I can do to keep from drooling at the sight of his mouth moving around the food. I feel as if the weight of the ocean is on my shoulders and we're all just floating listlessly under water.

Minnie is clearly freaking out because on her other side casually sits the big white-haired Siberian tiger they call Yeti. She stops eating completely.

"Don't stop on our account, Minnie Mouse," Xander drawls. "Eat up. You'll need your strength."

"For the next kidnap attempt?" Minnie blurts.

We all go still. Then Savage and Xander laugh and everyone relaxes. "No," Savage says as if it's all very funny, "we're not doing it that way again."

My heart plummets into my stomach, but I try and maintain my calm. Swivelling around in my chair, I turn to face Savage front on. "Are you going to try something else, then?" We're so close, and clearly he's feeling it too, because his eyes drop to my lips and he licks his own. Heat pulses all around my entire body and I feel like I'm going to pass out.

But it's Xander who spits, "We don't have to. The trial will do that for us."

Oh no, he didn't! I flip my hair over my shoulder,

431

catching Savage in the face as I do, but he doesn't so much as flinch. "Yeah, well, enjoy this while it lasts then, *scales*, because you'll miss me when I'm thrown into Blackwater."

Everyone around the table stares at me, shocked.

"What did you just call me?" Xander's voice is dangerously low.

I mean, it's not the *worst* dragon insult out there—to compare him to a reptile—but Xander already hates me enough that I suppose that makes it worse. I recline in my chair. "I never *did* see your animus out there, dragon-man, but I sure heard you."

Xander sneers at me. "You won't be going to Blackwater, *snake*. When you're found guilty, you'll be going back to your father to be executed according to the Old Laws. You won't even get a choice."

I blink at him as everything else in the room disappears.

"What, Pardalia didn't tell you that?" he finishes irritably.

No, not that part he hadn't. Xander knows how this world works and so do I. My father will *make* this a certainty.

I think that there's a tether all beasts place upon ourselves. A chain of our own making that keeps us from losing our human side completely. Some beast's tethers are made of fine metal, intricate but easily breakable. Some beasts' tethers are made of wood. Sturdy but breakable with right pressure.

Mine?

I had a tether on myself that was as cold as a steel chain and hard as bone. I'd wrapped that grip around my body and mind until it kept me upright. And I'd relied upon it to keep me standing on my feet for the last seven years.

And with Xander's words, a hairline fracture forms in that tether. And it makes my mind and body stumble where I sit.

Scythe abruptly stands up. "Let's go." It's a command for the entire table and everyone scrambles to obey. Except me. I just stay seated while my entire world opens like a death maw before me. Savage leisurely gets up, his fingers lazily tracing up my bare arm like he can't help himself. When he leaves, I feel his absence like a cold wind at my side.

It's not my anima who screams this time, but my heart.

"Lia?" Minnie hisses. I can't even look at her, I just stare into space as my dad's face and form swim into my vision. *One thing you must learn is that we don't always get what we want.* "Lia, you're scaring me." Minnie rushes around to my side of the table, pulling me up by the arm and hisses, "Bestie, if you're going to have a breakdown, let's do it where we don't have enemies watching us!"

Henry squawks sharply in my ear.

"Enemies," I repeat absently.

There has only ever been one enemy.

Chapter 43

Aurelia

The Old Laws are the tenets we brought with us when we appeared in this world hundreds of years ago. They're mostly misogynistic and brutal ways that dictate how animalia should live their lives. The right for my father to give me away in a bridal contract without my consent is one of those laws. The right for my father to execute me for crimes against my family is another of them.

Not everyone in modern times follows these laws, but there are parts of the modern constitution that allow those of us who want to practise the option to do so.

I know my father and the awful things he's capable of. I know he wants to use me for my 'market value'. Xander's words are clear to me. If I'm found guilty in the trial, they'll return me to my father. He'll no doubt give an official notice for my execution to kill me off legally. Then he'll do what he did with Halfeather—start a bidding war for me and kill the winner off to take their money.

Then, he might breed me with one of his highest-ranking serpent generals, one of the rarer snakes, an anaconda, or there was a rumour he found a basilisk.

With an army of warriors like that, he'll be unstoppable.

A court to take over the world.

While I'm at the academy, I'm safe. But afterwards? I need to win this trial. End of story.

It's just my luck that before class on Wednesday morning, Scythe saunters in. Savage is not present in classes today as Class B is focusing on their literacy, but the other two have been a dark presence wherever I look.

"Shark incoming," Stacey mutters, sliding down her seat as if she can escape him by going under the table. Minnie audibly gulps, but I remain still, determined not to let him get to me.

Still, the memory of him slicing my shields like paper weighs heavily on me. He could have done it at any time, if it were not for his shackles. And it's only this that has me sitting still and not crying out for the guards.

A female beast behind me sighs as Scythe approaches. He *is* stunning to look at. But if he's an angel, he's lucifer; beautiful and deadly. The devil of the water. Cold and lethal. Even his walk is mesmerising, made to draw a woman's eyes. It's fluid, like he's gliding through water, but a prowl that screams strength.

He pauses a polite distance away, though he's so tall that he still manages to loom over us.

"Can I have a word, Aurelia?"

Not a question, but my name on his heavy rasp makes me tingle all over. I squeeze my thighs together and to my horror, Scythe notices, his ice-blue eyes flicking down and back up to my eyes.

His eyebrow twitches and I sit there horrified, as my mind goes to the time he cornered me against the wall, with his hand around my throat and his—

A low warning growl coming from his chest makes me startle as I realise the entire room is staring at us now.

I push my hair over my shoulder. "I'm not going anywhere with you alone. You tried to abduct me, remember?" Then I silently scream, *"You made a blood covenant with my father, remember?"*

Scythe flinches, and I frown at his response.

I watch the muscle in his jaw tic before he gestures at my body and says, "This is not appropriate clothing."

Is he serious?

I'm extremely offended. Also, I *curated* this outfit with careful thought, creativity and planning, to be inappropriate. Mission accomplished, really. "What business is it of yours?" I say viciously. "And you sound like Lyle. No animus will tell me what to wear."

"Lyle?" he repeats. "You mean your *deputy headmaster?*" His voice is dark as he states Lyle's title, and I hear the warning in it loud and clear.

"The boss lion, yes." I turn my head in dismissal. "I'm not speaking to you or your brothers anymore."

Traitors. Betrayers.

His second growl is soft but laden with anger. Every

girl in the vicinity goes still at the latent threat in that sound and the six nimpins tremble where they sit. But I know scary men. My father is a scary man, and while he may have no qualms hurting me in public, I somehow get the feeling that Scythe would have qualms aplenty. Sure enough, after a moment of being a looming menace, he turns on his heel and leaves.

"Oh shit, that was scary," Sabrina says breathlessly.

"Was it?" I say mildly, examining my cuticles even as my heart thunders like a rhino. "I wasn't scared at all." I hope he hears that.

Raquel swears under their breath. "Fuck, L-Lia. You've g-got b-balls as big as the s-sun."

I deflate like a balloon as Scythe smoothly sits down next to Xander. The only men in this school with the powers of fire and water, just casually sitting there. "That's me," I mutter darkly. "Big balls bunny."

* * *

The next day, Minnie, Stacey, Raquel and I are in the library, with a massive stack of legal books Theresa has us reading, when I feel a sharp gaze like a pickaxe on me. I turn around to see Scythe sitting in one of the armchairs, a leather-bound book in his tattooed hands.

Of course he's chosen a chair where he has a good view of me, even if it *is* my back. But I can't sit here now that I know he's here. I glance at Ephram, the librarian, but he's tucking one of his thick twists into his beanie as he reads a text on advanced telekinesis.

"Why is he here?" I hiss at Minnie.

She sighs, rubbing at her tired eyes. We've been at it for hours and haven't found anything of much use. She looks at me pointedly. "You know why, Lee-Lee."

His shark is no doubt trying to get close to me, just like Savage's wolf. They can't help it. And who can forget that day he was prowling towards me in the lecture hall with *that gleam* in his eye? It was a supernatural focus the likes of which made me both enamoured and terrified.

But this just turns my irritation into outright anger.

"What's he reading?" Stacey whispers, squinting over my shoulder. "He doesn't seem like the reading type."

"It says," Raquel enunciates slowly. "M-myths of the Boneweaver."

Raquel frowns. "W-What's a B-Boneweaver?"

"Oh it's a mythical animalia that can turn into all types of beasts," Stacey says. "They used to exist hundreds of years ago but they died out. All they had to do was touch an animal and they could turn into them *and* use that order's powers. Pretty insane, huh?"

"Strange," Raquel says.

I stand up so fast, my chair crashes to the carpet. I whirl around and stomp right up to Scythe.

As I approach, he snaps his book shut and drags his eyes up my bare legs, my short black skirt of the day, and my pink corset top. I have a jacket on top against the air conditioning, but it doesn't leave all that much to the imagination.

But my eyes also cannot help but look at him. This shark who's spoken about in whispers.

"Scythe," I state coldly.

He doesn't miss a beat. "Aurelia."

Every time he says my name, it takes me off my guard. But I recover under his steady gaze by tossing my long ponytail over my shoulder. He follows the movement with pinpoint accuracy.

"I'm curious." I put my hands on my hips as I stand over him. "Since you so enjoy working for my father, will you be coming to my funeral?"

That pristine face changes from curious to stony. "I work for no one, least of all Mace Naga."

"Liar," I hiss. I lash out and grab his right finger, observing the foul magic inked there.

But of course, he's faster. Stronger. He yanks me forward by the same hand I'm holding him with and as I swing forward, wraps one of those big hands around the underside of my face, his fingers squashing my cheeks from both sides. His face is inches from me, his eyes boring into mine in a way that sends my heart into spasm.

"I needed you dead, Regina," he whispers. "Needed it like the moon needs the sun."

My hands are wrapped around his wrist, and his skin is smooth and warm under my fingers. He abruptly lets me go, and because I'm already pitched forward, I idiotically collapse right onto him.

His body is deliciously hard under mine, by the Wild Goddess. Angrily, I brace my hands on the armrests of the sofa and push myself up to standing. Of course, he makes no move to help me.

I'm flustered as I stand there, by his words, by the

sheer power I'd felt under me. I push my ponytail back over my shoulder to collect myself. "You *needed* me dead..." I repeat slowly, trying to pretend like that entire collapsing thing didn't happen.

He's leaning forward in his seat now and Henry, the traitor, has levitated himself to sit on Scythe's shoulder as he says, "Not now. Not yet."

I close my eyes and tilt my head back in exasperation. "Can you make up your fucking mind, shark-man, because I can't take this stress."

The corner of his lips twitches upwards as if he finds me funny. I glare at him. I glare at Henry too. Scythe's eye wanders in the space around me and I can't help but wonder...

"What do you see of me with your shark powers?" But his black shackles are on now. "What did you see when..." *when you unzipped my shields like a dress.*

He considers my question. "When you have your... protections up, I cannot see much."

I swallow and say begrudgingly, "But you can remove those whenever you want."

"Did it hurt?" he asks. "When I did that?"

"Why would you care whether it did or not?"

He doesn't answer and rather suddenly I wonder what it would be like to have him as my mate. Openly. What it would be like to live with the man, sleep in his bed, accept his gifts. Would he take me with his brother? Are they close enough to fuck me at the same time? Would they—

It startles me when he speaks again. "What are you thinking about, Aurelia?"

"Nothing," I blurt. Then the backs of my eyes burn as I crash back to reality and I centre myself. What's the harm in telling him, really? "Just... what it would be like if things had been different. If my father didn't want to—"

I snap my mouth shut because I'd been about to... *shit!*

"If your father didn't want to what?"

I suddenly find that I can't look at him.

"Aurelia." His voice is as sharp as a pairing knife, and I remember who the fuck I'm talking to. A beast who orders others to be killed without so much as flinching. A beast who's feared because he *kidnaps people in the middle of the fucking day*. What the fuck was I thinking that I could have a *normal* conversation with him?

I turn away because walking over here was a shark-sized mistake.

But he's on his feet and has a hand around the back of my neck, yanking me back and turning me around to face him. We're pressed together, my head forcibly up-turned as he calmly stares down at me.

His voice is a clawed hand stroking down my spine. "Would you tell me your secrets if I held your little kitten captive? If I threatened to kill her? If I made her bleed, would you tell me then?"

Fear fills me like a thousand tiny knives.

"Monster," I choke. "You fucking monster. I'd never be safe with you."

The aggression in his facade falters, but I don't care. I tear out his grip, snatch up Henry, and Scythe allows it. Minnie, Raquel and Stacey are already standing, stricken with fear as I bolt towards them, and together, we flee the library and the monster within it.

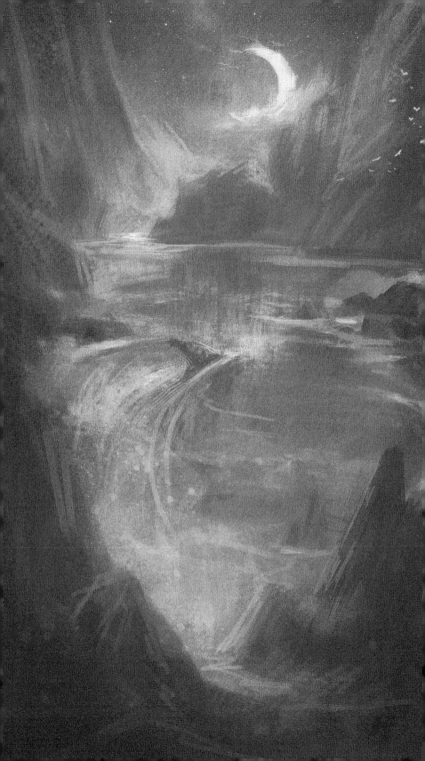

Chapter 44

Scythe

For the next two days, Aurelia and Savage continue to play their game of taking turns aggravating each other. One part of me is amused. It's cute to see her rebel against Savage's alpha tendencies in a way that no else could get away with. But another part of me heats up to see each risqué outfit gracing her body like a glove. The only time she doesn't wear anything showy is for her sessions with Lyle on Saturday mornings.

It also does something to me because I know exactly what this is, even if Aurelia doesn't. It's clear to me that she has lived away from her court, isolated. She is not entirely familiar with the ways of reginas and rexes.

The regina in her is pushing back, demanding the submission of her pack.

In another life, I would have enjoyed teaching her how to make us submit.

But Aurelia's scent has gradually become more and

more of a problem. She's now dropped all pretence of hiding it and uses it as a weapon. As a result, I've put a stop to eating at her table and we've taken to entering and leaving the dining hall early to avoid her.

I could almost laugh at the irony of that, but it's not at all amusing that she has this power.

Xander is unusually quiet and more aggressive than ever. He broke a jaguar's arm for 'looking at him crooked' and exhales smoke at anyone who so much as walks past him.

Us fighting it, fighting *her*, will be impossible for much longer. Even without her scent, she draws my eye. Her presence in this academy is a lure I can't deny my Great White. Even across campus, my animus knows she's here. My senses go beyond scent and sight and sound.

Aurelia has a power over us that's cunning and brutal. And that's a danger I can't stand by and just watch.

The day of her trial will be a relief for all of us.

It's on a night with no moon that Xander and I leave the academy. Just after lights out, we make our way up to the top of our dormitory building, where the black stone tiles are decorated with golden patterns of the ancient dragons and my star-bonded brother assumes his real form.

My shark eyes see well in the near dark and there are

a few floodlights on in the Hunting Games field that make the black tiles of the animus dorm gleam.

With a crunch of ligaments and a sigh of satisfaction, Xander's naked muscles burst outwards along with his powerful, colour-tinged magic. Orange like fire, red like pain.

In seconds, he becomes colossal muscle, broad sinew, and tendon covered in impenetrable blue-black scales. If this building wasn't dragon-wrought, it would have collapsed within seconds. He's easily bigger than the roof, his foreclaws gripping onto the sides of the building, making a clacking sound. He smells like power and something ancient that's probably the secrets all dragons keep. Glowing silver eyes flick at me through the night—an impatient order to get on.

I oblige him, quickly scaling his hind leg and bear-crawling up his thick scales to sit in front of his wing joint.

You have to be careful not to cut yourself on dragon hide. His scales are sharp, and if they catch you the wrong way, they can shred your palms and shoes.

My dragon-brother flexes and it's the only warning I get before we shoot up into the night like an arrow. Wind screams past my ears, burning my face with harsh intensity, and yet I love it. It's not unlike tearing through the Antarctic Ocean, and perhaps that's why I can take it when Xander doesn't hold back on his speed.

I can feel the joy in him as we breach the dragon-shields around the school and fly freely into the stars. It's times like these that I'm reminded that our bond runs deeper than blood. That we were made to be together.

There's plenty of cloud cover in the sky to hide us from prying eyes tonight and because the council prefers dragons to fly after dark, we have to be careful about fellow skyward travellers.

But the academy is in neutral territory, here in the regional area of the state, so the next two hours of southward flight go smoothly. I sit and enjoy the view of the clouds and the cold while Xander stretches his wings, swooping, banking, and occasionally plunging to see if he can unseat me.

He's never able to, however. Savage and I have had too much practice on his back, and there's something about the air that feels like the deep ocean. Vast space stretches out in every direction, with the wind currents sweep around us just as ocean currents do, and it can be peaceful if I block out the air rushing past my ears.

We begin our descent and my blood sings as I see the eastern coastline stretching out like a ribbon beneath us. Lights dot the coast like the hem of a jewelled dress, the ocean swells like its ruffles. I might be high on the smell of the ocean, but my mind shows me an image of Aurelia in a gown like that, a shimmery, puffy thing that cinches at her waist and flares out to sweep the ground.

I shake myself out of my delusional reverie as Xander circles lower and lower, looking for his mark, a bit of craggy stone that spears into the air like a weapon. A kilometre south of that, seated precariously on a shelf of rock, is a multi-story estate complete with swimming pool, tennis court and helipad.

Xander scouts the property, circling twice, lower and lower, to check for anything suspicious and to scent the air so we might know how many beasts are inside.

Xander lands right on the black X marked 'helipad' with a jarring thump and I leap off, landing in a crouch. Xander shakes his leathery wings and turns around to face the house, settling himself down to keep watch.

The house is dark with not a single light on inside, giving the place a mysterious air, well suited to its master.

The scent of human, wolf and bird is carried towards me on the wind. Stretching out my neck, I run my hand through my hair to settle it down after the flight, and head inside.

Along with the beastly scents, there is not only fear in the night, but terror. My shark perks up excitedly at that, just as one of my mental demons falls into step beside me.

"Blood," he hisses, prowling. "Sacrifice."

Animalia psychiatrists call them hallucinations, but I know better. They are figments of thought, emotion and memory that want to destroy me. But there is something darker in me that will not allow them to.

If you want to beat them, you have to be worse than them.

So as usual, I ignore him and climb up the steps to the main door.

The ten-foot stained glass doors are wide open and I step into the gaping darkness, following my nose into the dining room.

For some, it might be strange to see a supposedly extinct Caspian tiger sitting at the head of a candlelit dining table keeping six men captive, knives floating by their necks as they tremble with adrenaline. Stranger still that there are playing cards hovering before each of them and poker chips in the middle.

A lethal sort of game. My favourite.

The men stare at me as I circle the table and nod at the tiger. Two are human, the rest are a mix of felines and birds. But this is not my territory and I do not care to know them.

"Marduk," I say in greeting, pulling up the empty chair adjacent to him. "You are well, I see."

The tiger merely stares at me with obsidian eyes, the harsh shadows created by the candlesticks making his face look spooky. But his aura shines a jaunty yellow and orange. The bastard is having fun.

"T-Tell him to change back!" one of the human men says, his voice shaking. "Why is he doing this?"

I ignore him as he yelps like a pup, the knife against his neck pressing to draw blood. Pouring myself whiskey from the decanter across from me, I raise my brows at Marduk. He gives me a resigned blink and promptly prowls away from the table. The knives never falter, nor do the cards as a human male reappears by my side.

"Bloody is the night, Scythe Kharkorous," Marduk says. "Wild is the mother ocean."

"The tide is low, but it still feels good to be here." I get back onto my feet to face him.

Marduk's human form makes you feel like you've had

weights tied to your legs and you're about to be thrown overboard. There's a perpetual feeling of certain and precise danger. The type of beast who'll thank you after he cuts you. It's what makes him so good at what he does.

He's much shorter than me, but just as pale; lean but muscled. Where I've left my tattoos to start from my neck down, Marduk has numbers and ancient script along the planes of his face, neck and arms. No one except him knows what they mean, and I can only guess that they are ancient Sumerian. He's pulled on a black silk shirt and slacks, leaving his long black hair loose.

When he speaks, his voice is as dull and dry as dead branches, but it's also formal, as if he's come from another time entirely. "You will not have long, I imagine." His eyes flick in Xander's direction. "Come along, King of the Great Whites."

He gestures for me to follow him into the living room, but pauses and drawls over his shoulder, "If any here moves, they will die."

One of them lets out a whimper.

"One can only trust wild animals," Marduk says flatly. "Only they are honest."

"Truer words were never spoken."

He casts a look back at me and though there is no expression on his face—in ten years, I've never seen him smile—I get the impression he is pleased with my words.

Marduk leads me to the living room where a laptop, glass of whiskey and manilla folders are waiting.

He sits on the couch and picks up a folder full of paperwork. "Birth certificate, coronation certificate, death certificate, coroner's report—it is all in here, Scythe Kharkorous."

He hands it over, careful not to touch me and picks up his whiskey glass. "There are photos from the funeral."

I'm silent as I read the documents and commit the details to memory.

"Cause of death was declared suicide," I murmur.

"That is what it says."

I glance up at him and he shakes his head, precisely once. "I am still making inquiries."

"Is there a scent profile?"

He nods and taps the side of his nose.

As I read, a single word comes into view, the others fading away. The ghost next to me whispers it out loud and giggles madly.

"You understand the implications of this?" I ask, tapping the paper.

"There are many rare creatures that walk this great southern land, Scythe Kharkorous. I am one of them. You know this secret is safe with me, but... it will get out. These things always do."

I nod my thanks and hand him a wad of cash. He accepts it with both hands and a bowed head.

As I stride out of the house the night air fills with screams.

"*Crazy fucker,*" Xander laughs.

Chapter 45

Aurelia

The two weeks leading up to my trial pass a little too fast for my liking. The unmated animas train self-defence together in the large room with practice mats. Reuben, the seven foot tall wolf, teaches us basic moves, and for the moment, we only use our human forms.

We went to the village again, and I got to buy new underwear. With my massive stipend, Wednesday night drinks at one fancy café or another are always on me. Every other night, Connor joins us for coffee in the dining hall before we go to bed and we debrief or complain about the various goings on. Apart from the guards watching our every move, we could almost be having a normal time.

Until Minnie and I go to the library, occasionally joined by the others, to see what we can dig up, that is.

I work in the healing clinic on the next two Friday nights, where Hope is very impressed with my healing of the injured beasts who come in from the fights that happen at the academy. Because of all the injuries that come through there, I've been able to show my healing prowess that leaves Lyle positively befuddled by Hope's reports of my work.

Saturday becomes 'Lyle day', otherwise known as 'torture day' or 'control yourself, Aurelia day'.

My taunting of Savage by wearing scandalous clothes does not extend to the Saturday mornings I have with Lyle Pardalia. I struggle with his presence enough as it is, with the constant squeezing of my thighs, the damp armpits, the awful giddy feeling in my belly and *all* over. I don't need to be wearing a thong and a short skirt, making it worse for me.

I would have loved to see Georgia's face if I *did* rock up with my thong showing, but I couldn't stand it if Lyle saw.

So, when I get dressed to see him on the second last Saturday before the trial, I put on a nice pink dress—the colour of innocence to further my cause—cute sandals with diamantes on them, and do a full face of makeup with contouring and everything. I'm happy to say I've had a bit of a glow up because now I have access to makeup and no short supply of people to learn from. I'm pretty proud of it myself, and Minnie gives me an approving round of applause as I twirl around to show her.

The two guards glance at me and I can't see their faces, but I think they're raising their brows. I put my nose in the air and try to ignore them.

As Lyle and I do our walking meeting, the very first thing he says to me is a jab (no surprise at all). "Are you trying to impress me today, Miss Aquinas?"

I stiffen. "Definitely not."

"It's not working, in any case. The council will see right through it."

"I just happen to like pink," I say defensively. I channel my inner Elizabeth Bennet to match his haughty tone. "And you know, Mr Pardalia, you make it *really* hard to like you." I suddenly feel like I should apologise, but the blank look he's giving me is sending me off the rails, so now I'm definitely never apologising to him about anything.

"I'm not here to be liked, Miss Aquinas."

"Great technique. Must be peer reviewed and evidence-based. I'm sure it works well for you."

He stops walking and abruptly turns to glare at me. "Might I remind you that you have a trial for arson and murder next Monday?"

"I do not need reminding, Mr Pardalia," I snap.

"I think you do," he snaps back.

"You know," I say because now I'm riled up, and he's scraping on my nerves like a cheese grater, "I've been in a sort of jail before. *This?*" I wave my arms around his celebrated prison-school. "Is freedom for me, in some ways. If I ignore the guards, and my abductors, I'm actually, for the first time in my rotten, fucking life, having a good actual time! So you'll excuse me if I look like I'm doing okay, because in eight days, it's all over for me and I might as well enjoy it while I can."

His jaw goes slack and I think I've stunned him into shock.

I want to cry because this is the first time I've said any of this out loud to anyone and I thought he was supposed to counsel me, but really I've just counselled myself. I angrily wave my hand at him because no doubt he comes from a rich family with privilege and ease. "But you wouldn't understand that."

I turn away from him to start walking again, but he doesn't move. Sighing, I turn back around to raise my brows at him.

"Perhaps I might understand a little, Miss Aquinas." I blink at him. "But you shouldn't raise your voice when you're speaking to a staff member."

I dramatically hang my head back in exasperation. Like he's my superior! The nerve. Above me, the sky is a perfect periwinkle blue. Perfect, like Lyle Pardalia's blasted face. Perfect, like the feeling of a sweet easterly current beneath my wings. "Will I get to see the sky ever again?" I say to myself.

"That worries you?" Lyle's voice is *much* closer to me, and I snap my head back down and find him looming over me. His eyes are fixed on my neck and I realise, like any absolute idiot, I'm baring my neck to him like a submissive goon. His scent is drool-worthy and I force myself to take a step back.

"Didn't they teach you how close is appropriate to stand next to a lady?" I ask, a little irritated. A heat is spreading through my body and its origin is definitely between my legs.

Lyle reaches toward my cheek and I'm so shocked that my eyes goggle at him... only to have him take Henry off my shoulder into his big hands. Henry bops up and down, chattering a way too friendly greeting that Lyle has never deserved.

A traitor on many counts.

But I'm watching how gently Lyle is with Henry as he strokes the top of his head, then checks him over like a professional.

"*Are* you a lady?" he asks, but it's almost like he's actually considering the question as he checks Henry's eyes, then turns him over and checks his bottom.

"Sometimes they need their anal glands squeezed," he says softly. I gulp because people would pay good money to have their anal anythings be handled like that by Lyle's smooth, golden hands. "But he doesn't need that."

Shit. Focus. "Right now, in this moment, yes. I am a lady." And then I'm babbling because I'm feeling some kind of way. Hot. Very hot. "My father would refuse to let me eat until my back was perfectly straight. Snakes need to have high standards, he'd say. We can't give people a reason to hate us more. And I've had elocution classes and dancing classes and people who taught me history..." Why am I telling him this? It all ended seven years ago, and I barely remember any of it. I grumble under my breath because why do I have loose legs and a loose tongue all of a sudden?

Lyle rubs his jaw with his thumb as he considers me far too closely. I glance away from him and Henry to the passing guards as I flush under his attention. *Get a grip, Lia.* But I wonder what he's like to kiss. If he's rough or soft. I decide he's definitely the rougher sort, and my anima squeaks in excitement.

Clearing my throat, I slide my eyes back to him and find him still staring at me.

"If you're having that much fun here, Miss Aquinas, perhaps I *am* doing something wrong, after all."

I freeze at the low implication in that voice.

Slowly, like he doesn't want to startle me, Lyle puts Henry back on my shoulder. The back of his hand scrapes the bare skin of my shoulder, sending a direct shockwave through my stomach and right to my pussy. I take a sharp intake of breath and our eyes meet for a fleeting, hot second before he's a foot away from me again and we're walking like nothing happened.

He abruptly changes topic to similar legal cases I need to go to the library and look up, and I soberly listen so I can tomorrow with Minnie to make notes for my case. To my anima's dismay, the deputy headmaster doesn't touch me again.

That night, a letter slides under the door with Lyle's signature.

Notice of Detention
Name: Aurelia Aquinas
Crime: Disrespecting a staff member
Sentence: Communal bathroom cleaning duty
Duration: 1 month

"Why!" I screech in dismay.

Henry chirps in surprise. Minnie snatches the notice from my hand and her eyes widen as she reads. "Oooh, he's really got it in for you. You gave him lip at your session, didn't you, Lee-Lee?"

Her new pet name for me is fucking cute and I can't help but love it. "Yes, just a little bit, but it was justified. I shouldn't have told him I was enjoying myself here."

Minnie looks up at me with wide, shiny eyes. "You're enjoying yourself?"

"Yeah," I say with dismay.

"Aw!" She leaps for me, flinging her arms around my shoulders. "I am too! I think you're the best friend I've ever had."

We cling onto each other for a while before Minnie wipes her eyes and puts her business face on. "But... look at the date for when the detention starts."

I read the slip again and see that the start date is set the day *after* the trial.

"What's he playing at?" I say in anger. And the duration is set for one month. "Does he think this is some type of game?"

"Or maybe..." Minnie says, biting her lip. "He's trying to give you hope."

"That's twisted." I shake my head because Lyle isn't the hope-giving sort.

* * *

461

When we get to the library, I'm surprised to see Xander wandering through the stacks. He stiffens as we walk in, and immediately storms out.

"But how does he expect to read them?" Minnie whispers.

I shake my head because that's the question of the year. I don't know how long they're supposed to have their black shackles on, but I hope it's a while.

We sit down at the academy laptops and search through the case reports of the trials Lyle mentioned to me. It's not a half an hour until Minnie grabs my arm.

"This is a pretty big case involving the serpent court," she says nervously, turning the laptop towards me. "Do you remember it? It was five years ago."

It's a mass murder trial, the accused Black Mamba allegedly poisoned an entire family of pumas. Mother, two fathers, and their five adult children. My heart drops as I read about the case.

The serpent, a twenty-one-year-old male, was acquitted of all charges and a dingo got charged for it instead.

"How?" I gasp, staring at the screen. "How does a dingo get charged for what was clearly a serpent's job? The autopsy came back as a match for his venom!"

We can't tell if there was any media coverage of the event, because we're not allowed access to the wider internet, but I would have seen it on the Animalia Today news app.

My stomach churns at the thought of an entire family

being murdered, but more so because I don't remember the trial either.

I would have been fifteen at the time, and I hadn't heard anything close to it, and being so cut off from the world, I was always checking the news.

"I don't remember this trial at all," Minnie says. "It should have been big news, being in our own state!"

Something tells me to look for the name of the defendant's lawyer and I scroll up to find it. When I see it, I grab Minnie's hand.

"Kahliso Naga is my father's lawyer," I say in disbelief. "He's my great uncle."

My father was involved with this trial. Minnie turns her wide eyes towards mine. And her eyes are saying what I'm thinking. I push away from the table in disgust.

"So the trial was rigged. If my father can get a man off scot-free in what was a clear-cut case, then it's going to be easy for him to get me charged as guilty."

I nervously tug on my student lanyard, as the bold black letters stare back at me. *Flight Risk*. They still use that name in the hallways. Still tease me with it.

But opposite of that, the path I'm now travelling down leads me to one place.

At the end of a chain in a breeding pen.

Chapter 46

Aurelia

The Friday before the trial, things change for the worse. Honestly, I was just waiting for something to happen.

I have my shift at the hospital wing to distract me from the multiple threats coming at me from all directions. After my shift, as usual, the guards check my pockets and pat me down before they escort me back to the dining hall where Minnie is waiting for me. We have a quick hot chocolate with the other animas before heading back to our dorm.

Minnie is finishing up her turn in the shower when I flip my duvet back to climb into bed.

I'm met with a bloody red mess.

A dead python lies on my mattress. Its severed head is hanging by a single tendon, and its throat is bleeding out all over my sheets.

A scream tears from the depths of my lungs.

Minnie comes crashing out of the shower, naked and dripping wet, her pink curls coming loose from her bun.

"What in the godfather is that!" she screeches. "Call the guards!"

Gertie chatters by her ear and Henry joins in, panicking, and they both start zooming around the room.

"No!" I cry, waving my hand and throwing the duvet back over and rubbing my eyes like I can scrub the bloody image from them. "No, no, no. Wait, let me think. Oh Wild *Mother* Goddess." I stumble back from the bed and continue swearing until my head stops spinning, but the vision of all that blood just sticks in my mind like tar.

There's a dead snake in my bed. A corpse. I *know* it's animalia by its scent.

My entire body feels petrified, like someone has me in a vise. I can't move. I can't think.

This can't be happening.

But I know what I saw.

"Lia." Minnie's voice is shaky as she comes to my side, wrapping herself in a towel. "It's alright, Lia," she says softly. "We'll report it. They've taken it a step too far. This is a class-A offence."

Murder. He's murdered someone and put his body in my bed.

"Minnie." My entire body trembles like a leaf. "It's not—" I swallow. "It's not *them*."

Minnie looks at me like she can't believe what I'm saying.

"Lia." Her voice breaks. "This is a dead body. We need to report it."

It's a message to me. A clear fucking written-in-blood message. My anima shrieks inside at the soul-wrenching realisation.

There's a knock at our cell door and we both violently jump back from my bed.

But it's just Raquel, their face peering through the bars. "You g-guys screaming in here?"

"We're fine!" Minnie and I both say at the same time.

"Just a spider. Sorry, Raquel," I say.

Raquel frowns but says nothing as they leave and when we hear the door next to ours click shut, I breathe, trying to feel my body again.

It's my heart beating a thunderstorm in my chest. *My* burning eyes that saw that snake's corpse. *My* nose that can smell the clotting blood.

"If it's not *them,* then who?" Minnie hisses, tugging on her hair.

Slowly, reluctantly, I ease the duvet back. Minnie holds her breath as she sees what I'm pointing at.

There's a tiny piece of paper lodged under the snake's severed head. Written in blood is a single line of text.

You were always mine first, Aurelia

"W-Well, I know it's not Savage." Minnie gulps. "He can't write properly."

"Right." I whisper it because I can't bear that I'm actually saying this out loud. "This is my father's work." I cover the snake's body again and my mind shudders back online like an old, worn engine.

My father has owned me since the beginning. Even when he exiled me, he still held me on a chain. He *still* commanded me. This is him staking his ownership. Reminding me whose I really am.

Evil, manipulative, bastard. He would kill his own just to send me a message. Just to try and make me look bad. To set me up, yet again.

"No one can know about this," I say quietly. "If they find out, it'll hurt my case at the trial, I'm sure of it. Lyle will think it's all my fault. I'll be branded a murderer *yet again*. Everyone will think I did it. They already think I tried to kill my dad."

"So what are we gonna do? Hide a dead body?" Minnie hisses, pulling her towel tighter. "Please, don't tell me we're going to try to sneak it out of here unnoticed!"

I stare at her because she said 'we'. I don't deserve her, I really don't.

And it's like my mind shifts into an old, less-used gear. "I want you to pretend you never saw this," I say in a calm, deep voice that does not sound like my own. "I want you to go back into the bathroom and get dressed. When you come back, it'll be like it never happened."

"*Lia*." Minnie's eyes boggle out of her head. "Please don't tell me you've done this before."

"No, I haven't done this before." But I *have* seen it before. When your dad is the King Cobra, the princess sees more than her fair share of murdered snakes at court. It's the only way to deal with defiance, according to my father.

"What are you gonna do with the body, then?" she whispers. "He has a family. Friends. Who is this person?"

I gulp the very big lump in my throat. "I know, Min."

She looks at me like she wants to throw up, and honestly, so do I.

"Minnie, I don't want you involved in this. So please, I'm begging you, get back in the shower and we can pretend this never happened. Alright?"

She stares at me but sees something in my gaze that makes her nod slowly. "Alright, Lia."

"Henry, go with Gertie."

He chirps like he doesn't want to, but thankfully obliges.

Stiffly, I watch Minnie's retreating back, and when she clicks the door shut, I spring into action. Everything will have to go. All my sheets and my duvet. Thankfully, they have a mattress protector on these beds and I bundle everything up in it so I don't have to touch the dead body.

But I feel his weight in my hands like a judge's gavel.

There's no time to wonder who it is. I didn't recognise the viper, but it's likely they come from the academy. With my heart hammering in protest, I envelop myself and the bundle into my invisible eighth shield.

It's been weeks since I used the eighth shield, but it's like sliding into an old dance routine. A cloak of air surrounds me in a soft whoosh, and it feels good to know that no one will see or scent me as I run to get rid of this. Opening my cell door, I find the corridor empty and slip out and down the narrow stairs. I'm just lucky the night time locks have not yet activated. I estimate that I have a little over an hour left.

I loathed my father before, but I can now say that has

evolved into full-blown hatred. He's turned me into someone who hides dead bodies. He's turned me into an *actual* criminal. Goddess, it should be blood-curdling anger that I have coursing through my veins. Instead, I feel only terror. And it pulls at that tether of steel and bone I keep around myself...and the cracks already fracturing it.

There are two armed guards at our dorm entrance, so I have to wait a few torturous minutes for girls to return from their supper to sneak through. Once I'm out, I think fast.

My first instinct is to find the kitchen dumpsters and dump it in there. The good thing about being in my scent shield 24/7 is that my scent is not on my clothes or sheets, meaning the animalia police won't be able to scent me on the cobra at all. So I head around the back of the dining hall, and thankfully, the space between buildings is devoid of patrolling guards. I ease open the dumpster and stand there for a moment, just looking at where I need to put this snake's body.

"I'm sorry," I whisper. "I'm so fucking sorry. Whoever you are."

Realistically, if my father is killing a snake, it's for some reason—whether it was insubordination, disrespect or failing his duties. But whoever it was, they don't deserve to have their body put into a dumpster. No one does.

I can't do it.

Tears streak down my face and I try not to sob at what my life has come to. At the control that he has over me, even here, where there's a federal peace treaty. I sink down onto the cold concrete, breathing hard.

Something primal in me looks eastward.

Because I *do* know three beasts who know how to get rid of a dead body. Who've done such a heinous thing many times. Running around campus with a dead body is a new sort of low, and that devastation takes me over, turning my mind numb, turning my thoughts into nothing but smoke and shadows.

And then my legs are moving of their own accord. I'm out of the alley within seconds and turning down a familiar path. My anima keens and it's the only thing I can hear, the only force pushing me, steering me, right towards the unmated male dorms.

Before I know it, I'm standing outside the old building, trying not to pant, swaying a little on my feet to the sound of the cicadas chirping in the grass.

I'm vaguely aware that it's a half-moon, the silver-blue light hitting the gothic curves and intricate latticework of the dormitory in the most ethereal way.

This could be a dream. Another world entirely.

A world in which a figure approaches through the darkness.

My anima whines as the shadows part for the tall wolf prowling down the path. My lips part at the expanse of his naked torso just laid out for all to admire, like an exhibition at the Louvre. He gleams with sweat, so the wolf tattoo spanning his chest glistens under the night-time lights. He's come straight from the jungle gym because there's dirt on his arms and those dark curls are tousled in a way that tells me he's been running. He wears his black track pants down low so I can see his Adonis Belt—the deep V that runs into his pants where I can just see curls of hair. Thick veins travel all the way from his hands up his forearms and I almost whimper at the sight. He's a wild god, returned from a hunt.

My mouth is suddenly as dry as a desert plain.

I want to leap onto his body and devour him whole.

But there is a dead snake weighing heavy in my arms. I suppress a sob and follow close behind him as he swipes his student ID card from his pants pocket.

Immediately, I slip sideways and let the door shut behind me. Savage climbs up the steep stairs two at a time and I follow him like a ghost, determined to keep his perfect, glistening, muscled back in my line of sight.

I jog up the stairs behind him and with the five flights of steps up, I'm panting by the time we reach the top.

I smother my breaths with my forearm and tip toe behind Savage like a fool as he stalks down the wide corridor.

The male dorms are loud on a Friday night.

There's RnB music blaring from a speaker, and males are laughing and shouting. There's the audible sound of multiple people fucking, including a few animas outright screaming with pleasure.

The desire in the air swarms around my head like a predatory perfume, and it presses on my skin, thick as maple syrup.

The beasts lingering in the corridors part for Savage like water and somehow between the beginning of the corridor and the end, I'm fixed on the smooth skin of his back like my life depends on it.

Because right now, it does.

I barely notice the beasts I almost bump into. I barely notice the noise. Everything fades away at the sight of my mate walking up the dragon-trick stairs.

Deep into the primal depths of my anima self, I doggedly chase him all the way up the hidden stairs—

And promptly stop dead.

Because not four steps into the sixth floor, Savage has turned around and is waiting, staring straight at me with a face rendered into marble and an expression of utter focus.

A deathly seriousness clings to his voice. "Your breathing always gives you away, Regina."

Xander and Scythe step up behind him with their arms crossed like sentinels of all things morbid and dark, as if they too have been waiting for me.

Chapter 47

Aurelia

"Take *it* off," Savage commands. "Take it off or I'll drag you up here and bite your tiny neck until you do."

Before I can choke out an answer, Scythe strides forward, and raising a single finger, he slices downwards.

With lethal precision, my invisibility falls away. One set of eyes flashes and two sets of pupils dilate as they take me in from head to toe. Hazel, sky blue, glowing white. I do not move. I do not even breathe. I don't even care that I'm in my tattered pyjama shorts and T-shirt. All I can do is stare and tremble under the weight of the pure need that courses through every artery, capillary and vein. It's painful. It *burns*.

I allow the rest of my shields to fall to my feet like flimsy gauze.

They all take a sharp breath and so do I, because on their necks, three beautiful mating marks emerge for me to see. Beautiful, heavenly glowing marks that are right, *so* right.

But their eyes flick down to the bundle I hold.

Something makes me look at Xander. And I know that his eyes are glowing because his obsidian shackles have been taken off.

"Regina." Savage takes a step toward me.

"You." But I'm pointing at Xander. I step around Savage to the dragon with the blank expression. My voice does not sound like my own when I drop the bundle at his feet and take a step backwards. "Incinerate it." It is a command, raw and true.

There is only a millisecond before he responds against his will. He raises his hand and the bundle lights up in a blaze of hot red and orange.

I close my eyes, but the flames light up my lids in red and heats my bare limbs. Dragon fire will be hot enough to turn the entire thing to ash. There will be no body left. No bones to identify. No evidence to use against me.

My cheeks become wet before the tears turn to steam.

For a life lost, for my mates, for the impossible situation I face.

When I open my eyes, I know that Savage has stepped up to my back. With my shields down, I can sense him completely. His power is wild like white water rapids and as volatile and uncontrolled as the deep jungle. There is violence inside of him, and aggression, but it's laced with something else that lures me in.

There are also questions heavy as lead in the air, but I will not have them.

I whirl around. Savage's eyes widen in surprise, but his nostrils flare in awareness of my desire. I know that no truer words have ever been voiced when I snarl, "I *need* you."

Savage doesn't smile. Doesn't laugh. No, he grabs the back of my neck and pulls me into him with a purely feral growl, crushing his lips against mine.

Clawing at his bare chest, he lifts me up by the ass, and I wrap my legs around him in an utterly desperate way. I moan as our lips collide, our mouths part at the same time, and hungrily, we devour each other. We fight for dominance with a vicious push and pull. I bury my fingers in his hair and yank. He's all teeth and tongue and growl and the pure animalism of it is overwhelming.

He breaks it off. "Fuck!" he roars like he's furious and lifts me off, forcing me to step onto the floor. He grabs my hand and yanks me toward the bedroom where he lets go and grabs his own hair like he wants to tear it out.

I know he means the blood covenant he made not to mate with me.

"Just use your fingers," I say angrily, reaching for him. How dare he step away from me? "Or whatever, I don't care."

"*No, Regina.*" His voice is a guttural, wolf-deep and I watch in shock as he aggressively pulls open his bed-side table and brings out a switchblade, sets his hand on the table and presses the knife under my father's mark.

"Oh my God, no!" I cry, rushing over to him.

Strong hands grip my waist and roughly push me aside and Scythe steps around me. I stumble back in shock.

"Let me, brother," the shark rasps.

I gape at the two of them, looking over at Xander as if he's going to help. But the dragon just apathetically looks on.

"Do something!" I urge him as Scythe calmly takes the blade from Savage.

Xander's head snaps towards me, and he growls. "Don't fucking talk to me, *snake*." He stalks over to his bed, lies down with his hands behind his head and closes his eyes.

Ignoring him, I step forward to try and stop the two brothers, but just as I put my hand on Scythe's shoulder, he angles the knife on Savage's finger and pushes down with his other hand to snap the bone.

Savage grunts. Blood sprays across the table. I cry out, but Savage just whirls around and grabs me.

"Argh! Wait!"

Blood spurts from this wound.

"No waiting," he growls, stepping me backward.

"*Wait.*"

"*No.*"

I grab the wrist of his injured hand and raise it up. It's spraying blood, and I quickly place my hand over it to seal off the arteries. Savage pulls me against his body and runs his tongue up my neck as I try to process what the fuck just happened and heal him.

Scythe moves away with a sigh, and I hear the springs

of a bed creak as he sits down on it. When I open my eyes, Savage's stub of an index finger is no longer bleeding and is now only red raw.

But Savage is not paying attention. He throws me onto the third bed but it barely recoils under my weight before he's on top of me, tearing my T-shirt in two with a loud rip.

"Oh fuck, Regina," he groans, running his calloused hands over my stomach and up over my bare breasts. His mouth follows his hands, licking and sucking as if he wants to taste all of me at the same time, a beast starving for my skin. I writhe under him, gasping at the tingles his touch sends all over me. He reaches my mouth and we hungrily kiss, our tongues fighting, my hands fisting his hair, his weight hot and hard against my own softness. He rears back to kick his sweatpants off before yanking down my shorts and underwear in one go.

Without warning, he shoves his face against my sex, and I cry out as his tongue lashes across my clit, his lips sucking, tongue tasting. His groan is a broken thing, low and deep. His hands grab and squeeze my thighs and I'm completely undone.

"I need you inside me," I gasp, trying to get more air into my lungs because dear Goddess, this is too much and not enough.

He growls in approval and gives me one final, long lick before leaping up and caging me with his tattooed biceps. He fists himself in one hand and I get one look at his huge, erect cock before he's pressing his crown against my entrance.

Scythe's voice is sudden and deeper than I've ever heard it. "Be careful, brother."

I'm overcome, but I glance over at him. He's sitting on his bed, his eyes hard and hot on me, his pupils blown out, and I've never been so turned on in my life.

"She feels so fucking good, brother," Savage groans, rubbing his crown up and down, coating himself in me. I'm so wet and overwhelmed by my own need and the pure ache of my core that I wriggle myself against his cock.

Savage's chest rumbles low and deep and he closes his eyes, savouring the feel of my pussy. He eases his cock through my opening and it's a delicious burn that weaves around my lower stomach.

"Fuck," he groans, and sheathes himself in one stroke.

I scream, my back arching as stars explode behind my eyes and my world narrows onto Savage and only him. Ancient pieces of me are drawn together with bands of sparkling light and tears spill from my eyes.

Savage's palm finds my face and his thumb strokes my tears with a gentleness that surprises me. "Lia," he chokes out. "I waited so fucking long for you."

"Oh my God!" I groan as he pulls out almost completely and slams back into me.

Savage buries his nose in my neck and fucks me, hard and fast, moaning and grunting his pleasure in my ear. His body trembles with exertion, but I know it's not physical. It's one mate meeting another for the first time, and I feel tendrils of our powers twirling around each other, meeting and sensing. My body shudders under his touch, my pussy clenching around him as he whispers, "You take me so well, my regina. Oh God, you take me so fucking well." He shoves his cock into me over and over again, his hips telling me he's claiming me, owning me, *possessing me*, and I take it all willingly, the spiralling desire a whirlwind at the base of my spine, funnelling up and up. I cry his name over and over and he whispers mine.

And then he reaches around my back to press me closer to him and ruts against me, his pelvis grinding against my clit, sending me higher into a sweet, golden place I've never been before.

Savage suddenly puts his teeth around my neck and bites down. I come instantly, shuddering and sobbing his name, my pussy clenching over and over again. He comes in me a second later, roaring a feral animal sound that sends my pleasure into a new dimension. I arch and tremble beneath him as he pumps warm bursts of so much cum that it's pulsing out of me with each of his slow thrusts.

He stills, fully sheathed, panting as he looks down at me, one hand cupping my cheek. His handsome face is a mixture of awe and heavy elation, hazel eyes glimmering so brightly that it terrifies me. We stare at each other before he withdraws and sits back on his heels to stare at my pussy. I watch on as he licks his lips, hungrily eyeing my core, absently stroking his thumbs over my calves.

"So beautiful," he whispers. "Regina, your pussy wet with my cum is the most beautiful thing I've ever seen."

Movement from the corner of my eye makes me look

at Scythe, who, with hooded eyes, steps over to look as well. I should have the urge to close my legs and hide myself, but I don't. Instead, it's some type of thrill when Scythe's head cocks ever so slightly as he drags his ice-blue eyes down my naked body and stops at my pussy. Xander's bed creaks and I'm surprised to see him rising and walking over too. To my surprise, his white eyes glow with a brilliant opalescent sheen as they land on my centre.

I don't breathe as all three beasts raise their heads to look me in the eye.

What happens then is both terrifying and exhilarating. Both shark and dragon *lunge* for me. Scythe mouth goes for my throat and Xander bends over my right thigh.

Both of them bite down.

I cry out, fighting against them and the sting of their teeth, but alone, both men are freakishly strong. Together, they hold me down and mark me with a bleeding, claiming force.

As quickly as it began, it finishes, and both Scythe and Xander snap up to straighten, before striding right out of the room.

Savage's hazel eyes are soft on me as he crawls up my body and rolls me into him so he's cuddling me to his warm chest. His lips are soft on my mouth and it's in stark contrast to the vicious burning on my neck and inner thigh.

But the hurried departure of the other two men brings me to my senses. "I-I have to go."

The wolf's arms tighten possessively around me, and I stiffen. With an exhale, he lets me go.

My anima is quiet as I gingerly climb off the bed, and since my T-shirt is shredded, I grab up someone's discarded shirt and my shorts, pulling them on quickly. I keep my eyes on the floor as my heart deflates in my chest. My body is on a high, tingles and rivulets of pleasure still pumping through my veins. But the bitter taste of my situation suddenly fills my throat as I brace myself to leave.

"Lia." It's a low warning.

I lamely stand still for a moment before I slowly raise my eyes to look at his. He's a glorious, beautiful picture of male perfection lying on that bed, muscles glistening with sweat, his dark hair tousled, his cock still huge and wet with my slick. And yet his expression is dark. So dark that it sends me bolting.

"I'm sorry," I blurt, fleeing the room.

Chapter 48

Aurelia

The next day is the Saturday before the trial and I'm sitting across from Lyle in the armchair by the bay window in his office. My mental health has never been the best, and this morning I'm left to pick up the pieces of a regina's overactive libido.

My pussy burns a little in memory of the beast who claimed me last night, and I had to cover up the worst hickey I've ever seen, and yet my body is singing a song of pure joy. Henry has been sniffing me constantly, as if he knows what I did last night, and this morning, I woke up to the smell of incense and Minnie meditating in front of her altar for the Wild Goddess, no less than five candles burning. We all have our ways of coping, I suppose, and I'm certain I need new ways that are not moping and crying on the floor of the shower for half an hour.

Worst of all, the lion in front of me at the moment is not helping my cause.

Lyle frowns over Hope's latest report.

I think he's confused because it doesn't fit his picture of who he thinks I am: a bratty child who grew up spoilt and then ruined it by being a delinquent.

"Hope is... impressed by your last shift. She says that you re-attached an ear." He looks up at me, his amber eyes piercing right through the skin of my face. If he can see through to my brain, why doesn't he just pick me apart himself?

I shrug in a way that says 'I told you so'. "It was hanging on by the skin, a fresh wound, so it wasn't too difficult." I tried to look nonchalant as I internally cringe at the two hours I sat in the hospital reattaching the eagle's ear centimetre by centimetre, sweating and dizzy by the end of it. I even had to end my shift early.

"Quite a feat," he says in his special shopping-list voice.

"Will it go into your report for the trial?" I ask, sitting myself straight.

"Yes, Miss Aquinas, it's all going in there. However, whether or not they take it into consideration is a different matter."

Reality is a sharp barb through my chest. "What do you mean?"

Lyle's features go hard, and just for a moment he looks... disgruntled. I forget how young he actually is, because his bearing is so commanding you could mistake him for someone much older. But what he says next wipes everything from my mind. "Your father has built quite the case against you."

I knew he'd do anything to keep me under his fangs,

but as Lyle hands me the thick stack of papers that shows my assigned lawyer's notes on the case against me, I'm still gutted.

Flipping through the lines of the lawyer's predictions, old wounds are torn anew by the second. It shouldn't surprise me that my father would try to tarnish my name by exaggerating my faults, but making them up completely? Lying about harm I've caused?

This trial is my death warrant. Suddenly, in my mind's eye, I see the notice on the thick black vellum the wealthy animalia use to write proposals to each other:

Boneweaver female. 20yo. Prime condition. Unmated. Unbred. Offers over $20 M.

Panic is a serpent that constricts my neck and I clutch the sides of the armchair so hard my circulation cuts off.

"Miss Aquinas?" Lyle's voice is exaggerated as if this is the second time he's said it.

My hand moves to my stomach where my breakfast is trying to catapult out of me.

"N-No." I breathe. "I... I..."

"You're scared of him." Lyle sits back in his chair. That is not a profound thing to notice in itself. A lot of animalia fathers are terrifying to their young. But my father is no normal animalia. He is something much, much worse.

"I really thought I could get away from him." I don't even know why I say it out loud. Lyle doesn't care. He's had his revenge on me. Now he's just got a job to do.

But I keep coming back to the same fucking conclusion. I need to run. I need to go far, far away from here.

To another country. Fiji is supposed to be nice in the winter.

"Aurelia, you *cannot* run." Lyle grabs me by the shoulders and shakes me so hard the shock makes the running thoughts cease. I stare at him, his face too close to mine, his minty breath fanning across my face. Abruptly, he sits back as if he realises he shouldn't have done that.

Perhaps I needed the shock. "How did you know?" I say dully.

"I can see it on your face," he grits out. "You can't do anything stupid. You need to go by the book with this."

"My father will not go by the book, Mr Pardalia," I say. "He has me by the balls and a fate worse than death is waiting for me."

The venom in my tone makes surprise flashes across his face. "Miss Aquinas, I cannot help you if you don't tell me—"

"You can't fucking help me!" I'm on my feet before I realise it, gesturing madly at him. "This *whole time* with you has been a waste. I never had a chance, did I? You were never going to be able to stop this. I've been kidding myself this entire time!"

His jaw clenches and I'm so aware of every inch of his movements that I see it all. The nostrils flaring, the clench in his fists, the tension in his entire body. A dark feeling suddenly slithers through me for the first time. An ancient inkling. An intuition. But I brush that away because it doesn't matter anymore.

"Mr Pardalia," I announce formally. "We are done here. I wish you well. It was lovely to meet you. You've done rather well with your academy; you should be proud."

I think I just needed to say that before my day of doom. Before I never see *any* of these beasts ever again. Storming out of the office, I slam the door open and see Georgia frowning at me. I stomp past her, then on second thought, turn to look at her.

"Georgia."

Her perfectly laminated brows fly up.

"I think you're really pretty and I hope you find your mating group because you're wasting time with him." I jerk my thumb towards Lyle's office and her features darken as she knows at once what I mean. But I don't give a shit because I'm being nice.

I stalk over to the elevator doors and angrily stab at the button as Henry clucks a soft reassurance in my ear. I don't need Lyle. I need Minnie. I need my animas.

* * *

On Monday morning, I can't stomach going down to breakfast, so I let Minnie go to breakfast with Sabrina, Stacey, Connor and Raquel. All five animas come to my dorm and give me hugs, and even Sabrina pats my shoulder and says, "You'll do good, Lia."

Minnie lingers as if she's reluctant to leave me. "I really wish they'd let me come with you."

"At least they let me keep Henry," I say softly. We had to get special permission for an assistance animal as it was. When I approached Lyle about bringing Minnie with me, he looked at me like I was an idiot. Nothing new there, really.

She flings her arms around me. "I'll be waiting for you when you get back and we'll debrief together."

I cast them all what I hope is a confident smile as my stomach roils like the sea in a storm. Lyle told me to meet him outside my dorm, where he'll drive me to the trial in the city. I dress carefully, putting on the dress Minnie and I thought was best last night, a high-necked, no-cleavage dress in the lightest blue to show that I'm a sophisticated and classy young woman and not the arsonist feral murderer my dad is trying to make me out to be. I have white ballet flats with little blue bows to match and nothing else. I stare at myself in the mirror and take a deep breath.

"You can do this, Lia. You'll survive this. You're a predator. You're a—"

The cell door slams open and I jump, stumbling backwards as a furious Xander Drakos strides into my room.

Henry squeaks in shock.

"Xander, what the fuck—"

But a wave of pure dragon magic pummels into me like a hot storm. Charged and powerful. It locks me in place and all I can do is stare.

There is a teal paper bag clutched in one of his large fists and his eyes are glowing an unusual silver. But one thing makes my blood run cold. His headphones sit around his neck, not in his ears at all.

Xander dwarfs the room, cocking his head in a very animalistic way, and my own anima rears up in response.

"My regina." His voice has turned into something guttural, scathing and hot. Like fiery chambers deep near the Earth's core, and it falls upon my ears like a bloody furnace. Realisation shivers through me.

This is not Xander at all.

It's his dragon.

"Fuck, Xander..." I don't even know what to say as he prowls closer with a new sort of lethal, mythical grace and I can't help but step backwards.

I'm backed up against the wall next to my dresser as Xander looms over me. He leans down to inhale the side of my neck, opposite to Henry's side. My nimpin is quivering on my shoulder, but makes no noise. It's then that I realise my shields are down and I don't remember dropping them.

"Regina," he says in that dragon-voice that's even darker and rougher than Scythe's.

I gulp, because what the hell am I supposed to do with a dragon? I instinctively know I have to be careful because it's no man I'm dealing with, and Wild Goddess knows what could set him off. I've never seen him without his headphones and, this close to me, the whole effect is jarring.

But he sets the little teal bag on the chest of drawers next to me and says, "We endured pain, Regina. We endured suffering to meet you, at this time, in this place. And you think that I would let you slip away from me at the last moment? You think that I would allow you to turn me away? You have no right, Regina. *None*. Not when our union was determined before you were born, when the universe was still young and I breathed the light of the first stars." His words brush over my skin as his power pulses around us both, and the very room seems to shudder. "Not when I see in you something magnificent and bright and brilliant. Just like I saw that first time. The man I am cannot see it because he will not allow himself more pain. But he did not fall in his final hour and neither will you. Command me. I am your general of war. Let me lead us into blood and fire and then we will make love on the ashes of our enemies."

Holy shit. Something inside of me rears its bestial head.

"I know what you're saying," I say slowly. "I think I do, at least. But... I..." I'm actually at a loss for words. The fact that a dragon wants to help me is very unexpected.

But when I say nothing, he huffs and straightens. "Because you are mine, you will wear my gifts."

He pulls open the bag on the dresser and brings out a small teal jewellery box. When he opens it, my breath catches in my throat.

I watch him gently lift the very expensive diamond and sapphire necklace, open the clasp, and reverently drape it across my neck. I vibrate under his touch, adrenaline and desire rippling through me. He closes the clasp and slides it around so it sits properly, affectionately brushing a knuckle down my neck.

I never imagined, in my wildest dreams, that Xander was capable of a touch like this.

He stares at my neck for a moment, cocking his head again in thought before grabbing a second box from the bag. I remain still against the wall, frozen in time and space because I don't know what the hell is happening. But Xander continues, presenting me with a delicate bracelet of linked sapphires and pulling my wrist up so we can both see him loop it around and clasp it shut.

"Blue to match your eyes," he murmurs, his large fingers trailing over my skin. My stomach flops on itself.

He brings out a final box, this time a tiny square one, and inside are two sapphire drops. I suck in a breath as he removes the cheap crystal stud from my left ear and hooks the new one in. He does the same with my right.

The dragon steps back as if admiring his work, like he's an artist who's painted something meaningful and precious. Those eyes shine like opals, all the colours in them shining... just for me.

"When you go, Regina, I will be there with you. You will look at my jewellery and think of me." He turns to Henry. "Small creature, care for my regina."

My hand flies to my neck and I clutch the necklace that hangs there, heavy and reassuring.

Xander's dragon has given his regina the only appropriate gift it could think of, and I have no idea what the man underneath would think about that.

He'd probably only resent me further.

But I can't bear to take these gifts off. It's the most expensive thing anyone has ever given me, and right now, the most meaningful. I glance over at Savage's teddy bear

and the pink handbag sitting in their shadowy corner—
like I couldn't bear to hide them completely.

But today, if everything goes according to plan, my
beasts will never give me any gifts ever again.

Then, in the traditional way, Xander walks backwards a few steps, then turns around and heads for the
door.

"Wait." I don't even recognise my own voice, but it
makes Xander turn smoothly back around. "There is one
thing you can help me with."

Chapter 49

Aurelia

Lyle arrives in a black suit and tie with four armed guards behind him and I shiver at the sight.

Vaguely, I register that it's the first time I've seen him in all black.

How fitting.

"Miss Aquinas." He states by way of greeting. His eyes flick down my body and I see him take in my new jewellery, piece by piece. He's far too observant. I suppose I might even miss being observed so closely by him once this is over.

I might have been furious on Saturday, but... anger seems pointless now. My reckoning has come.

"Will it do?" My voice is quiet and I'm not even sure why I felt the need to ask.

"Let's go."

Cold Lyle is unpleasant, on this day of all days, and it's even worse when he puts the metal handcuffs on me.

himself. His hands are cold as he avoids touching me as much as possible. Henry gives a paced, low chirp in my ear that reminds me to slow down my breathing. And then the deputy headmaster is a foot away from me once again as I'm escorted out to the front of the school.

There are three black Animus Academy SUVs in the driveway. Two guards head to the first car and the other two to the third. I walk around to the passenger side of the middle car.

"No driver today?" I say to Lyle half-heartedly. The first day he came to get me, I thought him an arrogant asshole for bringing a driver.

"Not today, Miss Aquinas," he says.

I open my own door and am about to slide into the passenger seat when he says in a clipped voice. "Sit in the back."

"Pardon?"

"You heard me, Miss Aquinas. The accused sit in the back."

I don't know why it makes my eyes burn. Perhaps that title is a low jab. But silently, I obey, though it's a little difficult to do the seatbelt up with my hands restrained. Finally, our little criminal convoy is ready.

"What, no comeback?" he says as releases the handbrake and starts off.

"Not today, Mr Pardalia."

We sit in uncomfortable silence for the entire two hours it takes to get to the city. I end up just tilting my head back and closing my eyes, pressing my cheek against Henry's as he vibrates comfortingly.

I'm a little annoyed that Lyle won't even make conversation in the car, even just to berate me. He only speaks when he parks the car in front of the imposing glass and stone building that is the Court of Beasts.

When I open my eyes, the sight of the courthouse fills my heart with a full and complete dread.

Because what I didn't prepare for is the gaggle of journalists waiting before the marble steps.

I seize up, staring at the three sets of cameras and journalists pertly dressed with microphones at the ready. One of them is marked 'Animalia Today.'

But then Lyle is at my window, blocking my view, his face made of stone and cold as ice as he opens the door, reaches over me to unbuckle the seat. I get one delicious whiff of his cologne and it settles me, a tiny bit.

He tugs on my elbow. "Let's go, Miss Aquinas."

Henry croons and I nod, sliding out of the leather seat in the most ladylike way possible, keeping my knees pressed together. Lyle's hand is firm around my elbow as the guards surround me and we begin walking up to them.

Cameras are angled upon me from all sides.

"Aurelia!" one of the female journalists shouts. "Why did you kill Charles Halfeather?"

"Did you want his money, Miss Aquinas?" cries another.

"Would you like to make a statement, Aurelia?" A woman shoves her microphone at me. They never get far though, because luckily, Lyle chose the biggest guards for today and their big bodies won't let anyone through.

We're through the glass doors marked *Council of Beasts*, in gold and get checked through the metal detectors in no time.

Animalia have our own courthouse in the city because it needed to be fortified in case we throw a tantrum and break something. The front doors are fortified steel, and I know that inside, the benches and stands are made of titanium, not wood.

We're through the gates and walking through the intimidating marble hallway. The ceiling is arched, and because the council has a flair for the dramatic, there are intricate sculptures of lions, wolves, bears and dragons all eating each other. I can't help but notice, though, there are no serpents in the mix.

"You didn't tell me the media would be here," I say accusingly to Lyle, looking down at his hand still on my elbow.

His jaw tightens. "I didn't know they would be. Someone tipped them off."

"One guess as to who—"

From the other side of the corridor, a group of men step around the corner, all swathed in black. And in their lead is a man, tall and lean.

Dressed in a long black coat, business shoes, and black shirt and slacks, my father has always cut an intimidating figure. Though he stands straight at an intimidating height, his shoulders are sort of hunched and the shadows under his eyes are deep. Despite this, there is always a feeling of power writhing through him, like you can see the king cobra rearing up, staring at you straight in the eye, and that at any moment, he might strike.

A step behind him is my great uncle, the famous lawyer, a broad-shouldered man in his late sixties with a full beard and a gold hoop in one ear.

Flanking them both are five athletic men, rivalling my father's height. They wear half face masks painted to look like the bottom part of a skull, and all-black tactical gear.

To everyone else, these men look like the guards of the king of serpent court. But I instantly know that he's come here prepared for war.

Within my father's court, these males, while masked and their identities hidden, are famous. The five serpent generals. We don't know their names, but we know their breeds. One is a Black Adder, one is an Eastern Brown—the Snake Eater—one is a Saw-scaled Viper, the most dangerous snake in the Pacific, and the other two, I'm not familiar with.

My skin crawls, and I think it's a little dramatic, but this show of power is no doubt meant to intimidate me and anyone who might want to stand with me.

I'm a predator. I'm a beast like no other. I'm... seriously fucking intimidated.

Lyle abruptly stops and steps in front of me, obstructing my view of Mace Naga and the six serpents.

My hands start trembling, and I clench them, but the metal cuffs still rattle.

"Miss Aquinas," Lyle says. "Control yourself."

I gulp, not looking up at him and just nodding at his black tie as Henry guides me to slow my breathing down.

501

After a moment, nothing changes and my hands still don't stop shaking.

"Drink this." He holds an opened bottle of water up to my mouth.

Adrenaline floods my veins like cold fire and I shake my head because now my jaw is trembling, too.

Lyle sighs.

"I... I need the bathroom."

"Of course."

One of the female guards gestures to me and I'm taken into the female toilets where I have to sit with the door open as my guard stands and watches me. If you've never tried to use the bathroom with handcuffs on, you won't know that it's actually really difficult and I'm worried I'll get pee on my dress the entire time. That'll be a great look as I enter the courtroom.

Luckily, I just manage it without any splashage or spillage and quickly wash my hands.

"That your dad, Aquinas?" the guard grunts at me.

"Yeah."

She grunts. "I don't envy you."

I glare at her because I don't really need reminding of that right now.

Henry plonks himself back down on my shoulder and we walk back out, where Lyle is talking to a middle-aged man with long natural blonde hair and brown eyes.

"Good morning, Miss Aquinas," he says, holding out his hand.

Awkwardly, I shake it. "Good morning."

"I'm George Fontaine, your lawyer. I'd like to go

through a couple of things before we go in. Is that alright?"

My eyes slide to Lyle, but his expression is unreadable. "Of course," I say quietly. "Thank you, Mr Fontaine."

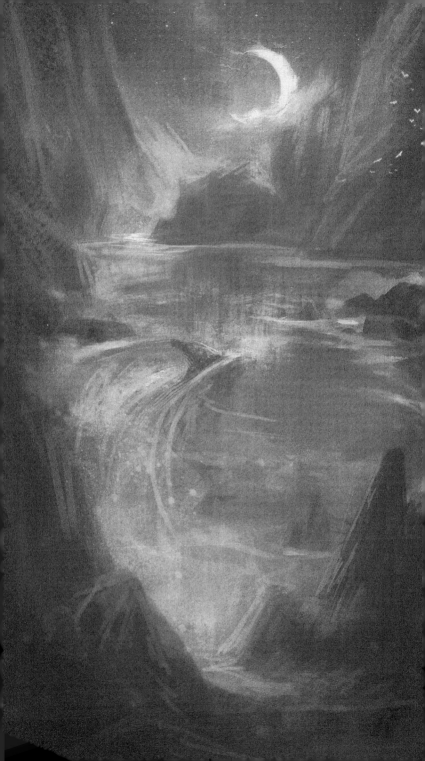

Chapter 50

Scythe

The fact that I have a seat at the council today is laughable.

But the usual holder of the marine seat didn't respond to the call, and since I'm the only marine beast in the state, old laws they can't ignore decree that I have a place here. Despite me being at Animus Academy and trying everything they could to circumvent the rule, they had no choice but to call me in for Aurelia's trial.

Conveniently, my attempted abduction of Aurelia went unnoticed. Corruption at its finest. If Mace Naga thought I would vote against him, he might have tried harder to get me killed. According to my informants, after Aurelia is his, the goal will be to remove all of Aurelia's mates from the world of the living. He knows of three of us, but not the identities of the other two. They've kept themselves so well hidden that I think they often forget

Alas, our little blood covenant has saved me trouble for the moment.

I shake hands with the other council members, say the pleasantries and talk as little as possible. The animalia royalty generally leave me alone, for fear of me getting a read on them, but their efforts are in vain.

There are seven seats of the Council of Beasts, and the marine seat is the only one that is not permanent or up for election, since there are none lucid enough to vote in the first place.

There is a seat for the regent of each of the major courts: dragon, feline, canine, feathered and marine. Tigers get their own place, and they save a single seat for the lesser courts to fight over. For the last twenty years, Mace Naga has held it for the serpents.

The dragon regent approaches me first. King Flores Drakos sort of looks like Xander with long black hair, almond-shaped eyes and striking green irises. He wears a deep green suit, and as a beast of fifty-five, he's still a force to be reckoned with—and will be, for another fifty-odd years.

"Scythe," he booms, offering me his hand. I doubt he'd be so polite with me if he knew I was his son's star-born brother. I barely suppress the urge to crush his fist into pieces.

Next, Ablo Obon grins at me, shaking my hand enthusiastically. The African king lion has always been the least corruptible of all the regents, but he's not above the old deal or two. He's brilliant in a white suit and heavy gold rings on his fingers, the long twists of his black hair stylishly kept with golden ornaments on the ends. He might be one of the council members who actually votes in Aurelia's favour.

The other might be the wolf matriarch, Queen Lunissa Darkfang, in a long flowing skirt and loose purple top. Her three long crescent moon necklaces chime as she breezes toward me, an aloof smile on her round face. She inclines her head, politely requesting entry into my mind. I allow it.

Her voice is as soft as an ocean breeze. *"The moon says much, Scythe Kharkorous. A joy to see you on land again."*

I respectfully bow my head. *"The moon listens to all, Your Highness."*

"Indeed, she does."

Queen Irma Goldwing turns her nose up at our telepathic communication. "Mr Kharkorous," she says sharply. "A pleasure." Her tone indicates anything but as she shakes my hand professionally. The space around her glimmers red and burnt orange, so I know she less than appreciates my involvement in the Halfeather business. And my other businesses.

"The pleasure is mine," I purr. She shivers at the sound of my voice and it's purely against her will.

Lastly, I shake the hand of the regent who holds the seat for the combined lesser courts. My hand tingles with recognition as Mace Naga silently shakes mine, staring me down. My blood thrums at the reminder, and the shadowed eyes of the Serpent King's flash.

"Shark," he states.

"Serpent King," I reply.

Mace and I pretend not to know each other, indeed few know my brothers and I were even at the Halfeather fire.

It doesn't matter that his daughter is involved in this murder, or whatever malicious games the Serpent King is playing, the council follows the Old Laws, and the regents are violently territorial about their claim to their seat. Whatever the ethics of it, right now that means Mace gets to speak on this case. As a result, two of us on this table know the truth of what happened the night Aurelia's supposed ex-husband's mansion went up in flames.

At least three votes will be cast against Aurelia, not including mine. But Albo's power now pulses with a blood red stain as he glances at Mace, and I know then that they have a deal. He will have been paid or coerced to vote against her. So that makes four.

As I take my seat at the long table, I discreetly sniff my glass of salt water for any poison.

There's none, luckily for them, and I scan the room to see who else is here. A spirit or two linger around those seated, but I'm not interested in them.

Beak sits with Halfeather's people. He's to testify as a security guard and pretends not to know me either, though really he's been on my payroll for the past four years. Even Savage and Xander didn't know that Beak was a double agent for me at first. He's an intelligent kid, and that means he's loyal to me at all costs.

Except for the fact that he lusts after Aurelia.

Though I can hardly blame him, or the other unmated animuses who stare at her. She's a stunning girl and they sense there is something unusual about her. Beasts are naturally enamoured by reginas, especially if they have not mated to one. Even if it *is* natural, I have to stay the irrational urge to snap necks during classes.

My mind skips to Friday night when I marked her with my teeth. She has a unique power over me, and *that* is dangerous. She has influence over *all* of us, and that is a level of power that no beast should have.

Sitting with Beak are Dirk Halfeather's widows among some other males and females who are distant family, nieces and nephews. Some of them glance darkly my way, likely hateful that I've taken any possible inheritance from them. The defendant's side is empty apart from some reporters and an artist who will paint Aurelia for the nightly news.

Lyle strides in with his personal lawyer, George Fontaine, behind him. A step behind them is Aurelia. Under the bright lights of the courtroom, time seems to slow down as my eyes hone in on her with a predatory acuity that my shark only manifests around our regina.

She's carefully dressed in a light blue dress. Her makeup is impeccable, though I can still see the dark circles under her eyes peeking through. I observe every perfect, black lash, covered in mascara, the powdered slope of her regal nose, the fine dark angle of her brows, the plush lines of her lips which she's tinted. She's smudged her lip-gloss a little, either from the ride over or from nervousness, but it's only something I would notice.

Her slender neck, ears and wrist sparkle with surprising additions that I know she didn't purchase herself. The power I sense in them is as familiar to me as my own and my animus rises in recognition.

Aurelia's shoulders are tense, her walk stiff, and her beautiful features are stuttered. But even then, she bears an unusual quality of light that should be impossible. And it's more than the fact that she is my regina. Phoenixes and dragons have a similar light, but hers is more nuanced, the fractals less defined.

She asked me once what I saw when I looked at her when I tore her protections down. Power prowls under her skin, heavy and deep. She is a beast of a different kind, but the pieces of herself are disjointed. As if she holds two magnets apart and is straining under the tension.

A part of me wonders what power she would hold if she just fully embraced those segments and let them come together.

I think then we would have a truly dangerous person of a kind we've never seen. It's alluring to me, that wild, covert strength, and I would be lying if I said I didn't want to steep in her presence. She's successfully covered the mark I gave her on her neck with makeup, but I can *feel* it there on her skin, and gives me a primal satisfaction I've never known was possible.

But it will be the closest I come to claiming her. Which is to say, not at all. She will never be mine and I will never be hers. That one thing is essential, however madly it makes my shark thrash.

That part of me is also a bit annoyed that Lyle gets to sit next to her. But if not me, better him than anyone else.

I watch Aurelia's head snap to the left where Halfeather's people sit and I know she hasn't expected to see them here. Let alone with accusing looks and tissues dabbing at their cheeks. It looks even worse that this supposed crime was done by one from their own order. Supposedly.

The moment Aurelia notices me, my animus thrashes about in triumph. She stiffens and blinks in surprise. I can't believe Lyle didn't warn her I'd be here, but he's too busy muttering with his lawyer to notice Aurelia's shock.

I pointedly look away, and after a moment, she does too. Do her shoulders relax an infinitesimal amount? Perhaps, but she's not as intelligent as I thought if my presence here *calms* her even slightly. I still hold her life in my Goddess-forsaken hands.

The council's tigress representative, Yana Chiu, the traditionally impartial, non-voting member, opens the trial and addresses the formalities of all those present for the minutes-keeper, a tigress typist at the front and centre of our bench. Yana then says, "Miss Aurelia Aquinas, you stand accused of one count of arson and one count of murder of the first degree of the eagle, Mr Charles Halfeather. How do you plead?"

Fontaine stands up. "My client pleads not guilty, Your Honour."

The Council of Beasts run their murder trials quite differently from the human ones. For our kind, violent crimes are commonplace and so there's less formality.

Some of it comes from the Old Laws, where a beast was tried and their sentence passed within minutes. Executions were done on the spot, with little fanfare.

In these modern times, we need to convince the humans we are not monsters, so they've added extra processes for show. The victims always go first with their lawyers, calling forth their witnesses to be questioned.

So as the next two hours pass, the tides inside of me become a tsunami as I watch Mace and his lawyer dismantle Lia's reputation piece by piece.

They call up Beak, who gives them only the information Mace has instructed him to give. Which is to say, nothing about Aurelia being there to do a healing for the beast in Halfeather's dungeon. The dungeon is not mentioned at all and Beak speaks of the day Aurelia got married to Halfeather. I was there for that, in astral form, so I know he's telling the truth about those parts.

Next, members of Aurelia's family are interviewed. Her Aunt Charlotte, a reedy woman with Marilyn Monroe blond curls and crimson lipstick that I dislike instantly. She has an aura of needy pink and orange tinged with the dishonour of black.

"Why did you take Aurelia in, Mrs Naga?" the lawyer asks. Charlotte Naga is regina to two snakes, therefore they take her name.

"She was a troubled girl," Charlotte says. "Mace thought a woman could get through to her and make her stable."

"Did it work?"

"No, she only got worse."

"In what way?"

"Going out all night and coming back at all hours smelling of cigarettes and... men. Humans and animalia both."

I glance at Aurelia and see her ashen and trembling. Henry is frantically rubbing himself against her cheek to try and get her to calm down. Even without the black and grey smoke I see coiling around Charlotte, I know she's lying through her teeth about these things. I've never smelled another man except Mace, her Uncle Ben and Beak on Aurelia, so I know she's not been with a male for a year at least. An animus always knows that about his regina.

Mace is called up and I, along with the rest of the court, hang onto his every word.

"She was always spending so much," Mace drones. "It was always cash, and we found pills and joints in her room. So eventually, I restricted her money."

"I have here the evidence of said transactions." Khaliso Naga holds up a stack of banking statements. "Miss Aquinas spent more than twenty grand in one month?"

"Correct," Mace says smoothly.

Lyle's typically stoic face becomes colder and colder as those of us who have observed Lia see what's happening.

Mace is a man with an agenda. Even with his strong psychic shields, I can see the darkness coiling around him the same as I did that first day I met with him outside Halfeather's burning mansion. I can see the shadow of his snake, which sits ready to strike at all times. It turns its hooded head, sees me and hisses threateningly. With defences like that, a beast has a lot to hide.

Of course he does, if he's tracked down his daughter's mates to help execute her.

Even if I cannot get a read on whether he is lying or telling the truth, the paper Khaliso is brandishing bears the characteristic brown-blue haze of forgery.

I'm not surprised. I've seen Lia's cottage. It was barely liveable. There was no evidence of drug use either in her room or on her person. I would know. I now control the drug trade within Animus Academy, and Aurelia has never sought any.

Then Fontaine calls up Lyle to the stand. He reads out his report from the last four weeks of observation. Lyle is honest and talks about Aurelia's escape from him before she got to the academy and how he captured her in eagle form. He mentions her healing and her good marks, that she made many friends with the animas. Fontaine asks for clarification on some points and Lyle answers them in a clipped voice, staring down Mace Naga as he does.

I might not like Lyle Pardalia all that much, but the one thing about him is that he never lies. He also never cowers in the face of the power at this court. I can't help but respect a beast like that.

When Khaliso Naga calls Aurelia up to the stand, I almost break the armrest of my chair for the grip I have on it.

The questioning from both sides is intense, but

Aurelia sits stoically in the witnesses' seat, as if the very moment she moves will be the moment she shatters. Her body quivers when Kahliso asks, "Were you aware of how much money Charles Halfeather had to his name, Miss Aquinas?"

"No, Great-Uncle. It was a surprise when I saw his house." Aurelia's voice is cold and something lifts in me at her addressing of her father's lawyer. She also does not mention the dungeon—the reason she was there in the first place—which is an unwritten rule amongst these beasts and it proves her awareness of that life, as well as a sort of maturity, which I would expect from the ex-heir to the serpent throne.

"But you saw his house and would have known how much he had?"

"Objection," Fontaine snaps. "Leading the witness."

"Sustained," Yana says. "Next question, Mr Naga."

"Miss Aquinas." Kahliso casually strolls in front of her metal stand. "The losing of your virginity was quite the... event, was it not?"

My shark goes still. Aurelia blinks and her cheeks flush.

"Objection," Fontaine sighs. "Leading the witness. Relevancy? This is a character assassination."

"Sustained," Yana says.

"I'm coming to my point," Naga says.

"Sustained," Yana says firmly.

"You've had a beast killed before," Kahliso presses.

Aurelia swallows. Her throat sounds dry.

"No, Great-Uncle, I have not."

"Does the name Theo Krait ring a bell, Aurelia?" Kahliso says. But he doesn't let her answer and speaks so quickly no one stops him. "The beast you lost your virginity to was named Theo Krait. You knew, your father follows the Old Laws. And according to the Old Laws, Theo would be killed for the deed. Yet, you allowed him to touch you anyway. Many times, in fact, over *months*, did you not? You knew exactly what the consequences were, and you did it anyway. *You* signed Theo's death warrant, Aurelia. *You* had sex with him, no one else. *You* forced your father's hand."

My body goes cold. The entire court stares in a sort of shock. According to our Old Laws, a parent can kill a person for having sex with their daughter for her first time. And apparently, Mace Naga did just that. I glance at the Serpent King and splotches of joy colour his auric field in yellow.

My animus roars.

Aurelia, who has gone ice-white, opens her mouth, but nothing comes out. Pain flashes across her face. A memory, I think. Perhaps the memory of Theo's execution. It would have been nasty. She clears her throat and tries again. "I—"

"That is all, your honour."

The damage is done.

As his daughter is publicly embarrassed, my shark hones in on Mace Naga's body, his face, memorising every single line and sweep of his form. I memorise his scent. The way he breathes. The velocity of his blood pounding through his arteries. The exact colour of each strand of hair. The cadence of his voice. The primal psychopathic beast in me marks the great hooded cobra under his skin in the same way. My shark commits those things into a part so deep in my brain that an ancient part of me shifts. And it whispers only one thing. *"Prey."*

Once all witnesses have been questioned, Yana Chiu rubs her brow and I see the surprise and wariness in her. She knows what has happened here. She also knows that she holds no real power. The power belongs to those who have taken it.

"The council will meet and vote as per the laws of our kind," Yana says. "A decision will be announced at the close of business today." Yana thumps her gavel. "The council will now vote. Court is dismissed."

Chapter 51

Savage

I stride down the dormitory corridor, hunting for my little messenger. Beasts scatter when they see me coming with my murderous face and intention.

I'm not happy.

Not since Aurelia *ran* from my room with my scent still on her skin, with my cum dripping from her, with my brothers' marks on her skin.

The sound of a woman moaning funnels through the air like a soft song and I frown.

Following Rocky's scent to a dorm with an open door, I lean my shoulder against the doorframe and watch.

Mating groups don't mind audiences, even possessive beasts wanted to show off their rex or regina. Wolves, especially.

Rocky was between a woman's legs, licking and sucking at her pussy while another animus thrusts into him from behind. I watch them for a minute, but really my mind is on Aurelia and how she'd made sweet noises in my ear. She'd been soft under me, submissive, even. As if she'd *wanted* to open for me and be mine, body and soul.

Just for a moment I'd given into the feeling of having a regina. Of having a woman own me.

And by fuck, was it like nothing else.

Finally Rocky notices me and lets out a yelp. The she-wolf opens her eyes and the animus fucking Rocky groans and rolls off to the side.

There's a chorus of "Sorry, Mr Savage!" As Rocky flings a blanket over his woman.

Ordinarily, I wouldn't have a problem with this, but for some reason, this scene is grating on my nerves and they all know it.

"I didn't know you had a regina," I mutter as Rocky tugs on his jeans. He's a skinny kid at only eighteen and wears bulky denim to try and look bigger. I have him sparring with the younger wolves to try and get him stronger, but I think I might train him personally. I crook a finger at him to follow me and though the others give him sulky looks, he rushes to obey.

I should feel bad about interrupting but I don't.

"Y-yes, Mr Savage," he says, shutting the door behind him. "Sherry is regina to Jeremiah and me."

"I didn't know that," I mutter again. Why didn't I know that?

"I met Jeremiah on our first day and he brought me to meet Sherry. Did you have a message for me to take somewhere?"

I whirl around to face him and Rocky stops short and

blanches, blubbering an apology yet again. The corridor around us empties.

"What was it like?" I snap

"W-what?"

"Meeting her. How did you get her to like you?"

Rocky's smile is lopsided and I stare at it as he rubs the back of his head like he's remembering it. Must be a good memory then. "Aw, sir, well it was love at first sight, wasn't it? She smiled and it was like I was falling through space. Her cheeks went all pink and then—"

Rage is an inferno bursting out of my chest. Rocky cuts himself off.

"Get the fuck out of my sight, Rocky."

He turns and bolts back down the corridor, skidding in his trainers before lurching into his room. I stalk down the empty corridor after he's gone, headed straight for the fighting mats. Lunch will be over soon but in that hour, Reuben holds sparring sessions for those of us who need them to control ourselves.

The image of Aurelia's back, running away from me flashes through my mind over and over again.

She is going to be leaving me. They're going to take her away.

By the time I get to the fighting hall, I'm riled up, jittery and ready for blood.

"Who wants to fight?" I roar. "Who wants to fucking fight?"

Everyone on the fighting mats freezes like prey

"I want to kill someone," I snarl, curling my hands

into fists. "I want flesh in my teeth and blood in my claws. In my fucking mouth."

Reuben steps out between me and the others, his tall frame towering over them. "You always had a way with words, Sav. It's a wonder how you're illiterate." He barks to the rest, "Clear out."

I'm breathing hard and staring as they all walk away as slowly as they can, although I sense they want to run. They don't want to activate my prey drive. It's on a hair trigger as it is.

Reuben takes a drink from his bottle but doesn't take his eyes off me.

"You wanna fight, Sav?" he asks, wiping his mouth. He puts on the boxing pads, never taking his eyes off me. He beckons with them. "Come and fight, then."

I charge at him.

He bares his teeth as I hit the pads, pummelling them with vicious speed. I'm hitting him harder than I should, but my blood is screaming, my head is pounding, and my wolf wants to see blood spattering his skin. It doesn't even matter I'm missing an index finger; I enjoy the pain of the amputated finger, that sheer, hostile burn. Aurelia healed it before I came in her so hard that my body is still wired from it. Somehow, she made my body even stronger, and now my wolf is all feral madness.

Reuben keeps up, but it's not enough for what I need.

"Take the fucking pads off and hit me!" I roar.

He ignores me, knowing it's the only thing keeping my wolf at bay. "It's over that eagle anima, isn't it?"

Reuben huffs, stepping sideways as I jog on the spot. "The one who went to court today."

I snarl and lunge at him.

He deflects, smacking me over the head. My head snaps to the side, but the pain feels so fucking good.

"You have an unusual amount of rage, even over a pretty anima," Reuben grunts. "It's not healthy. It'll get your ass killed, pup."

Agree to disagree.

"Your obsession over this girl is not normal," he presses. "Let her go."

It's my wolf who roars, "SHE'S MY REGINA!"

Reuben rears back in shock, his brown eyes wide. "Your *regina*?"

She whimpered my name. *Mine,* in *my* ear, from the way my cock was inside of her. Her sweet sounds resound in my head, and I want more.

But I know what Reuben is thinking, a beast like me is usually rex to a pack of females. It makes sense given my power. But he doesn't know Aurelia, doesn't know how well she took me last night. How she made me feel.

"What do you mean?" he asks carefully. "Why is she not—"

"Because she doesn't want to," I growl. "She Doesn't. Fucking. Want. Me."

Reuben sighs, falling back on his ass and staring at me. "She thinks you're too dangerous."

I shrug.

"She'd be right, Sav."

I glare at him, but he's right. I'm not really stable in

523

any way. "I don't know what to do." Those words have never come out of my mouth and it almost feels like another man is saying them.

"I'm sure she wants you too," Reuben says quietly. "Reginas have an unquenchable need for their pack. She must be worried about all the other shit she has going on."

He has no idea.

"Yeah, but she should have come to me about it. I've never wanted to help anybody. But she won't let me."

"She doesn't know you."

"It doesn't matter."

"It's harder for the women, pup." Reuben strokes his long brown beard and I don't even care that he's calling me that. "We are their natural predators. A relationship has to be built on trust. Regina or not. You can't trust someone you don't know."

I frown at him and then shake my head. "But I'm her mate. I would never—"

Reuben arches a brow at me.

"Shit." I *did* want to hurt her. I wanted her dead.

Reuben's voice is soft. "My regina rejected me at first."

I gape at him. "What?"

"Yeah, I know. I used to be a bad, bad guy," he smirks. "You might not remember, but I did all sorts of shit. Once I landed in prison, I thought she'd reject me for good. But..."

Getting onto my knees, I press him. "What did you do? How did you win her back?"

He tuts at me. "It's not about winning her; it's about

growing trust and mutual respect. You need to *earn* her, Sav."

Earn her?

Reuben must see my confusion because he barks a laugh. "You'll figure out what you need to be for her. If you really want to care for her and be her mate, you need to find out what she needs and give it to her. You... need to put her first, Sav."

I fall onto the mat with a dramatic thump. "They're going to take her away from me."

"Who?"

"Her father. Mace Naga is going to execute her under the Old Laws."

Reuben swears under his breath. "He's involved in dark serpent magic. You need to be careful."

Mother Wolf, I know that. I chopped that magic off my body. Mace wants to get rid of her because of her power. He doesn't want a rival.

I say absently, "The day Scythe and I got our mark, it felt like something more than destiny."

Reuben sucks in a shocked breath. It's common for brothers to share a mating group, but brothers of different orders usually don't. Reuben doesn't question it though, and instead says. "What happened to your dad, Sav? Did you do it? Or was it Scythe?"

I stare at him, the massive wolf who was friends with my dad. Friends, and yet he stood up to him on more than one occasion. There is no anger in him now, only curiosity.

But the thought of death, the thought of Lia on an

execution block, makes me so violently angry that I throw myself at Reuben again.

Pain explodes in my left thigh and I stop short. A second pain bursts down my side and I grunt in surprise before the rage hits me.

There are only two beasts in this world that could sneak up on me.

With pain spreading up my torso, I recognise the fiery magic lacing the bullets. Slowly, I swivel around to see Xander standing at the entrance to the gym, a cigarette hanging from his mouth and in his hands, an automatic dart firearm.

"I'm sorry, brother," Xander says over his cigarette. "It had to be done."

The pain reaches my chest and I break out into a sweat as my heart pumps the poison up to my brain.

My legs stop working and I allow myself to fall to my knees.

I only have seconds.

"I'm going to fucking kill you," I grunt.

"I know."

My vision narrows, before everything goes black.

Chapter 52

Savage

Ten years ago

I'm thirteen when women start to call out to me at my fights like they do Scythe. I'm strong and tall, ripped from fighting, and Dad takes me to the barber to have my hair done all nice. They make comments about my body at the fights, and one day Dad starts to look at me with a weird thinking sparkle in his eye.

We get home from training one day and Dad says, "Are you still a virgin, Savage?"

I look up at him because it's the first time he's used my name and not 'pup'. But also, what the hell?

"Yeah?" I say. "Scythe said I should wait until I'm at least twenty, so I don't hurt the other person by accident."

Dad shoots a lethal look at Scythe and I know he'll be in trouble for my stupid mouth. I punch myself in the head, but Dad seizes my arm when I go for the second punch. "Stop that. You'll make yourself even more stupid."

I drop my arm.

"You want to though, I bet?" Dad says, intently looking me up and down. "You want to fuck someone?"

My face goes hot and I shrug. "Yeah, I suppose. One day."

"You like any of the girls at school?"

I look up at Dad because this conversation is weird and Scythe is standing by my side, all stiff like he's ready for a fight. But that doesn't make sense because Dad beats me all the time. But he's never used this voice on me either. I'm automatically suspicious and glance at my brother, only to find him as white as a ghost.

"What's this about, Dad?" I ask.

"Don't ask questions," he snarls, shoving my face down to make me submit. Then he pulls something out of his pocket. "You know what this is?" It's a small blue plastic square and heat fills my face because Scythe's told me about it.

"Yeah," I mumble. A cold draft wafts from Scythe and I know he's super mad about something, but I can't fucking tell what.

"What's it called, Savage?" Dad's voice is dead serious and I know he's losing patience with me.

"A condom."

I'm more than aware of mom on the couch and Lily sitting in her cage in the living room behind me. But all Dad says is, "You know how to use it?"

"Yeah," I mumble.

"Good. Get out." He turns away from us and reaches for the phone.

As we leave, my mum says in the slurred voice she has when she's shooting up, "How much more will we make?"

It hurts because my mum is always asking about how much money I make and not how much I bleed. Sometimes she calls Scythe to her bedroom, but she never calls me in there. I'm jealous of that and I shoot an angry glare at him. I don't really hate him, but I now know my mom definitely loves him more than me. Dad is trying to make another baby with Lily, but it's not working. I tried to tell him that they need to feed her more, but it only landed me a jab to the windpipe. Lily has stopped talking at all now. She mostly just sleeps and blubbers. Scythe cleans out her cage and holds her after dad is done with her, but the last time he did that, she almost clawed his eyes out.

I think she thought he was going to hurt her. I snuck her a chocolate after that, but she didn't eat it.

As we walk out of the living room, Scythe grips my arm and I whirl to look at him, about to tell him to fuck off or I'll break his arm. But I can't because the pure terror on his face stops me dead. He's so white he *could* be dead except for the way he's shaking. His blue eyes are wide and his hand on mine is so fucking cold it's burning me.

"Sy?" I whisper, wondering if he's turning out to be mad like his mum. He's always been scared of that.

His eyes never leave me when he says, "I'm *not* going to let them."

Our parents' screams pierce the night, hitting me right between the eyes. But the sound is sweet music. The other wolves in our street run out of their houses to stare at our blazing house and the thick black smoke that fills the black sky.

Scythe walks out of the blaze, his bare skin covered head to toe in ash, his clothes burned away.

He coughs and it's a rough sound like a saw on wood. I rush forwards and yank him by the arm so we can get out of here, but he places a sooty hand over mine and his grip is like steel. He wants to stay. He wants to feel their pain, their suffering. And so, I sit with him on the sidewalk and with his arm around me, we watch our dad and my mum go to hell.

When the screams stop and the wail of sirens replace it, we walk away from the house together. Scythe, with the wad of cash he's been saving—tips from the people he calls *clients*. Me? I walk away with knowledge that sits like a curse at the front of my mind, because Scythe told me everything our dad let strangers do to him since he was eight.

Scythe puts his arm around me. "I'll never let anyone hurt you, pup."

My big brother always means what he says. I turn to look at him and it's then that I see the mark on the side of his neck for the first time. A mark made by a divine hand, made of light that does not come from this world.

A skull with five beams of light curling from it.

We both gasp, reaching for one another.

We are not only bound in blood, but in soul, too. Brothers of the same mating group.

"When we find our regina," I breathe in wonder, touching his neck, "we'll take over the world."

Out there is a girl just like us, made for us, who will love us. Will she be a shark or a wolf? I hope a wolf.

But Scythe doesn't look so sure, and I know it because that muscle in his square jaw pulses like a heartbeat.

"First," he says seriously, "we're going to kill everyone who ever hurt us."

Chapter 53

Aurelia

I jerk awake with a start, only resting my head when I remember I'm in the car with Lyle and not in front of a burning house with Savage and Scythe. I've come to accept that these are not just dreams I'm having. That every time I've been physically intimate with Savage, I see his memories in my sleep.

And this last one sends my heart racing.

Henry clucks softly against my ear and I lean into his tiny warmth for comfort.

The rest of the car ride back to Animus Academy is just as quiet as the ride to court, only there's a dark undercurrent that creeps all over my body—as if I'm already locked away. As if my father's jaws are already fixed around my neck. The tether that I have around myself groans under the strain of my emotion.

I'd thought I was loopy back when I was running and starving. But that seems like child's play compared to this. Compared to certain doom. I clasp my hands to stop them from tembling.

Lyle's hands are clenched on the wheel, making his knuckles bone white. I wonder if he's angry or embarrassed about the trial. Maybe he thinks I wasted his time.

He likely believes what he's heard today, and it affirms what he thought he knew about me all along.

I want to cry. I want to tear my hair out. I want to scream at the top of my lungs.

My father will win this case. He structured the entire thing so carefully. Brought out my dirty old laundry and aired it for all to see in the worst way. I was sixteen when I had sex with Theo Krait, a quiet boy who was kind and gentle with me. We met at Aunt Charlotte's store and he bought a packet of gummy bears and cigarettes and I was enamoured by the tattoo on his neck.

My father marks the most venomous snakes of Serpent Court, and the Common Krait is the most venomous snake in the world. But they are also the least aggressive. Perhaps that's what lured me towards him. Both the inherent danger and the lack of it. He was a contradiction, just like me.

I made him read smutty scenes in my favourite paranormal romances. We ate badly made spaghetti and had sex like rabbits for weeks. He was clumsy, but a fast learner, and we had orgasms aplenty together.

It makes my stomach turn now, to think of how he was executed in front of our entire court. Father used his own venom, as was tradition. He made me watch, as was tradition.

Just for a moment, it occurs to me that I deserve my fate. I knew my father and what the consequences of getting found out were. But the attention of one boy had been impossible for me to toss away. For those six weeks, I wasn't alone in the world.

* * *

When we get to the academy, it surprises me the relief I feel at seeing those massive, curling black and gold gates. The two dragons rearing up on either side, the animus crest in the centre. This has been home for a little over a month, and I will remember these weeks for the rest of my life.

We pull to a stop in the driveway and it feels like an age before Lyle walks to my door and lets me out. I don't look at him or the guards who loiter around us before we walk back to the anima dorm. There is the fate my father would have for me and the fate I would give myself, and those twin threads weave about me like snakes, swaying to the sound of my heartbeat.

Dun-*dun*.

Dun-*dun*.

Dun-*dun*.

The long rays of the afternoon sun cast the dorm in gold and there is a sharp growl in my inner ear, low and unhinged.

Running is pointless, Miss Aquinas. There is nowhere I could not find you.

Lyle has no idea what he's led me into. No fucking idea. And he wouldn't believe it if I told him.

"Miss Aquinas." Lyle's voice is taut, like a leash pulled tight.

Can he hear that warning growl too?

I turn around and stare at his broad chest. Despite the long drive, his shirt is crisp, his tie smooth. I want to run my fingers down its silken length. He undoes my handcuffs, careful to only touch the steel as if my very skin is venomous.

Perhaps it is.

Lyle says nothing for a moment and then, "Look at me."

Reluctantly, I oblige.

His amber eyes are darkened though the rest of his face remains blank. I don't know what he sees in my eyes, maybe a cornered beast. Maybe the anger I feel stoking deep within the base of my stomach.

I think that he's going to say something inspirational. Something nice, like 'well done. You did well. We tried'. That's what a normal person would say, isn't it?

Apparently, all he has left is apathy, because he says, "I'll call for you when I have the verdict."

"How long?" My voice is as dull as old brass.

He blinks, staring into my corneas. "A few hours."

I can't help it. My vision blurs and a tear slips from one eye. I'm not even embarrassed because the growling inside my head only gets louder.

Without another word, I turn around and swipe myself into the dorm.

Heaviness clings to my frame, threatening to drag me under the stairs of this old building and bury me underneath. I fought. I ran. I sat at that tribunal and suffered the public humiliation. By tomorrow, those journalists will put everything they saw into the state newspapers.

The growling inside my head spreads through my entire body. Henry makes a frightened noise. When I reach the third floor corridor, I stare at the portrait of the dragon flying happily above the mountains. Freedom. Blue and shiny. That is what that painting represents.

In my room, Minnie, Raquel, Sabrina, Stacey and Connor are all waiting for me. Their nimpins chirp a greeting. But the grins of their owners all slide off their faces when they see me through the open doorway.

"Oh, Lia." Minnie rushes for me and pulls me into her arms. "It's alright. It'll be alright."

I squeeze my eyes shut just before the other animas huddle around us. I'm squashed on all sides. Someone's boobs are pressed against my cheek and I know it's Sabrina. It's sort of comforting, actually. Raquel's arm is around my back and Stacey's cheek is pressed against mine. The growling quietens, just a little.

Connor rests his chin on the top of my head. "Those bastards are ruthless," he mumbles into my crown. "Fucking council bastards. Who do they think they are?"

"Fuckers, the lot of them," Sabrina mumbles.

"We should s-set fire to their c-cars," Raquel says.

The laughter comes tumbling out of my mouth because a fire is just what this is. When my father set fire to Halfeather's mansion, he set fire to my life too.

Minnie squeezes me tighter, as if she can hold me together by sheer force of will. Stacey swears and admonishes Raquel for the fire remark.

Eventually, we ease apart.

"When will you get the result?" Minnie asks quietly.

I wipe my eyes. "Lyle thinks it'll be a few hours."

"Lia," Stacey says quietly, "these things were here when we got back to your room from lunch."

Sniffing, I look over at what she's pointing to. There is a pile of items on my bed.

"I told them not to touch any of it," Minnie says nervously.

But I can barely hear her. I can barely hear the tentative questions they're asking, or Raquel and Connor's discreet sniffing, because the growling in my head turns into something an inch less than rabid.

On my bed is a neatly folded set of black trackpants. On top of that is an old USB and a tiny square of red foil that once held chocolate.

Slowly, I slide to the floor, my knees suddenly weak, my very marrow *burning* with something heinous.

My anima screams, and it rattles my very skull.

"Lia," Sabrina whispers, like she can't believe what she's saying. "Why are the Slaughter Brothers sending you gifts?"

"Are they even gifts?" Stacey says.

"Of c-course they are," Raquel says softly.

But my mates aren't giving me gifts. They are *returning* gifts to their regina.

"I can't do this," I choke out, clutching at my stomach

540

as if I can cling onto my anima, hold her in my arms and stifle her screaming with a hug. "Oh Goddess, I can't do this."

I rejected my mates, quite clearly, by physically running away from them. But now, they rejected me in the most concrete way an animus could.

Traditionally, a regina or rex is the first to gift something to the members of their pack. It's a sort of claiming, and even without knowing, I gave these gifts to them. The fact that they kept them all this time, and were now returning them...

I sucked in a breath through a constricted throat and I sounded like I was dying.

"Oh, Goddess!" Minnie rushes over to me. "Calm down, Lia. Calm the fuck down. Breathe. Breathe!"

Henry smacks his entire body into my cheek and I'm so shocked by the sudden pain that I do take a full, unrestricted breath. I stare at him in shock, but his inky black eyes are angry on me. He squawks forcefully with his whole body.

"He said that with his whole chest, too," Connor says. "Listen to Henry, Lia."

The nimpins squeak in agreement.

"Fuck," I sob. "Fuck!"

"What's going on, guys?" Stacey asks frantically.

"I-It's obvious, isn't it?" Raquel says behind me.

"It's not possible," Stacey says, and it sounds muffled, like she's covering her mouth. "The lockdown starts tomorrow, so she must be a little riled up! It has to be that."

541

"That's not it," Connor says quietly. "No fucking way."

Minnie comes to my rescue. "Look, guys. Whatever the truth is doesn't matter anymore. We've only got a few hours left."

"You're r-right," Raquel grunts. "We n-need to be c-clear-headed."

I hold Henry to my chest to try and reassure him that I'm not completely losing it.

But the thrashing and snarling inside my body tells me otherwise

"It *is* a mess," I whisper.

The room is silent as they all stare listlessly at me, no doubt coming to a conclusion in their minds about what this means.

"What do you want to do, Lia?" Sabrina asks, smoothing my hair down. "Want me to do your hair?"

I shake my head. "I want to bath Henry." One last time. I don't say it out loud, but they all hear it. The nimpins all bob up and down excitedly at the thought of their favourite thing, but Henry just stares at me like he's trying to tell me something. I climb to my feet as the animas gather the towels and brushes.

Those twin snakes sway threateningly. The growling in my body makes my whole body tremble.

Each way I turn leads to running. And at the end of each path waits an apex predator, determined to sink their teeth into me. Xander's dragon was wrong. We would be parted, whether he liked it or not.

Always running. Always hunted. Always prey.

Minnie is eyeing me as she soaps up Gertie, but I avoid her eyes and concentrate on massaging Henry, who is also staring me down.

We wash and groom our nimpins quietly, the other animas voices no more than murmurs. The nimpins love the water and find it relaxing. They recharge their batteries this way, dozing off in between massages, and it makes them smell like soap and bubble bath.

It's a good distraction from what's to come.

And the entire time, I keep my back turned to the bundle still lying on my bed.

* * *

It's well and truly dark by the time the knock comes at our door. Georgia is standing there with two guards flanking her and Theresa behind them. "You need to come with me, Miss Aquinas."

It's not her words that make my blood run cold, but the absence of any smirk. Of any attitude. Her face is dead serious.

A dark feeling solidifies in my chest. "Right."

I turn around, but Minnie is already at my side and wraps her arms right around me. "I'll be right here, Lia," she says. Then her voice trembles and she meaningfully squeezes my hand. "Waiting right here for when you come back."

My heart. How is it possible that I feel it cracking open and swelling at the same time? I take her hands in mine because I want to look at her as I say this.

"Minnie, you've been a good friend to me," I whisper. "The best. Thank you for your friendship."

I turn away from her before the tears spill from her eyes because if I see that, I might lose my nerve completely.

"I'll come with you, Lia," Theresa says, but there is also a shimmer to her eyes. "I'll be with you all the way."

"Thank you."

She hasn't noticed anything different about the room. I zip up my jacket.

I turn to look at my friends one last time. Minnie is holding Raquel's hand, her pink hair bright, her eyes shining. Raquel grabs Sabrina's hand as if they need to and my leopard friend bites her lip. Stacey is wiping her nose on her sleeve and she too grabs Sabrina's hand.

I'm glad they have each other.

But Connor bites his lip as he clasps Stacey's, and the conflict in his eyes beams right through me. He knows they're my mates. I wonder if my secret will be all out now. I wonder if it matters anymore.

"I love you guys," I say. "You've been more like family to me than anyone ever has in the last seven years."

"Don't say it, Lia," Raquel bites out. "Don't fucking say it."

I smile at them because it's the first time since I've known her, Raquel did not stutter. "I'm not going to die," I reassure them with a weak smile. "That's not the way it will go."

Minnie nods eagerly and I force a smile for her.

The guards put steel handcuffs on me and I'm followed out, Theresa falling into step beside me.

The walk is quiet, but immediately I see that we're not headed towards Lyle's office. Instead, we're walking the opposite way, towards the medical wing. I say nothing as we walk through the double locked doors and the familiar smell of hand sanitiser and disinfectant wash hits my nose, both comforting and anxiety-inducing at the same time.

Adrenaline cuts through my veins like glass and I barely suppress the full-body shake that's trying to tear me apart. I've only known terror like this in nightmares.

Only known it as waking up sweat-soaked with rib-crushing heart beats.

But now the real thing is here.

We arrive through the assessment centre, and I find Lyle standing there by himself.

But as I look through the now open glass front doors of the entrance, it's immediately apparent why we're meeting here.

Nestled between armoured black SUVs, a black Rolls Royce awaits in the receiving bay marked on the driver's door with a coat of arms I know well because it was on my childhood bedroom wall. I woke up every morning, seeing it as if my father was reminding me of who I was. Who he wanted me to be.

Two rearing cobras. In the middle, a shield with a snaking black 'N'.

Chapter 54

Aurelia

I freeze, every cell and nerve and movement in my body going into a standstill. Except the growling at the centre of me.

It turns into a roar.

"Aurelia." Lyle's voice is deep and commanding, but there's a strange bite to it. "Come here."

Stiffly, I obey.

The deputy headmaster hands me a letter and I open it, knowing what it will say already. Henry leans down to look as if he wants to read it too, so does Theresa.

Miss Aurelia Aquinas
The Council of Beasts has found you GUILTY of the
crime of grand arson and one count of murder of the
second degree.
According to the OLD LAW, you are ordered to return to
the custody of your paternal blood, His Royal Highness,
King Mace Naga of Serpent Court,

Where you will be punished with Venomous Execution.
May the Wild Mother have mercy upon your soul.

Even knowing that this would happen, reading the words verbatim on the page sends the animal in me thrashing, lashing, *raging*.

"Oh, Lia—" Theresa begins.

"It's fine," I bite out. My hand is still shaking as I crumple the letter in my fist and throw it at Lyle's perfectly shiny shoes.

Lyle starts, "Miss Aquinas—"

"No." My head snaps up to stare daggers at the deputy headmaster. I won't fucking have his attitude. *Not* today. *Not* now.

The outright violence in my eyes makes him press his mouth into a thin line and Henry whines on my shoulder.

I frown across at him because I've never heard him making that sound before. Perhaps he knows what's coming. But I'm proven wrong in an instant because behind Lyle walks out familiar hulking figures. Broad shoulders and silver hair like a full moon. And long hair as dark as midnight. I wait to see the third figure, only he doesn't appear.

Something made of sinew and fangs roars in the back of my mind. I scramble for control. I can't lose it and embarrass myself here. I nervously tug at the zipper of my jacket.

Dully, I turn away from three men staring down me.

Outside, males in all black are now streaming out from the Serpent Court vehicles. A tall, wiry male steps out from the central car, straightening the collar of his long black jacket. At the end of summer, my father is the only serpent wearing a coat like that. Perhaps it's to protect his cold, dead heart. He is immediately flanked by his five imposing generals.

My father turns and through the glass, our gazes lock. His eyes glint under the floodlights of the carport. The slight twitch of his lip tells me he is satisfied.

A malicious voice slithers into my mind.

Boneweaver female. 20 years old. Prime condition. Unmated. Unbred. Offers over $10 million.

No.

No.

No.

One of the Animus guards presses a button beside the glass. They smoothly slide open and stay there. Next, the steel bars slide silently apart.

There are less than twenty paces between me and my father. Less than twenty paces between me and a tomb.

Two guards stand on either side of me, but they stay a distance away. Frowning, I look left and right, only to have Scythe and Xander take up positions next to me. Scythe flicks out a finger and I look down to see he's indicating my father's mark.

I realise that they need to fulfil their blood covenant to return me to him. They don't miss a beat and grab me by the arms, and I have no choice but to walk forward with them.

Beside my father stand the five tall combat-ready serpents, their skull masks covering their noses and lower faces, eyes pinned on me in death stares that make my skin crawl.

My father's gaze is fixed on me with a dark malevolence I've seen many times before. There is satisfaction there. Deep, righteous satisfaction that turns the roaring in my head into a *scream*.

His betrayal might sting deepest of all.

We stop right in front of him and I do my best to stand tall. I'm sweating. I'm shaking. My vision is going blurry. Xander and Scythe drop my arms and I let them fall like dead weights.

I'm suddenly surrounded by towering, threatening males, danger bearing down on me from all sides and I grit my teeth. My anima thrashes madly.

"Aurelia," my father says. Such overt promise in that one word.

"Father." I raise my chin and look him in the eye.

From the corner of my vision, I see Xander raise his hand. I glance at him and see the black ink of the blood covenant dissolve before our eyes. From Scythe's shift, I'm guessing his is gone as well.

Xander scoffs and strides back towards the medical wing.

"It's done then, Naga," Scythe says evenly.

I turn to glare at him.

Metal clanks and my father produces obsidian handcuffs.

I'm not ready for the ingrained terror that lashes through me like a dragon's tail.

But I have one last thing up my sleeve.

Actually, make that five.

"*Go,*" I mentally command.

From under my jacket, the five hidden fluffballs wriggle free and zip into the air.

And open their beaks.

The nimpins' combined psychic cry pierces the night sky like a sonic blast. The sound sears my eardrums and animuses all around us cry out and crumple to the ground.

The serpents all reach for their ears, struggling to reinforce their psychic shields.

Scythe alone remains unaffected. He just cocks his silvery head, and in his gaze, I see a single question. "*What will you do now?*"

Take my fucking chance, that's what.

I let my open handcuffs drop to the ground along with the bobby pin Minnie palmed me during our last hug.

But something happens that I don't expect. A force greater than me takes over. The beast in me screams, shattering all seven of my shields. Suddenly, I'm out of control. I'm burning up like a nuclear bomb, but I can't contain it and... I don't want to.

Like a magnet being forced by a counter-magnet, I'm swung around.

And then I'm standing across from Lyle, on his knees, his eyes huge and fixed upon me like he's seeing me for the first time. And on his neck, five points of light burst from a golden skull.

But Lyle's angelic face morphs into fear and someone's psychic fingers grab me from behind. A voice like death and darkness slithers into my ear.

"Boneweaver Female. Fertile. Unbroken. Unmated. Offers over ten million. That is your asking price, Aurelia Aquinas."

That thought steals the breath from my lungs. It steals reason and logic and reduces me to instinct.

Faces blur, sounds distort. My very body is not mine.

And that tether, that tether of sinew and bone had been holding onto me by her claws and talons and teeth, *snaps*.

It reverberates like a gong in my ears.

The sound that comes from my throat can't be my own because it's vicious and rabid and shakes the ground beneath my feet. The foreign psychic hands are blown off me as a pure blast of my uncontrolled power sweeps outward.

Someone is roaring and I realise it's me. It's my voice, my feline larynx and feline whiskers on my cheeks. I land on four paws. Paws that are honey yellow, with sharp claws created to maim and kill.

There is a shot and it rings through the air as my bones crunch for a second time.

Logical thoughts are wiped from my mind as all I know is that there are no chains around me, no voices around me, and I'm weightless on feathers and wings. There is light and crisp air and freedom, but I know it is borrowed. I know that I am still in a cage.

A beastly intuition tells me many shots are being fired directly at me, but that same intuition follows a thread of old thought and clings to it like a fresh kill. Up and east, where old power meets newer magic, where a second, matching, dragon-trick door lies nestled in the anima dormitory, opened by a dragon because his regina asked him to.

Chapter 55

Lyle

As my eardrums pop under the pressure of the energy Aurelia is exerting, she lights up. Or rather, her neck lights up with a symbol I've been seeing on my own neck since I hit puberty.

The five nimpins cut off their shrill cry, but I remain on my knees.

I've known that Aurelia is my regina for weeks, but to see that celestial skull on her neck with my own eyes is a new kind of nightmare.

But then her body shifts and she is neither eagle nor serpent. Her fur is as golden and her claws are as sharp as my own.

With another burst of impossible power, she's off into the air, into the night with beating wings and there are shouts and shots and pounding feet.

Impossible, my mind roars. *Impossible*.

In my horror-ridden mind, multiple threads suddenly fall into place.

Mace Naga is shouting to his team. Shouting at me. It's too much, my power bursts out in a wave. There are more screams.

Where is Aurelia?

Legs in black slacks calmly step before me and I know without looking that it's Scythe, towering over my kneeling form.

"Boneweaver," he says to his bond-brothers. To me. "*Our regina is a Boneweaver.*"

* * *

If you haven't read the prequel *Her Vicious Beasts: The Beginning* yet, you NEED to check it out because it's delicious and you see what Aurelia's life was like when she met her men. You can get it for free here: <u>www.ektaa-bali.com/herviciousbeasts</u>

About the Author

Ektaa P. Bali was born in Fiji and spent most of her life in Melbourne, Australia.

She studied nursing and midwifery at Deakin University, going on to spend eight years as a midwife in various hospitals.

She published her first novel in 2020, the beginning of a middle grade fantasy series, before going on to pursue her true passion: Young & New Adult Fantasy.

Her Vicious Beasts is her fourth series set in the Chrysalis-verse and the first in a new New Adult series.

She currently lives in Brisbane, Australia.

facebook.com/ektaabaliauthor

instagram.com/ektaabaliauthor

youtube.com/ektaabali

Also by E.P. Bali

<u>New Adult Fantasy Romance</u>

A Song of Lotus and Lightning Saga:

#1 *The Warrior Midwife*

#2 *The Warrior Priestess*

#3 *The Warrior Queen*

#1 *The Archer Princess*

#2 *The Archer Witch*

#3 *The Archer Queen*

Her Vicious Beasts

#0.5 *The Beginning*

#1 *Her Feral Beasts*

#2 *Her Rabid Beasts*

#3 *Her Psycho Beasts*

#4 *Her Tortured Beasts*

#5 *Her Monstrous Beasts*

<u>Upper YA Dark Fantasy</u>

The Travellers:

#1 *The Chrysalis Key*

Made in the USA
Middletown, DE
03 December 2023

44429621R00316